River of Fallen Angels

ALSO AVAILABLE BY LAURA JOH ROWLAND

Victorian Mysteries
Garden of Sins
Portrait of Peril
The Woman in the Veil
The Hangman's Secret
A Mortal Likeness
The Ripper's Shadow

Sano Ichiro series
The Iris Fan
The Shogun's Daughter
The Incense Game
The Ronin's Mistress
The Cloud Pavilion
The Fire Kimono
The Snow Empress
Red Chrysanthemum
The Assassin's Touch
The Perfumed Sleeve
The Dragon King's Palace
The Pillow Book of Lady Wisteria
Black Lotus
The Samurai's Wife
The Concubine's Tattoo
The Way of the Traitor
Bundori
Shinjū

Secret Adventures of Charlotte Brontë
Bedlam
The Secret Adventures of Charlotte Brontë

RIVER OF FALLEN ANGELS

A VICTORIAN MYSTERY

Laura Joh Rowland

This is a work of fiction. All of the names, characters, organizations, places and events portrayed in this novel are either products of the author's imagination or are used fictitiously. Any resemblance to real or actual events, locales, or persons, living or dead, is entirely coincidental.

Published in the United States by Crooked Lane Books, an imprint of The Quick Brown Fox & Company LLC.

Crooked Lane Books and its logo are trademarks of The Quick Brown Fox & Company LLC.

Library of Congress Catalog-in-Publication data available upon request.

ISBN (hardcover): 978-1-63910-151-1
ISBN (ebook): 978-1-63910-152-8

Cover design by Melanie Sun

Printed in the United States.

www.crookedlanebooks.com

Crooked Lane Books
34 West 27th St., 10th Floor
New York, NY 10001

First Edition: January 2023

10 9 8 7 6 5 4 3 2 1

To Lena Joh, my beloved mother.
Thank you for everything.

London, April 1891

Chapter 1

At the edge of the River Thames, I position my camera on its tripod and aim it up at the man who dangles from the high walkway of London's Tower Bridge. Only a rope twisted around his ankle keeps him from plunging some hundred and fifty feet into the water. He's one of the many workers on the bridge, which has been under construction for the past five years. The bridge will be magnificent when completed, but now the two towers that rise from stone piers are mere steel skeletons.

"This is better than our usual job of photographing dead bodies," Lord Hugh Staunton says. "The poor fellow still has a chance."

"If someone don't rescue him before he falls, there will be a dead body," Mick O'Reilly says.

Hugh, Mick, and I are crime photographers and reporters for the *Daily World* newspaper, covering mainly the East End. Because of a recent, rare lack of notable crimes on our beat, we're temporarily assigned to other events, such as accidents. Today, chance has brought us to Bermondsey, on the Thames's south bank, to the foot of the Horsleydown Stairs. The narrow stone staircase, green with algae, descends from an alley directly to the water. The low tide has exposed a strip of mud on which we've stationed ourselves amid rocks, broken shells and glass, dead fish and wooden timbers, machine parts and torn nets. Brown foam soils the water's edge; drainage from sewers and cesspools flows directly into the Thames. The crowd around us includes the publican, barmaids, and customers from the Anchor Brewhouse beside the stairs. Smoke from nearby factories darkens the fog and clouds. On this cold April afternoon, the river's foul, fishy stench isn't as bad as in summer—a blessing. Wind that smells of coffee, tea, and spices in the warehouses blows the dangling man as if he's a toy on a child's mobile. His screams echo up and down the river, across the city, while men on the towers watch helplessly.

"Why don't they pull him up?" someone in the crowd asks.

"The part of the walkway he's hanging from looks pretty flimsy." Hugh, tall and blond, elegant in smartly tailored clothes, points to the short segment connecting the two spans that have grown daily, inch by inch, from each tower, to join in the middle. It looks like a thin, horizontal ladder. "If the other men go out there to rescue him, it might collapse, and they'll all fall."

Women in the crowd gravitate toward Hugh. That often happens because of his strikingly handsome looks. He smiles as he introduces himself and interviews them. "What do you think of the accident, miss?"

"Oh, terrible, sir!"

From his gallant, flirtatious manner, one would never guess that he's not interested in women. A bolder one asks him about me: "Who's your lady with the camera?"

"She's my dear friend and colleague, Mrs. Sarah Barrett," Hugh says.

I keep a careful, protective watch over him. During our last investigation, he was seriously injured, his right arm almost crippled by a knife wound. His arm is still weak and tender, and he holds it close to his side, lest someone bump it. I hope nobody here recognizes him from the newspaper stories published a few years ago, after he was caught in a vice squadron raid on a club for homosexual men. His family disowned him, his aristocratic friends dropped him, and the public's hostility can be brutal.

Below the bridge, water traffic halts as the crews on barges, ferries, and other boats gawk at the dangling, screaming man. Steamships are backed up behind them. Horns blast, in vain. I see photographers among the crowds massed on both banks of the river, on rooftops and the wharves outside St. Katharine's Docks opposite us. Word travels fast in London, from the streets to the public houses, to the newspaper offices. Mick greets two shaggy-haired street urchins who come running to see the spectacle. When I first met Mick almost three years ago, he was one of them, an underfed, undersized, grimy boy. Now fifteen, he's a tall, lanky, handsome youth, but his red hair still sticks up, and he has a raffish air.

One boy jingles pennies in his hand. "Wanna bet he dies?" He points at the dangling man.

"You're on," the other boy says.

"That's cold," Mick protests.

"Aw, you got deep pockets. Don't be tight," the first boy says, his voice sharpening.

Mick hesitates. I perceive that these boys, his friends from the old days, resent his good fortune of having a well-paid job and a respectable place in the world.

"I'm in." Mick obviously doesn't want to be thought a snob. "I bet he gets saved."

I duck under the black drape attached to the back of the camera and peer through the viewfinder. I'm using a special lens, purchased at a high price from an inventor, that functions as a telescope and magnifies far-distant objects. It gives me an amazingly clear, close-up view of the dangling man. He's young, muscular, and clad in rough, dirty clothes. He waves his arms as if in an attempt to fly to safety. The rope twists. For a moment his panic-stricken gaze turns directly toward my camera, and he screams, "Help!"

My heart clenches. This is in some ways worse than photographing murder scenes at which the victims, the blood, and the gore are still present. For those folks, the worst has already happened. With crimes, I at least can seek justice for the victims. With fatal accidents, there's no justice, no consolation. All I can do for this man is pray.

He wails as I snap the shutter. The wind blows the cap off his curly brown hair. The cap falls the long, long way down. The spectators groan. I imagine myself in his place, suspended in empty air, help beyond reach, with only the thin, straining rope tethering me to life. The mud beneath my feet feels less solid, and I tremble with vicarious terror as I change the negative plate. I imagine the snap as the rope breaks, then the heart-stopping plunge, the explosive collision with the water.

Sometimes I find danger thrilling and alluring—a quirk of my personality. I seek it out, as if my day is incomplete unless I find a sleeping wolf to poke and wake up. I never feel more alive than when danger threatens. But sometimes its sensations evoke memories of past dangers I've experienced. Now my vision darkens, a gunshot blares in my mind, and I smell sulfur as the old bullet wound in my shoulder throbs. Breathless, I fling the drape off my head.

I see a miniature steamboat—a police launch—chug down the river toward the bridge. A constable on board speaks through a megaphone, ordering the logjammed watercraft to move. Within half an hour that seems like forever, the logjam clears. A barge stops under the walkway. Atop the barge, a man operates a crane equipped with a steam engine and a long boom. Smoke puffs from the boiler as the boom rises. I photograph the expression of dawning hope on the man's face. The boom stops at its full vertical height, its tip level with his upside-down knees. The man wraps his arms around the boom and sobs with relief. But the rope still tethers his ankle to the bridge. He reaches in his pocket, brings out a knife.

"God, please don't let him drop it," Hugh murmurs.

A hush descends. The crowds are silent, paralyzed by suspense as the man contorts his body into an impossible position and saws at the rope. I take photographs, barely able to watch him. The rope frays, fiber by fiber, then breaks. Suddenly released, the man loses his precarious balance. He drops the knife, yells, and slides down the boom. My cry of alarm joins those from the other spectators. He's about ten feet above the water when he falls in with a big splash. The barge crewmen fish him out and drag him aboard. He stands on the barge, dripping wet and shaking violently, but safe. Applause erupts amid cheers and whistles.

"Whew," Hugh says, and wipes his brow.

I clasp my hand against my pounding heart. Mick says triumphantly to his friends, "Pay up," and holds out his hand. They fork over pennies. The barge moves toward shore. Photographers and reporters rush toward the pier to meet the rescued man and his saviors.

"C'mon, we gotta get photos." Mick grabs my flash lamp and the valise full of blank negative plates and other supplies.

"And interviews." Hugh packs up my camera, then carries it in his strong left hand as he and Mick and the spectators hurry toward the pier.

I fold the tripod and sling my satchel over my arm. As I race after my companions, a steamship thunders up the river. The wake swells and rolls. A huge wave laps the shore, hurling debris and foam. Amid wood scraps, rusted tins, and broken bottles, a larger shape washes up at my feet. It's about fifteen inches square and seven thick, a pinkish-gray color, red at the edges. A chunk of butchered cow or pig that fell off a boat? My photographer's eye takes a closer look. The shape is wider at one end, curved inward near the other, disturbingly familiar. Two pink circles top two round swellings near the middle.

Breasts.

My heart and my stomach lurch simultaneously.

The shape is a woman's torso. The red at the top, sides, and bottom are raw flesh where the head, arms, and legs are missing. A yell of horror bursts from me. Accustomed to grisly sights, I can view them with aplomb when braced to photograph them, but this has caught me off guard. I clap my hand over my mouth as sour bile rises in my throat.

Hugh and Mick hear my yell; they stop and turn. I beckon frantically. They come running, and when I point at the torso, Mick exclaims, "Gorblimey!"

Hugh retches, drops the camera on the mud, doubles over, and vomits. Two years of crime scenes and murder investigations haven't toughened his stomach.

My own stomach will fail me unless I distract myself. I resort to speculating about what happened to the poor woman. "She must have fallen in the river and gotten cut to pieces by a steamship propeller." I don't believe it, but it's better than the alternative.

"It weren't no propeller." Mick voices my terrible thought: "It's the Thames Torso Murderer again."

Dread coils through me as I recall the case. In spring 1887, a sack was found floating in the Thames at Rainham, a town some sixteen miles upstream from London. The sack contained a woman's torso. Over the next two years, severed torsos, arms, legs, and hands from three other women turned up in various locations in or near the river. Their heads were never found, and only one of the women was identified. The cause of their deaths was presumed to be murder but never proven. The police investigated, but they had so little to go on, and the killer was never arrested. The newspapers covered the case, but without developments other than the discoveries of more remains, the press and the public quickly lost interest, their attention diverted by a more notorious case.

In Whitechapel in 1888, Jack the Ripper began his reign of terror. He savagely murdered and mutilated Martha Tabram, Polly Nichols, Annie Chapman, Liz Stride, Kate Eddowes, and Mary Jane Kelly, one after another, between August 6 and November 9. His malevolent shadow fell across all of London. The police interviewed multitudes of witnesses and arrested dozens of suspects. The investigation had all the high drama that the Torso Murders lacked.

I didn't cover the Ripper case for the *Daily World*, as my employment there didn't begin until April 1889. My interest in that case was personal.

My personal interest, shared by Hugh and Mick, led us to undertake our own private, illicit investigation, which was so engrossing and life transforming that we had no attention to spare for the Torso Murders.

Now excitement dawns on Mick's face. "We wanted a big case to investigate."

Hugh gags, spits, says, "Sorry," then, "Yes, I thought a big case would be just the thing to brush up my detective skills." He had taken time off while recovering from his injury. "We should be careful what we wish for," he says ruefully. "Oh God, any case but this one!"

"I agree." I too had wanted a new challenge, but I quail at taking on the Torso Murders, and not only because of the gruesome corpses. What kind of person could butcher a woman like a piece of meat? For Hugh, Mick, and me, the Ripper is a known quantity—merely mortal, no matter how vicious—whereas the Torso Murderer is a nameless, faceless, unfathomable evil.

"We solved the Ripper case. We can solve this one." Mick speaks with the brash confidence of youth.

"With the Ripper, we had a special advantage," I remind him. "We knew who he'd chosen as his next victims. With the Torso Murderer, all but one of his victims are still unidentified, and nobody knows who's next."

Hugh wipes his mouth on his handkerchief and keeps his eyes averted from the torso. "We're getting ahead of ourselves. It's Sir Gerald who decides what cases we investigate." Sir Gerald Mariner, our employer, owns the *Daily World*.

"He'll put us on this one," Mick declares.

I hope so, despite my misgivings. We put the Ripper out of action, but not before he killed all those women, and I feel responsible because a mistake of mine had brought them to his attention. If not for me, they might still be alive! The Torso Murder case offers a chance to replay the Ripper investigation with a better ending, to atone for my mistake.

"For now, I'd better fetch the police." Hugh runs toward the launch moored by the barge.

I set up my tripod, mount the camera on it. Mick opens the trunk and hands me a fresh negative plate. We're going to photograph a dead body today, after all.

The clouds thicken; the sky grows darker; drizzle threatens to turn into a rainstorm. I work as fast as I can. Mick loads powder into the flash lamp. White explosions light up the torso. Looking at it through the viewfinder distances me from the horror. My nausea fades even as I take close-ups of the severed white neckbone, the ragged flesh where the limbs were amputated. I move the tripod to capture the torso from different angles.

Who was she? What led her to this terrible fate?

The Ripper victims had traits in common, which included their association with me. What traits did the Torso Murder victims share?

What kind of woman ends up cut to pieces and dumped in the river as if she were mere garbage?

Other reporters and photographers charge toward me, the crowd of spectators close behind them. People exclaim. Photographers block my view of the torso, jostling for position, setting up their equipment. I've enough pictures, so Mick and I lug our equipment to the edge of the crowd. In the distance, the rescued man and the barge crew stand alone, forgotten.

Hugh returns with a police constable. In his late forties, with graying brown hair under his helmet, the constable wears the oilskin trousers and mackintosh of the Thames River Police. The crowd parts to let him approach the torso. He frowns and shakes his head but seems neither shocked nor sickened. The River Police mostly handle thefts on the ships and docks, but the Thames has a long association with dead bodies—from wars, accidents, and murders, from the recent and distant past. Skeletons from the Roman period have surfaced, and when the *Princess Alice* pleasure steamer sank in 1878, some seven hundred people drowned. The Thames is also a popular place for suicides. I once heard that more than five hundred bodies in total are recovered every year. The constable must have seen his share of corpses.

He yells and gestures. "This is a crime scene. Everybody, stand back!" Reporters and photographers grumble as they move. "Who found this?"

I nervously raise my hand. I've an ingrained fear of policemen, no matter that my work puts me in frequent contact with them, and no matter that I'm married to one. My fear dates back to the time when I was ten years old, and police came to my house and interrogated and threatened my father, Benjamin Bain. I didn't understand why. Many years later, I learned he was the prime suspect in the rape and murder of a teenage girl. The shocking discovery contradicted everything I'd ever believed about my family and altered the course of my life.

Hugh and Mick stand protectively beside me. The constable asks, "What's your name?"

"Mrs. Sarah Barrett."

The constable raises his eyebrows as he recognizes my name. Voices among the crowd repeat it. Reporters pepper me with questions:

"Have you seen your father since his trial for the murder of Ellen Casey?"

"Are you certain he didn't kill her?"

"What's he up to now?"

His trial, concluded four months ago, was a public sensation, and some people still think he's guilty despite overwhelming evidence to the contrary and the fact that the judge dismissed the charges. My past escapades as a crime investigator had already made me notorious, and the trial has increased my unwanted fame.

"No comment," I say coldly.

My father lives in Brighton, where he operates a photography business. As a result of his own notoriety, he never comes to London, and I haven't visited him. We're estranged, a sad development in our troubled history. I'm thankful he's a free man, but the trial drove a wedge between us, and he's as absent from my life as if he'd been convicted and executed.

"You just happened to be here when these remains washed up?" the constable asks me.

"That's correct," I say.

"You oughta be glad she spotted 'em," Mick says. "You can tell your bosses the Torso Murderer's struck again."

The constable glares at me as if I've tossed him a handful of worms. I doubt he wants to bear the bad tidings about a new murder in an unsolved series that everyone thought ended two years ago.

"PC Wilson," Hugh says, "Mrs. Barrett, Mr. O'Reilly, and I work for the *Daily World*. We would appreciate it if you would let us observe while you examine the crime scene."

The charming manner that wins over other people doesn't work on PC Wilson, who says to us, "Get lost." He waves away the other reporters and photographers. "The rest of you too."

The reporters shout questions at him: "Any new leads in the four previous Torso Murders?" "Are detectives still investigating, or have they given up?" The photographers snap pictures of the torso. The spectators loiter.

"We can help you look for the other body parts," Mick says eagerly.

"No thanks," PC Wilson says.

"Seems like you could use some help," Mick says. "You ain't caught the Torso Murderer yet. You couldn't even find all the other victims' parts."

Anger flushes the constable's cheeks.

"You didn't catch the Ripper either," Mick taunts.

"Mick, that's enough," I say. Jabbing the police's sore spot won't gain us favors, and to mention the Ripper is to enter dangerous territory. My friends and I number among the few who know why the Ripper has never been caught. It's a deep, dark secret that, if made public, would condemn us to death.

"You owe Mrs. Barrett five shillings," Mick tells the constable. "Anyone finds a body in the river gets paid five shillings—it's the law."

Hugh smoothly talks over him. "We've solved some major cases, including the Hangman Murder and the Sleeping Beauty mystery. We'd be happy to lend our expertise."

"The *Daily World* has a special arrangement with the police," I add. "We're privy to their investigations, and in exchange they get publicity that helps them catch killers."

"That's not my business. Move along, or I'll arrest you." The constable then addresses the crowd: "The same goes for everybody else."

More policemen arrive; they must have been watching the rescue from other vantage points and come to see what's caused the commotion here. Their presence backs up the constable's threat. My friends and I escape ahead of the disgruntled crowd.

"Let's hurry back to the *Daily World*," I say, "so we can get our pictures published before anybody else's."

Chapter 2

Fleet Street is the center of London's news publishing industry, where all the major papers have their offices. It's named after the river that once ran along its course and is now channeled underground. I think of it as still a river, akin to the Thames. Whereas the Thames gathers the detritus of the city and sweeps it downstream, Fleet Street absorbs the populace's stories and pours them out in a flood of printed pages.

At three o'clock this afternoon, when Hugh, Mick, and I arrive, the fog smells of the ink and machine oil that lace the water in the gutters. Fleet Street is so clogged with omnibuses, wagons, and cabs that when we cross, we risk bites and kicks from horses. A train thunders along the Ludgate Hill railway bridge. We weave through the crowds flocking to taverns and coffeehouses near the *Daily World* headquarters. It occupies a huge corner building whose Moorish arches, Baroque turrets, and Greek columns trumpet the newspaper's claim to a place in international history. Above the giant clock protrudes a marble sculpture of a ship—the Mariner trademark, in honor of Sir Gerald's first business venture, a mercantile firm. The man puts his stamp on everything under his power.

Inside the building, Hugh goes to the editorial department to write up the stories about the rescue and the torso. Mick helps me carry the photography equipment to the darkroom and pour chemical solutions into trays. He doesn't chatter as usual; lately he's prone to silent brooding. At age fifteen, a broken heart seems like the end of the world.

Despite my concern, I don't fuss over him. He thinks himself a grown man and doesn't like being babied. When I turn off the light and put negatives in the developer, I can feel his lonely anguish, as if the space he occupies is a darker presence in the darkness.

A knock at the door interrupts. I call, "Just a moment," put the negatives in the fixer, light the gas lamp, and then say, "Come in."

Hugh enters with Sally Albert, my younger sister. Sally works for the *Daily World* as a junior reporter. She wears her self-styled uniform of plain gray skirt and high-necked white blouse. Although we were born to different mothers, we look so much alike that people sometimes mistake one of us for the other. At twenty-four, Sally is ten years younger than me and also prettier, but we're both tall and slim, with hazel eyes and ash-blond hair. I wear my hair in a coronet of braids; Sally's is in a casual topknot skewered with a pencil.

Hugh holds his hand in front of his eyes. "Please don't make me look at the pictures of the torso."

"We haven't printed 'em yet," Mick says.

Hugh sighs with relief.

Sally says, "They'll have to wait. Sir Gerald wants to see you."

"I thought it was your day off," I say to her. "What are you doing here?"

"I came in just in case there was a big story." Her normally fresh, rosy complexion is pale, with dark shadows under her eyes, and she smells of tobacco smoke from the room where male reporters puff pipes and cigarettes while they pound typewriters.

Concerned about her, I say, "You shouldn't work so much." We try to spend leisure time together, but other than when our paths cross on the job, I haven't seen her in weeks.

"Oh, I don't mind. I love my job." Her smile sparkles. "And it's a good thing I did come in. Hugh told me about the new Torso Murder."

"It's why Sir Gerald wants to see us," Hugh says. "As soon as I finished typing the story, the editor sent it up to him, and the summons came down. We'd better not keep our lord and master waiting."

As we all hurry down the corridor, Mick says, "Looks like he's gonna assign us to investigate."

Sally, tagging along, says to me, "Have you heard from Father?"

"No. He hasn't answered my letters." I gather from Sally's mournful expression that he hasn't answered hers either.

His silence must pain her more than me, even though our histories with him are so similar. When I was ten, Benjamin Bain disappeared—left my mother and me—and for more than twenty years afterward, I believed him dead. During those years, he remarried, and he and his new wife had Sally. He disappeared on his second family when Sally was ten. Without him, Sally and I and our mothers lost our places in respectable middle-class society. My mother worked factory jobs, and we moved from one cheap lodging house to another. Sally and her mother went into domestic service. We two half sisters share the same experience of mourning and yearning for our lost father. And now we've lost him again.

But I have the comfort of a new family of sorts. My husband and I live with Mick, Hugh, and Hugh's valet, Fitzmorris. Sally has a room in a lodging house for young single women. Her housemates are mere casual acquaintances. She lost touch with her old friends when she began working at the *Daily World*, and she's estranged from her mother, an unfortunate consequence of our father's trial. Sally believed Benjamin Bain was innocent, but her mother believed him guilty, and even now that the charges have been dismissed, she thinks he's evil and Sally shouldn't have a relationship with him. Sally works hard because she wants to advance her career, but I know that loneliness is another reason for her long hours on the job.

"Come to my house for dinner tonight," I say.

"Thank you, but no," Sally says regretfully. "It'll be late, and I need to get home before my landlady locks the door at ten o'clock."

Her landlady's curfew is just an excuse. Sally once let on that the conviviality of my household makes her even lonelier when she goes home. If only there were room for another person, I would move her in with us. She's said she wishes she could meet a man who would be as wonderful a husband for her as mine is for me, but she's afraid she never will, and she needs to make good at her job so she can support herself if she never marries. I wish I were the kind of big sister who could introduce her to eligible bachelors and teach her how to capture their interest. But I'm not. It was by pure fluke that I attracted the one man who's right for me.

We take the elevator to the top floor. We're accustomed to the iron cage that bears us upward with its huffing, grinding, steam-powered mechanism, but Hugh and Mick always laugh like little boys on a carnival ride. I'm glad Mick has temporarily shed his bleak mood.

In the corridor that leads to Sir Gerald's office, Sally says, "I'm going in too." Before I can point out that he didn't summon her, she enters through the open door with the rest of us.

The office's condition startles me. The telescope on the windowsill and the stand that held a globe have been replaced by stacked ledgers and back issues. Crumpled papers overflow the wastebasket and litter the floor. Sir Gerald rises from behind a desk that's buried under documents, proof sheets, photographs, and letters. The man himself has undergone a disturbing transformation since I last saw him some two months ago. His dark brown hair has more gray streaks than I remember, and his stout figure has lost weight; his expensive suit hangs loosely on him. He must be close to seventy, and he's begun to look his age. Rumor says his wife, Lady Alexandra, has cancer, and her illness has taken a toll on him. But the stern expression on his broad, permanently tanned face forbids any word or look of sympathy.

Noticing Sally, he says, "What is it, Miss Albert?" He doesn't have much to do with the junior staff, but he knows Sally because she's my sister, and he hired her on my recommendation. My relationship with him is complicated.

Sally squares her shoulders, lifts her chin, and says, "Sir, I'd like to be assigned to the Torso Murder investigation."

I'm flabbergasted. Sally has come a long way from the shy, timid girl she once was, but I never thought she possessed the nerve to make such a bold request of Sir Gerald. Mick and Hugh look equally startled. On second thought, I shouldn't assume I know my sister well. We first met only two years ago, after I discovered her existence.

Sir Gerald, taken aback by her boldness, drops into his chair and frowns. He's one of the richest, most powerful men in England, and he doesn't like other people calling the shots. "Why do you think I want anyone to investigate the Torso Murders?"

"Because it's a big story," Sally says. "And because the *Daily World* needs a big story. Circulation has fallen by five percent during the last two months. The *Chronicle* has replaced us as London's top-selling paper."

It's true. Rumors of pay cuts and firings dominate conversations among the staff. Sir Gerald flares his nostrils like an angry bull. Hugh, Mick, and I are too aghast to speak. Sir Gerald won't like his business problems aired at a time of crisis in his personal life. The lone painting on the office wall—a ship in a storm at sea—once seemed intended to remind him of trials overcome, but now it seems a harbinger of rough seas ahead for everyone present.

Sally barrels on, heedless. "The Torso Murders could put us back in first place."

A moment of tense silence passes, then Sir Gerald bursts into good-humored laughter. "You're right, Miss Albert. Well said."

Hugh, Mick, and I sigh in relief. Sir Gerald is unpredictable, and sometimes he admires people who dare to speak unpleasant truths to him. He started out as cabin boy on a merchant ship, and he must have taken some daring risks on his rise to owner of his own fleet, a banking empire, and the *Daily World* and other newspapers around the country. Maybe he sees his younger self in Sally.

I feel a mixture of dread and anticipation.

We are going to investigate the Torso Murders, for better or worse.

Sir Gerald crosses his arms on his desk and fixes a challenging stare on Sally. "Why should I put *you* on the investigation?"

Fearful that Sally's involvement would complicate matters, I say, "Perhaps it would be better not to."

Sally looks at me, surprised I didn't stand up for her. Sir Gerald says, "Mrs. Barrett, if I want your opinion, I'll ask for it. I'm talking to Miss Albert."

"I've conducted three hundred and fifty-one interviews for the *Daily World*." Sally's voice quavers, but she radiates pride in her accomplishments. "I can get answers to questions that people don't want to answer. Which I think is a good skill for a detective."

"I agree," Sir Gerald says.

I haven't kept track of how many people I've questioned, but it's probably far fewer than three hundred and fifty-one, and often I don't get answers.

Steadier now that she's scored points with Sir Gerald, Sally says, "I know I've never investigated a murder. All I'm asking for is a chance to prove I'm capable."

"You've got it." Sir Gerald makes up his mind fast, based on long, varied experience and confidence in his ability to judge people.

"Thank you, sir!" Sally is breathless with delight. "I'll do my best."

Although I don't want to spoil her triumph, I feel duty bound to say, "This case won't be easy to solve. The police haven't gotten anywhere with the first four murders."

"I don't expect miracles," Sir Gerald says. "Just dig as hard as you can, and whatever you find out, I'll make hay with it."

That doesn't mean he won't be disappointed if we don't solve the case. And the consequences of disappointing him are dire.

"Get to work," Sir Gerald says. "Don't let the *Chronicle* break any news before we do."

After we leave Sir Gerald's office and we're back in the elevator, Mick says to Sally, "Good job twisting Sir G's arm."

"Thank you." Sally turns a quizzical look on me. "Why did you try to keep me out of the investigation?"

"Because murder investigations are dangerous," I say.

"I have to admit, Sarah is right." Hugh points at his injured arm, then at my shoulder where I was shot.

"I'll be careful," Sally says.

"I've had to eat those same words," Mick says glumly. During our last investigation, he and his former girlfriend Anjali were almost killed after they'd promised to be careful.

"We'll be hunting a killer who cuts his victims to pieces. I'm afraid of what could happen if and when we confront him," I say. Our last confrontation ended with four violent deaths.

"Why is it all right for you to be in danger, but not me?" Sally asks as we exit the elevator.

Nonplused, I stammer. Hugh says with wry amusement, "She's got you there, Sarah."

"I love you, Sally," I say. "I don't want you to get hurt." It's an awkward moment; we usually express our affection through deeds, not words. We both blush.

"I love you too," Sally says. "Do you think I like it when *you* get hurt?" She shakes her head. "If you're going to chase killers, I want to be in on it and help you stay safe." She adds wistfully, "It would be so much more interesting than reporting about new schools and railway lines."

"Can't argue with that," Hugh says.

I shush him and tell Sally, "You can write up the information we collect."

"No." Her objection is swift, vehement. "I want to interview witnesses and suspects and hunt for clues, just like you do."

"I'm not the best example to follow." Not for the first time, I regret that my example lured Sally out of a menial, low-paid, circumscribed, but safe existence as a housemaid. Her relationship with me is also a factor in her estrangement from her mother, who's the housekeeper in the same mansion where they'd lived and worked together. Her mother is furious because Sally followed me onto precarious ground.

"If we solve this case, I could be promoted to senior reporter. That would mean more money, better assignments, and I would be the top-ranking woman at the *Daily World*!" Sally shines with excitement.

"A great goal," Hugh agrees.

"You'll have other chances," I say. "You needn't endanger your life for this investigation."

"There ain't been any danger so far," Mick says.

I glower at him and Hugh. They love Sally as if she's their sister, and they have difficulty saying no to her.

Sally studies me closely. "Don't you want me to get ahead?" A frown wrinkles her smooth brow. "If I'm promoted, I'll outrank you. You're not afraid I'll show you up, are you?"

"Of course not. I want you to have everything you want." But I'm shaken by the new idea that perhaps there is rivalry between us, and perhaps the younger sister will surpass the elder.

Sally smiles. "Well, then. Let's get started."

As we walk down the hall to the darkroom, I say, "You don't understand what you've gotten yourself into. If we don't solve the case, Sir Gerald will fire us. Now your job is in jeopardy, as well as Hugh's, Mick's, and mine."

Sally rolls her eyes. "Sir Gerald is always threatening to fire you. He hasn't yet. We'll just have to make sure we solve the case."

I've lost the battle; all I can do is protect her as best I can. "I have to print the photographs of the torso. Do you want to learn how?" That should keep her safe for a while.

"I'd rather see the place where the torso was found. And start looking for clues and witnesses there."

"I'll take you," Mick says, eager for action.

Sally is already slipping out of my control, and Mick is abetting her! Hugh casts a guilty look at me and says to her, "We should review the information about the previous Torso Murders. There must be articles in the back issues of the *Daily World*. I could use some help pulling them out of the archives."

"Oh, I pulled them already," Sally says. "They're in a box on my desk. Sarah, if I don't see you again today, let's meet at Peele's Coffee House tomorrow morning at eight to compare notes and plan our next steps." Then she gaily skips off with Mick.

Chapter 3

After I print the photos and give them to the editor, I head for the Whitechapel Police Station to ask my husband what he's heard about the new murder. The police's telegraph system must have been clicking busily all afternoon, spreading the word to every precinct. Laden with photography equipment, I emerge from the underground train at Aldgate Station to find newsboys hawking broadsheets from the *Chronicle* to the crowds.

"New Torso Murder! Read all about it!"

The *Daily World* is nowhere in sight. Our rival has gotten the news out first, and Sir Gerald won't be pleased. This is a bad start for a new assignment.

Trudging down Whitechapel High Street, I bump pedestrians with my tripod and camera case. The late afternoon traffic is heavy, the day already fading into dusk. Streetwalkers dressed in ragged finery crop up under the gas lamps, outside the public houses, and at entrances to alleys. The Ripper victims were all streetwalkers, living on the fringes of society. I wonder if the same was true of the Torso Murder victims. Poverty forces many women into prostitution, makes them vulnerable to the strange men with whom they couple in dark places. I hate to think how close I came to such an existence. Impoverished by my father's desertion, alone in the world after my mother died, all I had was my modest trade as a photographer. But for sheer luck, I could have ended up on the streets, a fallen woman, prey for the Ripper.

I turn right on Leman Street and pass the carpenter and bootmaker shops, the printer and haberdasher's, the Brown Bear public house. Photographers and reporters block the street outside the five-story brick building that contains the H Division headquarters. When I move closer to see what the press conference is about, I hear a familiar, authoritative male voice speaking. The temper that lurks behind my sedate facade begins to fume even before I see the man himself at the door of the building. Dressed in a gray overcoat and black derby, he's in his mid-forties, his short brown hair, mustache, and beard flecked with gray.

Inspector Edmund Reid.

Reid and I have been bitter enemies since we first clashed during the Ripper investigation almost three years ago. He's been out to get me ever since, and for his latest ploy, he arrested my father for the murder of Ellen Casey and testified at his trial in an attempt to get him wrongly convicted. Even though the trial is four months past, my antipathy has waned not a bit.

"The Metropolitan Police has formed a new task force to investigate the Torso Murders," Reid says. "I will be heading it up here at H Division."

What a nasty surprise! During our own investigation for the *Daily World*, my friends and I will likely cross paths with Reid. But this turn of events is news for me to cover, so I set up my camera and photograph Reid and the six officers standing beside him. He introduces them as the members of the task force, detectives from various divisions. Among them is my husband.

"Detective Sergeant Thomas Barrett," Reid says.

Nowadays, Barrett wears civilian clothes instead of a uniform. His tough, handsome face is grim. Probably he would be glad to be chosen for this important investigation if it were headed by anyone but Reid. The bad blood between them is just as poisonous as between Reid and me, and I'm surprised Reid put Barrett on the task force.

I wave at Barrett. His clear gray eyes brighten, and we smile. My heart flutters. Although we've been married six months and lovers for two years, I still thrill to the sight of him.

Reid spies me. He scowls. Amid white explosions from the photographers' flash lamps, reporters shout questions. "Inspector

Reid, why are you leading the task force when only one previous Torso Murder victim was found in Whitechapel?"

"That was the Pinchin Street case. I was in charge of it. I was also on the team that investigated the Ripper murders. And the two sets of crimes are related."

I stare, appalled. Barrett tightens his jaw, as if to keep himself from shaking his head. Reid is so wrong!

"Do you mean you think the Ripper and the Torso Murderer are the same person?" a reporter asks.

"Yes, indeed." Reid speaks with utter confidence. But of course he doesn't know what happened to the Ripper. He's so obsessed with that case, so anxious for another chance to solve it. Now he thinks hunting the Torso Murderer will help him snare the Ripper. I suppose he's also hoping for new leads in the Pinchin Street murder, another he failed to solve. "I ask you to publish this message in your papers: Anyone with information that might help us identify the killer should report it at the Whitechapel Police Station. Anyone with knowledge of a missing woman who might possibly be the latest victim, please come and view the remains in the mortuary at St. George-in-the-East Church. The mortuary will be open for viewing between nine AM and six PM. In the meantime, I assure you that we will leave no stone unturned in our hunt for the killer. Thank you."

Reid waves off more questions. The group disperses, leaving me alone with Reid and Barrett. I can't resist taking another picture that captures Reid glaring at me. Reid is a wolf that someday I'll poke one time too many.

"I had a bet with myself that you would turn up." Reid's eyes remind me of a muddy pond glazed with ice.

"It's your lucky day." Barrett bristles at his superior's rudeness toward me.

Controlling my temper, I say, "I'm just doing my job."

"Well, you and your motley gang can forget about reporting on this case," Reid says. "I've made an exclusive arrangement with the *Chronicle*. Their reporters and photographers will accompany the task force during the investigation. Whatever developments arise, you and the rest of the press and public can read about in their paper."

I'm disconcerted, and so, obviously, is Barrett. Trust Reid to blindside both of us. Now I deduce how the *Chronicle* got the news out first: They'd been informed by the police.

"But the police and the *Daily World* made a deal," I say. "We're supposed to have access to information about cases, in exchange for providing publicity."

"Hasn't Sir Gerald told you?" Reid regards me with sly satisfaction. "The deal is off. I pulled some strings."

How could Sir Gerald let that happen, and why didn't he tell Hugh, Mick, Sally, and me? He knew full well that we'll be at a disadvantage while investigating the murders. But I'm angrier at Reid. "You pulled strings because of your grudge against me!"

Reid shrugs, not denying it. "Word is, Sir Gerald's lost a fortune on bad investments. He doesn't have the influence he once had. The men behind the *Chronicle* swing a lot more weight."

Dismay fills me as I begin to understand why Sir Gerald wants a big story so badly. He needs to shore up his whole empire, not just boost the *Daily World*'s circulation.

Cunning glints in Reid's eyes. "But I could cut the *Daily World* back in and tell the *Chronicle* they're out. It depends on you."

My heart sinks in a mire of dread and déjà vu. "What terms are you going to offer me this time?"

"I'll never trouble your waters again if you tell me what you know about the Ripper and the Torso Murderer."

It's a familiar proposition. Last time, for his half of the bargain, he offered to get my father acquitted. My half is the same as usual, but with a new twist: Since he thinks the Ripper is also the Torso Murderer, he expects information from me to help him solve both sets of crimes.

"She's already told you—she doesn't know anything," Barrett says.

"I've a special assignment for you, *Detective Sergeant*." Reid emphasizes the rank that he tried his best to prevent Barrett from attaining.

His abrupt change of subject disturbs me. So does the fact that he hasn't said what he'll do to me if I don't tell him my secret. Not knowing what form his revenge will take is more frightening than knowing.

"You'll guard the torso at the morgue," Reid tells Barrett.

"What?"

Reid smiles at Barrett's discomfiture. "We can't have anyone tampering with the torso. It's important evidence."

"You want me to hang around the morgue all day?"

"Nine AM to six PM."

I'm as indignant as Barrett. Guarding a piece of a corpse is not only the dullest job in the investigation but also one that offers little chance of solving the crime.

"You could give that job to a rookie constable," Barrett protests.

Reid pretends not to realize how demeaning the assignment is to a detective sergeant who's solved major cases. "Oh, you'll do more than stand guard. People will come to view it. You'll write down their names and information. This time's the charm!"

Meaning, the remains of previous victims were put on public display with no luck identifying them. Barrett says angrily, "You're shunting Sarah and me to the sidelines."

Reid points his finger at Barrett, grins, and nods. "You have your wife to thank for your assignment. I can't have her meddling like she did with the Ripper case, so I need to distance both of you from the investigation. You might cock it up to protect her."

We glare in helpless outrage. Reid pulls his watch out of his pocket, glances at it, and says to Barrett, "It's four o'clock. You'd better get to the morgue. You have two hours on duty before it closes." He tips his derby at me. "I'm off to start turning over stones."

⋆ ⋆ ⋆

Barrett and I hail a cab, load up my photography equipment, and climb aboard. As we ride, I raise my voice over the clatter of wheels and horses' hooves. "I'm afraid of what Reid will discover under those stones."

"Don't worry. Nobody who knows what happened with the Ripper will talk." Barrett sounds as if he wants to reassure himself as well as me. "If they did, they would be in trouble too."

"But what if someone we don't know about saw something?"

We're quiet as we remember the night at the slaughterhouse. I think of the extra police constables on duty, the citizens who patrolled Whitechapel during the Ripper's reign of terror, the vagrants who live on the streets.

"They would've said something by now," Barrett says.

"Maybe they didn't think it was important at the time, and they forgot, but when Reid starts asking questions, they'll remember."

"That's the trouble with cover-ups. You never know if everything you thought was hidden will stay hidden." Barrett's expression is troubled.

I'm surprised to learn that he's not as at ease with our secrets as I'd thought. He's always seemed strong and stable enough to carry the weight of the past on his shoulders, but now I realized he's as afraid of exposure as I am. He clasps my hand, offering physical comfort when words would only lend a false sense of security. The new murder has cracked open the lid of a coffin we'd thought was sealed and buried, and who knows what Reid will flush out? If it's our secret, we'll be hanged for murder.

"The police department's failure to catch the Ripper is personal for Reid," Barrett says. "He thinks that if he can solve this case, it will make up for things he didn't do, or did wrong." Regret inflects Barrett's tone. "I hate him, but I understand how he feels. Because he's not the only one who flubbed up. Remember, *I* made a mistake during the Ripper investigation. I was a constable on patrol the night Martha Tabram was murdered. I saw a soldier loitering in George Yard shortly before her body was found there. His uniform looked like the one for the Grenadier Guards. I reported him, and he became a suspect. At the identity parade at the Tower of London, I picked a private who looked like him but turned out to have an alibi. The whole fiasco wasted time that could have been used for finding real clues. If I hadn't focused my attention on that soldier, I might have spotted the Ripper. I might have prevented all six murders."

The anguish in his voice surprises me. I knew the mistake still bothered him, but until now I hadn't realized how much. Probably as much as my photographs of the Ripper's victims still plague my conscience.

"Why did Reid put you on the task force?"

"He didn't," Barrett says. "Police Commissioner Bradford did. For services rendered in the past."

Last fall we'd investigated and solved a special case for Commissioner Bradford. He's a former military officer and civil administrator who served in India, and his most notable physical feature is his missing left arm. He lost it when mauled by a tiger during a hunt. He obviously considers the task force assignment a plum job, a reward for Barrett.

"I hoped the Torso Murder investigation would be my chance to make up for my mistake," Barrett says.

"I hoped it would be my chance to make up for mine."

We hold hands, thankful for our mutual understanding and love. "We still have a chance," I remind both of us.

"Yes, and if we catch the Torso Murderer, the task force will disband," Barrett says. "Reid will have to go back to his regular work and stop turning over stones."

"I'll never accuse you of not thinking big," I say with a wry smile.

"Thinking wishfully is more like it," Barrett says. "The Torso Murderer has stumped everyone for three years."

"Mick said, 'We solved the Ripper case. We can solve this one.'"

We laugh, heartened by Mick's bravado.

The cab stops at St. George-in-the-East. The Baroque white stone church with pepper pot towers stands in spacious grounds through which we carry my photography equipment. Fog droplets glisten on the pale green spring foliage of the trees. We pass the old graveyard, with its tilted, moss-covered stones, and arrive at the morgue. In this modern era when office buildings have elevators and sometimes electric lights, morgues still tend to look as they must have in the Middle Ages. This one is a small, dingy brick building crouched amid tall shrubs planted to conceal it. Gaslight shines through the open windows and door.

"I shouldn't be here," I say. "Reid won't like information about the case leaking to me."

"I'm not worried," Barrett says. "You know how to keep secrets."

Truer words were never spoken. But I'm uneasy about keeping secrets from Sir Gerald.

Within the stained plaster walls of the morgue, Barrett and I find Dr. George Phillips, a police surgeon we know from previous investigations. Wearing rubber gloves and boots, he lays out sharp instruments on the worktop near a table covered with a sheet.

"Welcome, Detective Sergeant and Mrs. Barrett." Dr. Phillips bows. I'm glad he remembers me, as he knows I'm a reporter, so I don't need to justify my presence. With his gray mutton-chop whiskers and wearing a high-collared white shirt and black stock tie under a brown smock, he looks like a portrait of his own eighteenth-century ancestor. His gallant, old-fashioned manners match his costume. "Have you come to watch the autopsy of the Torso Murder victim? I was just about to start."

I'd hoped to miss the autopsy and would have been satisfied to be among the first to know the results. Barrett says, "I'm also here to guard the torso. Inspector Reid's orders."

"Ah." Dr. Phillips's tone says he knows about the feud between Reid and Barrett. He walks to the sheeted table.

I'm glad I know what to expect, but when Dr. Phillips pulls back the sheet, I behold a grotesque surprise—the torso has sprouted a left leg with a bare foot attached. I shudder. Barrett winces. The cold, fresh air from the open windows and door doesn't dispel the odors of dead fish, sewage, and spoiled meat.

"The police found the leg downstream." Dr. Phillips points to the red cuts where the leg had been amputated at hip, knee, and ankle. "The parts match. They're from the same person."

They bring to mind Dr. Frankenstein's monster. And now I see something terrible that the foam on the riverbank had concealed. A deep gash runs down the torso's center from breastbone to pubis. The edges of the flesh have shrunken and parted to reveal an empty red cavity.

"The organs are missing," Dr. Phillips says.

Barrett gulps. To distract myself from my own nausea, I set up my tripod, mount my camera, and insert a negative plate.

Dr. Phillips probes the gash with long forceps. "This looks like a surgical incision. The organs were cleanly removed by human hands, not scavenged by fish or other animals." He points to the stump of the neck, then the shoulders where the arms are missing. "The limbs and head were precisely amputated at the joints."

"The same as the previous victims," Barrett says. "So it is the work of the same killer."

"It seems likely," Dr. Phillips says. "The theory was that the killer is a doctor, butcher, or someone else with a knowledge of anatomy and dissection. I tend to agree. But the causes of death in the previous cases were ruled as undetermined. It may be the same for this one. There's no sign of violence inflicted before death."

I slip under the black drape on my camera and focus the torso and leg in the viewfinder. Dr. Phillips says, "Let's see what she can tell us."

The switch from considering the victim as a woman rather than a collection of body parts is disturbing. What terror and pain did she suffer? Has she a family wondering where she is and praying for her safe return? Or was she alone in the world, lacking anyone to protect her? Again I wonder if she'd been a streetwalker, like the Ripper victims, and one night she went with the wrong man, her killer. Barrett takes off his hat, as if he's at a funeral. He rumples his dark, unruly hair, his habit when he's disturbed. I hold up the flash lamp and snap the shutter. The white burst lights up Dr. Phillips as he studies the remains.

"She was white, pale-skinned, slender, with medium-blond hair." He points at the hairs on her pubis and armpits. "From the condition of her skin, she was between thirty and forty-five years old and in good health before she died." He unrolls a measuring tape and measures her from her foot to the point where the top of her head would have been. "She was approximately five feet seven inches tall."

An eerie sensation ripples my skin. He could be describing *me.* But for the grace of fortune, my remains could be lying on the table.

"She was from the upper or middle class." Dr. Phillips points to her foot as I take its picture. "It's clean and in good shape. She didn't go barefoot or walk long distances and stand for long periods of time in ill-fitting shoes."

I remember Annie Chapman lying on a morgue table. Her feet had been dirty, disfigured by callouses and ingrown toenails. Life on the streets wasn't kind to them. I'm surprised to learn that this woman was neither poor nor likely a prostitute. How did she get from the drawing room to the morgue?

"She doesn't fit the description of the Ripper victims," Barrett says. "Which Reid won't like to hear because it contradicts his theory that the Torso Murderer and the Ripper are the same individual."

Dr. Phillips examines the torso's abdomen. "I don't think she ever bore children. There are no stretch marks. To be certain would require an invasive examination, to look for marks on the pelvic bone from ligaments torn during childbirth."

"Better hold off until the public has had a go at identifying her," Barrett says.

Would that this murder didn't leave children without their mother! When I have enough photographs, I fling off the black drape.

"Did you work on the previous Torso Murder cases?" Barrett asks Dr. Phillips.

"Yes, number four—the torso found under a railway arch on Pinchin Street."

Reid's case, I recall.

"At first, I thought it would be the break that solved all the murders," Dr. Phillips says. "The torso was found on dry land and not altered by submersion in the river. It was wrapped in a torn chemise, a possible clue. The arms were attached, and the victim had a smallpox vaccination mark and an injured right finger. A hundred extra policemen were brought in from other divisions. They went house to house, searching for evidence and focusing on butchers. Alas, nothing came of it. I think the investigation suffered because of the theory that the Ripper is the Torso Murderer. The police stopped the inquiries in favor of sifting through evidence and witnesses from the Ripper cases."

Barrett and I exchange a somber glance: Thanks to Reid, the new investigation is bound to take the same wrong approach.

"At the inquest, the coroner asked me if there was any similarity between the Pinchin Street murder and the murder of Mary Kelly. I had performed Miss Kelly's autopsy, and I testified that her injuries resulted from wanton savagery, whereas the Pinchin Street corpse suggested careful dismemberment for the sake of disposal."

Obviously, the differences hadn't been enough to change Reid's opinion that both murders were the work of the same person.

"Have you any theories?" Barrett asks.

"Other than that the Torso Murderer is a seriously deranged individual?" Dr. Phillips shakes his head. "I will say the timing is of interest. The Pinchin Street murder happened in September 1889. Why did the killer wait until now to kill again?"

Barrett and I have no answer to the question.

"But it seems that a multiple murderer who's lain low for a year and eight months is back in action," I say.

"And this new murder promises more to come if he's not caught," Barrett says.

Chapter 4

Whitechapel, in the East End of London, was the notorious hunting ground of Jack the Ripper. It's also home to S. B. Barrett Photographer & Co., the name of which is emblazoned in gold letters on the window of one in a row of eighteenth-century buildings on the high street. I, Sarah Bain Barrett, am the proud proprietress; "& Co." is Barrett, Mick, Hugh, and Fitzmorris. My studio occupies the ground floor, and we inhabit the living quarters above.

I've been alone for most of my adult life, and sometimes I can't believe I live with four other people, all men, in close, often fractious camaraderie. We're a family, albeit an unconventional one, bound as strongly by love and loyalty as if we were blood kin. And I owe them more than the affection they've shown me. They rescued me from loneliness on the margins of society. Mick came along first; then Hugh, along with Fitzmorris; and then Barrett, the cornerstone of my secure place in the world. No other person provides a woman as much respectability as a husband. That I'm passionately in love with Barrett is a bonus. Not every woman can afford to marry for love; not every love match is as blessed with compatibility as ours.

At six thirty in the evening, the high street is a river of lights from windows, cabs, and streetlamps, all blurred by the misty rain. Barrett and I walk home past the peddlers and newsboys, shopkeepers welcoming late customers, and patrons entering public houses. Behind the prosperous, respectable commercial zone lie some of London's most poverty-stricken slums. In their dark alleys and courtyards amid the squalid lodging houses and tenements, none but the streetwalkers, the homeless, and the predators are abroad after dark. From the butcher shops and slaughterhouses wafts the odor of blood and decay, an ever-present reminder of mortality.

Is the Torso Murderer hunting his next victim now?

Giggles emanate from the alley between the Angel pub and our house. Peering inside, I see Mick flirting with a pretty blond girl—the grocer's teenage daughter, Nancy. In recent months, the neighborhood girls have woken up to the fact that Mick, the scruffy former street urchin, has matured into a handsome, rakish charmer.

Barrett chuckles. "Romeo is at it again."

I'm less amused than sorry for Mick. During a previous case, he fell in love with Anjali Lodge, but the outcome of our investigation led her to end their relationship. Mick tried to win her back, with no luck. I think he romances other girls in an effort to forget Anjali. I only hope nobody gets hurt.

Mick bends his head to kiss Nancy. An irate male voice calls her name, and I turn to see her father, in shirtsleeves and apron, coming down the street. He goes into the alley, seizes his protesting daughter by the arm. "You're coming home now, girl." He glares at Mick as he drags Nancy away.

When Mick was a street urchin, the neighborhood men disliked him because he stole from their shops. Now, woe betide him if he gets their daughters with child. I can't blame the men. Illegitimate pregnancy is a disaster that has been the ruin of many girls. Unwanted by respectable men, they're consigned to remain single, working for a meager living if their families can't or won't support them and their children. The descent down the social and economic ladder could eventually put them on the streets with the likes of the Ripper victims.

"Hullo," Mick says cheerfully to Barrett and me, unabashed by the little drama we witnessed. "I just took Sally home. While we were at the river, the coppers found a leg."

"We know," I say. "We saw it at the morgue."

Barrett, Mick, and I enter our house. Three stories high, plus an attic set beneath a gable, the whitewashed stucco building is the sanctuary to which we return after days often plagued by strife and violence. In the studio, a sense of peace calms me as soon as I see the carved furniture and gas chandelier, the Turkey carpet and cabinet full of props, the rolled backdrops on a stand, and my gallery of framed photographs on the wall near the darkroom. I put away my equipment and follow Barrett and Mick upstairs to our living quarters. There, Hugh sits in the dining room, with a large sheet of heavy white paper spread on the table, drawing in different colors of ink. Fitzmorris, officially his valet and unofficially our housekeeper, cook, accountant, and manager, is in the kitchen preparing supper.

"I read up on the Torso Murders, and I thought a map that shows where the body parts were found would be useful," Hugh says.

A thick, curving blue line marked "River Thames" snakes lengthwise across the paper. In black ink, Hugh has labeled the bridges—Hammersmith—the farthest west, Wandsworth, Battersea, Albert, Chelsea, Vauxhall, Lambeth, Westminster, Waterloo, Blackfriars, Southwark, London, and Tower. Red dots, numbers, and notes mark various locations along the river.

"It's a work of art," I say with sincere admiration.

"I do say so myself." Hugh smiles as he draws tiny figures and arrows by the red dots. The figures are arms, hands, legs, feet, and torsos. It's morbid, but I'm glad to see him so enthusiastic about his work. For months after his injury, he had no interest in anything.

Fitzmorris, thin, gray-haired, and dapper, appears with a stack of dinner plates. "You'd better move your creation, Lord Michelangelo. Time to eat." His family has served Hugh's for generations, and he loves Hugh like a brother. No one was more devastated by Hugh's almost fatal injury, and no one is happier now that Hugh has regained his high spirits.

Hugh clears away his pens and inks, takes down the watercolor paintings that decorate the wall, and tacks up his map. We sit down to fried lamb chops, mashed potatoes, and peas. While we eat, Hugh turns in his chair to read off the map, briefing us on the previous Torso Murders.

"May eleventh, 1887. The first victim's lower torso was found off Rainham, near the Victoria Dock. On June fifth, a thigh turned up by Temple Pier, and the upper torso on the south riverbank by Battersea Park pier. June thirtieth, two legs in Regent's Canal."

Hugh points at the locations on the map. "Autumn 1888, the second Torso Murder. The torso, the arms, and the left leg with attached foot were found in Whitehall, at the site where the New Scotland Yard headquarters were under construction."

"On the coppers' own territory!" Mick says.

"And during the Ripper investigation," I say.

Barrett groans. "I remember. It felt like a slap in the face."

"I'll skip ahead to victim number four," Hugh says. "September 1889, a torso with arms and hands was found under the railway arch on Pinchin Street." It's the one Dr. Phillips mentioned, Inspector Reid's unsolved case. "No other parts turned up. And now for number three. This is where things get interesting. Her lower torso was found on June fourth, 1889, in Bermondsey—near Horsleydown Stairs, where Sarah found the new torso. The same day, a thigh turned up on the Battersea shore. Upper body, June sixth, near the Albert Bridge. Left leg, June sixth, Copington's Wharf. Right leg and foot, June seventh, Limehouse. Left arm, June eighth, Southwark. Pelvis and buttocks, June eighth, near Battersea Park Pier. Other thigh, Chelsea Embankment; right arm, June tenth, Southwark Bridge."

The litany of dates and body parts is a sobering reminder of how horrible the crimes are. I picture the Thames's dark, oily water afloat with severed limbs. They gradually sink to the bottom, decompose, and join layers of ancient skeletons.

"We don't know if any of those locations are actual crime scenes," Barrett says. "The remains could have been dumped anywhere upstream from where they were found."

I perceive why Hugh thinks the third murder is the most interesting. "Was victim number three the only one identified?"

"Right," Hugh says. "She was seven or eight months pregnant before she died, and the baby was removed."

I wince and feel a pang in my own stomach. I wonder if the pregnancy had anything to do with her murder. Was she killed by the father because he didn't want the child?

"She also had a distinctive scar on her wrist," Hugh says. "Her mother came forward to report her missing and identify her. Her name was Elizabeth Jackson."

How awful for her mother! Not only to learn that her daughter had been killed, but to see remains akin to those now lying in the morgue.

"Wasn't there a suspect in the Elizabeth Jackson case?" Barrett says.

"Yes, a miller named John Faircloth, the father of her child," Hugh says. "Neighbors said he beat Elizabeth regularly, but he had an alibi."

So much for my idea about her killer's identity and motive. I'm losing hope that the old cases will cast light on the new. "Were any clues found with the other victims' remains?"

"The Whitehall torso was wrapped in a black dress with a label from a factory in Bradford," Hugh says. "Nobody came forward to identify the dress. It could have been purchased secondhand by the victim or the killer."

"I remember that the victims had little in common besides their murders," Barrett says.

"Unfortunately true," Hugh says. "They were within the same age range—twenties to thirties—but that doesn't narrow it down much. The Rainham and Whitehall women were brunettes; Elizabeth Jackson had sandy hair. The Rainham, Whitehall, and Pinchin victims had been in good health, and their hands were unaccustomed to manual labor, which indicates middle or upper class. Elizabeth was a streetwalker who'd been sleeping rough on the Thames Embankment. And she was the only one confirmed to be pregnant when she died."

We're silent as the sheer improbability of solving the case sinks in.

"But here are some interesting facts," Hugh says. "The Rainham torso had been in the water longer than the limbs. And the Whitehall victim's torso hadn't been at the construction site as long as the other parts. Which means the killer hung onto some parts and disposed of them later."

Revulsion fills me as I picture remains stored in trunks. *"Who does that?"*

My companions respond with bewildered looks. The killer we're hunting is not only elusive but of a breed which we've never before encountered.

"Barrett and I have bad news," I say. We tell Hugh and Mick what happened with Inspector Reid. All the while, Mick jiggles his foot and glances at the clock. I say, "Are we keeping you from something?"

"I got a date to the Oxford Music Hall."

"With Nancy?" I ask. "Her father wouldn't approve."

"That's putting it mildly," Hugh says.

"Not her," Mick says. "Maureen Howard."

"The barmaid at the Angel? But she's older than you," I say.

"Only five years," Mick says.

Hugh laughs. "Well, Maureen should know how to look after herself."

"Gotta run. See you later." Mick bolts down the stairs. The door slams.

It's occurred to me that my cherished living situation isn't permanent. If Barrett and I have children, we'll need more room, but Mick may be the first to leave. He spends less and less time at home, he earns enough money to support himself elsewhere, and he likes independence. The thought of my family moving on, growing apart, fills me with apprehension, an echo of the loss I felt as a child when my father disappeared.

Thank God, I'll still have Barrett. He promised to have and hold me until death do us part. He's the man who won't leave me.

The doorbell jangles. Hugh says, "That's Dr. Lewes. I invited him over."

He goes downstairs and returns with Dr. Lewes, an extremely thin, youngish man with sharp cheekbones and prominent nose. Black clothing and shaggy, unfashionably long black hair emphasize the paleness of his complexion. Barrett and I greet him warmly. Joshua Lewes is the psychologist who helped Hugh recover from his injury and severe depression. If not for him, my dear friend probably would have committed suicide. And I'm glad Hugh has gained a confidant after losing all his longtime friends during the scandal precipitated by the vice squadron raid.

"I asked Dr. Lewes to help us with the case," Hugh says.

"I would be glad to," Dr. Lewes says in his clear, Welsh-accented voice. He's not handsome, but his smile and the intelligence in his deep-set black eyes render him attractive. "It sounds most intriguing."

The news is a rather unwelcome surprise. It's one thing for Hugh to bring Dr. Lewes into our household, another to include him in our work. But Sally barged into the investigation without asking our permission, and Hugh didn't object, so I smile and keep mum.

"What kind of help?" Barrett asks in a neutral tone that suggests he's reserving judgment until he has all the facts.

"Joshua is an expert on the psychology of criminals." At first, Hugh had been skeptical of Dr. Lewes's profession, but now he's a fervent believer. I still have my own reservations about psychology, although I can't dispute the benefits for Hugh.

Dr. Lewes smiles modestly. "I wouldn't say *expert*, but I have interviewed criminals and studied cases—at Broadmoor and the Salpêtrière. I've written monographs and presented them to conferences in New York and corresponded with psychologists and police in other countries."

Broadmoor is England's famous prison for the criminally insane, and the Salpêtrière a French asylum. "How impressive," I say.

"He can give us a psychological profile of the Torso Murderer," Hugh says.

"I've never heard of doing that." Skepticism tinges Barrett's voice.

"It's a relatively new science," Dr. Lewes says.

"I think it's worth a try," Hugh says. "Sarah?"

"Yes," I say, willing to take a chance for Hugh's sake. Barrett hesitates before he nods.

We move to the parlor. Barrett and I take our customary seats on the divan, and Hugh claims the chaise longue. Dr. Lewes sits in one of the two armchairs by the hearth. He's sat there before, but tonight he seems an interloper. Hugh fills Dr. Lewes in on the Torso Murders past and present. I don't know anything about Hugh's therapy; Hugh doesn't talk about it, and Dr. Lewes refused to tell me, saying it was confidential. I wonder, not for the first time, what Hugh has told Dr. Lewes.

Does Dr. Lewes know our secret about the Ripper?

I trusted him with Hugh's life. Can I trust him with my life—and Mick's and Barrett's?

"The only case I know of that's similar to the Torso Murders is the Battersea Mystery of 1873," Dr. Lewes says. "Severed body parts of a woman were found in the river, in various locations between Hammersmith and Woolwich."

I frown in surprised dismay. "I wasn't aware that the recent cases weren't the first."

"Now that you mention it, I remember my father talking about the Battersea case," Barrett says. His father was a police constable at the time. "I was only fifteen in 1873. I'd forgotten."

Now I understand why I hadn't heard. "I was away at school."

"So was I," Hugh says. "Not that I'd have paid attention to crimes even if I'd been in London. I was oblivious to anything outside my own social circle. Was the Battersea killer caught?"

"Unfortunately not," Dr. Lewes says.

"Might he be the same person who killed the five other women?" I wonder aloud. "He could still be alive."

"So where's he been for eighteen years?" Barrett asks Dr. Lewes, "Why stop killing and then start again so long afterward?"

"I don't know," Dr. Lewes says.

Barrett ponders, then nods. He seems to like that Dr. Lewes gave him a straight, honest answer.

The more I hear, the more disturbed I am. The criminal we're seeking may have evaded capture for not just four years, but seventeen. "Were there any clues from the Battersea murder?"

"Almost all of the victim was recovered," Dr. Lewes says, "but her face had been mutilated, and she was never identified.

The only clue was a tattoo on her arm, which indicated that she may have been a prostitute."

Was she the Torso Murderer's first victim? I doubt any evidence would be left to find after seventeen years. The case is looking to be an even harder nut to crack than I'd thought.

"Since the Battersea killer was never caught, the case doesn't tell us anything about him that might apply to the Torso Murderer, if they're not the same person." Barrett's expression challenges Dr. Lewes. "How is psychology going to help us?"

Unfazed, Dr. Lewes says, "My research shows that every crime sheds light on the criminal, even if he didn't leave any physical clues. The Torso Murders tell us something about the man behind them. He planned his crimes; they didn't result from a sudden violent impulse. He neatly, surgically dismembered his victims—he's meticulous. He didn't dispose of all the parts at once. Chances are, he kept some back because that would delay their discovery and decrease the likelihood that the victims would be identified."

"Which means he's patient," Hugh says, anxious to champion Dr. Lewes.

"The fact that the body parts turned up in such far-flung locations suggests he didn't dump them all in the river at the same place," Dr. Lewes adds.

I'm gaining enthusiasm for psychology. "He dumped them in different places to make it harder for the police to figure out where he killed the women, so there's no murder scene to give away clues. He covered his tracks. He's intelligent."

"Also, daring enough to risk carrying body parts around the city and down to the river on multiple occasions," Hugh says.

"A more impulsive, less disciplined person would yield to the temptation to get rid of the incriminating evidence as quickly as possible," Dr. Lewes says. "He also has a place where he can cut up bodies in privacy and store the parts without anyone noticing."

"He could be wealthy enough to own his own house," I say.

"Wealthy and insane?" Hugh looks to Dr. Lewes.

"I don't think he's insane. His effort to avoid detection shows that at least he understands the law and he's aware of the consequences he would suffer if he were caught. That's not to say he's normal. He lacks empathy. Other people are nothing to him except as they serve his own selfish needs. His actions show no remorse toward his victims."

I've met such men. I dread meeting another.

"But he must appear normal enough that nobody suspects what he's up to," Dr. Lewes says. "He may even be married."

"Like Bluebeard," Hugh says.

I shiver as I recall the fairy tale about a wife who sneaks into her husband's forbidden chamber and discovers the corpses of his previous wives.

"The Torso Murderer may have lured the women to the place where he killed them," Dr. Lewes says. "Which reminds me of a case in France. Between 1855 and 1861, a man named Martin Dumollard approached young women and told them he was looking for a servant. He offered them a high-paying job. Then he led them to deserted places, such as the woods. He violently attacked at least twelve women and murdered three."

Unfortunately, it seems that serial murder is a worldwide phenomenon, not confined to Britain.

"His life of crime came to an end when he attacked a girl named Marie Pichon. She managed to escape, and she described him to the police. They searched his house and found clothing that belonged to his victims. He was put to death on the guillotine in March 1862." Dr. Lewes has a remarkable memory for names, dates, and details. "His wife was convicted as his accomplice and sentenced to twenty years' labor in prison because she had sold some of the victims' belongings."

"How is that case relevant to the Torso Murders?" Barrett asks.

"Martin Dumollard was personable enough that the women trusted him," Dr. Lewes says. "The same could be true of the Torso Murderer. He may even be attractive and charming."

"I don't disagree with anything you've said," Barrett says, "but it doesn't tell us what he looks like or where he is."

"Psychology has its limits," Dr. Lewes readily admits.

"I'm sure it will come in handy at some point," Hugh says.

I add my support for Dr. Lewes. "When we meet the Torso Murderer, maybe we'll recognize him from Dr. Lewes's profile."

"*If* we meet the Torso Murderer," Barrett says. "First, we have to find him—and how are we supposed to do that without any clues besides a description of his personality?"

"I'm sorry I couldn't be of more help," Dr. Lewes says, regretful but not offended.

"Thank you anyway," Barrett says with sincere gratitude. Whenever we in this household thank Dr. Lewes for any favor or courtesy, we're also thanking him for saving Hugh's life.

Soon Dr. Lewes takes his leave. Hugh walks him to the door, and Barrett and I help Fitzmorris clean the kitchen. Then Hugh goes up to bed. It's only eight o'clock, but he still tires easily. Fitzmorris retreats to his room, leaving Barrett and me alone in the parlor.

"I have to go out," Barrett announces.

Surprised because he hadn't mentioned any plans for tonight, I say, "Why?"

"To look for the Torso Murderer."

Chapter 5

"You're going to look for the Torso Murderer *now*?" I say, puzzled as well as surprised.

"When else?" Barrett stands up from his seat on the divan beside me. "I'll be stuck in the morgue all day tomorrow."

"How do you even know where to look?"

Barrett smiles with mixture of bravado and mischief. "I've a trick up my sleeve."

Even after two years together, he can still astonish me. He explains, "When I was a patrol constable, I made a list of suspicious folks that I thought could be the Ripper. I spied on them, hoping to catch someone red-handed." Barrett chuckles. "I dreamed of being the hero who arrested the Ripper."

I admire his initiative. "You never told me."

"After everything that happened later, it didn't seem important. But now . . ." Barrett's eyes gleam with excitement. "Maybe one of them is the Torso Murderer."

Intrigued by the possibility, I say, "Let me see the list."

Barrett reaches in his pocket and pulls out a folded paper. "I keep it updated, out of habit." He unfolds it to reveal seven handwritten names, all but two crossed out. "The crossed-out ones are dead. Of those, three were hanged for unrelated murders. So I was right in thinking they were bad apples, even though they turned out not to be the Ripper."

The remaining two are "S. Klosowski" and "V. Pearcy." Neither name is familiar to me. I imagine Barrett standing on one side of a deep canyon and the Torso Murderer hidden somewhere on the other. The list seems like a bridge Barrett is building on a shaky foundation. I feel compelled to say, "It's a long shot."

"What other shot do we have?" Barrett grabs his coat and hat from the stand.

"Wait." I'd rather gamble on his list than sit idle. "I'm going with you."

"No." Barrett's opposition is quick, adamant. "It's dangerous for a woman to be out on the streets after dark."

Whitechapel is rife with crime, even now that the Ripper is gone. "You'll protect me."

"One of these people could be a murderer," Barrett says.

"We've confronted other murderers and lived to tell," I say.

"Barely! I would rather not have to worry about your safety."

I mustn't say I'm worried about *his* safety. For his wife to doubt his ability to take care of himself would insult a man who's been on the police force twelve years and spent most of that time patrolling Whitechapel alone.

"You won't have to worry about me." I go to the side table, open a drawer, and take out my pistol.

Barrett frowns. In our previous investigations, guns figured disastrously. But when I offer him his own pistol from the drawer, he takes it. Better to be prepared than not.

⋆ ⋆ ⋆

On the Whitechapel High Street, shops are closed for the night, the traffic reduced to a lone cab that rattles past Barrett and me as we walk in the haloes of yellow light from gas lamps and through the dark stretches between them. The fog renders everything more than ten feet ahead of us invisible. Cold droplets tainted with soot and chemicals fill each breath I take, as if I'm submerged in polluted water. Sounds drift and disorient; I can't tell where the footsteps, the train whistle, and the laughter I hear are coming from, whether the danger I take for granted is near or far. In the autumn of 1888, I spent nights such as this following the Ripper's next victims, trying to protect them and catastrophically failing. Now I'm on the hunt again, for a killer who's even more elusive and perhaps more dangerous.

"Severin Klosowski," Barrett says. "A Polish immigrant, age twenty-six. He was a surgeon's apprentice in Poland."

"Which means he has the right skills to be the Torso Murderer." I begin to think that maybe Barrett's list isn't such a shaky bridge after all.

"He's a barber now." Barrett stops outside the White Hart pub. "His shop is in the basement."

We loiter outside the narrow, three-story building. Lights in the windows show customers drinking at the bar. On the right is an alley lit by a gas lamp at the entrance.

"Why did you think Mr. Klosowski might be the Ripper?" I ask.

"He's a regular customer of the streetwalkers. And wait till you see him."

We don't have to wait long. In the alley, the White Hart's side door opens. A man appears, dressed in a black coat and black top hat. His boots must be rubber soled, for they don't make noise as he walks toward us.

Barrett whispers, "That's him."

Klosowski moves past us with a furtive, slouching posture. He has heavy dark eyebrows and a thick black mustache. A shiver runs through me. He fits the description of a man whom multiple witnesses claimed they saw with the Ripper's victims immediately prior to their deaths or near the crime scenes. If I didn't know better, I would think I was seeing the Ripper now. Barrett and I follow Klosowski at a distance from which his black figure is a mere hazy shape in the fog. He slinks past warehouses, the Bull Inn pub, and Aldgate Station, then pauses at St. Botolph's Church. The tall, square tower dwarfs the brick building; fog shrouds the steeple. Around the iron fence that encloses the churchyard marches a slow, ragtag parade of women. St. Botolph's is nicknamed "Prostitutes' Church" for the streetwalkers who congregate outside at night. Unless they keep moving, the police will arrest them. They walk in down-at-the-heel slippers or bare feet. Layers of tatty clothing with dirty hems keep out the cold; paper flowers smarten up frayed straw bonnets. Men eye the women and take their pick. Couples vanish into the fog.

Barrett and I watch Klosowski scan the parade. Two women walking together catch my attention. One wears a black-and-white-checked scarf and a red silk rose. The other, small and slim in a fur-trimmed coat over a green skirt patterned with daisies, has curly auburn hair.

Liz Stride and Kate Eddowes!

My heart seizes. Liz and Kate look just as they did when I saw them here the night the Ripper killed them. The next time I saw them, they were both dead, Liz with her throat cut, Kate horribly butchered. I gasp and blink. The woman I thought was Liz is a haggard blonde in a gray coat; "Kate" is a plain young redhead in a velvet jacket, striped frock, and scuffed work boots. The redhead makes eyes at Klosowski and beckons. He strides up to her. She steps out of the parade, and they negotiate terms. She takes his arm, and they walk away together. Barrett and I follow as they proceed down Aldgate High Street, then turn right on Duke Street between rows of tenements. I suddenly know where they're going, and I shy like a horse alarmed by a thunderclap.

"Hurry, or we'll lose them," Barrett whispers.

I press forward as my nerves shrill in protest. Just as I intuited, Klosowski and the woman turn down Church Passage, a narrow alley. Barrett and I trail them. The lamp over the entrance illuminates dirty cobblestones and the obscene words scribbled in chalk on the walls. I steel myself for the sight of the place I've avoided since the last time I was there, in 1888.

Barrett says under his breath, "Mitre Square. Damn."

He too realizes where Klosowski is taking the woman. Mitre Square is frequented by streetwalkers and their clients. Convenient to St. Botolph's, deserted at night, and private enough for a quick transaction, it's where Kate Eddowes met her death at the hands of the Ripper.

Klosowski and the woman outpace us. Their bawdy laughter echoes from the square. Barrett and I emerge into a large, dim courtyard surrounded by warehouses, tenements with boarded-up windows, and a picture frame factory. My memory fills the space with an ambulance wagon and glaring lights from bullseye lanterns. Policemen stand in the corner. At their feet, Kate lies in a puddle of blood, her skirts pushed above her waist, her face slashed. Her bowels ooze from a cut that sliced her abdomen.

Screams jolt me, dispelling the terrible memory. The square is dim, deserted except in the corner where Kate died. There, Klosowski fights with the woman. He tears at her clothes, growls like an animal. She punches him, screaming, "Lemme go! Help!"

As we rush to her rescue, Klosowski shoves her up against the wall and closes his hands around her neck. Barrett shouts, "Severin Klosowski!"

Startled by the sound of his name, the man relaxes his grip on the woman. She wrenches free of him and runs away. Klosowski yells angry words in a foreign language that I take to be Polish, then glares at us.

"What the hell you think you doing?" A heavy accent inflects his guttural voice.

"Stopping you from hurting that woman and getting yourself in trouble." Barrett's voice is quiet and steady, the one he uses to calm dangerous situations.

Under his thick black brows, Klosowski's black eyes glitter with a fierce, maniacal light. "I teach you to mind your own business." He dips his hand into his coat pocket and pulls out a small, thin object. I hear a click, and a steel blade flashes in the meager light.

Without conscious thought or mutual decision, Barrett and I draw our guns and aim them at Klosowski. "Drop it," Barrett says.

Klosowski gapes, shocked that the busybodies who interrupted his pleasure are armed. His out-thrust jaw and huffing breaths signify an aggression that's barely under his control. My gun trembles in my hand. I've never shot anyone, and past experience has shown me that I can't. I pray to God that if shooting is necessary this time, Barrett will do it, and he won't miss.

Klosowski opens his fingers and lets the knife fall. It clanks on the pavement and skitters to rest at our feet. My breath seeps from me with tentative relief. Barrett cautiously bends and picks up the knife, his gun still aimed at Klosowski.

"Who the hell are you?" Klosowski demands.

"Detective Sergeant Barrett, Metropolitan Police."

Recognition gleams in Klosowski's eyes. "I've seen you before." Suspicion draws his heavy brows together. "Were you following me?"

"It's a good thing I was, for her sake." Barrett glances in the direction the woman ran.

"I wasn't going to hurt her. I was just having little fun."

Angry on her behalf, I say, "It didn't look like she was having fun."

Klosowski fixes his smoldering stare on me. "You are that photographer lady from the high street."

I flinch. This violent man knows not only who I am but where I live.

"I think you like to hurt women," Barrett says. "Ever killed one?"

"No." Klosowski sounds offended.

Barrett examines the knife. "Ever used this on anybody?"

"Is for defending myself only. Is dangerous here. You police, you should know."

Barrett turns the knife so the blade flashes. "You could cut up a body with it."

"I never!" Klosowski says, indignant.

"You were a surgeon's apprentice," I say. "You must have dissected bodies."

"That was long time ago. I am barber now. I only cut hair." Klosowski pantomimes snipping with scissors.

"Do you know Elizabeth Jackson?" Barrett asks.

"No." Klosowski answers promptly but warily.

"She was once a streetwalker," Barrett says. "Did you have 'fun' with her?"

Klosowski shifts his weight from one heavy black boot to the other, as if uncomfortable with the direction the conversation has taken. "I said I don't know her. What is this about?"

"Elizabeth Jackson was murdered in June 1889," I say. "Her body was cut in pieces and thrown in the river."

Klosowski beholds Barrett with appalled, angry enlightenment. "You trying to pin it on me? Well, I did not do it."

"Maybe you think you didn't know her because you didn't ask her name before you killed her," Barrett says. "Elizabeth Jackson was seven months pregnant. Does that ring a bell?"

"It wasn't me," Klosowski says stubbornly.

I begin to think we're barking up the wrong tree. He sounds insulted by the accusation and not as scared as he would be if it were on the mark.

"Or maybe Elizabeth slipped your mind because she's only one of five murders, and you can't keep track of them all. Maybe you'll have a better memory of the woman whose remains turned up in the river today." Barrett demands, "Who is she?"

Klosowski stares at Barrett as if he's gone mad; then his expression turns slyly cheerful. "I have heard of these murders. First one, 1887, no?"

"Yes," Barrett says, a hint of a confusion in his voice.

"In 1887, I still in Poland," Klosowski announces triumphantly. "I not come to England until 1888. Somebody killing and cutting up women before I get here. Someone doing it again now. Not me."

Being in a faraway foreign country is a good alibi, and some quick arithmetic tells me that even if Klosowski had been in England at the time of the Battersea murder, he was only eight years old in 1873.

Barrett, undaunted, says, "You were here for the four other murders, including the latest."

Scorn twists Klosowski's mouth under the heavy mustache. "You got wrong man."

"Who is she?" Barrett repeats.

"Hell if I know. You gonna arrest me?"

Barrett hesitates; I sense him imagining what Reid would say if he brought in Klosowski on a mere hunch.

Klosowski emits a gruff bark of laughter. "You got nothing on me. I'm going now." He holds out his palm. "Give me my knife."

"I'm confiscating it," Barrett says.

His black eyes burning with fury, stymied by our guns, Klosowski curses in Polish. Then he stalks off.

Barrett folds the knife and tucks it in his pocket. "I'll give it to Dr. Phillips. Maybe he can tell if it matches the knife that was used on the latest victim."

As we retrace our steps back through Church Passage, I say, "If the murders are connected, then Klosowski isn't the killer."

"*If* they're connected."

"You don't think so?" I'm surprised that he could disregard their similarities.

"They appear to be, but I'm not convinced they're the work of one person."

Our investigation has barely begun, and we're already disagreeing.

"For now, I'm not ruling out Klosowski," Barrett says.

I think he's grasping at a flimsy straw because he hasn't much chance of finding better leads. "We just saw Klosowski pick up a random woman, in front of many witnesses, and attack her minutes later in a public place. He never even looked behind him to see if anyone was following him. One could hardly call him patient or careful. He doesn't fit Dr. Lewes's profile."

"I don't put much stock in Dr. Lewes's profile."

"I gathered that. But I think he made some good observations about the Torso Murderer."

"It seems like guesswork."

He's in a bad mood because his confrontation with Klosowski went nowhere, and I don't want to aggravate him, but I say, "Dr. Lewes based his profile on cases he's studied and criminals he's met."

"He's not a police officer. And he can't have met as many criminals as I have."

So this has turned into a contest, his expertise versus the psychologist's. Men can be so exasperatingly competitive. "He's trying to help us. We can use all the help we can get."

"Now that I'm stuck on morgue duty, you mean." An edge harshens Barrett's voice. He walks faster, as if he could outrun the unpleasant truths.

I hurry to catch up with him. "We're both on the sidelines because of Inspector Reid. I meant we can't afford to ignore Dr. Lewes's opinions."

"Well, he has his opinions. I have mine."

Barrett's tone says the matter is closed. If I push him, we'll quarrel, and a few months ago, a bad quarrel nearly ended our marriage. I hesitate before asking, "What are you going to do about Mr. Klosowski?"

"Keep an eye on him. Meanwhile, there's one more name on my list."

"I remember. Who is V. Pearcy?"

"It's getting late. I'll introduce you tomorrow."

* * *

On the way home, Barrett refuses to answer more questions. I'm left wondering why he doesn't want to talk about V. Pearcy. We trudge up the stairs to our room, weary from the long, difficult day. When we're in bed together, we kiss and say, "I love you."

After our last case, during which we both were almost killed, we promised never to go to sleep without first kissing and voicing our love for each other. It's become a ritual that reminds us that we're fortunate in our marriage, our life together. No matter what happens during the day, at the end of it, we have these blessed private hours of intimacy. My desire for my husband kindles, and I press myself against him. No matter who or what else I lose, I'll have Barrett, and lovemaking can soothe many worries.

"Not now." He rolls onto his side, facing the wall.

I'm surprised because he rarely turns me down. It's my first inkling that he's more upset about our dispute, and Inspector Reid, than I'd thought.

"I'm tired," he says. "I'm sorry."

"It's all right." But I can't help feeling rejected. Hurt and cross, I stare at the ceiling and brood until the ache of desire fades and I fall asleep.

Chapter 6

At seven the next morning, Barrett and I are at breakfast with Fitzmorris when Hugh comes downstairs. "Where's Mick?" I ask. "We'll be late to meet Sally."

Yawning, Hugh pours himself a cup of coffee. "I just woke him. He didn't get in till two."

Barrett stands. "I'm off."

"I thought the morgue didn't open for viewing until nine," I say.

"I want to stop at the station before Reid gets there, and find out if there've been any new developments in the case. I have friends who'll keep me posted."

"Good luck," I say.

"I'll let you know if any leads come up at the morgue."

"I have a hunch someone will identify the victim," Hugh says, optimistic as usual.

"Even if they don't, their missing persons could be the previous victims," Barrett says.

I remind him, "Reid doesn't want you leaking information to me."

Barrett snorts in disgust. "Reid wants to hoard clues, but the investigation needs more people rather than fewer. I'd rather aggravate him than give up a chance at getting justice for those women." He kisses me, says, "See you tonight," and departs.

"I admire his principles," Hugh says.

I do too, but I'm thinking of Martha Tabram, the soldier in George Yard, and the botched identity parade. There's more at stake for Barrett besides catching the Torso Murderer. He's often accused me of recklessness, yet how far into jeopardy is he willing to step?

Mick runs in, buttoning his waistcoat, his hair damp and streaked with lines from combing. He gulps coffee and bolts down a piece of toast. "Let's go."

★ ★ ★

At Peele's Coffee House on Fleet Street, Sally, Hugh, Mick, and I claim our favorite table by the window, where we can watch passersby. The room is warm and cozy from the steaming coffee urns and the fire in the hearth. On the chimneypiece, a portrait of Dr. Samuel Johnson looks down his nose at us while we greet fellow reporters who also frequent Peele's. Guests from the hotel that occupies the building's upper stories tuck into hearty breakfasts of chops, steak, and fish. I wonder which folks are witnesses for trials at Old Bailey. The hotel capitalizes on its location near the courthouse and advertises its accommodations for witnesses who live out of town.

Hugh opens a copy of the *Chronicle*, taken from Peele's stock of the latest newspapers. "Let's see what our rival has to say about the Torso Murders." He reads aloud, "'Were the victims fallen angels expelled from heaven after they sinned against God? Were they rendered mortal and hurled into the river? Are their broken bodies a lesson to mankind?'" Hugh snorts in derision. "How's that for purple prose?"

"I'm afraid the *Chronicle* has the advantage over us," I say, and inform Sally that Inspector Reid cut the *Daily World* out of the police investigation.

"Why didn't Sir Gerald tell us?" Sally says.

That's exactly what I've been wondering, and I voice a possible answer. "I think he figured we'd find out soon enough, and it's our problem, not his."

"He might have forgotten." Ever compassionate, Sally says, "The poor man has a lot on his mind."

"Maybe he don't know," Mick says.

This simplest answer is the most worrisome. Sir Gerald being in the dark would be a sign that he really is losing his power.

"Should we tell him?" Sally says.

"Not unless we wanna be the messengers that gets killed," says Mick.

We agree to keep quiet. I'm already not telling Sir Gerald about my visit to the morgue, and I just hope we won't regret our decision.

"Look on the bright side," Hugh says. "The police are just as much at sea as we are. All they have is bits and pieces of the latest victim. And I have the information about the previous cases." He taps his finger against his head. "Thanks to Sally and the *Daily World* archives." He bows to Sally; she smiles. "I'll look into the possibility that there's a connection between the victims. Since Elizabeth Jackson is the only one who was identified, her background is the place to start."

"I bet I can scare up some leads," Mick says. "I got friends all up and down the river." When I first met Mick, he was a sometime mudlark—one who scavenges the mud along the Thames at low tide for coins and saleable items that fell in the water. "They might've seen something. They won't talk to coppers, but they'll talk to me."

I can't think how to make myself useful. I have brought camera equipment, but photography won't be of any help. Then Sally says, "I've an idea for something Sarah and I can do."

* * *

At the *Daily World* headquarters, Sally and I climb the stairs so that we won't run into Sir Gerald in the elevator. "We'll look through the *Daily World*'s personal ads," Sally says. "Some of them are from the families of missing women, begging their wives or sisters or daughters to come home and asking for information regarding their whereabouts. If we follow up on the ads, maybe we can identify the Torso Murder victims."

I regard Sally with surprised admiration. "What a bright idea!" Even as she smiles with pleasure at my praise, I have to say, "Won't the police already be investigating missing women?"

"These women wouldn't have been reported to the police. Families like theirs think a small, discreet ad in the personals is less likely to cause a scandal. I know because when I first started at the *Daily World*, I sometimes worked in the personals department when it was shorthanded."

I hadn't known that, and I realize I don't give Sally enough credit for experience, initiative, or cleverness. Now I'm glad she's part of our team. I'm still concerned about her safety, but what harm can come from looking at personal ads? "Your idea might save our jobs."

"We'd better not count the chickens before they've hatched." On the third floor, Sally leads me to a room filled with rows of tall cabinets, each divided into labeled drawers. "These are the archives, known as the morgue. A suitable nickname for dead stories." She walks along a row, reading the dates printed on labels. She stops and pulls out a drawer to reveal file folders categorized according to subject matter. "In here are articles clipped from the newspaper. They go back to 1870, when the first issue was published."

I look around, marveling at the wealth of information. By the window, an older woman wearing an apron, spectacles, and gloves uses scissors to cut columns from newspapers. "I didn't know this was here."

"I know because the men reporters send me here to fetch clippings for them. They treat me like a secretary."

"How obnoxious." I'm thankful that my own job takes me away from the office. It exposes me to dangers in the outside world but allows Hugh, Mick, and me to avoid bosses and difficult colleagues.

"Well, maybe all the time I've spent getting black fingers will pay off," Sally says.

We gather the personal ads that were placed within two months before the Rainham, Whitehall, Pinchin Street, and latest murders. As we carry them out of the room, the woman clipping articles says, "Be sure to return them. And give them to me; don't refile them yourself. You reporters always put things in the wrong places."

"Yes, Miss Clay." Sally whispers to me, "She's been the archivist for twenty years."

We go next door to the library, which I've also never had occasion to use. Shelves hold encyclopedias, dictionaries in various languages, almanacs, atlases, and other reference books. We sit at a table, and I sort through the most recent ads, hoping for a lead to a missing woman who could be the most recent Torso Murder victim. I soon discover what Sally meant by black fingers and why the archivist wears gloves. The ink from the newsprint smudges our hands. I skim ads from people seeking jobs, men seeking female companionship, and parties seeking to buy or sell all manner of items.

"Here's one dated last month." I read aloud, "'Dear Susan, where are you? Please come home. Love, Mum and Dad.' But how are we supposed to find out who 'Susan' is?"

Sally sifts through ads placed before the Rainham murder. "See the little number in the corner? It corresponds to a record of the person who placed the ad."

After a dozen more columns, I say, "Here's another from six weeks ago: "'To anyone who knows the whereabouts of Louisa N: Please write care of this newspaper."

"That's a possibility. And look." Sally shows me ads that mention a Jenny, a Margaret, and a wife named Frederica.

I find ads pleading for a word from a Peter, a William, an Ernest, and a Seth. "I never knew there were so many missing men."

We're silent, thinking of our father's disappearance. I'd never thought to place an ad because I'd been led to believe he was dead.

By the time we've finished searching all the ads, we have four possibilities for the Rainham victim, three for Whitehall, five for Pinchin Street, and four for the most recent.

"I think that's enough to start." We'll be traipsing around town all day, and I'm glad I brought my smaller camera, lightweight tripod, and a minimum of supplies that fit in my satchel.

Sally gathers up the other ads to return to the archives. "It's hard for me to believe that all these women were victims of crimes. I wonder if some of them ran away. And if they did, what were they running from?"

My mother wanted to escape the scandal after Ellen Casey's murder and my father's disappearance. She took me away from Clerkenwell—from all my friends and the only home I'd ever known. I'd felt so lost, lonely, and miserable, but things had turned out all right for me. One might say that my father's disappearance had set me on a journey toward my current life with the husband, sister, friends, and work I love.

"Maybe the women were running to something better than what they left," I say.

"Maybe so." Sally is quiet, perhaps thinking of how she'd escaped domestic service to begin a career as a reporter, and the cost of her independence. Cleaning up after rich people is neither fun nor well paid, but it gave her a stable place in the world as well as a roof over her head—not trivial benefits.

We return the ads to the archives, then go downstairs to the office, where two women are taking new ads from customers. Sally looks up the records for the ads about our missing women. I write down the names and addresses of the people who placed the ads.

"Do you know," Sally says as we walk along busy Fleet Street, "I hope we find out that all these women are alive and well."

"So do I." Although that would thwart our quest to identify the Torso Murder victims, I can't wish those women dead or their families devastated by their murders.

We take the underground train west to Kensington High Street Station and walk the few blocks to Essex Villas. The neighborhood is affluent, the shops along the high street expensive, the clean pavement free of the beggars, peddlers, and street urchins who abound in the East End. The people we pass are fashionably dressed; they speak in well-bred accents. Essex Villas consists of several short, parallel roads on which terraces of white stucco houses face semidetached brick houses. Pine shrubs fill the small front gardens. A nanny pushing a pram is the only person in sight.

"When I was younger, I used to walk by houses like these and pretend I lived there," I say. "They seemed so cozy and serene." Compared to my transient existence in shabby lodgings after my father disappeared.

"Life in those houses isn't always as nice as it looks from the outside," Sally says.

She should know, and I nod to her superior wisdom. But I have difficulty believing that a woman from a home in Essex Villas would leave it voluntarily. I think it's more likely that the latest Torso Murder victim was kidnapped.

I set up my camera and photograph number ten—a three-story, semidetached house built of pale brown brick, with white trim and bay windows. We open the iron gate and walk up the front steps. I employ the knocker on the black front door.

A tall, dignified, gray-haired man answers. He's dressed in a dark suit and starched white shirt. "Good morning." His cultured voice is polite, but he looks down his nose at Sally and me as he offers us a silver tray.

I deduce that he's the butler, he thinks we're visitors and expects us to put our calling cards on the tray. I thought Sally would do the talking—after all, this expedition was her idea—but she stands frozen and mute, like an unprepared student suddenly called on by the schoolteacher.

I introduce us and drop my *Daily World* business card on the tray. "We're here to see Mrs. Margaret White." Her husband had placed the ad that requested information regarding her whereabouts.

A woman appears in the hall behind the butler. "Who is it, Crawford?" She's gaunt and pale, clad in a mauve dressing gown, slippers on her feet. Her hair is disheveled, and as she sees Sally and me, her eyes bulge with a strange mixture of fear and hope.

"Are you Margaret White?" I call.

"Yes?" Wringing her thin, spidery hands, she extends them as if to plead with us.

The butler says, "Mrs. White isn't receiving visitors." As he closes the door, I hear a faint cry from the woman.

Sally runs out the gate. I follow her half a block down the street until she stops. "I'm sorry," she says, breathless and agitated.

"What's wrong?"

"That man reminded me of the master at the house where I used to work. He has an awful temper. Everyone walked on eggshells around him. For a minute, I was a ten-year-old maid again, terrified that I would make a mistake." She forces a self-deprecating laugh. "The cat got my tongue. A fine detective I am. I'm sorry, Sarah."

"It's all right." I pat her arm. Of all people, I understand that the habits of a lifetime are hard to unlearn. As we walk back toward the station, I say, "Well, Margaret White isn't a Torso Murder victim."

"Lucky for her," Sally says. "Not so lucky for us."

Glancing over my shoulder at the house, I wonder about the circumstances under which she went missing and later returned home. She didn't look well.

"But don't worry—I have a feeling we're going to identify the victims and catch the killer." Undaunted by our first dead end, Sally says, "Just imagine the headline in the *Daily World*: 'Sisters Solve the Torso Murders and Jack the Ripper!'"

An uneasy sense of foreboding trickles through me. "Not both."

"Why not?" Sally sounds surprised. "They're the same person."

"No, I don't think so." I'm disturbed that she believes the theory, and I can't tell her why it's erroneous. Her knowing the secret would not only make her an accomplice after the fact and put her in jeopardy but also ruin her good opinion of me and permanently damage our relationship. Moreover, the secret isn't mine alone. I can't break the vow of silence that Barrett, Hugh, Mick, and I made.

"The Torso Murderer and the Ripper have completely different methods of murder," I say instead. "I spoke with Dr. Phillips, the police surgeon who performed the autopsy on the new torso. He also performed the autopsies on the Pinchin Street torso and Mary Kelly, the Ripper's sixth victim. He said Mary's injuries were a result of wanton savagery, whereas the Pinchin Street corpse was carefully dismembered for the sake of disposal."

"Is that the real reason you don't believe they're the same person? Or is it because Inspector Reid believes it, and the two of you don't see eye to eye?"

I bristle at the idea that she thinks I'm so petty. "Of course not."

"If he said the sky is blue, you would say it's green."

"Reid has been wrong about other things." My temper heats up as I defend myself. "He once arrested an innocent man for the Ripper murders."

Sally looks unhappy and flustered; she doesn't like to disagree with me, but she says, "You told me you dabbled in the Ripper investigation." That's all I told her. "Reid knows it, and he thinks you're hiding something about the Ripper. But of course you aren't."

I force my eyes to meet hers and not look away.

"Just because he was wrong once, doesn't mean he's always wrong," Sally says. "I think he's right about the Torso Murderer and the Ripper."

Angry as well as troubled that Sally is taking Reid's side against mine, I say, "Forget about Reid. Why do *you* think they're the same person?"

She blinks, startled by my challenging tone. "Because . . . because neither has been caught. And how could there be *two* such vicious madmen killing women in London during the same period?"

"That's not evidence. That's just speculation. If you want to solve crimes, you need to be objective."

Sally's cheeks redden; she's as stubborn as I am, and she too has a temper. "Well, I suppose *you've* never lost your objectivity or made a mistake."

If she only knew! The fact that I can't tell her puts me in a grievous position. When our father was on trial for murder, she thought he was innocent while I had my doubts. That almost caused a permanent rift between us. Perhaps I shouldn't be surprised that we're at odds now, still experiencing the aftereffects of that serious conflict.

"I think you're making a mistake now," Sally says.

I'm tempted to say that if she's so determined to believe in theories unsupported by facts, then Sir Gerald made a mistake by assigning her to the investigation. I hold my tongue rather than start a quarrel that would end badly. "Shall we agree to disagree? And focus on our missing women?"

Sally frowns, opening her mouth as if for a snappy comeback. Then she sighs and nods—she wants to avoid a quarrel as much as I do. Anyone watching us must see two slim, blond women who look alike, each with shoulders squared, head high, and an obstinate expression. The argument is far from over.

Church bells ring noon, and I discover I'm hungry. Figuring that Sally must be too, I say, "Let's have lunch." Food soothes the prickliest tempers.

"I know where we can go."

Sally leads me to tearoom named Frances Allen's, off the Kensington High Street. It's decorated with chintz curtains, lace tablecloths, and fresh flowers. All the customers are women. A waitress in a black taffeta uniform and starched white apron pours tea for us. "Good to see you, Miss Albert. The usual?"

"Yes, please, Betsy."

I consult the menu and order Welsh rarebit. The waitress departs, and I sip the tea, which is hot, strong, and fragrant. "How do you know about this place?" I ask Sally.

"I'm sent all over town to cover little stories that none of the men reporters want. I've had to find good, cheap places to eat, or I would starve."

I'm getting a better idea of how hard she works and how much she has to put up with. "I understand why you want to investigate crimes."

Sally nods emphatically. "I'm sure it requires just as much running around, but it's for a worthy cause."

"I'm glad you're working with us."

Sally smiles, pleased. "So am I."

The food arrives. My Welsh rarebit has rich, plentiful cheese on crusty bread that tastes home baked, with a tangy ale, cheese, and mustard sauce—delicious. Sally's chicken salad sandwich looks good too.

"This is nice," I say. "We hardly ever have a proper meal together these days. Why don't you come over for dinner tonight? Hugh, Mick, and Barrett may have news."

"All right." Sally seems glad to be invited.

The tearoom's proprietress comes to our table to greet us. Frances Allen is a tall, handsome woman with a profile that would suit a ship's figurehead. Sally introduces me. "Mrs. Allen, this is my sister, Mrs. Sarah Barrett. She's a crime photographer and investigator for the *Daily World*."

The pride in Sally's voice moves me. How nice to have a sister who's proud to show me off to her acquaintances. After exchanging pleasantries with me, Mrs. Allen asks, "What are you ladies up to today?"

"We're investigating the Torso Murders," Sally says.

"Then you'll be interested to hear what our local constable told me not an hour ago. An arm was just found at Chelsea Pier."

Chapter 7

Half an hour later, Sally and I arrive on the Chelsea Embankment, the wide, tree-lined promenade along the Thames. Behind us is the Golding's Pier Hotel. To our left, a ramp slants down to the Chelsea Pier, which floats on the water. High above us to our right, cabs, carriages, and omnibuses rattle across the Albert Bridge. Seagulls perch on the bridge's cables and Gothic iron support towers. I glance inland at the row of mansions along Cheyne Walk.

"Isn't that where your mother works? Maybe you should stop in and see her when we're finished."

Looking over the stone wall of the embankment, Sally pretends not to hear me. Her determination to maintain the chilly distance from her mother vexes me. She doesn't realize how fortunate she is to have a parent who loves her and cares about her! And her mother is as stubborn as she is. Rather than let bygones be bygones, Sally nurses her grudge against her mother for believing our father was guilty, and her mother won't admit she's wrong and ask for forgiveness. Perhaps something similar happened to the new Torso Murder victim. Did she find herself on her own after a family quarrel? Did that put her on a collision course with a killer? Broken families were a common theme among the Ripper victims.

Some fifteen feet below Sally and me, the tide is out, and a small crowd of men occupy the swath of exposed mud. Two police constables are wading in the shallows, scraping the mud with rakes.

"There's Hugh." Sally points.

Among the men watching the constables, Hugh sees us and waves. Two of the other men have cameras, and I gather the rest are reporters or spectators. Sally hurries down the steps to join Hugh. I follow with my camera equipment.

"Fancy meeting you here," Hugh says. "I suppose you heard about the arm. News travels fast."

Sally explains how we heard. Hugh says, "I was on the Thames Embankment. That's where Elizabeth Jackson used to sleep rough." Homeless streetwalkers and vagrants often spend nights camped on embankments along the river. "I was talking to some folks who'd slept there last night, asking them if they knew Elizabeth. No luck, but they told me about the arm."

"Where is it?" Not that I'm eager to see more severed body parts.

"By the time I arrived, the police had rushed it to the morgue, to see if it matches the torso. They're looking for other parts now." He points down the shore. "Trust Mick to beat us to the scene."

Mick is talking to three men armed with rakes, poles with hooks at the ends, and fishnets. Their clothes and rubber boots are black with river mud. "Those are old friends of his," Hugh says. "Dredgermen."

Whereas mudlarks scavenge along the banks, dredgermen pull things up from the river bottom and sell whatever they can. One of Mick's friends has what looks to be machine parts piled by his feet. In response to questions from Mick, the men shake their heads. He's apparently asking them, in vain, if they saw anything that might pertain to the Torso Murders.

Hugh points at photographers and reporters grouped around a constable. "Surprise—our friends from the *Chronicle* are here."

Sally heads toward them, pulling her notebook and pencil from her handbag. She asks the constable, "Have you found other parts besides the arm?"

"The *Chronicle* has exclusive access to the police investigation," a reporter says. "She's from the *Daily World*."

"Run along, then, Miss," the constable says.

Sally stands her ground. "Our readers have a right to hear the news!"

"They can switch to the *Chronicle*." The reporter advances on Sally. "Better do as the nice officer said." He reaches out and pushes her shoulder.

"Don't you touch me!" Offended by his impertinence, Sally shoves his chest.

"Hey!" He stumbles backward, slips in the mud, and falls on his buttocks.

Hugh laughs, but I drop my equipment and hurry toward Sally, spurred by the same dismay and concern that Barrett must feel when I engage in physical altercations. Sally is proving herself to be as temperamental and reckless as I. Photographers and other reporters laugh and jeer at their fallen comrade. He scrambles up, furious, and lunges at Sally. I put myself between them. Hugh grabs the reporter's arm, twists it, and the man crumples with a yell of pain.

"Simmer down, old chap." Hugh is still an adept fighter despite his wounded arm. "That'll teach you to put your paws on the ladies."

I steer Sally away from the crowd. "You shouldn't have pushed him."

"I'm all right." Sally giggles with delight at her own nerve.

"Imagine what might have happened to you if Hugh and I hadn't been here!"

"I was only trying to get information we need. Remember, if we don't solve the murder, Sir Gerald will fire us."

"If you do that again, I'll tell Sir Gerald that you're a danger to yourself. He'll take you off the investigation rather than have you get hurt."

Sally glares at me with more ire than the situation merits. Then she turns, trudges up the shore, and stands at the water's edge with her back to me, facing across the river. She's still angry at me because I doubted our father's innocence, and every new disagreement further threatens our sisterly harmony. I'm scared to think how easy it would be to lose each other. From such quarrels come permanent family estrangements.

Hugh joins me. “I smoothed things over with the boor from the *Chronicle*.”

I never cease to be glad of his social skills. “Thank you.”

Loud barking startles us. A large black-and-white dog charges at Sally. As she turns, it springs up on its hind legs and plants its paws on her chest. She shrieks, loses her balance, and falls sideways into the shallow water with a thud and splash.

“Sally!” I cry, alarmed.

The *Chronicle* reporters and photographers double over with laughter. Hugh, Mick, and I rush to Sally. Gasping with shock, dismay, and embarrassment, she pushes herself to her knees. The dog scampers around her, barking and wagging its tail.

“Go away!” As I lend my sister a hand, the dog licks her face. Sally stands, her clothes dripping wet and fouled with river mud.

“Smoker!” A man hurries up to us. He’s stocky with short, neat blond hair, mustache, and beard. He carries a leash. “Here, boy.”

The dog runs to him, barking joyously. Sally demands, “Is this your dog?”

“Yes. I’m terribly sorry.” The man is in his late twenties, with bright blue eyes in an open, honest face. His smooth forehead creases with what seems like genuine remorse. His dark gray wool business coat and black derby are of good quality, but not new, and he wears knee-high rubber boots. “Are you all right, miss?”

Sally exclaims in disgust. “Do I look all right?”

She tries to wipe the mud off her clothes, but her hands are muddy too. I scrub at her with my handkerchief, which immediately becomes wet and black.

“Sir, you ought to keep that dangerous beast under control,” Hugh says.

The man fastens the leash to the dog’s collar. “He’s not dangerous. Just playful.”

“Oh, so you think it’s ‘playful’ for your dog to jump on strangers and knock them in the river.” Sally wrings out her skirts, twisting them violently as if she’d like to strangle the dog’s owner instead.

"I'm sorry." He sounds anxiously, sincerely contrite. "I'll pay to have your clothes laundered."

I see a notebook and pencil tucked in his breast pocket. "Are you a reporter?"

"Yes. I'm Jasper Waring, from the *Chronicle*." He extends his hand to me, then Sally, then Hugh. When nobody shakes it, his fair skin blushes rose pink.

Sally glares, furious. "You sent your dog to attack me. Because I'm a reporter with the *Daily World*, and what fun to play jokes on your rivals."

"That's not so!" Mr. Waring protests. "I didn't know you were with the *Daily World*. I didn't even know you were a reporter. And Smoker didn't mean to knock you down. It was an accident."

I think he's telling the truth; both he and his panting, smiling dog seem innocent of malicious intent. I could take pity on him if they'd offended someone other than my sister. "Why did you bring your dog to a crime scene?"

"To help the police find body parts." Mr. Waring says proudly, "After the upper arm turned up, Smoker found the lower arm with the hand. And back in 1888, he dug up the leg of the Whitehall victim."

Sally beholds the dog with horror. "You mean, he's been nosing around severed remains, and he *licked* me? *Ugh!*"

"I'm sorry," Mr. Waring says. "Please let me make it up to you."

"Get away from me! Don't ever come near me again." Sally stalks past the other *Chronicle* men, who are still laughing and jeering.

Hugh and I follow her to the steps. She's shivering violently, and I sav, "You'd better go home, take a hot bath, and put on dry clothes, or you'll catch cold."

"We'll take you," Hugh says.

"No! You have to investigate the murders. We can't let that scoundrel from the *Chronicle* get ahead of us." Sally reaches in her wet handbag and takes out the list of missing women. She tears the paper in halves and gives me one. "Go. I'll work on my half later." She runs up the steps, onto the embankment, and hails a cab. As she jumps in and rides away, I hope she doesn't forget about dinner at my house tonight.

Hugh points at my half of the list. "What's this?"

I explain while we walk back toward the river to fetch my camera equipment. At the water's edge, Smoker strains at his leash, sniffing the ground, towing Jasper Waring. Reporters, photographers, and constables trudge after them. Mick and the dredgermen watch from a distance.

"If more parts are found here, Mick will let us know," Hugh says. "Why don't I help you look up your missing women?"

A steam launch roars up to the pier. "Wait," I say. "Something's happening."

The crew ties the launch to the pier and lowers a dinghy into the water. The three passengers on deck—two men and a woman—climb into the small wooden craft. A River Police constable rows them to shore, and the crowd hurries to meet the newcomers. Mick runs ahead of everyone else. As I move closer and the three passengers disembark, I see that one man is Inspector Reid, the other a tall, gaunt fellow, both dressed in hooded mackintoshes. The woman is actually a teenage girl. A mackintosh that's too large envelops her small, slim figure. Her long black hair is done up in an elaborate, braided twist, but the wind whips loose strands around her delicate, lovely face, which is the color of coffee with a little cream.

"Do my eyes deceive me, or is that Anjali Lodge, your lost love?" Hugh asks Mick.

"What on earth is she doing here with Inspector Reid?" I exclaim.

Now Anjali sees Mick. Her lips part. Her black eyes widen, and she freezes in her tracks. He skids to a stop and regards her in flabbergasted silence while the other man urges her forward. Tall and spare, the man has short gray hair and the bony, ascetic features of medieval statues of saints. He's her father.

The reporters and photographers hurry to meet the three, calling questions: "Inspector Reid, are there any new developments in the Torso Murders case?"

"Yes indeed." Reid smiles with self-satisfaction. "Gentlemen, allow me to introduce Dr. Everett Lodge and his daughter Miss Anjali Lodge. They will be assisting the task force with the investigation."

Hugh and I join Mick, and we all stare in shock at Anjali. Her attention remains fixed on Mick for an instant before she looks away. Mick says, "What the—?"

Reid glances at my companions and me but otherwise doesn't acknowledge our presence. Jasper Waring, dog in tow, pushes his way to the front of the pack while photographers set up cameras.

"Dr. Lodge will give a statement," Reid announces.

"I am a scientist and professor at University College and president of the Society for Psychical Studies," Dr. Lodge says in a deep, resonant, upper-class voice. "My daughter, Anjali, is blessed with the gift of psychic powers. We volunteered her services in the hope that her visions can help the police identify the Torso Murderer and his victims."

"Well, this is an unexpected kettle of fish," Hugh says.

Mick's face shows the same wonder and dismay that I feel. I've been aware of Anjali's "gift" since I met her last fall, and although I'm a longtime nonbeliever in supernatural phenomena, my experiences with her have shaken my skepticism. But why did Reid engage her? It goes against standard procedure for detective work. Why did her father allow her to volunteer? It's very public-spirted of them, but they can't have forgotten that a previous murder investigation almost cost her life.

"Inspector Reid, do you really believe a psychic can solve the case?" Jasper Waring says.

Sally will be vexed that Waring caused her to miss this newsworthy event.

"I'm willing to let Miss Lodge have a try," Reid says. "I promised I would leave no stone overturned. Maybe she'll overturn some stones that I can't."

"So he's desperate enough to try anything," I say to Hugh and Mick. Otherwise, I'm sure the pragmatic Reid would think psychics should stick to performing in carnival acts.

As photographers snap pictures and flash powder explodes, Anjali flinches. Mick waves to her, but she won't look at him. I don't try to take pictures, lest I start a new brawl with the *Chronicle* men.

"Is she going to hold a séance?" a reporter asks. Laughter bursts from skeptics among the crowd. Anjali moves closer to her father, who puts his arm around her. Mick scowls, angry because they're mocking Anjali. He has complete faith in her, no matter that she cast him off.

"A séance won't be necessary," Dr. Lodge says. "Anjali will visit the places where the body parts were found and touch the remains at the morgue."

Hugh winces. "I believe in her psychic powers, but I hope her stomach is as strong as they are."

"She'll describe the impressions she receives," Dr. Lodge adds. "Our hope is that they will contain clues that Inspector Reid can follow."

"Now if you gentlemen will step aside, we'll get on with it," Reid says.

As he and Dr. Lodge escort Anjali along the water's edge, the reporters and photographers follow close behind. He flaps his hand at them. "Give her some room."

I think he doesn't want the press to hear what Anjali says. The visions she describes sometimes sound bizarre, and if they are published in the newspapers but don't lead to the killer, he'll be a laughingstock. He's taken a big risk by engaging her; no wonder he wants to exercise control over whatever information she provides.

The photographers, Jasper Waring, and the other reporters stand back, but Mick runs forward, calling, "Anjali!" His face shines with love and hope.

Dr. Lodge puts himself in front of Anjali and raises a warning hand at Mick. "Don't come near her. You've caused her enough trouble already."

Anjali stands mute, hands clasped, her face averted from Mick. Because of her mature hairstyle and aloof manner, she seems older than when I last saw her in November, almost a grown woman now.

"Begone, or I'll have you arrested," Reid tells Mick. "You too, Lord Hugh and Mrs. Barrett."

"I just want to talk to her a minute." Not about to let his chance slip away after four months of pining for her, Mick tries to maneuver around Dr. Lodge. *"Anjali!"*

She moves down the riverbank and stops to stare at the mud at her feet. Reid beckons the constables; they advance on Mick. Hugh and I run to him, seize his arms, and drag him away. As he resists, Hugh says, "Whoa, there. You won't be able to win her back if you're in jail."

Mick flings our hands off him, but instead of pursuing Anjali, he halts and stares at her. Yearning and anguish contort his face. To distract him and keep him from doing anything rash, I say, "You should go to the *Daily World* and report the new developments."

He takes one last look at Anjali, then stalks away and flees up the steps to the street.

"Shall we investigate the missing women?" I ask Hugh.

He's watching Anjali, his expression filled with surprise and wonder. "That's the spot where the police found the arm. She zeroed right in on it."

Chapter 8

At five o'clock in the evening, Hugh and I find ourselves in Berkley Square. Our investigation of missing women has led us all over London's fashionable West End, and finally to Mayfair, one of the most expensive, prestigious districts. Outside townhouses even larger and statelier than in Kensington, private carriages let out gentlemen returning home from their clubs and ladies from a day spent visiting. Fog shrouds the gazebo at the center of the garden, in which marble statues loom like ghosts.

"There's Gunter's Tea Shop," Hugh says. "They have the best ice cream. In summer, when I was a child, we rode over in our carriage, and they brought it out to us, and we could eat it under the cool shade of the trees."

He sighs, and I can tell he's regretting that such innocent family treats are no more since his parents disowned him after the scandal. "I'm sorry," I say.

"Don't be," Hugh says with a quick smile. "I was living a lie then. I'm not now."

I think he's actually happy, which I'd feared was impossible. My mind drifts back to my thoughts about families. Hugh is another example of broken ties, a soul cut loose from kith and kin. But perhaps losing his place in high society was worth the freedom to be who he is.

We walk toward house number forty-five, the address of a Miss Louisa Nussey, the last name on my half of the list. The advertisement read, "To anyone who knows the whereabouts of

Louisa N.: Please write care of this newspaper." The records at the *Daily World* contained the address to which the newspaper should forward the replies, but none have come.

"This has been an education," Hugh says. "All these women born with silver spoons in their mouths, who ran away from a sweet life."

"Maybe not so sweet." I remember Sally's remark about life inside affluent households. None of the women Hugh and I investigated today had turned out to be crime victims. Two were debutantes who'd eloped with unsuitable men. The other was the companion of her rich old aunt; she'd emigrated to America. The servants had been delighted to tell us how outraged the relatives had been when they'd discovered what the women had done. I think the women must have found freedom sweeter than being trapped by servitude or social constraints.

"At any rate, they're all accounted for," I say. "Let's hope we strike lucky this time."

Number forty-five is Georgian style, faced with white ashlar, four stories high. Eyelid dormers jut from the slate mansard roof. Classical pediments and balconies with stone balusters adorn the second-story windows. I take a photograph with little hope that it will ever appear in the *Daily World*. Then I knock on the recessed black front door.

A stout, dignified, older woman in a white apron and black frock answers. I immediately step backward, and Hugh steps forward. After working together for more than two years, we've learned that he gets on better with women than I do.

Hugh tips his hat and speaks with his best smile and most aristocratic accent. "Good evening. I'm Hugh Price, and this is my cousin, Miss Sarah Price." When on investigations, we often use aliases, so nobody will recognize his name from the scandal, and I often pose as his relative in order that nobody will think our relationship is improper.

A smile thaws the housekeeper's stern countenance, a typical feminine reaction to Hugh's good looks and charm. Hugh says, "We're friends of Miss Louisa Nussey. We'd like to see her, if she's available."

The housekeeper's smile vanishes. "She isn't." The door closes firmly.

Startled, Hugh says, "I haven't been given the gate so fast since I was nineteen and showed up falling-down drunk at Annabelle Lawrence's coming-out party."

My intuition tells me there's something amiss in this house, and it concerns Louisa. Excitement quickens my heartbeat. "I wonder if she's the one woman on our list who's still missing." I state a principle that Hugh, Mick, and I have employed ever since we began investigating crimes. "When thwarted, try the neighbors."

We go next door, a similar house. The butler who answers my knock is ancient and wizened. After I introduce Hugh and myself and say we're old friends of Louisa Nussey and we're looking for her, a high-pitched, quavering voice inside the house calls, "Show them in, Perkins."

The butler escorts us into a marble-tiled foyer with a grand staircase. He takes our coats and hats, then ushers us into a parlor that's so full of carved furniture, fringed lamps, porcelain knick-knacks, and painted screens that at first, I don't see the two elderly women seated on a velvet divan by the fireplace. They look alike, with frizzy outdated hairstyles, bony figures, and faded dark taffeta frocks. Introductions reveal them to be Mrs. Weston and Mrs. Palmer, widowed sisters. They quiver with delight at having new acquaintances to enliven their day.

When Hugh and I are seated on the divan opposite them, sipping tea, Mrs. Weston asks Hugh, "And how did you come to be acquainted with Miss Louisa Nussey?"

"We met on holiday in Brighton when we were young."

Our hostesses accept his answer without question. They ignore me; they've noticed my accent and inexpensive clothes, and they've categorized me as his poor, insignificant relation.

"Then you've not heard the news about Miss Nussey?" Mrs. Palmer sounds eager to share gossip.

"I'm afraid not. I've been abroad for some years, and we lost touch." Hugh puts on the expression of a concerned friend. "Has something happened to her?"

Mrs. Weston speaks in the sort of whisper meant to evoke scandal and titillation. "She ran away last December."

I tingle with anticipation. Hugh says, "Where did she go?"

"Nobody seems to know," Mrs. Palmer says. "She just packed a bag and slipped out of the house in the dead of night, without a word."

"And she hasn't come back?" Hugh says.

"She is still missing." Mrs. Palmer speaks with more relish than concern.

I'm excited because the remains found in the river could belong to Louisa Nussey, but dismayed by the thought of her possible suffering and her family's bereavement.

"Has anyone heard from her?" Hugh asks.

"Not that we're aware of, and we're aware of most everything that happens in the square." Mrs. Weston's expression turns cunning, mischievous. "We have our sources."

I suppose gossip circulates as vigorously in Berkley Square as in Whitechapel and passes freely between the rich folks and the help.

"What could have happened to Miss Louisa?" Hugh asks.

"The general sentiment is that she ran off with a man," Mrs. Palmer says, "but we don't believe it."

"She's such a plain, mousy girl," Mrs. Weston says. "And she's thirty-five years old."

So am I! Stung by the conventional wisdom that women of our age are unattractive to men, I say, "She could have met someone who fell in love with her." Better that than she crossed paths with the Torso Murderer.

Our hostesses look at me as if the teapot had spoken. Mrs. Weston says, "Louisa was always very bookish and religious. If she had any interest in men, it was hard to tell."

"What do *you* think happened?" Hugh asks.

"At one time, Louisa wanted to become a Roman Catholic nun. Imagine!" Mrs. Weston and her sister exchange scandalized looks. "Her father put a stop to that, of course. We think she joined a convent."

After Hugh solicits the names of Louisa's friends, we manage to get away only after I photograph the sisters and promise to send them prints. As we leave Berkeley Square, Hugh says, "I'm afraid the new Torso Murder victim is Louisa Nussey."

"So am I, but we should investigate further before we jump to conclusions."

"You're right. I'd rather find out that she's tucked away in a convent than lying in pieces in the morgue. Even if it means we've spent the afternoon on a wild goose chase."

I glance at the Nussey house. Lights in the windows shine through gaps between closed curtains. "Someone in there must know something about Louisa."

"We'll come back tomorrow. Meanwhile, we'd better head home. Mick and Barrett might have news. And I invited Dr. Lewes to dinner."

* * *

When Hugh and I arrive at home, Sally is helping Fitzmorris cook, and Mick is sneaking tastes of the food. I'm glad to see that Sally has recovered from her dip in the river.

"I tracked down three of the missing women on my list," she says. "Two are wives who returned to their husbands. They didn't seem very happy, but at least they're alive. The other was a maid who stole the silver, went home to Ireland, and was arrested there. Because of that Jasper Waring, I didn't have time to investigate the last two. I still think he set his dog on me. When I think of him, I get so mad!"

"I musta talked to every dredgerman and mudlark between Chelsea Pier and Tower Bridge, and nothing," Mick says.

I tell Mick and Sally about Louisa Nussey. Hugh says, "Cheer up, everybody. Tomorrow could be our lucky day."

"I sure hope so." Barrett joins us. He's oddly dressed in a formal coat and trousers from the wardrobe of costumes I keep in my studio. His hair is wet, his chest and feet bare.

"Where are your clothes?" I ask.

"I bundled them up for the laundry. They smell like the morgue. I washed myself in your darkroom."

Everyone expresses sympathy and tries not to laugh. Barrett goes upstairs to dress. By the time he returns, Dr. Lewes has arrived. We all sit down to vegetable soup, fish cakes, potatoes, and sherry trifle. Sally, Hugh, Mick, and I tell Barrett and Dr. Lewes the results of our inquiries.

"It was a busy day at the morgue, but no luck." Barrett sounds rueful. "Seventy-four people came by. Ten had missing female relatives. They weren't able to make a match with the remains. The others were just curiosity seekers. I showed Dr. Phillips the knife I took from Severin Klosowski. He said it could have been used to slice human flesh, but the killer would have needed a cleaver or saw to cut through bone. So the knife doesn't incriminate Klosowski. I wish there were more clues."

"Scientists are working on a new method for identifying criminals from the fingerprints they leave at crime scenes," Dr. Lewes says. "Each person's fingerprints are unique. A print is indisputable evidence."

The idea intrigues me, but Barrett says, "Fingerprinting wouldn't do any good in this case. We don't know where the crime scene is, and even if the killer left prints on the body parts, the river washed them off."

I feel competition in the air again.

"Maybe fingerprinting will be advanced enough by the time our next case crops up," Hugh says in an obvious attempt to smooth things over.

Dr. Lewes smiles at him and passes him the tartar sauce. Their hands touch for a moment longer than necessary.

I freeze with my fork halfway to my mouth. The moment is over so fast that I'm not certain I saw what I thought I saw. I glance around the table. Everyone else is eating and talking; no one except me seems to have noticed. Hugh and Dr. Lewes aren't looking at each other or behaving any differently than usual.

It never occurred to me that Dr. Lewes might be a homosexual; he's given no hint of it, nor has Hugh. Yet a budding love affair could explain why Hugh is happier.

Dr. Lewes catches me watching him. He raises his eyebrows in a pleasant, quizzical manner.

Instead of rudely blurting, "Are you and Hugh more than doctor and patient?" I scramble for other words. "Inspector Reid thinks the Torso Murderer is Jack the Ripper. What do you think?"

That was the wrong thing to say. I feel Hugh, Mick, and Barrett tense up because I've broached a sensitive subject.

If Dr. Lewes notices, he doesn't let on. "Based on psychological profiles, I don't believe they're the same person. As I said, the Torso Murderer is careful and meticulous. It appears that he lured his victims to a private place where he killed and dismembered them and stored their body parts. There's no evidence of a sexual motive. The Ripper picked up streetwalkers, murdered and mutilated all but one of them in public places, and left them there. The nature of the mutilation indicates that sex was a major factor. And the crimes seem to be ones of violent impulse."

Barrett and I nod. Dr. Lewes's analysis supports the police surgeon's comments regarding the surgically dismembered remains in the morgue versus Mary Ann Kelly's savaged corpse. And of course, Barrett, Hugh, Mick, and I know the truth.

"But isn't it possible that a murderer could behave differently on different occasions?" Sally asks. "I mean, nobody is completely consistent."

My heart sinks. She still believes the Torso Murderer is Jack the Ripper, and I'm afraid nothing short of telling her the secret would change her mind.

"It's possible," Dr. Lewes says. "When I was conducting research at the Salpêtrière, I met a convicted murderer who behaved as though he were two different men who took turns inhabiting the same body. One was sedate and rational; the other, a raging, violent lunatic."

"Like Dr. Jekyll and Mr. Hyde," Hugh says.

"Two different men in the same body." Sally aims a pointed glance at me, as if to continue our argument. "A careful one who plans ahead; an impulsive one who takes risks."

"But he was a rare case," Dr. Lewes says. "A likelier possibility is a killer who switches methods to throw the police off his track. But I've found criminals to be tediously consistent. Their crimes reflect their basic natures. They do the same things over and over until they're caught. For the careful, private man to kill streetwalkers in alleys would be difficult. Even more difficult for the impulsive daredevil to stalk and lure his victims, surgically dismember them, and dispose of the remains little by little. One's basic nature is hard to subvert."

"I'll second that," Hugh says. He must be thinking of his preference for men, which he couldn't change no matter that it's caused him a world of trouble.

Dr. Lewes regards Hugh with sympathy in which I can't detect any stronger, more personal feeling. I can't begin to fathom all the possible ramifications of a love affair between them; I just know the idea worries me.

"Until evidence rules out the theory that the Torso Murderer and the Ripper are the same person, I think we should keep an open mind," Sally says with another sharp look at me.

I sway between vexation because she's accusing me of close-mindedness and regret that I have to keep her in the dark.

"Do you think all the Torso Murders were the work of one person?" Barrett addresses his question to Dr. Lewes but glances at me, as if to say he wants our disagreement settled by an objective third party.

"I do, based on the similarities in the conditions of the remains," Dr. Lewes says. "It's hard for me to believe there's more than one killer with the same distinctive pattern."

Before the Ripper investigation, I had found the same thing hard to believe.

"I'm not ready to rule out the theory of multiple killers." Barrett sounds vexed that Dr. Lewes has taken my side of the argument. "The Battersea Murder was eighteen years ago. I think it's more likely that was a different killer than that the same person waited so long to kill again."

"*I* still think there's only one killer," Sally says, "and he's both the Torso Murderer and the Ripper."

Mick fidgets with his knife and fork; no matter that he considers himself a grown, independent man, he's afraid of arguments that threaten the security of the only family he's had since his mother abandoned him and his grandparents put him in an orphanage. I hold my tongue. I don't want Sally laboring under the same delusion as Inspector Reid. I hate to see Barrett steering our investigation down what I believe is the wrong track, but I stay silent because I don't want a quarrel. The situation reminds me of the Greek mythology I learned in school. Eris, the goddess of strife, had a golden apple, and wherever she tossed it, friends became enemies, and enemies waged war. Dr. Lewes might help us solve the case, but he's like Eris's golden apple of discord. He frowns with concern as he looks around the table. Obviously, he realizes he's widened the fissures that threaten the foundations of our group, and it bothers him. But he doesn't know their root cause, our secret.

Or does he? Again, I wonder what Hugh has told Dr. Lewes. If they're lovers, he might have spilled everything.

"How about if we go about our investigation and reserve judgment until we see what transpires?" Hugh says, anxious to make peace.

"Good idea," Barrett says, but his voice is tight.

Mick pushes back his chair and stands. "'Scuse me—I gotta go."

"Another engagement with Maureen Howard?" Hugh sounds as glad as I am to change the subject.

"No. I'm goin' to see Anjali."

"That's a terrible idea," I say, "after what happened this afternoon. Her father wouldn't let you see her then. He surely won't now."

"If I talk to him, maybe I can convince him that I've changed and it's okay for her to be around me." Mick speaks with youthful, unrealistic confidence.

Just when he might have begun to get over Anjali, she showed up. I wonder about her motives. She must have known that if she became involved in the Torso Murder investigation, she and Mick were bound to run into each other. But right now my primary concern is keeping Mick out of trouble.

"Inspector Reid ordered you to stay away from Anjali. If you go to her house, Dr. Lodge will tell him, and he'll have you arrested."

"Sod Reid."

I regard Mick with pity and exasperation. He hasn't changed at all, except to collect a bevy of new girlfriends, and that certainly wouldn't please Anjali or her father.

"When it comes to love, I'm all for 'try, try again,' but enough is enough," Hugh says.

Mick glowers. "Yeah, well it's not up to you."

Sally, Fitzmorris, and Dr. Lewes busy themselves clearing the table. Barrett says, in an obvious effort to divert Mick, "Sarah and I are going to investigate a possible suspect tonight. Why don't you come with us?"

"I'm goin' to Anjali's house," Mick says, stubbornly determined.

I make a quick decision. "Then I'll go with you."

Mick reacts with dismay at the thought of my intruding on what he thinks will be a romantic reunion. "No, thanks."

"Dr. Lodge might be more willing to talk if I'm there than if you show up by yourself." I have my own reasons for wanting to see Dr. Lodge and Anjali.

"Investigating my suspect can wait until you come back," Barrett says.

Mick frowns, then considers and nods. "I guess it won't hurt to have someone there who's on my side."

Chapter 9

Anjali and her father live in Bloomsbury, near the University College where Dr. Lodge teaches. Their house is in Burton Crescent, a Regency-era terrace built of brick, with white stucco facades on the ground floors that curve around a semicircular garden. The terrace once served as luxurious abodes for the wealthy, but now many of its houses bear signs advertising rooms to let. Adjacent to Dr. Lodge's house is the Home for Deserted Mothers.

That's where Anjali and her mother once lived.

Her mother, while enrolled at the college, had become pregnant by an Indian man, a fellow pupil. He returned to India, deserting Anjali's mother, whose family disowned her. After she gave birth to Anjali, the Home for Deserted Mothers took the two of them in. She went to work as a charwoman for Dr. Lodge, who fell in love with her, married her, and adopted Anjali. She's another woman who threw away propriety to follow her own desire. But it wasn't all happily ever after. Dr. Lodge's family disowned him for wedding a woman who had an illegitimate, half-Indian child, and she died of consumption when Anjali was eight.

Mick knocks on the door. After a few minutes, Dr. Lodge answers. When he sees us, the muscles of his bony face tighten, his eyes flare, and he holds up his hand to ward us off.

"So it's you again." He looks like a medieval saint confronting the devil. "What are you doing here?"

Mick takes off his hat and holds it in both hands in front of his chest. He looks like an altar boy with a candle. "Please, sir, may I have your permission to talk to Anjali?"

"No, you may not. I have made that clear on exactly thirty-eight occasions."

He's cold and pedantic, but I have to admire him. He defied propriety and sacrificed his familial ties for the sake of love; he's raising his half-Indian stepchild as his own; and he couldn't love Anjali with more devotion if they were blood kin. He's determined to protect her because she's all he has, and he's all that stands between her and the cruel world. He thinks Mick is an untrustworthy cad who would ruin Anjali and then desert her, just as her natural father did to her mother.

"I understand why you're ticked off—I mean, displeased with me," Mick says. "You got every right to be. But I ain't—I'm not—the rotter—I mean, the scoundrel—I once was. I've turned over a new leaf. All I ask is a chance to prove it to Anjali, and to you, sir." Mick sounds so earnest that he's half convinced me, and I dare to hope Dr. Lodge will relent.

"I don't care how many leaves you've turned over, you're a juvenile delinquent underneath," Dr. Lodge says. "I shan't let you near my daughter."

Mick's face falls. Before he can lose his temper, I push him behind me and say, "Can you and Anjali and Mick and I sit down together for just half an hour?" That's the most time I think I can ask for, and Mick and I will have to cram in everything we want to say. "Then, if you still feel unfavorably toward Mick, he'll promise never to bother you again."

I hear Mick mumble that he'll make no such promise, and I wave my hand behind me to shush him. Dr. Lodge says, "That's out of the question. The boy almost got my daughter killed! Mrs. Barrett, you should be ashamed of yourself for trying to help him push his way back into her life." He points at the street. "Begone, both of you!"

"Dr. Lodge, what has Anjali told Inspector Reid?" I ask.

"That information is confidential, not for release to the press or the public. Inspector Reid's orders."

"Did she have a vision at the river today?"

"You heard me." Dr. Lodge's gaze darts away from mine for an instant.

"I must warn you that working on the Torso Murder investigation is dangerous for Anjali."

"I'll be with her every moment, and so will the police," Dr. Lodge says. "We won't let any criminals near her."

"It's not the criminals you should worry about," I say. "Inspector Reid is dangerous. If she says the wrong thing to him, or if her visions fail to solve the case, she'll be in serious trouble."

Dr. Lodge looks skeptical. Then his gaze sharpens. "Where's the boy?"

I look over my shoulder. Mick is gone. Then I hear rustling noises from the left side of the door and look over to see Mick climb a pine shrub in the garden. He scales the thick ivy branches that cover the wall, up to a lighted second-floor window.

"Mick! Don't!" I hurry to stop him.

Dr. Lodge gets there first. "Come down from there!"

Mick raps on the window and calls, "Anjali!"

Anjali appears and opens the window. "Mick? What . . .?" Her voice is filled with a strange combination of disbelief, irritation, and hope.

"Anjali, I have to talk to you," Mick pleads.

"Get away from my daughter!" Dr. Lodge grabs Mick's ankles and pulls.

Mick clings to the ivy with his hands while he tries to kick free of Dr. Lodge's grip. "Anjali—"

The ivy peels away from the wall. Mick falls backward and crashes in the shrubbery. Dr. Lodge drags him out, hauls him to his feet, and shoves him into the street.

"If either of you come back, I'll call the police."

* * *

On the way home in the underground train, Mick sits scowling at the floor. His face is scratched from the pine needles, and when I try to dab off the blood with my handkerchief, he pushes my hand away. He escorts me home, unlocks the door, lets me into the studio, and says, "See you later."

He stalks away, probably to drown his sorrows at a pub with Maureen or one of his other girls. I feel sorry for him; I wish he would get over Anjali, but I know that love stubbornly persists in the absence of all hope.

Upstairs, I find Barrett waiting for me, and I tell him I wasn't able to find out what Anjali told Inspector Reid, or convince Dr. Lodge to remove her from the police investigation. Thirty minutes later, we're standing in the dark fog on Commercial Street at the corner of White Lion Street, half a mile from our house, outside the Peabody Building. Five stories of yellow brick, it's a model dwelling—one of many tenements built in the past ten years to replace a slum of cramped, squalid houses and courtyards. Peabody Building houses respectable working people of modest income in two hundred eighty-six flats, with rent ranging from three shillings a week for a one-room unit to six shillings for three rooms. I know this because when it opened, I needed a place to live, and I applied for a flat, but I learned that they lack plumbing and residents share the lavatories, kitchens, and sculleries. That wouldn't have accommodated a photography studio.

"So this is where your second suspect lives?" I ask.

"Right." Barrett has steadfastly refused to provide further details about said suspect. "By the way, the inquest is tomorrow, at St. George's vestry hall at ten AM. You have to testify because you found the torso."

I think he deliberately saved that piece of information to spring on me when he wanted to distract me. Instead of quizzing him about his suspect, I worry about testifying at the inquest. Public speaking terrifies me. I envision the coroner badgering me and reducing me to helpless incoherence before a huge, hostile audience.

Barrett leads me up to the building's third floor and down a plain but clean, gaslit corridor. When he knocks on a door, there's no answer. We hear voices from behind other doors, the sound of families settled in for the evening. When Barrett knocks again, a young man opens the door of the adjacent flat. They regard each other with mutual surprise.

"PC James?" Barrett says.

"DS Barrett?"

"I didn't know you lived here."

"We just moved in." From behind PC James comes the sound of children squabbling. "If you're looking for Violet, she's not home."

Violet Pearcy? Surprise lifts my eyebrows as Barrett says to James, "Would you happen to know where she went?"

"I met her going out as I was coming in. She said she'd been called to the Providence Row Refuge."

After we leave the building, I say to Barrett, "You thought a *woman* was the Ripper?"

"Why not? 'Jill the Ripper' was a theory at the time."

I recall the speculation in the newspapers and in the gossip around Whitechapel, but I'd never put much stock in it. "I can't believe anyone thought such violent murders were the work of a woman." And of course Barrett and I now know they weren't.

"The theory offered a reason why the Ripper was so hard to catch. Everyone was keeping an eye out for suspicious-looking foreign men like Severin Klosowski. A female killer could come and go without anyone noticing. And the victims would let their guard down because they didn't expect an attack from a woman. But the theory was scrapped due to a lack of evidence."

"Now I know why you wouldn't tell me about your second suspect. Because you thought I would say you were daft."

"No. Because I wanted you to see her first. If your first sight of her is like mine was, then you'll understand why I put her on my list."

We walk a block up Commercial Street and turn left on Brushfield. At the corner of Brushfield and Crispin streets stands the Providence Row Night Refuge, a shelter for the homeless. The massive, three-story edifice of beige brick and arched windows also houses the Convent of Mercy. The nuns who live there run the refuge. At the door, a guard turns away a few men and women, dressed in dirty, ragged clothes, their possessions carried in bundles.

"Sorry, we're full. Come back tomorrow."

Barrett identifies himself to the guard. "I'm looking for Violet Pearcy."

"She's in the women's infirmary." The guard waves us through the door.

Inside, a female warden with a ring of keys at her waist patrols a dimly lit passage that smells of disinfectant. Muted screams come from the far end, and Barrett walks straight toward them. Open doors reveal dormitories with rows of cots in which human figures lie. The screams grow louder. At the end of the passage, Barrett pushes through double doors, and we step into the brilliant glare and sulfurous fumes of gaslights turned up high. The screams blare at a shrill, deafening pitch that freezes my blood. They come from a woman who lies propped in a bed, covered in a sheet from neck to breasts, her knees raised below the round, naked, swollen mound of her stomach. Between screams, she grunts and strains. Barrett and I stop short, alarmed to realize that she's giving birth.

Three nuns in black habits and white wimples stand at the foot of the bed. One holds a basin, another a towel, the third a long, curved pair of tongs. On a cart beside the bed are medical instruments and supplies—knives, a hypodermic syringe, scalpels, bottles of medicine, scissors, needles, and gauze pads. A midwife clutches the hand of the laboring woman, whose face is a red, open-mouthed mask of agony with tangled hair plastered to her damp cheeks and forehead. The room smells of urine, feces, and stale body odor.

I've seen scientific illustrations of childbirth, but never the actual event in the flesh. This is a nativity scene with all the morbid detail that artists leave out of religious paintings.

"Push, Julia," the midwife says. Her voice is authoritative, calm, and soothing. She wears a white apron over a brown frock, her hair wrapped in a white kerchief. She's neither young nor pretty, but in the harsh light, her face glows as if she's an angel of salvation.

I look at Barrett. As he stares at the scene, his Adam's apple jumps. He turns to me, and the shock on his face says he's thinking what I'm thinking: *Someday it will be* me *in childbed.*

The laboring woman heaves herself up on her elbows and shrieks as she bears down, again and again. Even while pursued by murderers, I've never had such an overwhelming impulse to run. Even when confronted by spectacles of extreme beauty or horror, I've never felt so compelled to behold, so rooted to the spot. I can't bear to watch for however long the agonizing labor takes, but I stay, and so does Barrett. We're like the shepherds in a nativity painting, immobilized on the canvas.

"I can't do it!" the mother cries.

Childbirth is hazardous. Cemeteries contain countless graves of mothers and their infants. Although every person alive entered the world via a tiny orifice, at this moment it seems impossible.

"Yes, you can," the midwife says.

The confidence in her voice reminds me that childbirth is successful most of the time; otherwise, the human race would have become extinct a long time ago.

A spasm convulses the woman, and she screams, "It won't come out! Oh God, I'm gonna die!"

"I won't let you." The midwife grasps the woman's hand and says, "Look at me." The woman's eyes are red from burst veins, huge with terror as she stares up at the midwife's serene face. "We'll get through this together. I promise you."

A visible change comes over the woman. Her perspiring face shines as though from the reflected glow of her savior. Determination replaces the hopelessness in her eyes even as she emits guttural yowls that sound torn from her very soul. Her face contorts as she strains harder and harder. She grips the midwife's hand hard enough to crush the bones.

The midwife's expression remains serene. "Push!"

I sense strength flowing from her to the woman through their clasped hands. She voices encouragements while the woman pushes, yowls, and gasps. It's as if she's working a magic that inspires faith and endurance in the time of greatest pain and despair. The yowling gives way to a shout of triumphant release. The nuns lean toward the woman, avid witnesses.

"Here it comes!" The midwife reaches between the woman's legs.

I hear a wet, slithery, gushing sound. Blood reddens the sheets from which she lifts the baby. The mother lies limp, gasping with relief. The baby in the midwife's hands is as small as a puppy, eyes and tiny fists closed, its translucent skin covered with a white, creamy substance and bright red blood splotches. The cord dangles from its navel like a gray snake. My mind flips backward to the memory of Kate Eddowes lying eviscerated in Mitre Square. The beginning of life seems as gory as its violent end.

The midwife slaps the baby's behind. Its mouth opens and emits a surprisingly loud cry. "It's a little girl." The midwife smiles as she lays the baby on the mother's breast.

The mother holds the baby and sobs. Whether she's overcome by joy or stricken by the reality of a child to raise, I can't tell. If she's at the refuge, she must be a vagrant, her child born into hardship. The nuns clasp their hands in prayer. But when Barrett turns to me with glistening eyes and a smile that combines incredulity and elation, I feel the same emotions. The beginning of a life is miraculous no matter how that life might turn out, and the midwife seems no less responsible for the miracle than God.

Now the women become aware of our presence and turn to us. "Violet Pearcy," Barrett says, "I'd like a word."

The midwife raises her hands as if to defend herself. Her hands and apron are as stained with blood as a butcher's.

CHAPTER 10

The passage outside the infirmary has a row of chairs against each wall. Barrett and I sit side by side and wait for Violet Pearcy to finish attending to the mother and child. I ask, "Is that how she looked the first time you saw her?"

"Yeah, when I was on patrol one night. Before the Ripper, the blood wouldn't have spooked me, and I wouldn't have bothered to stop her."

Bloodstained people aren't a rare sight in Whitechapel; it has its share of butchers and slaughterhouse workers as well as midwives. That could be another reason the Ripper wasn't spotted near the scenes of his crimes: Anyone who'd seen him would have assumed he had a legitimate explanation for the bloodstains and immediately forgotten him.

"Now I understand why you put her on your list. She looked like a murderess caught literally red-handed."

"That's not the only reason. When I stopped her, she acted as guilty as any criminal I've ever caught. All I did was ask her who she was and where she was going, and she turned and ran. I chased her five blocks before I caught her. She was crying when she told me her name and said she was going home from delivering a baby. She sounded as if she were confessing to a crime. I remembered I'd seen her before and that she was a midwife, so I let her go. But later, I investigated her. She drinks, and she behaves strangely."

"Strangely, how?"

"She talks to herself, and she's jittery. Always looking over her shoulder, as if she thinks someone's after her. Word is, she used to be a popular midwife. Now, only the poorest, most desperate women use her." Barrett nods toward the infirmary door. "I recognized that mother. She's a streetwalker. She sleeps at the refuge or the casual wards when she can get a bed, and in the alleys when she can't."

She's another woman doomed by misfortune. Out on the streets at night, she could have been a victim of the Ripper. I pity her and her child, whose future seems no brighter.

Violet Pearcy comes out of the infirmary and darts a furtive glance at Barrett and me.

"Don't make me chase you again," Barrett says. "Sit down."

She perches on the edge of a chair across the passage from us. She's washed her hands and removed her apron, but there's a red fingerprint on the kerchief on her head. She sits with her feet together, arms close to her side, fingers knotted. All the serene confidence she displayed during the birth is gone. She seems a smaller, timid person now, and I comprehend what Barrett meant—she acts guilty, even though we've not accused her of anything.

Barrett introduces Violet to me and tells her, "This is my wife, Sarah."

Violet gives me a brief, wary glance. "It's an honor to meet you." Visibly bracing herself, she asks Barrett, "What do you want?"

"I'm investigating a murder. Maybe you can help."

"I told you last time, I don't know anything about the Ripper."

I experience the unsettling sensation that I'm watching a play based on events in my own life. This situation reminds me of all the times Inspector Reid pressured me for information about the Ripper. Barrett has taken Reid's role; Violet, mine.

"It's not the Ripper this time," Barrett says. "It's another murder case."

"I don't know anything about any murder."

I must have spoken a similar line to Reid dozens of times, my voice tremulous with the same fear as Violet's.

"All right." Barrett's tone conveys disbelief and accusation.

Violet looks down at her hands and rubs them together, and I see blood under her fingernails. "I haven't done anything wrong."

I never believed in "Jill the Ripper," and I can't imagine the Torso Murderer as a woman, but I can't help wondering if Violet is lying, for *I* certainly lied to Inspector Reid.

"If you haven't done anything wrong, why are you so afraid?" Barrett says. "Why did you run away last time?"

She utters a breathless, nervous laugh. "You accosted me on a dark street in the middle of the night."

"Oh, I think it's more than that," Barrett says.

Other scenes from my life flash through my mind: the police interrogating and threatening my father about the murder of Ellen Casey; the times I crossed the street to avoid patrolling constables. Whether or not Violet has something to hide, her fear of the law taps into my own. I feel a sudden dislike of my husband. He's the law, and he's doing to another woman what Inspector Reid persists in doing to me.

"I think it's natural to be scared when the same policeman who jumped out of the darkness at you suddenly pops up again two years later," I say.

Barrett frowns at me; I've spoken out of turn. Violet gives me a grateful smile and musters enough courage to ask Barrett, "If this isn't about the Ripper, what is it about?"

"The Torso Murders," Barrett says.

Violet purses her lips and covers them with her hand. The sudden paleness of her face emphasizes the dark crescents under her fingernails and the red fingerprint on her kerchief.

"You trained at the Nightingale School for Nurses at St. Thomas's Hospital, didn't you?" Barrett says.

"How did you know?"

"I know all sorts of things about you. You must have studied anatomy."

She drops her hand. "Have you been checking up on me?"

"Did you perform dissections as part of your studies?"

Her eyes are a warm, soft brown, but anger kindles in them. "Why do you care?"

"The Torso Murder victims were dismembered by someone who has knowledge of anatomy and dissection," Barrett says.

I picture the torso and leg at the morgue, the surgically neat amputations. I mentally add the arm and the hand that Jasper Waring's dog found today.

"And you think it's me?" Indignant, Violet points to her chest.

"Is it?"

"That's ridiculous!"

I imagine the quickening throb of her heart and the cold sweat dampening her clothes. Those were my own physical responses whenever I responded to Reid's accusations by lying through my teeth. But I can't reconcile the cruel murders and mutilations with this midwife I just watched deliver a baby.

"Did you know a woman named Elizabeth Jackson?" Barrett asks.

His sudden change of topic startles and confuses me.

"No." Violet looks equally confused. "Why?"

"Elizabeth was the Torso Murderer's third victim, in June 1889," Barrett says. "She was pregnant when she died. Did you deliver her baby?"

He's drawn the possible connection between a midwife and the only known pregnant victim. I can't argue with his logic.

Violet squirms, then makes an obvious effort to sit still. "I didn't know her."

"Are you sure?" Barrett says.

"Yes."

"Elizabeth was a streetwalker who'd been sleeping rough on the Thames Embankment. She was twenty-six, with fair skin, sandy hair, and she had a scar on her wrist."

Violet shakes her head.

"You must have delivered babies from hundreds of women. It would be easy to forget some."

"No, it wouldn't." Violet's expression combines fear of his aggressive manner with scorn for his ignorance. "After I spend eight or twelve or twenty-four hours with a woman in labor, I don't forget her name."

"She was decapitated," Barrett says. "Her arms were amputated. Her torso was severed across the chest and the waist. Does that ring a bell?"

"No!" It's a plea for him to stop, as well as a denial.

"How about this? Her womb was cut open, and the baby was gone."

His brutality appalls me. He sounds just like Reid, describing the Ripper victims in an attempt to force me to talk.

Violet rubs her hands together, lacing and unlacing her fingers. "I could never do such a thing. Ask anyone who knows me."

Why didn't she say, "I didn't do it?" That would seem the logical answer from an innocent person.

"The new victim's remains turned up yesterday," Barrett says. "Who is she?"

"I don't know!" Violet stands up. "I've nothing more to say to you." She pushes through the infirmary door.

"We're not finished." Barrett starts after her.

Jumping from my chair, I hold him back. "Let's just go." I'm frightened to see a new side of him—a man who's as capable of becoming as obsessed and cruel as Reid, as liable to go down the wrong track to his own detriment, as well as to other people's.

"She's hiding something," Barrett protests.

"I think so too, but you can try her again later. You know where to find her."

He throws me off with an impatient motion. I stumble against the chairs, shocked and all the more frightened because his aggression has turned on me. He looks horrified to realize he could have hurt me, and Violet. Then he reluctantly accompanies me out of the refuge.

"I'm sorry," he says as we walk home.

"It's all right." But I'm shaking, upset.

"No, it's not." He removes his hat and rakes his hand through his hair so roughly that the ends stick up. "I don't know what got into me."

He's always been in control of himself, reliably good-natured. No matter how angry or upset, he never takes it out on others. Those are some of the reasons why I love and trust him. But everyone has a breaking point, and I'm disturbed to think he may be nearing his. Are the events of the past three years to blame?

I like to believe that when we hunted down murderers together, faced death, and survived, it was a triumph of justice over sin, life over mortality—cause for rejoicing. I prefer not to dwell on the terror, violence, and bloodshed. But those things changed me, I have to admit. My temper is quicker and hotter. Once prim and ladylike, I'd never raised a hand to anyone, but in recent years I've found myself involved in any number of physical altercations. How could Barrett not have changed too?

The experiences we've shared are on top of the half a lifetime he's spent on the police force, encountering violence and death on a regular basis.

He once told me that the Ripper investigation changed Reid from an honorable, by-the-book law officer to a corrupt man willing to cross every line in pursuit of someone he believes is a criminal.

Are our investigations changing my husband into Reid?

"Let's forget it for now," I say in an effort to put aside worrisome thoughts for now. I tuck my arm around his.

Barrett flinches at my touch. "You shouldn't have interfered while I was questioning Violet Pearcy."

Even though I don't regret it, I hurry to placate him. "I'm sorry. I just thought you were being unnecessarily harsh with her." Anger darkens his face, and I try to justify my actions. "It reminded me of Inspector Reid grilling me."

Barrett recoils from the comparison. "Then I'm sorry you had to see it. But in all fairness to Reid, you are hiding information about a crime."

I exclaim with indignation. "'Fairness to Reid?' After what he's done to us, he's the last person on earth who deserves fairness." That he would defend Reid is another alarming sign that Barrett has changed.

"I admit Reid has gone too far. But when it comes to pressuring suspects and witnesses, that's what we policemen do. Our job is to solve crimes, bring criminals to justice, and protect the public. We're not reporters who can pussyfoot around, coaxing people to tell stories we can publish in the newspapers."

His description of my job stings. With great effort I forgo telling him that I too solve crimes and bring criminals to justice. "Do you really believe Violet Pearcy is 'Jill the Torso Murderer'?'"

"Why not? The Torso Murderer has gotten away with four murders. That could be because he—or *she*—doesn't fit everyone's idea of what someone who kills people and cuts up their bodies looks like."

He has a point, but I say, "Does Violet Pearcy look like a person who lacks empathy and feels no remorse about killing women, cutting them up, and dumping the parts in the river?"

Barrett grimaces in exasperation. "Dr. Lewes and his profiles. I'm taking them with a grain of salt. You should too."

I counter his argument, even though I don't want to quarrel. "There's a practical reason why Violet Pearcy can't be the Torso Murderer. She lives in the Peabody Building. It has no facilities for tenants to dismember bodies without being noticed. I know because I went on a tour when I thought I might rent a flat there."

"She could have access to another place," Barrett says.

I try to explain the less tangible reasons why I don't think Violet is a murderess. "I saw how she was with the woman who was having the baby. I can't believe she's a killer. She practically radiated goodness and healing, like a saint."

Barrett gives me a puzzled look. "I don't know what you're talking about."

Apparently, he didn't see the phenomenon I witnessed; perhaps no one of the male sex would have. Or maybe I imagined it. I'm left with confused impressions of Violet Pearcy.

* * *

When we arrive at home, the house is quiet. Fitzmorris and Hugh are probably asleep, Mick is probably still out. Barrett goes straight up to bed, but I'm still rattled by the night's events. I go to the kitchen, make a cup of weak tea with milk, and sip it until I calm down. When I go upstairs, Barrett is in bed, motionless under the blankets. Quietly, so as not to wake him, I undress, wash, and slip in beside him.

He turns to me and mumbles drowsily, "I love you."

"I love you," I say.

After we kiss, he moves his mouth from my lips down my neck. He unbuttons my nightdress, baring my breasts. I'm glad he wants me after he didn't yesterday, and his desire is arousing, but into my mind flashes the memory of the woman in childbirth at the Providence Row Night Refuge. It's hardly conducive to sex, and I'm also ill at ease with Barrett because he shoved me. My body freezes. I clutch the collar of my nightdress to cover myself.

Barrett immediately desists. "Never mind, then."

Coldness edges the disappointment in his voice. He turns his back on me. Last night he spurned my advance, but I don't want us to go to sleep at odds with each other. "We can do it," I say, even though I know that if we make love, my mind won't let my body relax, and I'll lie awake tense from lack of release.

"If you don't really want to, neither do I," Barrett says crossly. "Good night."

Chapter 11

Early next morning, Hugh and I stroll up and down the alley behind Berkley Square. Rain pelts the umbrella he holds over our heads while I carry my camera, tripod, and satchel. He offered to carry them, but on account of his wounded arm, I won't let him. We shelter in the back doorways of the townhouses when horses and wagons splash past us in puddles on the cobblestones, bringing coal, vegetables, milk, and other supplies to the residents. Servants come and go from other houses, but the Nussey family's back door remains closed.

I pass the time by fretting about the inquest. In less than two hours, I'll have to testify.

"What's going on between you and Barrett?" Hugh asks.

He must have noticed Barrett and I weren't speaking at breakfast. Loath to air our intimate business, I say, "He's upset because he has another day at the morgue and his two suspects haven't panned out." I seize the opportunity to ask, "What's going on with you and Dr. Lewes?"

Hugh replies with suspicious haste. "Nothing." When I look askance at him, he says, "We're just friends."

"Last night, I sensed something more."

He flushes and averts his gaze. "He's like me. He's helped me accept myself. That's all."

"That's all" sounds like an understatement. Hugh just confirmed my notion about Dr. Lewes, and two men of the same inclination, joined by the intense closeness that psychological therapy must entail, seem headed for a love affair—if they aren't already in the thick of one.

Before I can question Hugh further, he points to the Nusseys's back door. "Look!"

A boy exits the house. About eleven years old, he's short and wiry, brown-haired, and carrying a large wicker basket. "Pardon me," I call. He stops to regard Hugh and me with curiosity. "We're looking for Louisa Nussey. Can you tell us if she's at home?"

The boy starts to sidle away. "We ain't supposed to talk about Miss Louisa."

My pulse quickens as I begin to think the hunch that brought Hugh and me back to the Nussey house was on target. "Why not?"

"Who're you?"

Hugh cups his hand around his mouth and speaks in a low, confidential tone. "We're detectives, and we're investigating a murder."

"Really?" The boy's eyes pop with excitement.

"Yes," Hugh says. "Maybe you can help us."

"How?"

"An unidentified woman's body has been found. We understand that Louisa Nussey has gone missing, and we think the body might be hers."

The boy's excitement deflates. "Aw, it can't be. Miss Louisa ain't dead."

I'm glad for Louisa, disappointed for myself. Hugh says, "Thanks anyway." But as the boy starts to walk away, the hunch nudges me again.

"Wait," I call. "Where is Miss Louisa?"

"I can't talk about her anymore." Nervous again, the boy walks faster.

As Hugh and I hurry along beside him, I say, "Please. This is very important."

"I already said too much."

"There's a murderer out there," Hugh says. "We need to warn Miss Louisa. She's in danger."

The boy stops at the end of the alley, his curiosity engaged. "Really?"

"Yes, really," Hugh says with a conviction that would persuade me if I didn't know he was making it up. "If you direct us to her, you could be the hero who saved her life."

The boy glances back toward the Nussey house. "You won't tell 'em I told you?"

"Our lips are sealed." Hugh runs his finger across his mouth.

"She ran away. They found her and brought her home," the boy whispers. "Then they sent her to a lunatic asylum."

The story of Louisa Nussey is more complicated than I imagined. "Which asylum?"

"It's called Ticehurst, in Sussex." The boy hurries away.

"Thank you for getting the information out of him," I say to Hugh, once again glad he's back in top form. I'm grateful to Dr. Lewes no matter the nature of their relationship.

"You're very welcome," Hugh says, "but I don't understand why you care where Louisa Nussey is. She's not the Torso Murder victim."

"I have a hunch that it's important."

"I'm the last person to dismiss a hunch, but it sounds like the usual story," Hugh says. "A woman behaves badly, and her wealthy family keeps her under control, out of trouble, and away from society's eye by shutting her up in an asylum."

"I feel as if I have to see Louisa. I can't explain why." I'm afraid I want to pursue Louisa because I can't think of anything more worthwhile to do.

"Then I'm all for a trip to Sussex."

I'm glad for his confidence in me, but I say, "It'll have to wait until after the inquest."

* * *

Hugh and I arrive half an hour early at St. George-in-the-East. "Let's stop at the morgue and see Barrett," I say.

The little brick building looks even more inhospitable with rain dripping off its eaves onto the sodden shrubbery. Outside the open door, three men and a woman stand in line under umbrellas. Hugh says, "I'll wait out here, if you don't mind. One look at the torso was enough for me."

When I enter the morgue, the foul smell of rot is stronger. Barrett and another man stand on opposite sides of the table where Dr. Phillips examined the remains yesterday. Now it holds a large metal trough filled with ice chunks. Nestled among them lies the torso and the leg, with the arm and hand found by Jasper Waring's dog. Although the ice has slowed the process of decay, the flesh has shrunken and turned gray, like meat kept too long. The arm and hand are in worse condition than the other parts. The skin is gone, the muscle tissue ragged, and the fingertips have been stripped to the bone, presumably by fish.

Barrett nods to me in greeting. The tension from last night does nothing to improve the unpleasant atmosphere. He holds a notebook and pencil. The man with him wears a derby, a black coat, and gray trousers, and holds a handkerchief over his nose and mouth.

"I can't tell if it's her." His voice sounds as if he's struggling not to be sick. He hurries out of the morgue.

Barrett calls after him, "If you hear from her, please let the police know." He pulls a rueful face and sighs. "He's the eleventh person who's tried and failed to identify the body today." He shows me his notebook, in which he's written the names and addresses. "Most of them just wanted to gawk, but I feel sorry for him and the others. They're desperate to find their missing relatives."

At least there are some people trying to claim the sheep that strayed from their fold. I wonder how many others prefer to act as though the lost one never existed.

"They had to look at that"—Barrett gestures toward the remains—"and how could anyone tell who it is?"

"I know, it must be terrible," I say. "For you too."

Barrett gives me a grateful smile; my sympathy narrows the distance between us a little. "Have you had any luck?"

"The last name on my missing persons list turned out to belong to a woman who's alive."

"That's too bad." Barrett doesn't sound particularly disappointed that we're both at dead ends. Misery loves company, even during a murder investigation.

I don't tell him that I'm planning to follow up a hunch about Louisa Nussey. He'll think I'm as misguided as I think he is regarding Severin Klosowski and Violet Pearcy. Then I feel bad because I'm keeping a secret from him. That's been a sore issue in the past. Suddenly I'm scared. Where is the frankness we once shared? I'm shaken to realize we'd been talking less even before this investigation started. Barrett hardly talks about his job, and when I tell him about mine, he seems distracted, preoccupied. We make love only once a week, if that. The change has been so gradual that I didn't notice, but now I can date its onset to our last murder investigation.

It ended with four violent deaths.

Barrett, Mick, Hugh, Anjali, and I barely escaped with our lives. How could that *not* change any of us? For Barrett, could it be the straw that broke the horse's back?

But now isn't the time to explore or solve whatever problem ails Barrett. People are waiting outside, and I hurriedly set up my camera and photograph the remains. Barrett says, "The coroner's jury has already viewed them. Do you want to keep me company until it's time for the inquest?"

I nod, and he calls in the next party in line—a youngish man and woman. The man is thin and pale, with spectacles and a receding hairline. The woman is taller, dark, and bright-eyed, towing him by the arm while he hangs back. The fit and fabric of their clothes indicates expensive custom tailoring. Her black hat has a little net veil, and a silver brooch shaped like a rose decorates the velvet lapel of her maroon coat.

When she sees the remains, she exclaims, "Good lord!" Her eyes sparkle with excitement despite her horror.

The man moans, bends over, and gags. Barrett grabs a pail from the worktop and positions it on the floor. The man falls to his knees and retches into it. My second look at the remains was bad enough; if I watch people vomit, I'll lose my own breakfast.

"I'd better head to the inquest," I say. "I'll see you tonight."

* * *

The vestry hall is located on Cable Street, around the corner from the church. It has Doric columns and pilasters around the porch, and tall windows on the second story interspersed with Ionic columns. A vestry is a place where church vestments are kept and the church wardens conduct business, but this one is big and grand enough to be a town hall. Hugh and I join the people streaming in through the door, and follow the crowd to the assembly room. Gas chandeliers illuminate a large space that has windows on two sides and a low stage at one end. On the stage, flanked by dark green velvet curtains, are a long table with chairs behind it and a line of chairs to its right. To its left, another chair behind a podium serves as the witness box. On the walls hang portraits of august-looking men, presumably church dignitaries from the past. Chairs arranged in rows fill the rest of the floor space. Most seats are already full. Hugh and I manage to grab three in the middle of a row near the back.

I put my camera equipment on the seat beside me to save it for Sally. The man on its other side says, "Hello."

It's Jasper Waring, dressed in a neat business suit, a notebook in his lap. Annoyed to see him again, I say, "Where's your dog?"

"At home. I didn't think his services would be needed here," Mr. Waring says with a nervous laugh.

Sally appears in the aisle, scanning the crowd for me. When I beckon her, she stops short at the sight of Mr. Waring. Displeasure clouds her face. "I'll sit somewhere else."

Mr. Waring hastily rises. "I'll move."

The look Sally aims at him could give him frostbite. "Don't bother." She must think his chivalry is either an attempt to buy her forgiveness cheaply or give himself an opportunity to make her the butt of more pranks.

"Hugh and I will change places," I say. We move so that I'm sitting next to Jasper, with Hugh beside me.

"Thank you." Sally takes the empty chair next to Hugh. She sits very straight, facing forward, chin up, ignoring Jasper.

"It really was an accident," Mr. Waring says to me. "Could you make her understand that Smoker and I didn't mean her any harm?"

I think he's sincere, but I'm in no mood to intervene in their spat. Officials are taking their places at the table on the stage, and the jurors seating themselves in the chairs on their right. Soon I'll have to testify, and my jitters are worsening.

"Leave me out of it," I tell Mr. Waring. I'm already on shaky ground with my sister, and I don't want to make it shakier by sticking up for a man she dislikes.

He leans forward, looking across Hugh and me at Sally. "She's quite a girl, isn't she?" Admiration colors his voice.

"Yes, she is." My frosty tone says she's none of his business.

The coroner is Mr. Wynne Baxter, a dignified man with spectacles and gray hair. I recognize him from the Polly Nichols inquest. He makes introductory remarks that I don't listen to; I'm preoccupied by the memory of Polly lying dead in a puddle of blood in Buck's Row, her skirts pushed above her knees, her throat cut. Horror and faintness wash over me. Through ringing in my ears, I hear Mr. Baxter say, "Mrs. Thomas Barrett."

Now it's shades of my father's trial, the endless walk to the front of the room, the frightening sensation of all eyes on me as I mount the steps to the stage and take my seat in the witness box. I remind myself that I'm not here to defend my father against a murder charge. This is an unrelated issue, not personal.

Mr. Baxter leads me through a recital of finding the torso. I'm so nervous, I forget what I said as soon as it's out of my mouth, but he doesn't challenge me. "Thank you, Mrs. Barrett—that will be all."

On quaking legs, I scurry back to my seat. Sally smiles at me, and Hugh whispers, "Excellent work."

Glad that my turn is over, I relax as the constable who was first at the scene testifies. Then Dr. Phillips gives a very detailed autopsy report. Hugh puts his hands over his ears; Sally and Mr. Waring take notes.

"Were you able to identify the victim and determine the cause of death?" Mr. Baxter says.

"Unfortunately, I was not," Dr. Phillips says.

After dismissing Dr. Phillips, the coroner says, "I must instruct the jury to return a verdict of 'Found Dead,' the same as for the previous similar cases."

Hugh, Sally, and I look at one another and shake our heads, disappointed by the lack of new evidence to help us solve the case. It appears that the coroner will close the inquest, and this investigation, like its predecessors, will end in a pile of yellowing pages in a police file. Then someone near the front of the audience raises his hand. I can't see who he is or hear what he says, but Mr. Baxter nods and says, "I call one more witness: Inspector Edmund Reid."

Startled, I watch Reid rise from his seat and take the witness stand. I'm glad I wasn't aware of his presence while I testified; I would have been even more nervous.

"Inspector Reid, what has the Torso Murder Task Force learned?" Mr. Baxter says.

Reid wears a pleased expression that I'm afraid bodes no good. "We have just obtained new information."

I wonder if Barrett knows or if Reid is keeping him in the dark.

"Would you care to elaborate?" Mr. Baxter asks Reid.

"Not at this time. It would be premature to make the information public. But I'm confident that it will lead not only to the identity of the victim and the cause of death, but to the identity of both the Torso Murderer and Jack the Ripper."

A stir of excitement ripples through the audience. Hugh says, "An old dog just won't learn to let go of the bone." Sally shushes him, and Jasper Waring regards us with curiosity. I'm afraid that Reid has twisted whatever clues he's found to fit his favorite, erroneous theory.

"That's a grand claim, Inspector," the coroner says. "Could you at least tell us how you came by the information?"

"I will as soon as I'm ready to name names. Meanwhile, I ask that you delay your verdict until then."

"Very well," Mr. Baxter says. "I adjourn the inquest until the task force's investigation is complete."

Hugh, Sally, and I join the exodus from the building. Reporters flock around Reid, shouting questions. "His information must have come from Anjali," I say, troubled because I know her visions are open to misinterpretation.

"I think you're right," Hugh says. "I don't see how evidence could have cropped up so quickly any other way."

"No comment," Reid says to the crowd. "You can read the story when it comes out in the *Chronicle*." He strides away, flanked by two constables and trailed by several *Chronicle* reporters, leaving me in terror that the information he's discovered will lead him to the secret my friends and I are hiding.

"I still have two more missing women on my list to look up," Sally says to Hugh and me. "What are you going to do?"

I tell her about Louisa Nussey, then say, "We're going to Ticehurst," and explain about my hunch.

"Well, I suppose it's worth a try," Sally says with obvious skepticism, "since you haven't any other clues to follow up."

Mr. Waring approaches her. "Pardon me, Miss Albert."

Sally glares at him. "What do you want?"

"I want to make it up to you for Smoker knocking you down."

"Then tell me what Inspector Reid knows about the murder," Sally retorts.

"Your sister drives a hard bargain," Hugh whispers to me. I'm surprised and pleased by Sally's cunning; I hope it works.

"Um, I was thinking of taking you to lunch," Mr. Waring says.

"Then you won't tell me?" Sally says.

"I can't," Mr. Waring says. "It would violate the *Chronicle*'s agreement with the police. I'm sorry."

"The fellow has principles," Hugh whispers. "That's a point in his favor."

"In that case, there's no use lunching together, because we've nothing to talk about." Sally flounces away.

Jasper gazes after her for a moment, then hurries in the opposite direction to catch up with Inspector Reid.

"I wish Sally would give him a chance," Hugh says.

"She's wise to avoid contact with him," I say. "He's the competition. He's more likely to pump her for information than give her any."

"You're probably right," Hugh says. "Are you ready for our trip to Ticehurst?"

Chapter 12

The 12:33 train from Charing Cross Station takes Hugh and me southeast over hilly, forested terrain, through tunnels bored into mountains. Two hours later, we alight on the outdoor platform at the small Ticehurst Station. Although only forty miles from London, Ticehurst has a blue sky and clean, warmer air. The windows of the cab we hire afford us a view of pastures and farmhouses, then a rustic stone wall that surrounds what looks to be a private park. The sign on the gate reads "Ticehurst Hospital." Beyond the gate, we ride past woodlands, rolling lawns, and a pagoda. Men on horseback gallop across fields. One raises a rifle, fires at the sky, and a bird plummets groundward, trailing feathers.

"I hope those men with guns aren't patients," I say.

We round a curve in the road, and the hospital is dramatically revealed, like a stage set. A palatial white edifice with a glass conservatory stands amid pine trees. A Gothic summerhouse and aviary decorate the grounds, with gardens, barns, and other outbuildings in the distance.

"Good Lord," Hugh says. "This would be fit for the Queen if she ever goes mad."

Accompanied by nurses in caps and blue capes, ladies and gentlemen stroll the scenic paths. Our cab lets us off behind a carriage parked by the main entrance. Uniformed liverymen help passengers into the carriage.

I pause to take a photograph of the hospital. "I don't suppose we'll need it, but as long as we're here, I might as well."

Inside, we find a hall with a reception desk below a high, vaulted ceiling and a bright, glittering gas chandelier. A doorway gives a view to a parlor, where people sit on plush divans, nibbling cakes, sandwiches, and scones from tiered silver trays on low tables. A waiter pours glasses of sherry; a man in evening dress plays a grand piano.

"If *I* ever go mad, put me here," Hugh says. "Of course, I probably couldn't afford the bill."

The receptionist is a stylish woman of about forty, every hair of her chignon lacquered in place. She greets Hugh and me with an artificial cheer that seems intended to convey the impression that Ticehurst is a hotel to which people come to enjoy a holiday, not an asylum where the insane are committed. When I tell her we want to see Louisa Nussey, her smile remains as fixed in place as her hair, but she says, "I'm terribly sorry, Miss Nussey isn't allowed to have visitors."

The now-familiar blend of relief and disappointment washes through me. Louisa really is here, alive, and not the Torso Murder victim lying in pieces at the morgue. But my hunch persists, like a stick poking my ribs. "It's urgent that we see Miss Nussey."

"We're from her family solicitor's firm in London," Hugh says. "We've brought papers for Miss Nussey to sign." He points to my satchel, which contains no such thing. "She's due to receive an inheritance, but if she doesn't sign, the assets will be frozen. Her bills won't be paid."

The receptionist hesitates, says, "Just a moment, please," and steps into the office behind the desk as if to confer with someone.

"Now that we know Louisa is here, we could leave," Hugh says.

"Not yet." I don't know whether my hunch is a real sign that there's something important to learn from Louisa Nussey or just a stubborn need to see this through after coming so far.

The receptionist comes back and summons a nurse, who leads us up a grand staircase to the third floor, along carpeted corridors lined with closed doors. She stops at a door and unlocks it. Hugh and I raise our eyebrows at each other.

It seems Louisa Nussey is a prisoner in this luxurious establishment.

Her room, larger than an entire flat in the Peabody Building, boasts pink rose-patterned wallpaper, a crystal gas chandelier and lamps, a Turkey carpet, and oil paintings. It smells sweetly rank, like unwashed hair, and contains enough divans and overstuffed chintz chairs to host a party. The four-poster bed wears a lacy white canopy, rose coverlet, and silk cushions. Pink velvet curtains cover the tall windows. Louisa Nussey kneels in a corner, before a little table that holds a framed picture flanked by two unlit white candles in silver holders. A coal stove exudes too much heat, and she wears nothing but a long-sleeved, high-necked white flannel nightdress. Her hands are clasped under her chin, her exposed feet bare, their soles dirty. Her long brown hair hangs in loose, greasy hanks over her thin, hunched shoulders. She prays in a voice that sounds like a dog whimpering. I move closer, the better to hear.

"The angel said to her, 'Behold, for the Holy Spirit has come upon you. You have conceived the son of God, and he shall be called Jesus.' For this child I prayed, and God granted my wish. The baby leaped in her womb, and she was filled with the Holy Spirit."

"Miss Nussey, you have visitors," the nurse says.

Louisa slowly turns and looks up. "But jealousy burns like fire." Her face is plain, all sharp bones and mottled fair skin. Her hair is gray at the temples; she must be near forty. "When Rachel saw that she bore Jacob no children, she envied her sister. She desired and did not have. Wrath is cruel, anger is overwhelming, but who can stand before jealousy? The thief came only to steal and kill and destroy. For where jealousy and selfish ambition exist, there will be every vile practice. Bloodshed followed bloodshed." Louisa seems dazed and troubled, as if just awakened from a dream of the events she's narrating. Her parted lips reveal large, yellowish teeth. "I said, 'Who knows whether God will be gracious to me, that the child may live?' But now he is dead. The dust returns to the earth, and the spirit returns to God who gave it. And she lifted up her voice and wept."

As she beholds Hugh and me, Louisa's hollow gray eyes light with rapture for no reason I can see. She brings to mind an early Christian martyr whose prayers have summoned angels.

"May we have a moment alone with Miss Nussey?" Hugh asks the nurse.

"I'll be waiting outside. I have to lock the door. Doctor's orders."

The nurse leaves, and the clatter of the key turning in the lock makes me feel as if I've been imprisoned. I suppress an urge to run to the door and beat on it. Louisa rises, her knees cracking audibly, and faces Hugh and me.

"Did he send you?" Hope brims in her eyes. Her well-bred voice is raspy, as though not often used in conversation.

"Who?" I'm confused by her question and her previous words, which seemed a hodgepodge of quotes plucked from the Bible and strung together in a bizarre rosary.

Louisa claps her hands and smiles. "I knew he would find me!"

"I'm sorry, we weren't sent by anyone." Hugh introduces himself and me. "We're detectives, investigating a murder, and we thought you might be able to help us."

Disappointment crumples Louisa's face. Then she seizes my arm and Hugh's. "You have to get me out of here." Her fingers dig into my sleeve, my flesh. She's quaking with anxiety.

Hugh and I look at each other, mystified. Whatever we'd expected to find, it wasn't a mental patient begging us to help her escape. I say, "I'm afraid that's not possible."

"Please! I don't want to be here. They kidnapped me and brought me here and locked me up against my will."

"Who kidnapped you?" Hugh asks.

"Mother and Father." Hatred burns in Louisa's eyes.

To accuse one's parents of kidnapping and imprisonment might sound outlandish, but perhaps not from a mental patient. "Why did they?" I ask, humoring Louisa.

"To get me away from him."

"Who is 'him'?"

"The Reverend Patrick Eden-Smith." Louisa speaks as if she can't believe I had to ask.

"I'm sorry, we don't know him," Hugh says.

"Soon you will. Soon everyone will." Louisa snatches the picture from her altar and holds it up for our examination. "This is Reverend Patrick."

Brightly colored, the picture at first looks like a typical print from a shop that sells religious items. Jesus hovers in a cloud, surrounded by angels, his hands extended to bless the worshipers below him. But instead of the typical long, fair beard and hair, this Jesus is clean-shaven with short black hair that grows from a widow's peak, his facial features handsome in the manner of dashing heroes in romantic fiction. His smile has a touch of arrogance. The angels and worshipers are all female.

Louisa notices the equipment I set on the floor, and her eyes brighten. "Is that a camera? Would you take a picture of me with Reverend Patrick?"

I oblige while she poses, smiling and holding his picture. It's another photograph that will probably never grace the pages of the *Daily World*.

Louisa kisses his painted face before she replaces the picture on her altar. "He's going to transform the world into heaven on earth." Her eyes are misty with adoration.

"If the Reverend is so splendid, why does your family want you away from him?" Hugh says.

"Because they think he was influencing my mind and stealing my fortune," she exclaims in disgust. "It's lies, all lies."

It's a common story—an unscrupulous man taking advantage of a rich woman. The clergy isn't necessarily above such base instincts, and a devout spinster would be an easy mark.

"Yes, I donated money to his church," Louisa says, "but I did it of my own free will."

I wonder how much "free will" she has when she worships his very image.

"I told Mother and Father so, but they wouldn't listen. They think he's an evil criminal."

I'm interested despite thinking this has nothing to do with the Torso Murders, and I begin to be concerned about Louisa's welfare. "So you ran away from home?" Not to enter a convent, as her neighbors thought, but to join the Reverend Patrick Eden-Smith's church.

"Yes. I moved into the rectory." Haggard, unwashed, and disheveled, Louisa sparkles with remembered bliss. "His church is called the Haven of Love. It's in Primrose Hill, and there's the most wonderful community. It's like a utopia."

"'Haven of Love,' eh?" Hugh looks interested too. "Your parents placed an advertisement in the newspaper, asking for information about your whereabouts. Why didn't they know where you'd gone?"

"I didn't tell them. I knew they wouldn't approve."

I suppose they wouldn't; it's highly irregular for a clergyman to move a female parishioner into his home. I'm more concerned for her than ever. "How did they track you down?"

"I don't know. But my father and brothers came and forced me to go home with them. I tried to run away again, so they brought me to this place and had me locked up." Louisa begs Hugh and me, "Help me get out of here and back to the church!"

We look at each other, and I can see that Hugh is as conflicted as I am. On one hand, I don't like to refuse aid to someone who's forcibly imprisoned; on the other, we can't return Louisa to a man who may be exploiting her. Perhaps her parents are right to think she belongs exactly where she is.

"I'm afraid we can't do that." And I can only imagine what would happen if we, with no legal authority, tried to remove a patient from the hospital.

"Please!" Louisa sobs, falls on her knees, and grabs Hugh's trouser legs and my skirts.

Stricken by her suffering, Hugh says, "We're sorry."

Louisa clambers to her feet, runs to the door, and bangs on it, screaming, "Let me out!"

The nurse opens the door. Louisa flies at her, punches her. The nurse grabs Louisa, who flails, kicks, and screeches. Hugh and I stare, astonished by Louisa's violent strength. The nurse calls for help, and two male orderlies come running. They restrain

Louisa, and she struggles in a frenzy of flying hair, emaciated legs, and clawing hands.

"You should leave," the nurse tells us.

As the orderlies pin her to her bed, Louisa calls to us, "Take a message to the Haven of Love. Tell Reverend Patrick to come and save me!"

Chapter 13

On the train to London, I say, "How about if we stop at Primrose Hill before we go home?"

Hugh looks askance at me. "We've a killer to catch, or have you forgotten? Reverend Patrick sounds a bit shady, but even if he really is duping women and stealing their money, it's a far cry from murdering and dismembering them."

"I know." Outside the window, sheep graze in a pasture, the bucolic scene such a contrast to my troubled thoughts. "But I can't just forget about Louisa. If I were in an asylum against my will, I would want someone to help me."

"Good point," Hugh says. "It's our job to solve the murders and get justice for the dead, but we can't ignore the living. We'll take time for a quick visit to the Haven of Love."

* * *

Primrose Hill, in north London, is a district that encompasses the park of the same name. Hugh and I exit the railway station after the ticket seller gave us directions to Haven of Love. Walking past stately villas, then terraces of brightly colored Italianate terraced houses, we hear distant roars from the lions in Regent's Park Zoo. At the junction of King Henry's Road, Primrose Hill Road, and Elsworthy Road, the Haven of Love Church stands in spacious grounds. It's of recent vintage; the brickwork and ornate stone trim are clean and sharp edged. Flanking the arched entrance are large marble statues that symbolize the four evangelists—St. Matthew, a winged man; St. John, an eagle; St. Luke, a bull; and St. Mark, a lion. Hugh and I tilt our heads back to look up at the pointed steeple that rises from a tall tower at the entrance. The same four figures, cast in bronze, perch on the corners of the steeple's base. They're a vivid blue-green color, chemically treated to look ancient. Little iron chariots crown weathervanes on the two smaller flanking towers. A stone wall, some ten feet high, conceals the area behind the church. Above the evergreen trees inside the walls I see the roof and chimneys of a large house, which I presume is the rectory.

"This must have cost a fortune to build," Hugh says.

"I wonder where the money came from." Perhaps Louisa Nussey and other women?

Lancet windows glow with stained glass. As Hugh and I walk up to the entrance, I hear faint music. Hugh says, "I think we're just in time for Evensong." He hesitates before he opens the door for me.

I know he hasn't attended a religious service since the scandal after the vice squadron raid. The pastor of his church, a lifelong friend he looked up to, told him that he was a disgraceful sinner who'd brought shame to his family. I also hesitate before I enter the church. I haven't attended a service since I was ten. After my father became the prime suspect in the Ellen Casey murder and then disappeared, the congregation at our church ostracized my mother and me. After one Sunday sitting alone in a pew while our neighbors whispered to one another and cast dark looks at us, my mother never took me again, and all throughout my adulthood, I shunned the religion that I felt had shunned me. Aside from my wedding, I've only been in churches to photograph the sights or investigate crimes.

Sonorous organ music and the smell of burning wax and incense greet us. Beyond the vestibule, a hammer-beam ceiling soars high. A black-and-white diamond-patterned tile floor extends between enough polished wooden pews to seat four or five hundred people. At least half the seats, those nearest the apse, are full. All I can see of the congregation are dark silhouettes against the light from the candles on the altar, which also holds a golden cross and vases of flowers. Women occupy the choir near the organ. They wear long white robes, tight in the bodice, cinched at the waist, with voluminous sleeves. At center stage, the minister, dressed in black vestments, stands beside a kneeling woman. He's handsome, with black hair that grows from a widow's peak—the man in Louisa's picture, the Reverend Patrick Eden-Smith.

"Come to me, you who are weary or carrying heavy burdens." His voice is a melodious baritone. "I will give you relief."

"God beyond us, God beside us, we seek your healing touch," the congregation responds.

The woman kneeling before him wails, "O God, I have offended Thee with my lustful thoughts and deeds!" Her frock is plain gray, but her braided chignon of auburn hair gleams red in the candlelight. "I fear the fire of hell. O God, cleanse me of my sin and my guilt!"

"There is no need to beseech God in the heavens, for He is present amongst you." Patrick Eden-Smith holds up his hands. On both palms are glistening red wounds.

The audience murmurs with wonder. The woman at the organ plays a thunderous chord, and the choir utters a harmonized exclamation that brings to mind angels singing in heaven. Hugh and I look at each other in surprise and disdain. We don't believe in mystical religious phenomena, and this show is far more theatrical than miraculous. In the space of a few minutes, Reverend Eden-Smith has proved himself to us an utter charlatan.

"My word is God's word," he intones. "I will save you with my love." He lays his hands on the woman's head, caresses her hair and her face. "Feel my love flowing into you."

"Lend me your strength and make my heart pure!" The woman kisses his hands in an ecstasy that verges on carnal. "Open my lips that I may proclaim your praise."

"May the Holy Spirit fill your whole being." Reverend Eden-Smith gasps as though physically aroused. "Let it purify your body and soul."

"Glory to God!" the woman shrieks while the organ thunders and the choir trills.

"I banish the darkness. Rise up and bathe in my holy light." Reverend Eden-Smith's hands gesture upward. "My spirit is within you, cleansing you of sin, restoring you to the purity with which you were born. I hereby pronounce you a vestal virgin, a keeper of the sacred faith, dedicated to chastity."

"Amen," cries the congregation.

The woman sobs with cathartic relief as she staggers to her feet. "Thank you!" The organ strikes up a hymn. The choir sings:

"Long my imprisoned spirit lay
Fast bound in sin and nature's night;
Thine eye diffused a quickening ray,
I woke, the dungeon flamed with light.

Amazing love! how can it be
That Thou, my God, should die for me?"

When the song is finished, Hugh scowls as he and I join the parishioners flocking to Patrick Eden-Smith. Now I notice that most are women. He extends welcoming hands to them as the choir gathers behind him. The scene resembles the picture in Louisa Nussey's room. After a lengthy period of chatting with his congregation members and bidding them farewell, Reverend Eden-Smith approaches Hugh and me.

"Hello. I don't believe we've met." His manner is genial, his smile warm. "I'm Patrick Eden-Smith. Welcome to the Haven of Love." He extends his hand to me.

Hugh intercepts Eden-Smith's hand and turns its palm up. The smooth skin is intact, devoid of blood. The pastor tries to pull away, but Hugh holds on tight.

"I want a closer look at your stigmata. Hmm, they're gone now," Hugh says. "Clever trick. Was it pig's blood or red paint?"

I'm shocked by his rudeness. I myself had planned to examine Reverend Eden-Smith's hand, albeit more covertly, but I'm dismayed that Hugh would affront a potential witness in our investigation when we need his cooperation. Eden-Smith gently, firmly extricates his hand. The church is almost empty; the only people who remain are the "virgin," three women from the choir, and three little girls. The women all glower at Hugh. Whispering among themselves, they sound like cats hissing.

Eden-Smith swiftly regains his genial poise. "I take it you're a nonbeliever," he says to Hugh.

"You take it correctly," Hugh snaps. "You aren't God, and you can't restore lost virginity." I think the anger and hurt caused by his own pastor is spilling over onto Patrick Eden-Smith, and we both despise folks who dupe the vulnerable and gullible.

"But he did!" the virgin cries. "I can feel the light and purity of God in me. Beloved Lamb is the incarnation of Jesus Christ our Savior."

The other women chorus, "Amen." Eden-Smith smiles a lofty smile and stands taller, as if their support is bearing him heavenward on a cloud. He apparently decreed that they call him "Beloved Lamb," as in "Jesus, the Lamb of God."

"I would be more impressed if you'd restored eyesight to the blind or made a crippled man walk again," Hugh says.

"I have done those things, and more. I perform laying-on-the-hands services every week." Reverend Eden-Smith continues with a touch of mischief, "Perhaps you should come and allow me to get that painful chip off your shoulder."

Hugh flashes him a teeth-baring grin, like a dueler drawing his sword. "I'd rather see you walk on water. How about it?"

The women buzz angrily. I'm torn between wanting to scold Hugh for his rudeness and commending his attempt to call the charlatan's bluff.

Patrick Eden-Smith turns to me. "What brought you to the Haven of Love, Miss—Mrs.—?" His eyes are a strange, deep violet hue, their gaze penetrating and mesmerizing. The force of his attention makes me feel as if I'm the most special person present.

Unsettled as well as unwillingly flattered, I say, "Mrs. Thomas Barrett. And this is my colleague, Hugh Staunton." On the train, we'd made plans to pose as newcomers to the parish, wanting to join the church, and discreetly find out the true nature of Eden-Smith's relationship with Louisa Nussey. Because Hugh's behavior has nixed that idea, I play it straighter. "We're reporters for the *Daily World*, and we're researching a story about women who've gone missing. We managed to locate one. Her name is Louisa Nussey. She told us about you. Do you remember her?"

"Ah, yes, Miss Nussey." If the Reverend is disturbed, it doesn't show, but I sense a heightened attention from the women, whose white robes rustle with their uneasiness. "She's a member of my congregation, but I haven't seen her in a while. How is she?"

"She's in an insane asylum." I don't tell him which. If indeed he's a dangerous con man, I mustn't help him get his hooks into her again. "Her parents committed her to get her away from you. They thought you were exerting too much influence on her and stealing her fortune."

"Let me assure you that nothing could be further from the truth," Reverend Eden-Smith says. "I admit that I accepted money from Louisa, but she donated it voluntarily."

"Here's a riddle," Hugh interrupts. "How many women does it take to build a fancy church? Answer: As many who are rich and foolish enough."

The women react with angry cries of, "How dare you?" and "Such blasphemy!" Reverend Eden-Smith, unruffled, pats the air, calming them down. "At the Haven of Love, we don't take advantage of anyone. Our mission is to transform the world."

Hugh laughs. "And how will you do that? With an army of refurbished virgins?"

"With love." Eden-Smith refuses to take offense; he speaks as if preaching a sermon. "Love is the ultimate, creative, healing, enlightening spiritual force. It can end wars, cure sickness of the mind and body, and lead lost souls into the light of God."

"Well, hallelujah," Hugh says.

I feel sad for him, as well as vexed by his rudeness. He must have listened to many sermons on the theme of love, from the pastor who later cruelly spurned him and made it obvious that "love thy neighbor" didn't apply to the likes of him.

Reverend Eden-Smith ignores Hugh and addresses me. "Here in our community at the Haven of Love, we set an example of living in harmony and peace." Turning to the women from the choir, he beckons. They step into his embracing arms, two on one side, the third on the other, while the virgin clasps her palms together and regards the group as if they're a banquet and she's hungry. He introduces the three, gesturing to indicate which is which. All of an age, in their mid-thirties, they beam up at him. "These are my wives—Merciful Saint, Light of Heaven, and Anointed One."

Hugh's expression blends amazement and derision. "First miracle cures, now polygamy."

"Merciful Saint and I are married in the usual, legal fashion."

She has a wide, plain face, a thick waist, and a jutting bust. Her mousy brown hair, liberally threaded with gray, is dressed in an unbecoming style—a fringe over her low forehead and curls over her protuberant ears. Her severe expression momentarily softens as she and her husband exchange intimate smiles. He says, "With the others, our union is strictly symbolic and platonic."

I can't automatically accept as fact anything said by this man who fakes stigmata, and his followers are giving me the creeps. "What are their real names?"

"These are our real names," Light of Heaven says. She's pretty in the manner of girls who bloom early and fleetingly, with faded blond hair in upswept ringlets. Her pale blue eyes squint as if she's nearsighted and too vain to wear spectacles. She has a pudgy face and a curvy, hourglass figure that looks permanently altered by too-tight corsets.

"Beloved Lamb gave us our names when he married us." Anointed One is slim, with black, glittering, watchful eyes, her dark, glossy hair wound in a braid above each ear. Delicate of feature, she would be attractive if not for the port-wine birthmark that spreads over her left cheek and down her mouth.

I'm liking "Beloved Lamb" less and less. It's easy to picture him wooing Louisa Nussey and these other unbeautiful spinsters and helping himself to their money.

"I'm Emily Clifford," the virgin says, as if eager for a share of attention. She's younger as well as prettier than the wives, in her late twenties. With her auburn hair, green eyes, and sly look, she brings to mind a plump, well-fed fox. I can believe she committed her confessed sins of lust in thought and deed.

Patrick Eden-Smith introduces the children. "These are my daughters—Fortitude, Humility, and Atonement." They're small, young, female versions of himself. But for their differences of height and of age—ranging from perhaps eight to twelve years—they could be triplets. Their black hair is smoothly drawn back from their widow's peaks and plaited in two braids, and they wear identical black frocks with white collars and cuffs.

"Did he name them too, or did you get a say?" I ask Merciful Saint.

She pauses before she says, "Their mother was Beloved Lamb's deceased first wife."

I sense a sore spot in her. "Have you children of your own?"

"Humility, Fortitude, and Atonement *are* my children."

"We wives are all their mothers," Anointed One says.

Patrick Eden-Smith smiles proudly. "If all men and women in the world followed our example and considered all the children in the world as their children, and loved and nurtured them as such, the world would be a better place."

"Amen," chorus the wives. The daughters wear identical prim smiles.

I wonder what they really think of the situation. Hugh says acidly, "Three mothers to boss them around. What fun."

I picture the six of them competing for the Patrick Eden-Smith's favor. What fun—for "Beloved Lamb."

"They must get teased a lot at school, on account of those names," Hugh says.

Eden-Smith's smile grows strained; Hugh's carping is getting to him. "They don't go to school. We educate them ourselves." To me he says, "Why are you interested in missing women?"

"We're investigating the Torso Murders," I say. "We're trying to discover the identity of the latest victim, whose body parts are in the morgue."

The Reverend raises his eyebrows, but he seems more baffled than disturbed. I hear a sound that combines a cough and a gasp. I look at the daughters. I can't tell which one uttered the sound. They all look at the floor.

"You shouldn't talk about such things in front of innocent young girls," Merciful Saint reproaches me.

"I've heard of the crimes," Reverend Eden-Smith says somberly. "They're a sad example of the ills of the world. The man who committed them must have experienced immense cruelty, pain, and suffering that twisted his character and drove him down a dark path. Now he seeks to visit his pain and suffering on others."

I think of Dr. Lewes and his profiles. Here's another profile of the Torso Murderer, and although I don't like or trust its source, perhaps it's equally valid.

"When my mission is complete," Eden-Smith says, "all the cruelty in the world will be transformed into love, all pain and suffering eradicated."

Hugh opens his mouth to utter another sarcastic comment, and I kick his foot. "Are there any women missing from your congregation?"

"Fortunately not, aside from Louisa Nussey." Eden-Smith smiles. The wives shake their heads, their expressions bland. I think they would corroborate anything he said. "And since you found her alive, she can't be the woman you're trying to identify."

⋆ ⋆ ⋆

Outside the church, we walk toward the train station. I carry my camera equipment and my satchel, which now contains negatives of the photographs that Reverend Patrick Eden-Smith let me take of him with his women and around the church. He said he hoped an illustrated newspaper story would help him spread his message. I'm collecting a whole album of photos that I doubt will ever be published. Hugh holds his handkerchief over his mouth, coughs, and spits.

"Are you ill?" I ask.

"No, the 'Beloved Lamb' and his harem left a bad taste in my mouth." Hugh glances back at the church. "After all that pious nonsense, I could use a drink."

I become aware that I'm hungry, and we stop at a public house called the Pembroke Castle, built above the railroad tracks. The taproom is crowded, noisy with chatter and the rumble of the trains passing below. Most of the other customers are men in railway uniforms.

"Sarah, I'm sorry I needled Reverend Eden-Smith," Hugh says as we seat ourselves at the lone empty table.

"It's all right." Although I'm vexed at him, I can forgive Hugh anything. Not only is he my dear friend who's stood by me through many ordeals, but he sustained the injury to his arm while saving my husband's life. If not for Hugh, I would be a widow now.

"No, it isn't all right. If I'd behaved myself, we could be sitting down to dinner with the good Reverend and his harem and ferreting out all their secrets." Hugh snorts in disdain. "'Spiritual marriage'—bah, humbug. I say it's nothing but a scheme that lets him commit adultery and extortion."

"I agree. But I can't picture him murdering or cutting up women."

"Nor can I. He wouldn't want to get his lily-white hands dirty. Now, if you'll excuse me, here's my chance to make up for ruining our chances at the Haven of Love." Hugh saunters to the bar.

I watch him strike up a conversation with the publican and the customers. He buys a round for them, and soon they're all chatting and laughing like old friends. Ten minutes later, Hugh returns to our table with glasses of ale and a plate of bread, cheese, and pickles. Accompanying him are a man and woman, both stout and with salt-and-pepper hair, dressed plainly but neatly. He has a full beard and mustache; her hair is done up in an outdated style with abundant curls and frizz.

Hugh pulls up chairs for them, introduces me, then says, "Sarah, meet Mr. and Mrs. Johnson."

"So you want to know what's what at the Haven of Love?" Mr. Johnson says to me. "The missus can tell you plenty."

"Yes, indeed," Mrs. Johnson says. "I was their charwoman when the church first opened."

"For three months, 'til the Reverend gave her the axe," Mr. Johnson says.

I'm so intrigued that I barely taste the food I'm eating. Here's an insider with ill will toward the Haven of Love, who might have valuable information. "Why were you dismissed?"

Mrs. Johnson smiles, sly and sheepish, like a cat with canary feathers on its mouth. "The Reverend's wife—the one they call Merciful Saint—caught me steaming open his letters."

"You shouldn't have." His fond, indulgent tone softens Mr. Johnson's rebuke.

"Well, I was curious," Mrs. Johnson says. "Who wouldn't be, with all the goings-on over there?"

"I meant you shouldn't have let yourself get caught."

"Yeah, I should've been more careful," Mrs. Johnson concedes.

More intrigued than ever, I say, "Can you describe the goings-on?"

"Well, those 'wives' are supposed to be like nuns, or so the Reverend explained it to me. He's in 'spiritual marriages' with them. Meaning, he doesn't go to bed with any of them except Merciful Saint. She's his real missus. But many a time I saw the one they call 'Light of Heaven' coming out of his room early in the morning. The same with 'Anointed One.' I could tell they were naked as jaybirds under their dressing gowns."

Mr. Johnson shakes his head. "Such language."

"I'm just calling it as I saw it."

Here's credible confirmation of polygamy, if nothing else. "Why did you steam open the Reverend's letters?" I ask.

"I wanted to know what was in 'em," Mrs. Johnson says. "Wouldn't you?"

"I certainly would." Hugh smiles encouragingly.

"Who were the letters from?" I ask.

"Women at his old parish. It's in Wiltshire, a village named Ashlade. They said they loved him and missed him. Sometimes they sent money. In one envelope, there was a bank note for five hundred pounds!"

Here's proof that he was taking money from women, if not proof of coercion.

"But the letter I got caught steaming open was from the bishop," Mrs. Johnson says.

"What did it say?" I ask eagerly.

"Something about complaints the bishop got from the villagers. That's as far as I read before Merciful Saint tore it out of my hands and the Reverend fired me."

Chapter 14

The couple at the Pembroke Castle couldn't provide any further information about the Haven of Love. After Hugh and I finished our food and drinks, we headed back to Whitechapel. Outside the train station, we're caught up in a crowd in which everyone seems to be hurrying in the same direction down the high street. We hear snatches of conversation: "Something's going on at the nick." "It's about the murders."

The warm glow from the ale I drank turns cold with sudden fear that Hugh puts into words: "Good Lord, has there been a new Torso Murder?"

Alarmed by the idea that the killer has struck again because we didn't catch him, we join the rush toward the police station. I couldn't protect the Ripper victims, and I pray that this isn't a new episode of my old nightmare. Leman Street is packed with people. Sally and Mick call to us from the mob, and we join them. I stand on tiptoe, peer through the crowd, and see Inspector Reid standing at the station entrance, flanked by Barrett and the other the task force members. With them are Anjali and Dr. Lodge. Photographers and cameras surround the company.

"Reid must be about to announce a clue from Anjali." My fear gives way to relief that no one else, as far as we know, has fallen victim to the Torso Murderer.

"I'm pleased to say that, thanks to Miss Lodge, we now have a possible identification of the victim and a suspect in the Ripper and the Torso Murders," Reid says.

The crowd exclaims. My companions and I gape at Reid. This is a far bigger and faster turn of events than we expected.

"Damn it, Reid beat us," Mick says.

"Don't be too sure of that." New apprehension fills me.

"If Anjali gave him the lead, it's good," Mick says with firm loyalty.

"If this means no more dismemberments and decapitations, then my hat is off to Reid, no matter how much I'd like to stuff it down his throat," Hugh says.

"Yes, I suppose we should be glad." Sally sounds disappointed at the thought of losing her opportunity to solve the crime and earn a promotion.

I fear Reid is going astray, as he did on the Ripper investigation. A mistake on his part now could leave the Torso Murderer free to kill again. I try to catch Barrett's eye and see how he feels about all this, but reporters shouting questions block his view of me. Jasper Waring is among them. Anjali cowers behind her father as flash lamps explode. People are packed so closely around me that I haven't room to set up my camera or get a clear shot of Anjali, Dr. Lodge, and the policemen. Reid holds up his hand; the crowd quiets.

"The possible victim is named Irene Muller," Reid says. "Her last known address is the Garratt Lane Workhouse. She went missing from there on April ninth. The suspect is her boyfriend, one Charlie Holt. His whereabouts are unknown."

My companions and I exchange glances and shake our heads in puzzlement. These names mean nothing to us.

"Mr. Holt is a sometime driver for the Simmons Horse Knacker Company."

Horse knackers transport horses that have died to rendering factories. Their wagons are a common sight on the streets, where many among the city's thousands of horses drop dead every day and block traffic until the drivers remove the corpses.

"Horse knackering is a perfect profession for the Torso Murderer," Reid says. "Simmons has a rendering factory. When it's closed overnight, it affords a private place to kill women, and it has the necessary equipment for butchering them. Mr. Holt would also have a means for transporting the body parts, and nobody who saw his wagon near the river would suspect anything amiss."

An earthshaking thought occurs to me. What if Reid discovers that this Charlie Holt is indeed the Torso Murderer? Surely, he'll pin the Ripper murders on Charlie Holt, no matter how strenuously the man denies the accusation. The police will close the Ripper case, and Reid will plague me no more. Elation buoys me up as I imagine the heavy weight lifted off my back. My family and I will suffer no more threats from Reid. Then I'm ashamed of my selfishness. A possible subversion of justice looms, and my care is all for my own personal interests.

"I ask that anyone with information regarding Irene Muller and Charlie Holt please report it to the nearest police station," Reid says.

His judgment is so impaired by obsession that I think him capable of pinning both series of crimes on Charlie Holt, even if the man is guilty of neither. Reid has persecuted innocent people in the past; what's to change him now? I can only hope his suspect really is the Torso Murderer; otherwise, God help him when he falls into Reid's clutches.

The press conference ends, and the crowd disperses. Mick shouts, "Anjali!" and runs toward her. A constable intercepts him. Dr. Lodge hurries Anjali into a cab that's waiting on the corner. Mick pulls free of the constable and runs after the cab. Barrett walks over to Hugh, Sally and me. Before I can ask him about Anjali's vision, Reid calls, "Mrs. Barrett! A word, please."

By now I should be accustomed to his attacks, but I as I turn to face him, I feel a twinge of the terror I experienced the first time we met, when I wasn't the hardened veteran of our many skirmishes.

"Where is Charlie Holt?" Reid asks.

His question is so different from whatever I might have expected; I just stare at him in confusion. "Why are you asking me?"

Reid's expression combines irritation and scorn. "Are you denying that you know him?"

"Yes." Flustered, I say, "I'd never heard of him until you mentioned him." Barrett, Hugh, and Sally listen, equally mystified.

"Is he a relative of yours? Or a former boyfriend?"

"No!"

"She told you, she doesn't know him." Anger darkens Barrett's face. "Leave her alone."

"Why do you think she does?" Sally asks Reid.

Reid turns a wolfish smile on her. "Hello, Miss Albert. Since either your big sister has been keeping you in the dark, or you're slow on the uptake, I'll spell it out for you. Sarah knows who the Ripper is, and she's protecting him. I think he's Charlie Holt."

I'm flabbergasted by this new twist in Reid's obsession. He's fixed his suspicion on a man against whom he has no evidence except a psychic's vision, and not only is he ready to pin ten murders on Charlie Holt, but he's painted me into his absurd scenario.

Bewildered, Sally says, "Why would Sarah protect the Ripper?"

"Because he's someone important to her," Reid says. "Because she cares about him, and she doesn't want him arrested and hanged."

"You're insane," Barrett says flatly.

Hostility sparks in Reid's eyes. "Watch your mouth, Detective Sergeant."

"Sarah wouldn't let the Ripper get away with murder." Sally flushes with angry vehemence.

"Maybe you don't know your sister as well as you think," Reid says.

Furious because he's roping Sally into his feud with me, I say, "I won't dignify your nonsense by listening to any more of it."

"You tell him, Sarah," Hugh says.

I start to walk away, lest I do something regrettable. As Hugh, Sally, and Barrett accompany me, Reid calls, "Wait, Miss Albert."

Sally stops and turns, as if she's Lot's wife and she can't resist looking backward at Sodom and Gomorrah. I tug her arm. "Sally, let's go."

She ignores me, her gaze fixed on Reid, who smiles like a fisherman with a big one on the hook. I realize with dismay that

Sally shares one of my traits—she's attracted to danger. That, as much as advancement and financial independence, is what led her to be a crime reporter.

"Sarah's in trouble," Reid says to her. "When I find Charlie Holt—and I will find him—I'll make him confess that he's the Torso Murderer and the Ripper and that Sarah helped him avoid capture. She'll be charged as an accomplice. Do you understand what that means?"

"Sally, don't listen to him," Barrett says.

"He's talking out of his behind, excuse my language," Hugh says.

Sally stares at Reid in horror as he continues relentlessly, "It means your sister aided and abetted a mass murderer. She'll be tried and found just as guilty as he is." Reid's eyes twinkle merrily. "They'll be hanged together."

Sally goes pale and turns her terrified gaze on me. I say, "That's never going to happen."

Reid smirks. "We'll see about that."

I hide the fear that rises in me as I remember that the law could be as grievously unfair to me as it was to our father. I picture myself in the dock in Old Bailey and standing on the wooden platform in the execution shed beside Charlie Holt, a man I don't know and whose face I can't see because our heads are covered with hoods, both of us with nooses around our necks.

Barrett puts himself between Sally and Reid. "That's enough."

Reid shifts position, restoring his view of Sally. "Here's the clincher, Miss Albert. You're in danger too. If the jury at your sister's trial thinks she told you who the Ripper is, and you kept quiet—well, *you* will hang for your role in covering up his crimes."

"I couldn't have told her, because there's nothing to tell!" I've never lied with such outrage or fervor.

Sally puts her hand over her mouth. Her eyes dart as if between her wish to believe me and her fear that what Reid says will come to pass.

Reid smiles, gratified by the rise he's gotten from us. "But I'll tell you what, Miss Albert—if you persuade your sister to come clean, I'll see that neither of you is punished."

I wondered what Reid's latest move against me would be, and here it is. In my distress, all I can think to do is get Sally away from him. I grab her arm, start walking, and pull her along so roughly that she stumbles. Barrett takes her other arm to prevent her from falling. Hugh follows close behind her, his hand laid protectively on her shoulder.

Reid calls after us, "Think it over, Miss Albert." Nasty mirth inflects his voice. "But think fast. If I find Charlie Holt, and he talks before your sister does, it'll be the gallows for you and her both."

* * *

At home, Barrett, Sally, our friends, and I have no opportunity to talk together about what happened, because Dr. Lewes is there with Fitzmorris. During the bustle of dinner preparations, however, Sally and I find ourselves alone in the kitchen for a moment while she slices bread and I take the shepherd's pie out of the oven.

"If you knew something about the Ripper, you would tell me, wouldn't you?" Sally speaks timidly, as though afraid of my reaction.

I almost drop the heavy baking dish of meat, carrots, peas, onions, and gravy topped with mashed potatoes. "Of course I would." I look Sally straight in the eye just long enough so that she won't think I'm lying. "But I really don't know anything."

Sally nods. I breathe a quiet sigh of relief as I set the pie on the stovetop and close the oven door.

"I just wondered if that's why you're so sure the Ripper and the Torso Murderer aren't the same person," Sally says. "Because you know who the Ripper is and there's some reason why he can't be the Torso Murderer."

I hear the question and the doubt in her voice. Luckily, Fitzmorris comes into the kitchen, interrupting our conversation. As I carry the pie dish to the dining room, the heat burns through the oven gloves on my hands. I'm furious at Reid, who's driven a wedge between Sally and me. Divide and conquer is a favorite ploy of his. He hasn't managed to break Barrett, Hugh,

Mick, or me, but he thinks that Sally can ferret the truth out of me, and he can break her.

He may be right.

At dinner, while we discuss the new developments in the Torso Murder case, Barrett, Hugh, Mick, and I skirt around the subject of the Ripper. Dr. Lewes eats while he listens in silence, watching us all. I uncomfortably wonder if we're material for a future monograph.

"And there I was, stuck in the morgue while Reid discovered the identities of the victim and suspect." Barrett stabs his fork through a carrot on his plate, as if he'd like to do the same to Reid's face.

"Irene Muller and Charlie Holt are the *possible* victim and suspect," I point out.

"If Anjali saw them in a vision, then it's them," Mick insists.

"She didn't say so," I remind him. "Reid may have twisted her vision, like he twists everything else."

"Well, we'd better hope he's right about this," Barrett says. "Only three people came by the morgue today, and the remains are deteriorating. Dr. Phillips says he'll have to put them in alcohol to preserve them, which will change their appearance. Then the chance of anyone recognizing the victim will be even less."

Sally turns to me. "*Do* you know Charlie Holt?"

I swallow a morsel of shepherd's pie, and it goes down the wrong way. "No." I cover my mouth with my napkin as I cough.

Sally studies me, and I see her trust in me eroding. "I'm going to look for him. The horse knackering company sounds like a good place to start."

I don't mention that Reid already must have checked there. Sally might think I'm trying to discourage her because I really am in league with Charlie Holt and don't want him found. Changing the subject, I describe Hugh's and my visit to the Haven of Love.

"Let me get this straight," Barrett says. "You found Louisa Nussey. She's not missing, but you investigated her anyway. And now you expect me to believe that this Reverend Patrick Eden-Smith might be involved in the Torso Murders?" He shakes his head. "And you think Violet Pearcy and Severin Klosowski are long shots."

I hurry to defend my position even though I know it's flimsy. "I think something's not right at the Haven of Love."

"So your hunches are worth more than mine?" Anger edges Barrett's tone.

"Of course not." But in this instance, I believe his are off the mark. "I just think Reverend Eden-Smith and his flock are worth further scrutiny."

"And I think you're getting sidetracked."

I look to Hugh. After a pause, he says, "Well, the Haven of Love definitely smells like a rat. Somebody needs to find out whether 'Beloved Lamb' really is bleeding money from women. If he is, that's one criminal we can put away."

I frown at Hugh, disappointed by his half-hearted support.

"I agree with Barrett." Sally speaks in a small voice, timid about getting in the middle of an argument between my husband and me.

We begin arguing about what our next step should be, which suspects to pursue first. I push for the Haven of Love; Barrett for Klosowski and Pearcy; Sally, Mick, and Hugh for Charlie Holt. Our voices grow louder, our opinions more entrenched and contrary. Hugh turns to Dr. Lewes. "Joshua, what do *you* think?"

As we all fall silent, my back goes up. Since when is Dr. Lewes the final arbiter? Still, we've reached such an impasse that perhaps I should be grateful for his guidance.

Dr. Lewes pauses, as though aware that he's on the spot in terrain where he's not entirely welcome. "It seems to me that all the theories have potential merit, including Inspector Reid's. I would suggest—"

"We've always managed to work out our differences and solve our cases by ourselves," Barrett says.

"Yeah," Mick says.

I feel both amusement and irritation as I realize what's happened. Barrett and Mick reacted like dogs in a pack when an interloper asserts authority. I can practically smell the male aggression in the air. They accepted Sally because she's female and seems no threat to their standing, but they perceive Dr. Lewes as a challenge to their own positions in our circle.

"An objective party could help settle things," Hugh says.

"Dr. Lewes is hardly objective," Barrett says. "He has his own opinions about the Torso Murderer."

I see that Barrett in particular feels threatened by Dr. Lewes, whose profiles of the Torso Murderer conflict with *his* own opinions.

"Why not listen to what he has to say before you reject it?" Hugh says.

His quick defense of Dr. Lewes makes it obvious to me that there's something more between them than mere friendship. Barrett and Mick look surprised that Hugh would take the newcomer's side. They apparently haven't noticed anything different about Hugh and his psychologist, and I haven't told them of my suspicions.

"All right," Barrett says, "I'm listening." He and Mick lean back in their chairs, fold their arms, and bend challenging looks on Dr. Lewes.

A shrewd glint in his eye says Dr. Lewes knows exactly what's going on. "To be clear up front, I'm not siding with one theory about the Torso Murders against the others." Mick and Barrett relax somewhat; Hugh looks relieved. "I'll just mention something I've learned from my research work. First, one is liable to go astray when one cleaves too strongly to a theory before it's been adequately tested. Second, the person who most wants to believe in it shouldn't be the only one to test it. The person who's most opposed to it should take a stab at it too."

A long moment passes while Dr. Lewes's words sink in.

Barrett and I lock gazes. He says, "I'm willing if you are."

Chapter 15

Sunday morning finds Barrett and me at Charing Cross Station. The platforms aren't as crowded as on weekdays, and church bells ring above the rumble of trains. Last night, we agreed that as much as we dislike admitting it, our stubborn adherence to our favorite theories about the Torso Murders puts us in danger of botching the investigation. We also agreed that since I had accompanied him while he investigated Severin Klosowski and Violet Pearcy, he should accompany me while I investigate Reverend Patrick Eden-Smith and the Haven of Love. Now, a tentative peace lies like sunlight upon the dark, turbulent waters of our marriage.

"I hope this little jaunt is worth the trouble I'm going to get into when Inspector Reid finds out I played hooky from the morgue," Barrett says as he buys our tickets to Ticehurst.

"I hope that today Louisa Nussey will be calm enough to talk," I say.

Two hours later, as soon as we arrive by cab at Ticehurst Hospital, I notice a difference. The weather is sunny and crisp, but a hush envelops the grounds, and no patients are visible.

"Yesterday it was like a holiday at a country estate," I say. "Something's wrong."

"Maybe everyone's at church?" Barrett says.

He tells the driver to wait for us, and we carry my camera equipment inside the building. The lounge is empty, and nurses huddle in anxious groups, conversing in low voices. At the desk, a middle-aged gentleman in a dark suit greets us, his manner courteous but unsmiling. He has the air of a store manager on the lookout for shoplifters.

"We're here to see Louisa Nussey," I say.

He frowns. "May I ask your name?"

A chill of foreboding runs through me. While Barrett stands by, I introduce myself with the cover story that Hugh and I used yesterday. "I'm from the Nussey family's solicitor. It's imperative that we speak with Louisa."

The manager lowers his voice and says, "I'm sorry to inform you that Miss Nussey passed away last night."

Shocked disbelief stuns me. "But I just saw her yesterday. How did it happen?"

"I've no authority to release information about her."

Barrett shows his badge and identifies himself. "My business with Louisa Nussey concerns a criminal investigation in London."

The manager's expression alters from obstinacy to anxiety. "What criminal investigation?"

"The Torso Murders," Barrett says.

"I'm sure Miss Nussey had no connection with that." The manager obviously fears for the reputation of the hospital.

"What happened to her?" Barrett asks.

"A full report will be made directly to her family. You can ask them."

Barrett hesitates before he forces the issue. "Unless you tell me, I'll have to launch a full inquiry and return with a squadron of police officers."

The manager glares, then capitulates. "Miss Nussey took her own life."

I reel with fresh shock, then dawning horror. Can it be a coincidence that Louisa committed suicide later the same day Hugh and I visited her? She'd been upset when we left. Was she upset enough to kill herself?

"I'm sorry to hear that," Barrett says, his own surprise evident despite his professional manner. "Where is her body?"

"Still in her room, where it was found."

"I'll need to see her," Barrett says.

After a pause, the manager buckles under the fear of London policemen overrunning the hospital, disturbing the patients, and causing a scandal. He beckons a nurse to take us to Louisa, but he points at my camera. "No photography. Leave that or stay here."

The nurse chatters nervously as she escorts Barrett and me upstairs. "Suicide can be contagious among the mentally disturbed. All the patients are confined to their rooms, guarded by staff members."

Louisa's door is ajar. The nurse precedes Barrett and me into the room. The velvet curtains are drawn back, the windows open. The pink color of the curtains, the bed coverlet, and the wallpaper roses is garishly cheerful in the sunlight. The cold spring breeze freshens the once stale, fusty air. A man with silver-rimmed spectacles and a dark beard and mustache sits at the desk, writing. His hairline recedes from a high, domed forehead, and the buttons of his dark suit coat gap across his paunch. Jarringly out of place amid the feminine décor, he frowns up at Barrett and me.

"Who are you?"

Barrett flashes his badge. "Detective Sergeant Thomas Barrett, Metropolitan Police, London. This is my wife. And your name, sir?"

The man loses his composure, as many of even the most self-confident people do when confronted by the law. "James Abernathy. I'm the attending physician for this floor."

"Mr. Warren told me to bring them up," the nurse says apologetically.

Dr. Abernathy's eyes narrow behind his spectacles. "What is this about?"

"Louisa Nussey was a possible witness in a murder case I'm investigating." Barrett shoots me a covert glance that says, *"Look what you've gotten me into."* He doesn't really think Louisa Nussey has anything to do with the case, and my hunch has put him in an awkward position—conducting an inquiry in a place where he has no jurisdiction. "I've just been informed that she committed suicide. I need to determine whether it's true."

"Oh, it's true." The doctor bristles because Barrett is questioning his professional judgment. "See for yourself." He gestures toward a closed door near the back corner of the room.

Following Barrett there, I see Louisa's makeshift altar. Reverend Patrick Eden-Smith smiles from his picture. Now that I've met him in the flesh, the arrogance in his expression seems more obvious.

Barrett cautiously opens the door. Cold air from a window inside the private bathroom wafts a rotten, metallic smell of blood and raw meat over us. I clap my hand over my nose. The bathroom has white fixtures, white paint and tile on the walls, and a black-and-white-tiled floor. Amid this lack of color, the clawfoot bathtub stands out like a tinted area in a photograph. It's filled nearly to the brim with bright red water. Immersed up to her chin, Louisa Nussey lies with her head propped on a folded white towel, her ash-blond hair hanging loose, her eyes closed, lips parted, face as white as the walls. Her left arm dangles over the edge of the tub, her spidery fingers dripping into a bloody puddle on the floor.

The red fills my vision and pulsates with the pounding of my heart. Through the roar of my own blood in my ears, I hear the doctor say, "She slit her wrists. I lifted her arm out of the water to check."

I blink hard, and the redness disperses into dots. I see raw gashes on Louisa's wrist. My stomach turns despite my abundant experience with terrible death scenes.

Dr. Abernathy points to the soap dish mounted on the wall beside the tub. In it lies a silver letter opener, its long, sharp, pointed blade stained with blood. "That's what she used."

"Why did she do it?" Barrett asks, calm and steady, the seasoned policeman.

"She was a very disturbed, seriously melancholic woman."

"If she was so disturbed, why was she allowed to have that letter opener?"

"She wasn't." The doctor's reply is quick, defensive. "But mistakes happen. Careless visitors leave things lying about, and patients find them and hide them from the staff. The insane can be very crafty."

"What was the time of death?" Barrett asks.

"About midnight, I estimate."

Louisa killed herself only hours after Hugh and I left. Without photography to distract me, nausea threatens to overwhelm my self-control. I stumble out of the room and into the passage. I lean against the wall, close my eyes, and breathe deeply until the nausea recedes. I see Polly Nichols lying in a puddle of blood, Liz Stride with her throat cut. I remind myself that Louisa's death was suicide, her own choice. But I can't forget that when I first met her, she'd seemed calm enough, and when I left, she was wild with desperation.

Visiting Louisa was my idea. Hugh isn't to blame; I twisted his arm.

Did I drive her to suicide?

If I hadn't been so stubborn about following my hunch, would she be alive now?

The tally of deaths that I can attribute to my actions, or lack thereof, threatens to rise. I feel a sudden, powerful urge to find out what happened after I left Louisa. Time is of the essence; I can't wait for Barrett. I look up and down the corridor. It's empty. I knock on the closed door of the room adjacent to Louisa's.

A nurse opens the door. I ask, "Were you here yesterday? Did you see Louisa last night? Did she say anything to you?"

The nurse blocks my view of whoever else is inside the room. "We're not supposed to talk about it." She shuts the door.

Spurred by my frantic hope that Louisa's death isn't my fault, I hurry to the other adjacent room. In response to my knock, a female voice inside calls, "Who's there?"

I keep knocking until the door is opened by a young, rosy-cheeked, brunette nurse. I push past her, into the room. She exclaims, "You can't come in here!"

I ignore her shooing motions and look around the room. Furnished in the same style as Louisa's, it's cluttered with books and candy boxes strewn on the bed, toiletries on the dressing table, letters on the desk, and bowls of flowers and fruit on the mantelpiece. The air smells of perfumed talcum powder and overripe apples. A woman, presumably the patient who occupies the room, stands by the window. Tall and buxom, perhaps forty years of age, with bold features, she has black hair arranged in an elaborate bouffant coiffure. She wears a teal silk frock and a necklace of diamonds so big that I wonder if they're real. She peers at me through a lorgnette.

"I'm Mrs. Thomas Barrett," I say. "I work for the Nussey family's solicitor. I need to find out what happened to Louisa and report back to him so that he can inform her family."

Although intimidated by my authoritative manner, the nurse bleats, "I can't talk about Louisa."

"Well, *I* certainly can." The patient has a fluty voice and dramatic manner to match her appearance. "I am Madame Claudia Orsini."

"Did you know Louisa?" I ask.

"Not really. She stayed in her room most of the time. I hadn't seen her in at least a week. But I heard plenty yesterday."

"Now, now, we mustn't gossip," the nurse says.

"Bah, you ninny! Gossip is the breath of life." Madame Orsini says to me, "Before they locked us all up, I heard that Louisa killed herself. How did she do it?"

"I'm going to fetch Matron." The nurse hurries out the door.

"Matron is like Cerberus at the gates of Hell," Madame Orsini warns me. "We haven't much time before she throws you out."

I hate to violate Louisa's posthumous privacy, but if I want information, I'll have to give some. "Louisa slit her wrists in the bathtub."

Madame Orsini gasps and clutches her bosom. "My word!" She staggers to a table and snatches a bottle of smelling salts, opens it, and inhales deeply.

I've no patience for hysterics. "What happened to Louisa yesterday?"

"She had a bad spell in the afternoon. I was taking my beauty nap. I woke up when I heard her screaming."

That must have been during my visit. "Did you hear anything else?"

"Not then. They probably gave her a sedative injection. That's what they do for bad spells. But someone went into her room at about eleven last night."

I tamp down fear, excitement, and the premature suspicion. "Who was it?"

"A man. I was in bed, and I heard the door open. When I got up and went out to look, he was already inside Louisa's room."

"Did you hear what they said?"

"No." Madame Orsini pantomimes eavesdropping with her ear pressed against the door. "But it sounded like they were praying. The only man who prays with the patients is the chaplain, but that wasn't him. He's old and his voice sounds like a tone-deaf musician sawing on a violin. This man's voice was deep, and he sounded younger."

Uneasy premonition ripples through me. "You didn't see him at all?"

"Just a glimpse. I waited until I heard Louisa's door open, then I peeked out my door and saw him walking away from me down the corridor. All I could tell was that he was tall with dark hair."

I can think of one man who fits that description, whom Louisa would have welcomed into her room to pray with her late at night. Fresh horror sickens me. The circumstances of her death indeed could be my fault, in a worse way than I thought, and I look for reasons to disbelieve it. Madam Orsini is a mental patient, perhaps not the most reliable witness. But I mustn't rush to doubt her story just because I want to absolve myself of blame. The man, his description, the praying, and the timing of his visit—it's too much coincidence to dismiss so easily.

The nurse returns with the matron, a stern older woman who seizes my arm in an iron grip and propels me out of the room. I protest as the nurse closes the door and locks herself inside with Madame Orsini. I try to explain why I was there, but Matron says, "I don't care who you are or what you want. You are leaving before you can bother more patients."

She marches me down the hall as if I'm a disobedient schoolgirl and she's the headmistress. I resist. Two men clad in black, wheeling a stretcher piled with folded dark canvas, block our way. They push the stretcher into Louisa's room. It's the undertakers, come to remove her body. I pull free of Matron and hurry in after them. Barrett and Dr. Abernathy are standing in the bedroom. The doctor somberly greets the undertakers. Barrett's wary expression asks me, *"What have you been up to now?"*

Matron tugs my arm. "You can't be in here."

"She's in the bathtub," Dr. Abernathy tells the undertakers.

I jump in front of the stretcher, spreading my arms. "You can't take her yet. She was murdered. This is a crime scene."

"What are you talking about?" Barrett regards me with dismay that says he thinks I'm chasing another baseless hunch.

The undertakers look to the doctor, who grimaces in annoyance and says, "Miss Nussey's cause of death was exsanguination from self-inflicted cuts on her wrists." He holds up the document he'd been writing when Barrett and I arrived. "For the sake of her family, I've written on the death certificate that she died of complications from pneumonia." He says to the undertakers, "Of course, I can trust you gentlemen to be discreet."

The undertakers murmur, "Of course."

I'm appalled that they mean to sweep the circumstances of her death under the rug. "But there needs to be an autopsy. And an inquest and an investigation."

Matron yanks me aside to make way for the undertakers. They move the stretcher near the bathroom, open the door, and wince at the sight of Louisa. One carries in the folded canvas while the other pulls the chain attached to the bathtub plug. As the water drains with a sucking, swirling noise, Louisa's naked body emerges—shoulders, then breasts—like a woman drowned in a red sea, exposed by the ebbing tide.

Dr. Abernathy slams the bathroom door and says to me, "You can't just walk in here and make wild allegations."

"Why do you think Louisa was murdered?" Barrett says in the patient, calm tone that men use toward hysterical women.

It has the effect of making me angry and incoherent. "Because he was here. Late last night."

"Who was?"

"Reverend Patrick Eden-Smith."

"That's impossible," the doctor says. "Visiting hours end at eight PM."

"He was in this room with Louisa," I insist. Things are looking even worse than I'd thought. I may not have driven Louisa to commit suicide, but I could be as responsible for it as if I had. I can't believe that her taking her life on the night after I went to the Haven of Love is a coincidence.

"How do you know?" Barrett asks.

"Madam Orsini next door told me. She heard them talking."

"Her name is Mrs. Orson, not Madame Orsini," Matron says. "She suffers from delusions, and she thinks she's a famous opera singer, which she most certainly isn't."

"Did she see this man?" Barrett sounds doubtful.

"Only a glimpse of him," I have to admit. "But her description fits the Reverend."

"According to Mrs. Orson, she entertains her own gentleman admirers every night," Dr. Abernathy says. "The man she saw was just another figment of her insanity."

It's as I speculated—Madam Orsini isn't a reliable witness. Now my own credibility is in question. Why should Barrett or the doctor believe me when I would take the word of a madwoman? But I persist because my intuition is telling me, loudly and clearly, that the facts about Louisa's death are yet to be determined. "Someone else may have seen the Reverend. Perhaps the people who were on duty last night."

"Our staff observes the rules," Dr. Abernathy says. "Louisa couldn't have had a visitor."

In frustration, I turn to Barrett. He asks the doctor, "Would you mind if I interview the staff?" I can tell that he doesn't think it necessary; he's only humoring me.

"I certainly would mind," the doctor says coldly. "You've no authority here."

The undertakers emerge from the bathroom, carrying Louisa's body wrapped in the canvas. They put it on the stretcher, fasten straps around it, and wheel it out of the room.

"Stop!" I grab the metal rail on the stretcher.

Barrett pries my hand loose, puts his arm around me, and says, "Sarah, we should go."

"If you don't go, you'll be forcibly removed from the premises," Dr. Abernathy says.

* * *

Outside the hospital, I stalk ahead of Barrett to our waiting cab. The driver opens the door for us. I stow my camera equipment, climb in, and tell him, "Take us to the police station."

"Sarah, no," Barrett says.

"I think a crime may have been committed, and since this isn't your jurisdiction, I have to find someone whose it is."

Barrett jumps into the cab beside me and tells the driver, "Take us to the train station."

I fume as we ride out through the hospital grounds. "We promised to keep our minds open to each other's theories and not dismiss them without serious consideration."

"You're asking me to do a lot more than keep an open mind." Barrett's voice is tense. "I draw the line at barging into the Ticehurst Police station and demanding an investigation of a death that I don't think was a murder."

I long to believe he's right and that neither Patrick Eden-Smith nor my visit to Louisa had anything to do with her death. "Please. I need to know the truth."

"The truth could be that Louisa committed suicide and Mrs. Orson imagined she saw a man because they were both insane."

I can't deny the possibility—and I would much rather not—but I say, "Even if Mrs. Orson has delusions, it doesn't mean that all the things she sees aren't really there."

Barrett draws a deep breath and exhales, mustering his patience. "So why would the Reverend have paid Louisa a visit in the middle of the night?"

I spell out my suspicions. "Because Hugh and I paid *him* a visit yesterday afternoon, and we told him we'd spoken with Louisa. I think he didn't want her to talk to us again, and he made sure she wouldn't."

To his credit, Barrett doesn't say that once Hugh and I learned Louisa was alive, we could have left well enough alone and not come to Ticehurst. "How could the Reverend have made her undress, climb in the bathtub, and slit her wrists?"

"Maybe he drugged her. That's why there needs to be an autopsy."

Barrett shakes his head, puzzled. "Why would he kill her? What's the worst she could tell anyone about him? That he sleeps with rich women, and they give him their money? Would he risk murdering her and getting caught, just to save his job?"

I'm horrified by the possibility that I'd meddled in affairs that had nothing to do with the case we're investigating, and possibly brought about poor Louisa's death. "She could have had information about the Torso Murders."

"You're stretching things way too far. Even if the Reverend did fake Louisa's suicide, that's hardly in the same league as cutting up women and dumping their body parts in the river."

When I stubbornly shake my head, refusing to admit that Barrett has a point there, he throws up his hands. "You're building a case against the Reverend out of thin air!"

I could say the same for him regarding his favorite suspects, but that would revive the issue of whose hunches are more valid, and another quarrel could lead to a blowup from which our marriage will never recover. "You agreed to test my theory that Reverend Eden-Smith and the Haven of Love are connected to the Torso Murders. Are you going back on your word?"

"No. At least, not as long as you stick to your promise to keep an open mind about Severin Klosowski and Violet Pearcy."

"I will." I'm disturbed that our marriage seems to have turned into a series of business negotiations. Where are the affection and intimacy? "We both want the same thing—justice for murder victims." I bite my tongue rather than add that if Louisa is a murder victim, then I want justice for her too.

Chapter 16

Back in London, Barrett accompanies me to the *Daily World* headquarters. Sir Gerald will be wanting reports on the progress of the investigation. I still don't know whether he knows about Inspector Reid's exclusive deal with the *Chronicle*, but I can't avoid him forever.

In the newsroom, we run into Sally, who says, "Sarah! Thank goodness you're here. I told Sir Gerald."

I'm glad I won't have to break the bad news. "How did he take it?"

"He turned so red with anger, I thought he was going to burst a blood vessel. But he just thanked me politely. He didn't say a word about firing anyone."

How fortunate that Sally can get away with saying things that Sir Gerald wouldn't tolerate from others.

"That's not all I wanted to tell you," Sally says. "There's a woman here to see you. She's been here since one o'clock."

Two hours is a long time to wait, especially with no idea of when or whether I might show up. "Who is she?" I hope it's not a curiosity seeker who wants to meet the notorious Sarah Bain Barrett. That's happened before.

"She wouldn't give her name. She said she would only talk to you." Sally pauses, all smiles, apparently to build suspense for a big announcement. "She says she has information about the Torso Murders."

Excitement and doubt battle in me. Barrett says, "The police have gotten hundreds of tips. We'd better not get our hopes up too high."

"I think she really does know something," Sally says. "She's in Sir Gerald's office. When I told him about her, he said she could wait for you there."

He probably meant to wring the information out of her. Barrett, Sally, and I rush to up to his office. We find Sir Gerald seated behind his desk, holding up a whiskey bottle.

"Another?" he asks the woman sitting in the chair opposite him.

"Won't say no." Her husky voice has a faint European accent that I can't place. She's dressed in layers of tattered clothes, surrounded by a carpetbag, a battered suitcase, and a bundle wrapped in a blanket and tied with string. Her gloves are dirty, their fingertips worn through. A ragged straw hat decorated with a red paper rose crowns her head. She and Sir Gerald clink glasses, and she says, "Here's to new friends."

"To new friends," Sir Gerald says. They laugh and drink.

If I didn't know better, I would think he wanted only her company, not the information she has. Sir Gerald is capable of using charm rather than fear to provoke cooperation, when he chooses. He and the woman turn, their faces rosy from the liquor, still smiling.

"Ah, here she is." Sir Gerald says to the woman, "This is Mrs. Barrett."

The woman scrutinizes me, suddenly wary. "How do I know it's really her?" She's younger than her voice sounds, in her twenties. Her eyes are bright blue in a square, pretty face that looks as though she'd scrubbed it clean before she came here.

I look around the cluttered office and pick up an old edition of the *Daily World*. The headline reads, *"Benjamin Bain Declared Innocent!"* The illustration shows the courtroom in Old Bailey, with my father in the dock; the jury, the lawyers, and the spectators all staring in amazement as the judge pounds his gavel. I point to my photograph among the others printed below the illustration. It's an unflattering but clear image of me, captioned *"Benjamin Bain's daughter, Mrs. Sarah Bain Barrett."*

The woman frowns as she studies the photograph, then my face. She nods cautiously.

"What is your name?" I ask. She glances at Barrett, Sally, and Sir Gerald. I say, "It's all right—you can talk in front of them."

After a long moment's hesitation, she says, "I am Irene Muller." Her foreign accent is more pronounced when she says her name; now I identify it as German. It distracts me, and at first the name means nothing to me. Then belated recognition makes me gasp.

"Irene Muller from the Garratt Lane Workhouse? Inspector Reid's Torso Murder victim?"

Irene nods, cringing with fright. Sally and Barrett look as shocked as I am. Sir Gerald leans forward, interested and alert. He gives Irene a reassuring smile and refills her glass.

She gulps the whiskey. "I saw the police notices. That is why I am here."

My doubts about Reid's identification of the victim were valid, for here is Irene Muller in the living flesh. She's not the dismembered remains at the morgue.

"Why didn't you go to the police?" Barrett asks.

"I'm afraid."

"You're not in any trouble," I say.

Irene looks unconvinced. "I came to you because I've heard of you. You stood by your papa when everybody thought he killed that girl, and you proved he didn't do it. I think you're a good sort."

I'm ashamed because I'd doubted my father's innocence, and I'm moved by Irene's words. Her praise is balm after the many ugly comments that rival newspapers have printed about my audacious, unfeminine behavior, and the ones people have made to my face.

"I thought if I showed you that I'm alive, then you could tell the coppers, and I wouldn't have to," Irene says.

"I can tell Inspector Reid." I can't wait to see his face.

"Not so fast." Sir Gerald says to Irene, "How do we know you're really Irene Muller?"

In the excitement of the moment, I was too quick to trust my intuition that she's telling the truth. A great detective I am.

"I can prove it." Irene reaches in her carpetbag and brings out a large, ivory-colored cardboard envelope, smudged with fingerprints. From the envelope she removes a document printed with calligraphy in what looks to be German. Below an etching of

Jesus among lambs, handwritten cursive fills in blank lines. Irene lays it on Sir Gerald's desk. "This is my baptism certificate."

Sir Gerald examines it. "I know a little German." He's traveled all over the world and learned bits of many languages. "This says Irene Muller was born November thirtieth, 1860, and baptized December thirteenth in Berlin." Handing it back to her, he says to Barrett, Sally, and me, "Unless she stole this, she's Irene Muller."

"I did not steal it," Irene says with wounded dignity. "It's mine. I brought it when I came to England."

"And you lived at the Garratt Lane Workhouse?" Barrett asks.

"Yes." Irene opens her coat. Underneath, she's wearing a gray smock over a knit jumper and blue-and-white-striped skirt. A label stitched in red letters on the front of the smock reads, "Garratt Lane Workhouse."

"I'll break the news to Reid," Barrett says.

I can see that his feelings are as mixed as mine. We share the satisfaction of debunking Reid's theory about the Torso Murders, and disappointment because the investigation has hit a dead end and the killer is still at large. But Sir Gerald finds the bright side of the occasion.

"This will make a good story." He rubs his hands together in excitement. "'Police Mistakenly Identify Torso Murder Victim.'"

"I'll write it up," Sally says.

"May I take your photograph?" I ask Irene.

Her frightened look returns, as if things are moving too fast in a direction she hadn't anticipated. "I didn't just come here on my own account. I have to tell you about Charlie."

"Charlie Holt?" This is more than I expected.

"Yeah. He isn't the Torso Murderer."

It stands to reason that if Reid was wrong about Irene as the victim, then he also is wrong about Charlie Holt as the killer, but I resist jumping to conclusions. "How do you know?"

"We went to Birmingham because his cousin offered us jobs in his shop. Charlie got in a fight and stabbed the other man. He was only defending himself, but he was arrested. He's been in Winson Green Prison since February. So he could not have killed that woman."

"Jail is a good alibi, if he's really there." Barrett says.

"I'll send a telegram to my bank in Birmingham and have someone go to Winson Green and look up Mr. Holt," Sir Gerald says.

"He still could have done the Rainham, Whitehall, Elizabeth Jackson, and Pinchin Street murders," Sally points out.

"He wouldn't kill anyone!" Irene cries. "He has a temper, but he's not evil."

"If he's not responsible for this murder, he probably didn't commit the others," Sir Gerald says, cleaving to the theory that all the crimes were the work of one man. "Mrs. Barrett, hurry up and take the photograph of Miss Muller. Miss Albert, tell the editor that as soon as the photograph and your story are ready, I want an extra edition on the streets today. This is our chance to outdo the *Chronicle*."

* * *

After photographing Irene Muller, I give the negatives to a darkroom assistant to develop and print. Barrett and I leave Sally at her desk, working on her story. Then we hurry to Whitechapel to alert Inspector Reid about Irene Muller and Charlie Holt before the *Daily World*'s extra edition comes out.

At the police station, Barrett asks the desk sergeant, "Where's Inspector Reid?"

"Conference room."

Barrett leads me upstairs. On a closed door in the dingy hallway, a handwritten paper sign reads, "Torso Murders Task Force." Barrett and I barge into the room without knocking. We find Reid and the five other task force policemen at the table with Jasper Waring and a *Chronicle* photographer. Their heated conversation ceases, and they look up at us. The air is smoky from their pipes and cigarettes; scattered papers, full ashtrays, and cups stained brown with coffee residue cover the table. One wall is covered by charts, lists, photographs of the body parts and scenes where they were found, and newspaper clippings.

"So you came to rub it in our faces?" Reid glares at us.

Confused, Barrett says, "Sir?"

Reid stands, grabbing a paper from the table. The paper is wrinkled, as if it's been crumpled and smoothed out. Reid smacks it against Barrett's chest. "Don't play dumb with me."

Barrett and I examine the paper—a telegram that reads, *Irene Muller alive and well at Daily World headquarters. Charlie Holt in prison Birmingham has alibi. You're welcome. Sir Gerald Mariner.*

We'd looked forward to debunking Reid's theory, but Sir Gerald beat us to the punch.

Barrett recovers from his shock. "*I'm* not the dumb one." He tacks the telegram on the wall, beside the photographs. "*You* misidentified the victim and suspect."

I glance at the hostile faces of the other policemen, then at Jasper Waring. He looks chagrined. The *Chronicle*'s photographer glowers at me as if this is my fault. Reid yells at Barrett, "You must have busted your tail looking for Irene Muller and Charlie Holt, just to make me look bad!"

"That's not what happened," I say.

Reid points his finger at me, says, "You stay out of this," then turns back to Barrett. "You were supposed to be guarding the morgue. I'm going to reprimand you for insubordination and dereliction of duty."

"You ought to be glad you found out instead of going further down the wrong track," Barrett says.

"You ought to have reported it to me before Sir Gerald. Did your wife make you wait so that he could get at me and beat out the *Chronicle*?"

"I didn't do anything," I say. "Irene Muller came to the *Daily World* building. She wants everyone to know she's alive and Charlie Holt isn't the Torso Murderer. She talked to me because she was afraid to go to the police. You can read about it in the *Daily World*'s extra edition tonight."

"You can wipe that smug look off your face." Reid's bright, malevolent cheer revives. "Because if you think this is a lucky break for you, think again. No matter that Charlie Holt isn't the Torso Murderer or the Ripper, you know who is. I could arrest you for obstructing two police investigations."

I'm dismayed but unsurprised that I'm still on the hook. Now that his case has fallen apart, he's more desperate than ever to solve it. "How many times do I have to tell you? I don't know anything!"

"We'll see about that. I've been checking your activities during the months of the Ripper murders."

Reid's words provoke fear that I struggle to hide. *What might someone in my neighborhood have seen, unbeknown to me, and told Reid?*

Reid turns on Barrett. "In the meantime, you're off the task force."

Barrett stares in outraged disbelief. "You can't do that!"

Reid grins. "I just did."

"You didn't put me on the task force," Barrett says. "You can't kick me off."

Unfazed, Reid says, "Oh, I know you have a friend in a high place. If you want to go over my head, be my guest." Apparently, he's willing to gamble that in a pinch, Commissioner Bradford will take his side against Barrett's because he's the superior officer. And he may be right. Barrett has the Commissioner's favor for only as long as he keeps solving difficult cases, and this one is stalled.

"You're the one who should be kicked off the task force because you ran it into a ditch," Barrett says.

Anger darkens Reid's expression. "I'm suspending you from duty for a week."

"Bollocks! You're making me pay for your mistake."

"Two weeks." Reid's smile dares Barrett to keep talking.

I grab Barrett's arm and pull him toward the door. We have to leave before things get worse. Reid says, "By the way, your little friend Anjali is in big trouble for pretending to be psychic. I'm charging her with fraud."

I stop and turn on him, aghast and furious. "But she's just a child!"

"Children who make mischief deserve to be taught a lesson."

"She was only trying to help you."

"Yeah, well, she sent me down a garden path, and she's not getting away with it."

"I won't let you harm her!" I lunge at Reid, too furious to know if I want to shake some sense into him or kill him.

As Barrett grabs me and restrains me, Reid laughs. "Go ahead, hit me." He thrusts his face toward me and taps his finger against his cheek. "Assaulting a police officer should get you at least two years in prison."

I struggle to pull free of Barrett. "You leave Anjali alone, or I'll . . ."

Barrett drags me from the room. I utter imprecations against Reid all the way down the stairs and out of the police station. I break away from Barrett, stumble across the street, and lean against a wall, panting with exertion and rage.

Barrett catches up with me. He clenches his fists and looks around for something to hit. "God damn Reid!" He kicks a beer bottle on the sidewalk, and it shatters against a lamppost.

Jasper Waring comes running up to us. "I'm sorry about what happened in there." He glances back toward the police station.

"Yeah, well, you're not the only one," Barrett says.

"I don't believe you went behind Inspector Reid's back and tracked down Irene Muller," Jasper says to Barrett and me. "I believe she really did turn herself in at the *Daily World*."

I think he's sincere, but I say, "Too bad it doesn't matter that *you* believe it. Inspector Reid isn't going to change his mind."

Jasper looks doleful, as if he's familiar with Reid's obstinacy. "I also don't believe Anjali Lodge was faking. At first, I was skeptical about her, but then . . ." He laughs uncomfortably. "She and I were alone together for a moment. She said she was sorry my grandfather had passed away recently, at age eighty-one, and I must miss him very much because we were so close." He blinks away tears. "How could she have known unless she really is clairvoyant?"

I smile despite my bad mood. Anjali often surprises skeptics into believing in her. I can count myself among their number.

"Maybe you could put in a good word for her with Reid," Barrett says, but without much hope that it will help Anjali.

"I certainly will," Jasper says.

"Thank you," I say, warming toward him.

"You're welcome." Jasper smiles, and as he walks away, I begin to think Sally really ought to give him a chance.

CHAPTER 17

At just past eight o'clock, Mick and I walk up to Anjali's house. "Hell or high water, we'll get in to see her this time," Mick says.

Earlier, Barrett had walked me home from the police station, and then he'd gone to the morgue to see whether anyone had come forward to identify the remains. I didn't remind him that he's off duty and the morgue is now off-limits to him. I think he wanted to get away from me because I saw Reid discipline him, and he's humiliated. But he still wants to solve the case, and since Irene Muller and Charlie Holt are no longer the possible victim and killer, the remains are the only clue left. I'd found Mick in the house, and when I told him what had happened with Inspector Reid, he'd insisted on going straight to Anjali. The fiasco must have resulted in bad consequences for her, and we must do anything we can to help.

The curtains at her house are all drawn, and I don't expect an answer to my knock, but Dr. Lodge opens the door at once. As I brace myself for another prompt dismissal, he says, "You needn't tell me you were right when you said Anjali shouldn't be involved with the police investigation." He looks shaken and humble. "We've learned our lesson."

"How is she?" Mick asks anxiously.

Dr. Lodge sighs. "You'd better come in."

The foyer is cluttered but smells of soap and furniture polish, as if someone who prizes cleanliness has tried to counteract someone else's untidiness. I recall that Dr. Lodge employs a woman to clean and cook for him and Anjali. The items on the table and ranged against the walls look to be his scientific equipment, replete with wires, gears, knobs, and dials.

"She's in her room." Dr. Lodge glances up the stairs, which are lined with piles of books.

Mick edges toward the stairs, but I put out my arm to stop him. Having breached the fortress, we need to be on our best behavior. We follow Dr. Lodge into the parlor. With its spindly, uncomfortable-looking furniture and lack of clutter, it seems designated for guests who never come. I also recall Anjali saying that his work keeps her father too busy for socializing, and she sees her few friends only at school because their mothers won't allow them to visit an Indian girl.

Dr. Lodge collapses into a brocade armchair by the cold, neatly swept hearth while Mick and I perch on the divan. "Things seemed to be going so well," he says. "Inspector Reid took Anjali to the places where remains were found. The visions were distressing for her. She's so sensitive to the emotional residue left by violence and pain. But she was brave. I was proud of her." Affection warms his voice.

"What did she see in her visions?" I want to know the starting point from which Reid wandered off track.

"She had many indistinct, fleeting impressions. Only one was particularly clear. It came while we were walking the riverbank near Horsleydown Stairs. Anjali said she was flying through darkness and fog, and the air smelled like rotten eggs. Below her were buildings that reminded her of Hampton Court." Dr. Lodge explains, "That's Henry the Eighth's palace in Surrey. She went there on a school tour last year. But she sensed that the buildings aren't far from where we were She saw a woman running away from them."

"Did she get a good look at this woman?" I ask.

"No. She was too far away, and it was dark. But she thought the woman was in danger. She felt her terror and panic. Inspector Reid seized on that vision."

"Of course he would, if that was the only clear one." Mick scornfully echoes my thought about Reid.

"Inspector Reid said some of the sites in London that fit her description are workhouses."

Workhouses, large complexes of dormitories, factories, and outbuildings, often constructed in Gothic style, do resemble palaces from a distance.

"He sent detectives to the workhouses," Dr. Lodge says. "One came back with the news that a woman had gone missing from the Garratt Lane Workhouse in Wandsworth. Her name was Irene Muller. He reported that the air in Wandsworth smells of rotten eggs from the paper mills, the dye works, and the gunpowder factories along the Wandle River. Someone at the workhouse said Irene had a man friend named Charlie Holt, who worked for a horse knacker."

Each step in Reid's process was logical, but logic only works when the first step is solidly grounded in reality. After Irene Muller turned up at the *Daily World* headquarters, his theory, biased by wishful thinking, had fallen down like London Bridge in the song.

"I explained to Inspector Reid that Anjali's visions aren't cut and dried, and they shouldn't be interpreted too literally," Dr. Lodge says, "but he wouldn't listen. I tried to make him understand that the vision might be about something completely unrelated to the murders. But he jumped to conclusions and called the press conference."

It's just as I feared: Reid's determination to solve the case had destroyed his objectivity. Now Reid has egg on his face, and of course he would blame someone other than himself.

"We were at the police station when Inspector Reid received a telegram from Sir Gerald Mariner," Dr. Lodge says. "It said Irene Muller is alive, and Charlie Holt is in prison in Birmingham. Inspector Reid blew up at Anjali. He said she'll be charged with fraud, and she'll have to stand trial. And if she's found guilty, she'll go to prison."

"The bastard!" Mick says.

I'm speechless with horror. Children even younger than Anjali often do go to prison for the pettiest of crimes, and with Reid hell-bent on punishing her for his own mistake, she might have to serve years. And conditions in prison are so miserable that even a short term could turn into a death sentence.

"All she did was try to help him solve the goddamned case," Mick says.

I'm afraid that Anjali's Indian blood will count against her in court, where a jury of white men will decide whether to side with her or Inspector Reid.

"I think she's upset about something else besides the possibility of going to jail," Dr. Lodge says. "Before I brought her home, Reid talked to her in private. I didn't want to leave her alone with him, but his men forced me out of the room. When she came out, she was crying. She was still crying when I checked on her a little while ago."

Puzzled as well as furious, I ask, "What did Reid say that was worse than the threat of prison?"

Dr. Lodge lifts his empty hands, then drops them. "She won't tell me."

"Can I see her?" Mick says.

Dr. Lodge frowns, clearly reluctant to let a bad influence back into his daughter's life or risk the two youngsters doing things they shouldn't.

"I'll go with Mick," I say.

Dr. Lodge sighs. "All right. Maybe you can comfort her. I certainly wasn't able."

Mick and I go upstairs. I hear weeping through the closed door on which Mick taps. "Anjali?" he calls.

The weeping stops. Anjali's voice, hoarse with tears, rising with eager hope, says, "Mick?" Her footsteps patter, and she opens the door. She wears a dark blue frock, her hair down, her feet in fur-lined slippers. Her face is red and swollen with tears. She and Mick fly into each other's arms.

"I've missed you so much!" Anjali cries.

"Me too," Mick says gruffly, burying his face in her hair. She sobs, and he pats her back. "Shh, it's all right, I'm here now."

"I still love you," she murmurs.

"*I* still love *you*."

They both sob with joy. I smile at them, close to tears myself. Their reunion is a heartening oasis in the midst of trouble. I give them a minute to enjoy it, then clear my throat.

They reluctantly separate. Mick grins sheepishly; Anjali is radiant, her cheeks pink, her eyes shining through her tears.

"Sarah. Thank you for coming," she says.

"Mick and I were worried about you," I say. My anger at Reid flares anew. That he would threaten this sweet, vulnerable girl!

"I'm better now." Anjali smiles at Mick. They clasp hands; they can't resist touching. "I shouldn't have gotten mixed up in the murder investigation, but I did it because I wanted to see you. In spite of the trouble it's caused, I'm happy that it brought us back together."

Mick blushes with delight. "Likewise."

"I'm sorry, I've forgotten my manners," Anjali says to me. "Please come in and sit down."

Her room is plainly furnished, with dark, somber colors and a lack of frills, as if her bachelor father didn't know how to decorate for a girl. Schoolbooks are stacked on a desk fit for a business office. But the shelves hold dolls and children's books, and stuffed animals sit on the bed. Dr. Lodge made sure she didn't lack for playthings, and they show how young she still is. I sit in the desk chair. Mick and Anjali sit side by side on the bed, his arm around her.

"Your pa told us what happened at the police station today," Mick says. "Don't worry about Inspector Reid. Everything will be all right."

"No, it won't. Nothing will ever be right." Anjali starts to cry. "Inspector Reid told me that by pretending to be psychic, I ruined not only my reputation but Father's too. He said Father will be fired from the university, and nobody will hire him or publish his books again. I'm so sorry for Father. Because of me, he's going to lose everything!"

Even in the midst of her trouble and fear, she's concerned about her father rather than herself. I'm all the more furious at Reid. She's of far better character than he is.

"Forget what that jackass said," Mick tells her. "He's mad at himself because he read the wrong meaning into your vision, and he's takin' it out on you."

Anjali looks up at Mick through streaming tears. "But what if he's right? What if I don't really have psychic powers?"

So that's part of what upset her, as well as the prospect of jail. I try to imagine how it feels to begin doubting something you've accepted as a fact about yourself all your life, a fact that set you apart from other people and made you special.

"He's wrong," Mick says, adamantly loyal.

"But maybe it's just make-believe that started when I was little, and I've fooled myself and Father into thinking it was true."

That sounds to be just as world shattering as for a religious person losing faith in God. For Anjali, her loss of her belief in her gift—indeed, the loss of her whole identity—may be a blow from which she never recovers. It strikes me that my intuition is somewhat like her gift. If her gift isn't genuine, is my intuition false too? The thought is sobering.

"It is true," Mick insists. "Your visions are always spot-on. They always will be."

Anjali sobs on his shoulder. "I wish I could believe you."

I wanted to ask Anjali if she'd had other visions at the places where body parts were found. I'd hoped for clues that would aid our investigation, but I can't risk having her come up with clues that lead to other dead ends. That would make her feel even worse.

Mick hugs her, his expression grim. "You ain't goin' to jail. I'll kill Reid first."

Anjali draws back from him and cries, "No! You would be in even worse trouble than I am. Inspector Reid said he won't charge me with any crimes, if I cooperate with him."

So Reid offered her one of his deals. I'm appalled that he's cruel enough to coerce a fragile child. Mick demands, "Cooperate with him how?"

Anjali turns to me. "I have to get you to tell me what you know about Jack the Ripper. Then I tell Inspector Reid. Then he'll leave me alone."

Mick and I look at each other, aghast. Reid has roped Anjali into our feud! Even as I boil with fury at him, I have to admire his cunning. This is the dastardliest form of pressure he's employed. Either my comrades and I maintain our silence and Anjali goes to prison, or we confess and send ourselves to the gallows.

Dr. Lodge walks into the room. I'd been so rattled by Anjali's bombshell that I didn't hear him coming. Mick and Anjali jump up from the bed and stand apart from each other, like soldiers at attention.

"I feel better now, Father, "Anjali says quickly. "Mick and Sarah cheered me up."

"You should go now," Dr. Lodge says to Mick and me. "Anjali needs her rest. I'll see you out."

At the door, he asks us, "Did she tell you what Inspector Reid said to her while he had her alone?"

"He scolded her for leadin' him down the wrong trail," Mick lies by omission.

Dr. Lodge glares at Mick and me. "This is your fault. Inspector Reid wouldn't have taken such umbrage at Anjali if she weren't associated with you. I don't know what you did to offend him, and I don't care, but you'd better mend fences with him, or Anjali will be the one who pays the price."

Chapter 18

"I have to tell," Mick says to Barrett and me.

We're seated in our parlor. The fire in the hearth burns bright and warm; outside, rain patters against the dark window. Fitzmorris and Hugh are out. I just told Barrett about our visit to Anjali and Dr. Lodge. He and I don't reply to Mick's announcement that he means to spill our secret about the Ripper. Protests and warnings aren't necessary; we all understand the consequences too well.

"I can't let Anjali go to jail," Mick says, as though we're arguing with him. "It would be the death of her."

Barrett and I nod in somber silence. Tender, innocent Anjali is no match for the physical and mental hardships of a prison workhouse.

"If I tell, it'll be the hangman for us. I don't mind dyin' to save Anjali, but how can I do that to you and Hugh?" Mick jumps to his feet, picks up the poker, and flings it across the room. It hits the lamp on the table, shattering the glass shade. "God damn it to hell!" He buries his face in his hands, and his shoulders heave with sobs.

Barrett and I avert our gazes from him. We know he's ashamed to break down in front of us, and words or gestures of sympathy would humiliate him all the more. At this moment I feel more sorrow for Mick than fear for myself. This would be a hard choice for anyone—his beloved or his friends. It's a choice that a fifteen-year-old boy never should have to face. I think of the times when I almost told, when the consequences of not telling seemed disastrous. Now Reid is investigating me, and how terrible if he not only discovered our secret but also destroyed Anjali!

Perhaps now really is the time to tell.

The doorbell jangles, and footsteps on the stairs herald the arrival of Hugh and Dr. Lewes. When they enter the room, Mick rushes out of it, without a word to them, and runs downstairs. The door slams as he leaves the house.

Hugh notices the broken glass on the floor and the worry on Barrett's and my faces. "Bad news?"

With Dr. Lewes present, we can't discuss Inspector Reid's latest scheme to wrest information about the Ripper out of us, and Barrett won't want to talk about his suspension. I'll have to tell Hugh later. Instead, I inform him about Louisa Nussey's death.

Hugh looks as if he suspects there's more going on, but he only says, "The poor woman. And you think the man who visited her was Reverend Patrick Eden-Smith, and he murdered her and staged it to look like suicide?"

"I do," I say.

"I don't," Barrett says.

Hugh drops the subject rather than wade into a marital tiff. "Any other developments?"

I describe Irene Muller's surprise appearance at the *Daily World* and Inspector Reid's plan to charge Anjali with fraud. I postpone mentioning Mick's and my visit to Anjali.

Hugh shakes his head. "Whew. This calls for a drink." He pours sherry into glasses and hands them around. The sherry is sour on my tongue, and I experience a pang of despair. Secrets and quarrels are like sharks swimming under the surface of our cozy harbor, and our lives are the price of saving an innocent girl.

"Not that I need another drink," Hugh says. "I've been hanging around pubs all day, chatting up my favorite sources of tips. But everyone's as in the dark about the Torso Murders as we are. The bookies are setting odds that the case will never be solved."

"Can you give us a new profile based on the theory that the Torso Murderer is a woman?" Barrett asks Dr. Lewes.

Exasperation provokes a humorless laugh from me. "You can't be still considering Violet Pearcy a suspect."

"I went all the way to Ticehurst to test your theory that Patrick Eden-Smith is the Torso Murderer. Suppose you humor me for a few minutes." A warning note edges Barrett's voice.

"What have we got to lose?" Hugh says with an apologetic glance at me.

Barrett bends a challenging look on Dr. Lewes. "Well?"

"There was a case in 1879," Dr. Lewes says.

I resign myself to a continuation of my husband's wild goose chase.

"The victim was a woman named Julia Thomas," Dr. Lewes says. "Her killer was Kate Webster, her Irish maidservant."

Barrett, who'd looked prepared to be skeptical, even though he'd asked for the profile, raises his eyebrows, his interest unexpectedly roused. "I remember. The Richmond Murder, wasn't it called?"

"Yes. Julia Thomas was a widow and a former schoolteacher who lived alone in Richmond in a semidetached villa. She had a reputation as a harsh, critical employer who had difficulty retaining servants. In January 1879, she hired Kate Webster. The two didn't get along. They quarreled, and friends of Mrs. Thomas stated that she'd told them she was afraid of Kate. She fired Kate on February twenty-eighth. Kate persuaded Mrs. Thomas to let her stay for three more days." Once again, Dr. Lewes displays a remarkable memory for dates and details. "On Sunday March second, the day Kate was supposed to leave, she got drunk at the local pub. When she came home, Mrs. Thomas scolded her, and they got into a furious argument. Kate threw Mrs. Thomas down the stairs. Mrs. Thomas screamed. To keep the neighbors from hearing her and finding out what had happened, Kate choked her to death. In an attempt to conceal the crime, Kate cut up Mrs. Thomas's body with a razor, a meat saw, and a carving knife."

Hugh winces and plugs his ears with his fingers.

"Kate realized that if the body parts were found, they might be identified, and the murder traced to her," Dr. Lewes says. "So she burned the internal organs in the stove. She put the other remains in the laundry copper and boiled the flesh off the bones."

The image of a bubbling soup of severed head and limbs is etched in my mind forever. Barrett glances at me, as if to say that since one woman was capable of such an atrocity, so might a certain other be. But I shake my head, unable to picture Violet Pearcy in Kate Webster's place.

"Kate packed what was left of the remains in a Gladstone bag and a hatbox and dumped them in the Thames," Dr. Lewes says. "On March fifth, a coal porter spotted the hatbox on the riverbank near the Barnes Railway Bridge. An inquest resulted in an open verdict, with the victim unidentified and the cause of death undetermined. Meanwhile, Kate went about her usual business as though nothing had happened—until the day she dressed in Mrs. Thomas's clothes and traveled to Hammersmith to visit old friends. She told them that she was now "Mrs. Thomas," having married and been widowed, and she'd inherited a house in Richmond. She continued to pose as Mrs. Thomas while living in the real Mrs. Thomas's house."

Hugh cautiously unplugs his ears.

"I remember she sold the lard and dripping from the body to a pub," Barrett says.

"Whoa!" Hugh plugs his ears again.

"That may be just a myth," Dr. Lewes says. "It didn't come up at the trial."

Now I'm willing to at least entertain the possibility that the Torso Murderer is female, if not Violet Pearcy. "How was Kate caught?" Perhaps the details will illuminate a path to the Torso Murderer.

"Kate sold some of Mrs. Thomas's possessions to a local tradesman. The neighbors grew suspicious because they'd not seen Mrs. Thomas in weeks, and now here came a deliveryman with a horse and cart to take away her things. They asked him who had ordered them removed. He said, "Mrs. Thomas," and pointed to Kate. Realizing that the jig was up, Kate fled to her family home in Ireland. The police searched Mrs. Thomas's house. They discovered bloodstains on the floor, burned finger bones in the hearth, and fat residue in the laundry copper. Kate was tracked down, arrested, and brought back to Richmond. The crime was a notorious sensation. Crowds packed the courtroom and jeered at Kate. She pleaded not guilty, and her defense lawyer claimed the evidence against her was circumstantial. But the jury convicted her after deliberating for less than two hours. She was hanged at Wandsworth Prison on July twenty-ninth."

"I've seen the waxwork of her at Madame Tussaud's," Barrett says.

"There have been books written about her, and songs, and a special edition of *Illustrated Police News* devoted to the case," Dr. Lewes says.

"She was certainly a bad apple," Hugh says. "If they hadn't put an end to her, she probably would have gone on to kill again."

"See?" Barrett says to me, as if he's scored a point in our argument.

I can't accept Kate Webster as evidence that justifies his suspicion of Violet Pearcy. "What sort of person was Kate Webster before she killed Mrs. Thomas?" I ask Dr. Lewes.

"Not a good sort. The murder wasn't her first crime. She'd been imprisoned for theft multiple times."

Kate's is the story of many desperate people who turned to theft in order to survive. "Does Violet Pearcy have a criminal record?" I ask Barrett.

"No," Barrett reluctantly admits.

"So that's one thing she doesn't have in common with Kate Webster," I say. "She's a trained midwife, gainfully employed helping people instead of stealing their property."

"There's a first crime for every criminal," Barrett hurries to say.

"A law-abiding woman suddenly kills and dismembers someone, out of the blue?"

"Research shows that perpetrators of serious crimes usually started out with minor ones," Dr. Lewes says.

"*Usually* doesn't mean *always*," Barrett says.

"True," Dr. Lewes concedes.

"Are there other cases in which a female killer dismembered her victim?" I say.

"Not that I know of," Dr. Lewes says. "It's rare even among male killers. Kate Webster is an exception."

Feeling vindicated because the facts are on my side, I say, "Well, I don't think Violet Pearcy is an exception."

"Whatever happened to keeping an open mind?" Barrett snaps.

"I could ask you the same question regarding Patrick Eden-Smith," I say.

"Just because Violet Pearcy doesn't fit the profile, it doesn't mean she's innocent," Barrett says. "How can the profile be accurate when it's based on only one example?"

"You're right," Dr. Lewes admits. "The best science requires more data."

Barrett seems less than pleased to have the doctor agree with him. "I don't think psychology is a real science at all."

Crestfallen, Dr. Lewes bites his lip. I feel sorry for him, even though he's been a source of discord in my family circle. Hugh springs to Dr. Lewes's defense. "Barrett, you need to study psychology yourself before you're qualified to rule on what is or isn't valid."

"I apologize," Barrett says, although he sounds more irate than sorry. "I didn't mean to put it down. I just don't believe studying criminals is a substitute for practical experience on the police force."

"I can't disagree." Dr. Lewes seems humbler than I've ever seen him. "My profession has its limitations, a major one being that people are extremely various, and they defy simple categorization." He says with a dejected smile, "I sometimes believe that psychologists will never solve the mysteries of the human mind."

His doubt about his profession strikes me as akin to Anjali's loss of faith in her psychic gift. Both must be painful to these two whose beliefs have guided the courses of their lives. I'm angry at Barrett for jabbing Dr. Lewes's sore spot, but I also sympathize with him because his own professional judgment has been called into question, and I'm ashamed of myself for denigrating his hunches about Severin Klosowski and Violet Pearcy.

My anger gives way to fear.

Am I so secure, and so justified, in my own beliefs?

Intuition tells me that Patrick Eden-Smith, the Haven of Love, and Louisa Nussey's death are connected with the Torso Murders. But what if I'm wrong? It's not that my hunches haven't led me astray before. But this time, I can't tell whether the hunch is more urgent than usual because I'm right, or because I *want* to be right. The thought that I've lost my internal compass disturbs me greatly.

The fire in the hearth has burned down to dull red embers. We all sit in dour silence, empty glasses in our hands. The Torso Murders case is the most hopeless we've ever encountered. And thanks to Inspector Reid, my sister and Anjali have been spun into the vortex of danger in which Barrett, Hugh, Mick, and I live. And things are worse for the lack of harmony among us. If external forces don't tear us apart, our own quarrels will.

"Look at us, moping as if we're at our own funeral," Hugh says with false jocularity. "Drinking on empty stomachs isn't exactly conducive to solving problems. How about if we see what we can rustle up for dinner?"

⋆ ⋆ ⋆

Later that night, in our room while we prepare for bed, I try to cheer Barrett up. "Since you don't have to report for duty tomorrow, we can work on the investigation together."

He utters a mirthless laugh as he unbuttons his shirt. "Small comfort. Do I need to tell you that two weeks of suspension means two weeks of no pay?"

I sigh because I've said the wrong thing. "At least you'll have a better chance to solve the case than if you hung around at the morgue."

"You're right, as usual," Barrett snaps.

Vexed by his ill humor, I hang my frock on the stand. "Your attitude isn't helping."

He throws his shirt on the chair. "All right. Tomorrow, we investigate the murders. I'd like another go at Severin Klosowski and Violet Pearcy."

Not them again! "I think it's more important to investigate Louisa Nussey's death."

"Whatever you say."

His tone tells me I've said the wrong thing *again*. I still believe Louisa's death was foul play that's connected to both the Haven of Love and the Torso Murders, and why waste time on two people that I think are lesser suspects? To placate Barrett, I say, "We'll question Severin Klosowski and Violet Pearcy first."

"Don't humor me as if I'm a child."

I squelch my impulse to say he's acting like a child. "Then we'll tackle them after we pay another visit to the Haven of Love."

"Let's make this fair." Barrett takes a coin from his trouser pocket. "Which do you want—heads or tails?"

He could have had his own way a minute ago. I reluctantly play along. "Heads."

Barrett tosses the coin in the air, catches it, and slaps it down on his hand. It's heads. He scowls. "Haven of Love first thing tomorrow, then."

What a sore loser! Struggling to control my temper, I turn my back to him as I unfasten my corset, step out of my petticoats, and remove my stockings, chemise, and knickers. I shiver in the cold. The discord between Barrett and me seems more frightening than the murderers we've encountered. After all we've been through, all the troubles we've surmounted, this case could be the rock upon which our marital ship founders. I feel sorry for Barrett, but I'm also angry at him for letting his problems get to him. It's as if Inspector Reid is between us in evil spirit, even though not in the flesh. Which probably is just as Reid would like.

Now in our nightclothes, we climb into bed, and I put out the light. Barrett turns to me. "I love you."

"I love you," I say.

Our voices are as flat as though we're reading from a script. Sadness overtakes my anger. I feel almost as bereft as I did as a child after my father disappeared. I relive the frightening sensation of being cast adrift in the world, into an uncertain future.

Barrett and I kiss briefly, our lips dry and cold. But before I can turn away, he presses his mouth against mine. I draw back, startled by his advance and my suddenly wakened desire.

"Sorry." He sounds chastened because he thinks I rejected him and angry at himself for approaching me while we're at odds.

The thought that he wants me so much that he risked rejection arouses me in spite of my wish to spurn him because it would serve him right. My body swells with the anticipation of pleasure denied for too long. I place my hand on his chest and slowly move it downward. I can't help myself. His skin is warm under his nightshirt. He flinches and pushes my hand away.

"Don't start anything you're not going to finish." His voice is at once surly and breathless.

We lie side by side, motionless, locked in a battle of will against desire. My heart beats so loudly, I think he must hear it. His hand cups my breast; his finger caresses my nipple. I can't stifle a gasp. I touch his penis. It's erect. He moans. We withdraw our hands and lie still.

This is a contest to see whose need is greater, who'll make the next move.

It's tantalizing, maddening, and thrilling.

It ends in a mad, hot scramble, our hands everywhere, our nightclothes torn off. His tongue is on my breasts, then between my legs. I groan and thrash. I take him in my mouth, and he pulls away lest he finish too soon. Now it's a contest to see which of us can give the other the most pleasure. I try to pull Barrett on top of me. He resists and drags me on top of him. We wrestle, playful yet fiercely determined to have it our own way.

I can't wait any longer.

Using all my strength, I haul him onto me, between my spread legs. He can't wait either. He enters me, and the wet friction makes us both cry out. He thrusts, and even as I buck underneath him and the bed pounds the wall, I try to delay myself. I mustn't succumb first and let him win. But the pleasure takes me. I yell, and he laughs in triumph. Before the waves of ecstasy subside, I'm pushing him onto his back, straddling him. I ride him until he thrusts high into me, his body convulses, and he shouts. I fall on him as we laugh and pant.

There's no loser in this contest.

Chapter 19

The next morning, Barrett and I stand in the drizzly fog that shrouds Primrose Hill, gazing at the Haven of Love Church. Its stone walls are dark with moisture; water drips from the statues of the eagle, the bull, the lion, and the winged man. The place is like a scene from a fairy tale about a magic kingdom risen from the sea.

"If this is a wild goose chase, it ought to be an interesting one." Barrett speaks with good humor.

Our lovemaking last night did wonders for our relationship. At breakfast, Hugh, Mick, and Fitzmorris smiled at us, and I blushed to realize they heard us. But I'm glad they're happy for us, and I'm glad our marital harmony is restored. Today we're both more optimistic about our chances of solving the crime.

Barrett tries the door of the church. It's locked, not a surprise during a time when there's no service. Churches used to be open at all hours, but the rising incidence of crime has required them to take precautions against theft. Barrett knocks, and a plain woman in a gray frock, white apron, and white headkerchief answers. She holds a wet, sour-smelling mop.

"I'm sorry, the church is closed."

Barrett shows his badge. "Detective Sergeant Barrett, Metropolitan Police. We need to see the Reverend Eden-Smith."

The woman hesitates, then lets us into the building. It's dim, lit by a few gas lamps and the meager daylight that filters through the stained-glass windows. Other women are polishing the brass candlesticks on the altar or kneeling on the floor, scrubbing the tiles.

"Beloved Lamb is in the chapel, performing his daily devotions." Our escort precedes us down the aisle.

She and the other women must be members of Patrick Eden-Smith's flock. I wonder if he pays them for their labor or if they toil in service to their faith. I expect the chapel to be the usual small room for solitary worship, with the Reverend praying amid religious trappings, but Barrett and I find him exercising at a portable gymnasium. The gymnasium is a square, heavy mahogany column about eight feet high, studded with pulleys, ropes, pedals, and other equipment. Stripped to his shirtsleeves, a towel slung around his neck, the Reverend stands with his back to the contraption, huffing and puffing as he yanks on handles attached to pulleys, straining his chest muscles. He looks mildly disconcerted to see us.

Our escort genuflects before him. "I'm sorry to interrupt, Beloved Lamb. They want to speak with you."

"That's all right, Sister Joan." He ceases his exercise and wipes his face with the towel. His perspiration smells too sweet and a touch fetid, like overripe peaches with a pinch of dung.

The woman genuflects again and leaves. When Barrett introduces himself, caution hoods Eden-Smith's expression, but he quickly regains his poise and smiles. "Pardon my deshabille." However, he seems unembarrassed, as though he thinks he can dress in whatever fashion he pleases, and if others take offense, it's their problem. "This is the only time of day when I have the leisure for my physical fitness regimen."

Physical fitness regimens are popular among men and women who don't get their exercise on the job. They flock to public gymnasiums, pump away at the apparatuses, and perform calisthenics. I think a little manual labor would be just as invigorating and much more useful. Only the wealthy can afford their own portable gymnasiums. Walking miles around town while lugging photography equipment is ample exercise for me. I hesitated before I decided not to bring my equipment today.

"Our bodies are temples that God gave us to house our souls," Eden-Smith says. "We must take good care of them. A strong Christian body can be an instrument to protect the weak, advance righteous causes, and defeat evil."

It's a popular philosophy, but I notice large mirrors mounted on the walls, and Eden-Smith glances at his reflections and smiles at himself as he flexes his arm muscles. Although I'm not attracted to him and his odor repels me, he is handsome. I think that no matter his lip service to religion, vanity is the primary reason he exercises.

"I hope you don't mind if I continue my regimen while we talk."

"Not at all," Barrett says, his voice tinged with distaste. He hasn't missed Reverend's preening or smell. "I'm afraid we have bad news, though. Perhaps you should sit down."

"Very well." Eden-Smith sits in front of the gymnasium, his feet against the base. Holding a metal bar attached to ropes and pulleys, he performs sit-ups.

"Miss Louisa Nussey died last night," Barrett says.

"Dear me." Eden-Smith finishes three more sit-ups before he lets go of the bar, stands, and crosses himself. "May God rest her soul. How did she die?"

It's the question an innocent man would ask. Eden-Smith doesn't seem to know the answer already, and his expression shows dismay, not guilt.

"It appeared to be suicide," Barrett says.

"Louisa slit her wrists in the bathtub." I speak bluntly, hoping to jolt Eden-Smith into dropping his innocent act—if it is an act.

He mournfully shakes his head. "It's a shame, but I'm not surprised. She was very troubled when I saw her last night."

"You mean, you were there?" Barrett sounds surprised that the patient in the room next door to Louisa's actually was a reliable witness.

"Yes." Eden-Smith addresses me. "After you came to see me, I was concerned about Louisa. I wanted to see how she was getting on."

I too am surprised because he freely admitted it. A man who'd committed murder wouldn't want to place himself anywhere near his victim shortly before her death. "How did you know where to find her?"

"Louisa had written to me and told me she was at Ticehurst Hospital."

That he didn't learn Louisa's whereabouts from me only partially relieves my guilt. If not for me, he wouldn't have gone to Ticehurst. His candor suggests that he's innocent, but I can't shake my hunch that he's responsible for her death, if not for the Torso Murders.

"What happened during your visit to Miss Nussey?" Barrett asks.

"She begged me to take her with me. But of course I couldn't. Her family had committed her, and the hospital wouldn't have allowed me to remove her against their orders."

I suppose that if he'd managed to sneak her out, her family would have brought the law down upon him, and he wouldn't want the police to arrest him for kidnapping—or to investigate the goings-on at his church.

"I tried to comfort her. We prayed together. She was calm by the time I left, and I thought she would be all right." Reverend Eden-Smith says with self-conscious pride, "I've had a special talent with women ever since my childhood. I was the youngest of seven children, a sickly, intellectual boy, and my mother's pet. She was a poor widow who took in lodgers. I knew early on that I wanted to go into the church, but I also knew there wasn't any money to pay for divinity school, and I would have to work to earn my keep as soon as I got old enough. But one of the lodgers was a spinster who doubled as my nurse. We studied the Bible and prayed together. She became devoted to me, and I became her spiritual counselor, even though I was only twelve and she, forty-five. She took me to her church, where I met other women like her. They soon became a loyal group of friends. Why, I was more popular than the vicar." Boastfulness swells Eden-Smith's chest. "That's when I discovered my calling—ministering to single, lonely, religious women. One of them was a wealthy widow who paid for me to attend Cambridge. That was my first step toward a life of service to people who need my special gift."

How offensively conceited he is! Not only is he using Louisa's death as an opportunity to tell his life story and aggrandize himself; he's not ashamed to admit that he's been using women his whole life. But conceited doesn't mean stupid. I can think of other reasons why he would admit he was at Ticehurst last night. Maybe he's afraid someone saw him there, and to confess it up front is safer than to deny it and risk being exposed as a liar.

Eden-Smith sighs sadly. "If Louisa had been allowed to stay at the Haven of Love, she would be safe and happy now."

Or maybe he's so arrogant that he thinks he can murder a woman, place himself at the scene, and not suffer any consequences. I ask him, "Wasn't Louisa happy to see you?"

"Of course." He radiates self-satisfaction. "The ladies generally are."

He doesn't seem to notice—or care—that his "talent" isn't working on me. But then, I'm not a lonely, religious spinster, the susceptible type. He probably sensed it the moment we met.

"When I matriculated at Cambridge, I started a prayer group that became very popular with the female students." Eden-Smith also has a talent for redirecting the focus of a conversation to himself. "I met Miss Julia Clark from Girton College, the woman who became my first wife. She belonged to a prominent family in Wiltshire. When we married, her father obtained for me the position of vicar at their local church."

Another rich woman, another rung up the social ladder. "If Louisa was so happy and calm, then why would she have killed herself that same night?"

"She did say that if she couldn't be with me, she didn't want to live." Eden-Smith speaks as though anyone, whether in her right or wrong mind, would feel the same.

He must be the most narcissistic person I've ever met. "Her death separated her from you permanently," I point out.

"At the Haven of Love, we believe that all of our flock will be reunited someday in Heaven when our time on earth is through."

"How was Louisa supposed to get to Heaven?" Barrett asks. "Isn't suicide a sin?"

"We believe there is no sin that love cannot redeem. Louisa is waiting for me in Heaven, along with my dear Julia." Eden-Smith seizes the opportunity to continue the story of his life. "Julia and I were in a carriage accident together. She died instantly, but I walked away without a scratch. The terrible tragedy brought me a revelation. At the moment of the crash, the Holy Ghost entered my body and saved my life. I was spared in order to carry out a new mission—saving other people through the love with which the spirit had endowed me. My preaching rose to new heights of eloquence and passion. I found myself able to perform miraculous acts of healing. My congregation grew by leaps and bounds. Thanks to generous donations from my followers, I was able to build a large spiritual community. People came from far and wide to hear my sermons and partake of my healing."

He makes me want to vomit. Either he thinks pride is another sin that his love can redeem, or he doesn't notice his own failing. I suspect the latter is true.

"Eventually, God rewarded me by sending me a new partner to share my vocation," Eden-Smith says. "I took a new wife, and her two sisters became my spiritual brides."

"Merciful Saint, Anointed One, and Light of Heaven are sisters?" I'm surprised; they don't look alike.

"All my brides are sisters," Eden-Smith says.

"Why settle for one wife when you can have three?" I remark.

Eden-Smith either doesn't notice my sarcasm or chooses to ignore it. With a smug glance in the mirror, he says, "I have an infinite amount of love to give, and it should benefit as many people as possible."

People meaning females. I can't believe there's no sex involved. I picture a donkey plow running wild in a field of corn.

Barrett clears his throat, obviously impatient with both the Reverend and me because the interview has gone off track. "If things were going so well, what brought you to London?"

"I wanted to spread the word farther and wider and grow my congregation bigger than I could in Wiltshire."

I dislike him so much that I want him to be guilty of Louisa's murder and the Torso Murders. Barrett aims a warning glance at me. I'm afraid my lack of objectivity toward Reverend Eden-Smith is as detrimental to our investigation as Barrett's dogged persistence in suspecting Severin Klosowski and Violet Pearcy.

"Your church is beautiful," Barrett says. "Would you mind showing me around?"

Eden-Smith frowns as his pride vies with his annoyance at having to postpone his exercises. Then he smiles and dons his coat. "It would be my pleasure." If he knows Barrett means to search for bloodstains, body parts, or other signs of murder, he doesn't care.

I dawdle behind the men as Eden-Smith conducts a tour of the church and expounds upon features of particular merit. He's so busy enjoying the sound of his own voice that he doesn't notice me leaving the church. Outside, I circle the property. I didn't bring my camera because I wanted to be free to maneuver. The brick wall that encloses the grounds is too high for me to see anything of the rectory except rooftops and chimneys. The one gate is solid iron, with neither handle nor lock. I push on it, and it doesn't budge; it must be bolted on the inside. The only way to the rectory must be through the church.

I go back to the front entrance, hoping Barrett will distract the Reverend while I sneak past him. Then I notice an iron gate behind the evergreen shrubs at the right side of the church. This gate has a lock. Concealed by the shrubbery, I remove my pick-locks from my handbag. In a few minutes, I have the gate open.

Chapter 20

On the other side of the gate is a large garden. Crocuses and daffodils bloom around a gazebo, and three little girls are seated on the swings. They're Patrick Eden-Smith's daughters—Fortitude, Humility, and Atonement. Three women who appear to be nannies stand behind the girls, each pushing one of them. As I watch from behind a pine tree, the scene at first seems innocent and pretty, but I experience a creepy sensation. The garden is too perfect, with nary a stray fallen leaf on the lawn, and too quiet, the noise from the streets muffled by the wall and trees. The girls, dressed in black, silently swing back and forth, perfectly synchronized, the nannies moving like automatons.

Humility, the youngest, emits a sudden, piercing whoop. She launches herself off her swing, flies through the air, and lands on her hands and knees on the damp ground. Her nanny rushes to her and cries, "You've dirtied your frock. Bad girl!"

She pulls Humility's skirts up and knickers down, then spanks her bare bottom, intoning, "'Withhold not correction from the child.'" Her hard, cruel blows leave red handprints on the girl's buttocks. "'Thou shalt beat him with the rod, and shalt deliver his soul from hell!'"

"Amen," chorus the other girls and nannies as Humility squeals.

Such harsh punishment for a minor infraction! I have to defend the girl, even if it gets me thrown out before I have a look inside the rectory or speak to the wives. Then the spanking stops. Humility pulls up her pants and climbs back on the swing, and the nanny resumes pushing. A sly smile twitches the girl's lips; otherwise, it's as if nothing had happened. The scene seems weirder than ever.

Staying in the cover of the trees, I move toward the rectory, which looks big enough to house twenty or thirty people in comfort. The architecture is Gothic style, with arched windows, tall chimneys, steeply pitched roofs and gables, and crenellated ramparts. Bay windows jut from its stone walls. I find an unlocked side door. As soon as I enter the passage, I hear women's voices. Loath to be caught trespassing, I dart down a staircase to hide. Up from the cellar waft the smells of cooking and bleach. Machinery clanks to the accompaniment of female voices raised in song. It sounds like a church choir in a factory. At the bottom of the stairs, I find the laundry. Women are using paddles to stir dirty clothes in tubs of steaming water and running sheets through mangles. While they toil, they sing:

"I want to be a worker for the Lord,
I want to love and trust his holy word,
I want to sing and pray,
Be busy every day,
In the vineyard of the Lord!"

In the scullery, more women sing along while scrubbing pots and pans. The song carries to the kitchen, where cooks chop onions and turn meat on a spit. Are these women members of Reverend Eden-Smith's flock? They're like servants toiling downstairs at a manor house. The laundry, scullery, and kitchen are the logical places to dismember a body, but with so many people around, I can't search for evidence. The staircase leads me back to the ground floor. A movement in the passage catches my eye. I turn, see the figure of a woman, and gasp with dismay—I've been caught. Then I realize it's my own reflection in a large, gold-framed mirror. Other mirrors decorate the walls. I picture Patrick Eden-Smith walking down the hallway, pausing to admire each of his reflections. Between two of the mirrors hangs a portrait of him, glossy, realistic, and flattering. His signature odor of peaches and dung faintly tinges the air. I follow the sound of women's voices to a doorway and peer into a dining room that's spacious enough for a banquet. At the end, above a marble fireplace, another, bigger portrait of Eden-Smith hangs. His smiling likeness presides over the two women who are setting the long, linen-covered table. They're his spiritual wives, Anointed One and Light of Heaven.

Instead of the white robes I saw at the church, they wear ordinary clothes. Light of Heaven's frock is a periwinkle shade that flatters her blue eyes and blond hair; Anointed One's maroon frock unfortunately matches the port-wine birthmark on her face. Both women are tightly corseted. Above their cinched waists, their bosoms swell large and full. While the pudgy Light of Heaven's bust may be natural, I suspect that the slim Anointed One's is padded. The Reverend must like big-breasted women.

Light of Heaven places two Wedgwood vases on the table.

"Not those," Anointed One says in a sharp, bossy tone.

Light of Heaven squints at her. "Why not?"

"We always use the Chinese vases."

"But I like these better."

"It doesn't matter what you like." Anointed One orders, "Put them back."

They bring to my mind the lilies of the field; they toil not except at dainty, frivolous tasks like decorating the table.

Light of Heaven pouts. "Why does everything always have to be the same?"

"It's Beloved Lamb's rule."

"Oh. Well, then." Respect for her lord and master doesn't quite eclipse Light of Heaven's contrariness. She puts the Wedgwoods in a glass-fronted cabinet full of dishware, takes out two brightly decorated porcelain Chinese vases, and thumps them down on the table. "But why do there have to be rules for things as trivial as what to use for holding flowers? And why do we need to follow them exactly all the time?"

"Everything we do is a ritual." Anointed One speaks as if quoting from their master. "All our rituals are acts of love that bring divine, healing mercy to the world."

"So if we deviate from them even a smidgen, the sky will fall."

Not every member of Eden-Smith's flock is a mindless sheep.

Anointed One regards Light of Heaven with exasperation and bewilderment. "You never used to mind obeying the rules. Now, all you do is carp. What's the matter with you?"

A troubled sigh heaves Light of Heaven's huge bosom. "Don't you ever wonder if this was worth it?" Her gesture encompasses the room, the house, the church that's visible through the window.

"Of course it is." Anointed One sounds puzzled, as if she's never questioned her faith.

"But we've given up so much," Light of Heaven laments.

A door slams somewhere behind me, and I hear the patter of footsteps. I turn to see Humility running toward me, giggling as her nanny chases her and shouts, "Stop, devil child!"

Humility skids to a halt and regards me with wary curiosity. "You're that lady who came to church the other day." Her voice is oddly deep for a child's. "What do you want?"

The nanny seizes Humility's arm and demands of me, "How did you get in here?"

Anointed One and Light of Heaven come out of the dining room to see what the commotion is about. Light of Heaven looks befuddled; Anointed One's black eyes glitter with ire. Humility looks slyly pleased that she exposed me.

"Reverend Eden-Smith sent me to call on you," I lie. "He said you're to let me interview you about yourselves and the Haven of Love." Seeing distrust in the women's expressions, I say, "You can ask him. He's in the church, showing my husband around."

The women hesitate, reluctant to question their Beloved Lamb's orders. Anointed One motions me into the dining room and says with a marked lack of enthusiasm, "Please come in and sit down."

"Come along, devil child." The nanny marches Humility away.

The girl looks over her shoulder at me, her expression at once surly and pleading. Anointed One and Light of Heaven ignore her. Seating myself in one of the heavy, carved chairs at the table, I say, "Why is she called 'devil child'?" It seems as bizarrely cruel as the way she's treated.

"A child makes herself known by her acts," Anointed One says. "She's willful, disobedient, and vexing."

In an obvious attempt to change the subject, Light of Heaven says to me, "May I offer you some tea?"

"That would be nice." The polite ritual will give me time to question the wives for however long it takes Patrick Eden-Smith to discover that I left the church, and come here looking for me.

Light of Heaven walks to the labeled mechanical bells mounted on the wall and rings one. In an instant, a woman in an apron and headkerchief comes running. Anointed One says, "Tea, please, Sister Ann."

Not a hired servant, but another of the flock. There's a hierarchy, which I presume is defined by wealth. The Reverend could hardly expect rich women to donate their fortunes and then do their own fetching and carrying. He must recruit women from the lower classes for the menial work.

Anointed One stations herself on the opposite side of the table, her mouth tight, waiting for me to initiate conversation. Light of Heaven is silent too. Neither woman sits; perhaps both hope I'll feel uncomfortable and go away.

I put aside my curiosity about the "devil child" and pursue another topic of interest. "I couldn't help overhearing your conversation," I say, and turn my gaze on Light of Heaven. "What did you give up when you married the Reverend Eden-Smith?"

"Our families." Light of Heaven answers readily, as though bottled-up emotions pushed the words from her. But a hitch in her voice suggests she's afraid of saying the wrong thing.

"Families." Anointed One snorts in contempt. "When I was a baby, my parents farmed me out to relatives because they couldn't stand to look at me." She touches her birthmark, then says to Light of Heaven, "And you told me that your parents and sisters were so selfish, they didn't care about you or want you to have

your own life. They wanted to keep you at home forever to wait on them while they lived off the money that your aunt left you."

I'm surprised to learn that even before Anointed One joined the Haven of Love, she was as estranged from her family as the Ripper victims were from theirs. And Light of Heaven was as little esteemed by her relations as Polly Nichols or Annie Chapman were by society. Their alienation must have made them vulnerable to the charms of Patrick Eden-Smith.

"But we also gave up the whole world outside the church," Light of Heaven says.

Bitterness twists Anointed One's mouth. "The world doesn't want me. Everywhere I go, people stare at me and shout insults. Being here is a salvation and a privilege. Marriage with Beloved Lamb is the most holy fulfilment a woman could aspire to."

"But don't you sometimes wish you had the normal things? A husband that you didn't have to share with other wives?" Light of Heaven's voice breaks. "A child?"

"Oh, the trappings of an ordinary woman's life. Even if I could have had them, I gladly renounced them when I married Beloved Lamb, for the sake of a higher purpose. Didn't you?"

"Yes . . ." The other woman's nearsighted eyes blink as if trying to see through a cloud of uncertainty.

Anointed One says to me, "Will you please excuse us? We've work to do." It's obvious that she wants to get rid of me because she thinks the conversation has taken a problematic turn.

Far from ready to leave, I say, "Your table decorations look lovely. What is the occasion?"

"Beloved Lamb is to be married tomorrow night. We're preparing for the wedding banquet." Anointed One's manner smacks of forced gaiety.

Light of Heaven scowls. At a disapproving glance from Anointed One, she puts on a syrupy smile. They can't hide the fact that they're not thrilled about the wedding. Eden-Smith's attentions, spiritual or otherwise, will soon be divided among four wives instead of three.

"Who is the lucky bride?" I ask.

"Sister Emily Clifford." Dislike permeates Anointed One's tone and sours Light of Heaven's fake smile.

I recall a vixenish, auburn-haired young woman. "Isn't Emily Clifford the vestal virgin from the ceremony the day before yesterday?"

"Yes," Anointed One says. "Now, if you don't mind . . ." She gestures toward the door.

Light of Heaven puffs her cheeks. I wish I could get her alone; she seems so filled with a need to vent her frustration that she's practically bursting her stays. Anointed One impatiently taps her foot; I'm running out of time, and I must cut to the chase.

"I'm afraid I have bad news about Louisa Nussey," I say.

Anointed One holds up her hand. "We don't talk about her. She is no longer of us."

What a nice attitude toward a woman who gave herself and her fortune to the church and ended up in an insane asylum as a result. I stare in disapproval that I can't conceal.

"What about Louisa?" Light of Heaven blurts, then cringes from Anointed One's reproachful glance.

"She's dead," I say.

"It is no business of ours," Anointed One says coldly.

Reverend Eden-Smith had been willing enough to speak of Louisa when he wasn't turning the conversation back to himself. I wonder if the ban only applies to his women—or if there's another reason why Anointed One wants to avoid this topic.

"Aren't you even interested to know what happened?" I ask.

"I know what happened. The wages of sin is death," Anointed One says, lowering my opinion of her. My suspicion toward her master increases, but I'm no more enlightened than before.

"How did Louisa die?" Light of Heaven's obvious hunger for information overcomes her fear of talking out of turn.

"She slit her wrists in the bathtub and bled to death," I say.

Light of Heaven gasps, turns white, and sways. She clutches a chair for support, then staggers out of the room. I hurry after her.

"Come back!" Anointed One's order is shrill with alarm.

Light of Heaven runs through the house, faster than I thought possible for a heavy woman on the verge of fainting. The rectory seems even bigger inside than outside. I chase her through a series of luxuriously furnished parlors, each with the Reverend's portrait above the hearth. They connect via arched doorways, nooks furnished with curio cabinets, or angled passages. The house is a maze in which I quickly lose my sense of direction, but I gain on Light of Heaven as she rounds a corner. Just when I catch up with her, she bolts through a door and slams it in my face. I hear Anointed One coming after us and her angry voice calling.

Is she afraid of what Light of Heaven might tell me about Louisa Nussey?

I see another door beside the one that conceals Light of Heaven. On impulse, I open it to a landing from which stairs ascend and descend. I slip in through the staircase door, close it, and wait.

CHAPTER 21

Anointed One bangs on Light of Heaven's door and calls, "Is that woman in there with you?" No reply comes from Light of Heaven. "Come out this instant!"

Light of Heaven whimpers inside the room.

"I'm going to tell Beloved Lamb you're having doubts," Anointed One says sternly.

"You mustn't!" Light of Heaven exclaims.

"We can't afford doubts within our family. A house divided cannot stand."

"Please, don't!"

"You need to be taught a lesson," Anointed One says with the pompous authority of a judge sentencing a criminal. "There is no mercy for the unfaithful. You shall suffer the wrath of the Beloved Lamb."

So Reverend Eden-Smith isn't only about love and healing. What form will his wrath take? An answer occurs to me with stunning force. Is the Torso Murder victim a bride who ran afoul of him? Did he kill her, cut her up, and dump her in the river? At the Haven of Love, is death the punishment for disloyalty?

These speculations horrify me but also thrill me. Even as I caution myself against jumping to conclusions, I think I'm getting close to the truth about the crimes.

Anointed One bangs harder and louder on the door, ordering Light of Heaven to come out and face her just deserts. Much as I long to wait in case the women say something that constitutes evidence against my favorite suspect, I run away up the stairs. I must make good use of whatever time I have until Anointed One discovers I'm not with Light of Heaven and tracks me down.

When I emerge in a passage on the second floor, my shoes sink into plush mauve carpet. The walls are decorated with gold-figured lilac wallpaper and yet another portrait of Reverend Eden-Smith. I smell his sweet, rank odor beneath the lighter scents of perfume and bath soap. Female voices lead me to an open door, and I peek in at a scene that resembles a cross between a tailor's shop and the changing room at a ladies' dress salon. A sewing machine occupies a table littered with spools of thread; shelves contain bolts of cloth; garments are strewn on chairs, hung on racks, and draped on dressmaker's mannequins. The wife named Merciful Saint kneels on the carpet, her mouth full of pins, beside Emily Clifford, the Reverend's new bride-to-be. Emily wears a white silk tulle gown with a full skirt and long train. The top is shockingly bare, exposing her plump, freckled arms and ample cleavage. Merciful Saint sticks pins along a seam in the bodice. Her own dowdy brown frock does nothing to flatter her thick figure. The bright light in the room emphasizes the gray in her hair and the severe lines on her face. Beside Emily's blooming youth, she looks plainer and unfeminine despite her large bosom.

"Hold still," Merciful Saint says as Emily turns to admire herself in the mirror.

"Can't you hurry up?" Emily says. "At this rate, my gown won't be ready for the wedding tomorrow night."

Merciful Saint glowers and mumbles around the pins. "Tomorrow is too soon for the wedding, if you ask me."

I get the idea that Merciful Saint dislikes Emily as much as Anointed One and Light of Heaven do.

"Nobody asked you," Emily says pertly. "Beloved Lamb proposed to *me*."

"You don't deserve to be a spiritual bride. You haven't been here long enough. Why, you only joined the Haven of Love three months ago."

Emily giggles. "Don't blame me if Beloved Lamb likes fresh cake better than stale."

Anger flushes Merciful Saint's sallow cheeks. "You were only made a vestal virgin the day before yesterday. Before *I* married Beloved Lamb, I was a vestal virgin for a year."

"So he didn't mind waiting for you." Emily smiles at her reflection in the mirror and pats her auburn hair. "But he can't wait to marry me."

Merciful Saint gives Emily's dress vicious tugs as she pins the seams. "I brought him a dowry of ten thousand pounds. What are you bringing? Your last week's wages from the music hall where you used to sing in the chorus?"

"Money isn't the only thing a man wants from a wife," Emily says with breezy indifference to the older woman's gibe.

"Of course you would know what else men want," Merciful Saint retorts. "You must have given it to hundreds of them."

Unfazed by this accusation of promiscuity, Emily says, "Oh, that's all in the past. Beloved Lamb purified my body and soul. Don't you remember?" She puffs out her bosom and tugs the neckline of her gown an inch lower.

"Charm is deceptive, and beauty is fleeting," Merciful Saint declares.

"Well, one needn't worry about losing one's beauty and charm when one hasn't any to lose."

Merciful Saint flashes a bitter glare at Emily. "You don't love him. You don't care a fig for our mission. All you want is a man to support you while you laze around and eat bonbons."

"Who wouldn't want that?" Emily sounds honestly puzzled. "It's better than working." Perhaps the slavish worship she showed toward Eden-Smith was mere pretense. "Oh, but you've never had to work. Your family's rich. You don't know what it's like for the rest of us."

"*You* are a greedy little tart. Greed is one of the seven deadly sins."

"So is envy," Emily says triumphantly. "The Bible says, 'Envy rots the bones.'"

"The sins of the flesh are written all over you." Merciful Saint jabs a pin hard into Emily's ribs.

Emily shrieks in pain and outrage. "Damn you!" She slaps Merciful Saint's face.

Merciful Saint screams as she rocks back on her heels. She jumps up, grabs the bodice of Emily's dress, and shouts, "'Pride goeth before a fall!'"

The flimsy silk rips, exposing Emily's corseted breasts. Emily gapes in dismay at her ruined wedding gown. "Bitch!" She hauls back her fist to punch Merciful Saint.

If this goes on, these two will be in no mood to give me any useful information. Bursting into the room, I yell, "Stop!" as I put myself between them and push them apart.

They pant and glare at me like boxers separated by the referee. Merciful Saint demands, "Who are you?"

"She's that lady reporter, stupid," Emily says. "Don't you remember?"

Merciful Saint lunges at Emily. I block her and say, "Whatever the problem is, beating each other up won't solve it. Let's sit down and talk."

"You don't belong here," Merciful Saint says. "Mind your own business."

"Sometimes an impartial person can help solve problems," I say, attempting to play peacemaker.

Merciful Saint points to the door. "Leave at once!"

Ignoring the older woman, Emily plops herself on the divan, pats the place beside her, and smiles at me. "Yes, let's talk."

I'm sure she wants to aggravate Merciful Saint more than she wants my company, but I seize the opportunity she's offered, and I sit. "Thank you."

Merciful Saint huffs like a locomotive engine, frustrated and furious because Emily has found a temporary ally. She turns her back on us and stands gazing out the window.

"I thought the Haven of Love was supposed to be all about love," I say.

Emily sniffs and jerks her plump chin at Merciful Saint. "Tell *her* that."

Merciful Saint clenches her fists.

"She doesn't want me to marry Beloved Lamb," Emily says.

"Why not?" I ask, even though I overheard enough to give me a good idea.

"She doesn't want to lose her place as his top wife."

I watch Merciful Saint tremble with her effort not to dignify Emily's goading with a reply. "What's the advantage of being the top wife?" I ask.

"She's his real missus in the eyes of the law, and she gets to boss the rest of us around." Emily raises her voice at Merciful Saint. "But that could change. There's such a thing as divorce."

Merciful Saint half turns, then stops herself. Emily smirks. I say, "Does Reverend Eden-Smith's church allow divorce?"

"Beloved Lamb is allowed to do whatever he wants. Including marrying someone who's only been a vestal virgin for two days," Emily says.

I steer the conversation to my topic of most interest. "Was Louisa Nussey a vestal virgin?"

Merciful Saint stiffens at the mention of Louisa's name, but Emily shrugs and says, "I don't know. I never met her. She was gone before I came."

"Did Reverend Eden-Smith plan to marry Louisa?"

"Of course not," Merciful Saint blurts.

"Why not? She donated her large fortune to his church. She was a faithful follower."

Merciful Saint replies with scornful condescension. "That's not all it takes to be chosen as a spiritual bride."

"It sounds as though you didn't like Louisa," I say.

"I only want what's best for Beloved Lamb and the Haven of Love."

Emily laughs. "She's just jealous. She wants him all to herself. She doesn't like Anointed One or Light of Heaven either."

"Well, you'll be pleased to hear that Louisa will never be able to marry him," I say. "She died last night."

"That's too bad," Emily says with the rote courtesy accorded to the death of a person one didn't know.

Merciful Saint snaps her head around so fast that I imagine the joints in her neck cracking. I can't tell whether she's surprised by the news of Louisa's death or the fact that I know about it. When she sees me watching her, she curbs her emotions. "The poor woman. I'm sorry." Her voice is steady, her expression pious. "It's sad when a life ends too soon."

"Hah! Butter wouldn't melt in your mouth," Emily jeers. "She's one less bird in the bush, and you're glad. Admit it!"

Unable to ignore her jibes anymore, Merciful Saint speaks between gritted teeth. "One *fewer* bird. You should learn to speak properly."

Emily laughs, gleeful because she finally got Merciful Saint's goat. "*You* should mind your manners toward me, or when I take your place, I'll make you pay."

Merciful Saint flushes so red with anger that she looks as if she's been dipped in boiling water. Jabbing her finger at Emily, she hisses, "You'll never take my place. Because you're not good enough to be Beloved Lamb's legal wife."

"We'll see," Emily says impudently.

"I'm his only bride who's allowed to bear his children." Merciful Saint exudes triumphant pride.

Evidently, the women at the Haven of Love are in competition for more than just Patrick Eden-Smith's favor. The right to have children is also at stake. Humility, Fortitude, and Atonement are his legitimate offspring by his deceased wife, and he must be aware that if he fathers children with women other than his current legal wife, it will cause a scandal, and the church authorities won't approve. As long as his other women remain childless, he can claim that his relations with them are platonic, and there's naught to prove otherwise. Moreover, I think Eden-Smith is so selfish that he would resent having bastards to support.

"How are *you* going to bear children?" Emily regards Merciful Saint with contempt. "You're too old."

Merciful Saint pretends not to hear, but anger reddens her sallow cheeks. "You'll never experience the physical union that the blessing of motherhood requires."

"Don't be too sure about that." Emily's sly expression makes her look more like a fox than ever. "Where do you think Beloved Lamb is at night when he's not in your bed?"

I watch Merciful Saint absorb the hint that Emily is having sex with Patrick Eden-Smith. Horror bulges her eyes. With an anguished shriek, she charges at Emily, grabs her arms, and yanks her off the divan. The two women are tussling on the floor before I can do anything but gape in consternation.

"God hates hands that shed innocent blood!" Emily cries as Merciful Saint claws red scratches down her cheeks. She punches Merciful Saint on the nose.

Merciful Saint howls. "God tests the righteous!" Blood oozes from her nostrils as she grabs Emily by the hair and bangs her head against the floor.

"God hates the one who loves violence!" Emily's fingers gouge at Merciful Saint's eyes.

"Whore! Jezebel!"

"Sticks and stones may break my bones, but names shall never hurt me!"

Merciful Saint sits astride Emily, wraps her hands around Emily's throat, and squeezes. Emily coughs and chokes.

Spurred to action, I seize Merciful Saint and haul her off Emily. "Don't fight over him. He's not worth it." Even if he isn't the Torso Murderer, he's vain, selfish, and he exploits women. And there's another serious reason why they should steer clear of the man.

Emily and Merciful Saint crawl toward each other, loath to quit their battle. I plant myself between them. "Louisa Nussey was found lying in a bathtub last night with her wrists slit. It looked like suicide, but I don't think it was. Reverend Eden-Smith was with her last night. I think he killed her."

The women pause, Emily on all fours, Merciful Saint coiled like a thick snake ready to strike. They gape at me in shock as I say, "Do you know if he murdered Louisa? Am I right?"

Merciful Saint whispers, "How dare you even suggest such a thing?"

She and Emily rise up as if buoyed by the anger that blazes in their eyes. They fly at me, grab my skirts, and pull me down onto the floor with them. I fall with a bone-rattling thud, and they pummel me with their fists. Shocked that they've suddenly turned on me, I fling up my hands to protect my face.

"Thou shalt not slander Beloved Lamb!" Merciful Saint cries.

"We shall not forgive blasphemy against His Holy Spirit!" Emily shrieks.

Although at odds with each other, they're united in defense of their master. They claw at my clothes and my hair as if they're harpies tearing me apart. A moment ago I'd pitied them—Merciful Saint for her slavish devotion to a man who's a charlatan at best and a murderer at worst; Emily because she's a young, foolish girl joining a sinister household that includes three women who don't want her in it. Now, their physical assault on me provokes my temper along with my will to defend myself. I grab Merciful Saint's wrist and twist it hard. She screams in pain. I ram my elbow into Emily's face. She howls. They fight back with the manic energy of the deranged, but they're no match for me, a veteran of life-or-death battles against more dangerous opponents.

Those battles instilled in me a hunger for more. My blood races with exhilaration because this is one battle that I know I can win. As Emily and Merciful Saint wrestle, kick, and punch me, I butt their faces with my head. I match blow for blow, scratch and kick like a wildcat. My hand flails in an instinctive search for a weapon to use. My fingers grope along the sewing table and snatch the scissors.

I could seriously hurt Emily and Merciful Saint, or even kill them. Unless I get out of here fast, I will. The knowledge is like cold water dashed on the fire of my battle lust.

Dropping the scissors, I thrash my way free of the women. I clamber to my feet, snatch my pocketbook from the sofa, and run from the room. They shout Biblical imprecations after me. In my haste, I turn the wrong way and get lost in a maze of passages. I finally see a stairway, run down it, and find a door through which I bolt. I find myself back in the garden. Humility is riding a roundabout while Fortitude and Atonement bob up and down on a seesaw. They and their nannies stare at me as I run for the gate as though fleeing the horsemen of the apocalypse.

It's my own tempestuous, violent nature I'm escaping.

Chapter 22

On the other side of the gate, sheltered by the shrubbery beside the church, I stop and inhale deep breaths of the cold, misty air. I reach in my handbag, pull out my pocket mirror, and look at my reflection. My hat is askew, my braids have come down, and loose hanks of hair frame my face, which is marred by a red scratch that runs down my left cheek to my neck. Taking a shameful pleasure in the fact that my opponents must look just as bad, I quickly comb, braid, and pin up my hair.

I hear the church door open, then Barrett and Reverend Eden-Smith bidding each other farewell. Donning a calm expression, I stroll over to meet Barrett on the sidewalk.

"Where did you go?" He takes a closer look at me, and his eyebrows fly up. He touches the scratch on my cheek. "What happened to you?"

"On my way to the rectory to visit the women, I ran into some thorn bushes." If I tell Barrett I got in a fight that could have proved deadly, he'll never let me out of his sight again. I cringe inwardly because this is another secret that I'm keeping from him after secrecy almost destroyed our marriage.

Barrett looks as if he doesn't quite believe me, but he accepts it rather than disrupt the fragile harmony we've restored. To forestall more questions, I say, "Did you learn anything from Reverend Eden-Smith?"

"Only that his favorite topic of conversation is himself," Barrett says as we walk down the street toward the train station. "No body parts or bloodstained knives in the church, but I didn't expect any. He may be vain, but he isn't stupid enough to show evidence of murder to a police officer. If in fact he is the Torso Murderer. Which I don't think he is."

"Why not?" I try to sound casual even as my heartbeat quickens with the urge to defend my theory.

"He wouldn't want to get his holy hands dirty."

"That's what Hugh thinks. Well, I just discovered that at least two of the Reverend's women aren't above shedding a little blood." I describe the fight between Emily Clifford and Merciful Saint, omitting my own role.

"It's a big stretch from catfight to murder," Barrett says.

I can't dispute that, but I say, "Jealousy is a powerful motive. The unidentified Torso Murder victims could have been vestal virgins that the wives didn't want their Beloved Lamb to marry."

"It's more common for a man to kill another man over a woman." Barrett speaks with the authority of an experienced police officer. "There aren't many cases of a woman killing another woman over a man."

"You didn't see Emily and Merciful Saint going at each other."

Barrett draws a deep breath as if to muster his patience. "Suppose the wives did kill some of the Reverend's prospective brides. Why would he let them get away with it?"

"Maybe he didn't know. They could have told him the women left voluntarily. Which means they would have needed to dispose of the bodies in a way that the murders couldn't be traced back to the Haven of Love."

Barrett stops walking. I stop, too, and wait for the moment until he starts again. He asks, "Can you picture those women carving up bodies?"

"Well, no," I have to admit.

"I don't see how they would know how to dismember bodies with surgical precision," Barrett says, "but I'll entertain the possibility. Did you find any evidence?"

"The laundry, scullery, and kitchen are the logical places to dismember a body, but I couldn't search them because they were full of women washing and cooking. And the rooms looked scrubbed clean."

"So much for the Haven of Love," Barrett says with satisfaction.

"So much for keeping an open mind," I say.

"Hey, I gave your theory a chance."

"Barely." I glance over my shoulder at the church, now partially obscured by the fog. "I think we should go back there. I'm sure they know more than they're telling."

"Later. It's my turn, and I want another crack at Severin Klosowski and Violet Pearcy." Barrett stops again. He lowers his voice. "Did you hear that?"

"Hear what?"

"Footsteps behind us. They stopped when we stopped. Don't look back."

It's too late; I've already turned. The street is momentarily empty; all I see is the fog that wreaths the lamps and drifts over the pavement and buildings. I hear the distant racket of carriage wheels and horses' hooves as well as footsteps coming and going in any number of directions.

"There's nobody following us," I say.

"Maybe not." Barrett doesn't look convinced.

In the underground train station, his gaze scans the crowds while we wait on the platform. I don't see anyone who seems to be watching us. When the train comes, we board. All the seats are filled, and I look for a strap to hang onto, but just before the train starts moving, Barrett takes my arm and hurries me out the door.

"Why did you do that?" I'm vexed because now we'll have to wait for the next train.

"Just in case."

* * *

In Whitechapel, Barrett pauses to survey the street before we enter the alley beside the White Hart public house. I haven't seen or sensed anyone watching us, but I don't know if it's because I'm not as observant as Barrett is or because he's imagining things. Is his troubled state of mind making him perceive spies where there are none? Now I'm more concerned about him than ever.

Although the Torso Murderer is still at large, I doubt if he's stalking us. He's been clever and careful enough to elude capture for at least the four years since the Rainham murder or, at most, the eighteen since the Battersea murder. Why would he risk calling attention to himself now? But of course, it's good to be cautious; Whitechapel is full of other dangers.

A man comes out of the White Hart and says, "Hello."

It's Jasper Waring. I'm surprised to see him alone and apparently idle. "Why aren't you tagging after Inspector Reid?"

Sheepishness tinges his smile. "I got fired by the *Chronicle*. The editor told me to write a story that said Anjali Lodge is a fraud who deserves to go to prison for deceiving the police, wasting the taxpayers' money, and helping a killer avoid getting caught. I refused."

"I'm sorry." Now I'm surprised he had the character to do what he thought was right at the cost of his job. "But good for you."

"Yeah, well." Jasper shrugs. "I've always wanted to be a reporter and nothing else. I won't let a little setback stop me." With more confidence than I think he actually feels, he says, "The *Chronicle*'s not the only newspaper in town. You'll see me back in business right quick." He saunters off.

In the alley, at the side door of the pub, Barrett pauses again. A hand-painted sign on the wall reads "Barber Shop," with an arrow pointing downward. Barrett glances both ways, toward the streets at either end. All I see is the glow of gas lamps diffusing in the mist.

Barrett opens the door for me. "I'd better go first."

He precedes me down a narrow staircase. The chill air smells of stale beer. At the bottom is an earthen-floored passage; on our right, a storeroom filled with kegs. On the left, light shines from a door. Barrett pauses at the threshold before he enters and gestures for me to follow. Inside, gas lamps suspended on pipes from the ceiling illuminate the barber shop, and an iron stove radiates heat. By the porcelain sink, a customer draped with a white sheet sits in the lone, leather-upholstered barber chair, a towel wrapped around his neck. Severin Klosowski dips a brush in a cup of hot suds and lathers the man's face. Looking up at Barrett and me, he frowns.

"Not you again! What do you want?"

"I've a few more questions for you," Barrett says.

I do a quick survey of the shop, a humble establishment for the working man who wants a haircut and shave between drinks at his local pub. The old wood-framed mirror and the two mismatched stools for waiting customers look like secondhand purchases. But the room contains a full range of barbershop necessities: a chart showing illustrations of the latest hair, beard, and mustache styles; ceramic basins; combs made of horn and ivory in different sizes and shapes; brushes, scissors, razors, and curling iron; bottles of shaving lotion and hair tonic. Everything is meticulously organized. In his white smock, Klosowski, the onetime surgeon's apprentice, looks like a doctor. The clean smells of soap and bay rum overlay those of beer, tobacco, and mildew.

"I told you, I didn't kill anybody." Klosowski sharpens his razor with a pigskin strop. His luxuriant black mustache and oiled black hair could be an advertisement for his skills.

"If that's true, you've nothing to worry about, and we can finish things up right now," Barrett says. "Do you remember Molly Sutter, Jane Murdoch, and Elda Pokorski?"

I'm surprised and confused by the question. Barrett has never mentioned those names before, and I don't recognize them. Where is he going with this?

"So what if I do?" Klosowski deftly maneuvers the razor blade over the customer's face and neck.

"Oh, you do," Barrett says. "They're all streetwalkers, and you're their regular customer."

Klosowski looks up from his work long enough to cast a wary glance at Barrett. "How do you know?"

"I've seen you with them."

"How long you been spying on me?" Klosowski demands.

"Since September 1888, right after the Ripper killed Polly Nichols, his second victim."

Klosowski blinks in surprised consternation. "Why?"

"At first, because I knew you went out at night picking up streetwalkers like Polly. I'd seen you often enough. Later, it was because you fit the description of the man that witnesses saw with the Ripper victims shortly before the murders."

The customer's eyes pop with sudden fear that the barber shaving him is the notorious killer. He shrinks from Klosowski's razor, jumps out of the chair. With streaks of soap and patches of unshaved whiskers on his face, he throws off the sheet and flees the room.

"Hey!" Klosowski calls after him, then turns on Barrett. Bristling with indignation, he says, "I am not the Ripper."

"Sorry you lost your customer, but you know, maybe I believe you," Barrett says. "Maybe you don't carve up women and leave them where they died. Maybe you carefully dismember them and dump the parts in the river."

Scorn twists Klosowski's mouth under his mustache. "I am not the Torso Murderer. You are just trying to put the blame on me because I am foreign."

"Then where are Molly Sutter, Jane Murdoch, and Elda Pokorski?" Barrett asks.

"I don't know. Why do you care?"

My surprise increases as I comprehend what Barrett is up to: He thinks those women are Torso Murder victims. He didn't mention that to me either.

"I've been looking for Molly, Jane, and Elda. Nobody's seen them since before the first Torso Murder victim was found at Whitehall in September 1888. They haven't been to their usual places or with their usual customers."

He must have investigated Klosowski in his spare time. This is all news to me. I'm not the only one of us who's been keeping secrets from the other.

Klosowski shrugs, but I sense the fear beneath his pretended nonchalance; he, too, knows where this is heading. "Women like them come and go. They'll turn up somewhere."

"*I* think they turned up cut into pieces in the river. Severin Klosowski, I'm arresting you on suspicion of murder." Barrett pulls handcuffs out of his pocket. "Put your hands behind your back."

Klosowski curses in Polish, his face so dark with rage that I instinctively step toward the door. If I didn't know he's not the Ripper, once again I could believe he is. He slices at Barrett's throat with the razor. Barrett yells and ducks. Even as panic seizes my heart, I grab a stool and hit Klosowski on the back. He falls to his knees. I hit him again and again until he drops the razor. Lying face down on the floor, he cries, "Stop! I surrender!"

Barrett kneels on his back, handcuffs him, and hauls him to his feet. He drags Klosowski up the stairs while I follow them. On the street, Klosowski shouts at Barrett, "You ass-licking whoreson!" He adds curses in English and Polish, calling Barrett every dirty name I've ever heard and some I haven't. The people we pass pay us little attention; criminals collared by police are a common sight in Whitechapel. At the police station, I wait outside while Barrett puts Klosowski in jail.

When Barrett comes out, he says, "Klosowski will be indicted for assaulting a police officer, and he'll be held in Newgate Prison until his trial. That'll give me time to connect Molly Sutter, Jane Murdoch, and Elda Pokorski with the Torso Murders." He's exhilarated, happier than I've seen him in months.

"What did Inspector Reid say?"

"He wasn't there."

"Why didn't you tell me about Klosowski and those women?"

Barrett gives me a roguish smile. "I wanted it to be a surprise."

"It was," I say tartly, miffed because I can think of a more probable reason: He was afraid I would think that the connection between Klosowski and the missing streetwalkers didn't mean anything, and I would criticize him for believing it did. Both cross and hurt because he didn't feel that he could confide in me, I say, "I'm starting to think you could be right about Klosowski." It's true; my own suspicion toward Reverend Patrick Eden-Smith took a steep downward plunge when I saw Klosowski attack Barrett with the razor. Klosowski is a man who wouldn't hesitate to get blood on his hands.

Barrett chuckles. “I won’t rub it in until I have evidence to convict him.”

“Does this mean we don’t need to investigate Violet Pearcy anymore?” I say hopefully.

“No. While I’m proving that Klosowski is guilty, I need to make sure she’s innocent. Just to be thorough.”

CHAPTER 23

Barrett tells me that Violet works at Guy's Hospital on Mondays. The information is the result of more investigating he's done without my knowledge. Guy's Hospital, located across the river in Southwark, on St. Thomas Street, consists of three palatial buildings that surround a forecourt, where carriages, cabs, and ambulance wagons are parked. Pedestrians stream in and out a wide iron gate crowned with a sculpted, enamel-painted coat of arms—a shield with three crowned leopard heads and three fleur-de-lis, flanked by golden-winged angels and surmounted by a mother with three naked infants.

"There she is," Barrett says.

I spot Violet among the crowd exiting the gate, a drab figure in a gray coat and plain dark blue felt hat. She carries a worn dark-brown leather bag. Head down, she has a furtive air, like a thief escaping with her loot.

"Miss Pearcy," Barrett calls.

As she looks up in our direction, Violet slows her steps but doesn't pause. Her eyes are red and swollen, as if from crying. They blaze with sudden fright as she recognizes us, and she starts running.

"Wait!" Barrett orders.

When she doesn't stop, we pursue her down the street. The crowds and fog hinder us, and twice we lose sight of her. "She's guilty of something," Barrett says as we pause to look around. "Why else would she run?"

"She's upset about something." At times, my own troubles plagued me so grievously that I wept in public.

"Criminals being chased by the police generally are upset," Barrett says.

"Maybe we should try her another time."

"There's no time like the present." Determination hardens Barrett's voice. "There she goes." He points to the blue hat bobbing amid the throngs on Great Thomas Street.

We follow her onto Borough High Street and under the shadows beneath the iron railway viaduct. A train thunders overhead. Violet leads the chase past the ancient St. Saviour's Church and runs onto the London Bridge, which crosses the Thames and connects Southwark to the City of London proper on the opposite bank. The heavy traffic of carriages, wagons, omnibuses, and pedestrians vanishes into the fog that obscures the view in both directions. On the far side, the tall stone column of the monument that commemorates the Great Fire of 1666 rises above the indistinct buildings. The gilded brass flames on top shimmer like a real blaze. Halfway across the bridge, Violet falters and clutches her stomach, as if she has a muscle cramp. We catch up with her as she hobbles to the side of the bridge, drops her bag, and leans against the stone parapet. Some twenty feet below, barges and boats move under the brick arches, along the murky, garbage-strewn river.

"What do you want?" Violet says, gasping for breath.

"I've a few more questions for you," Barrett says.

Pain contorts her face. "Not now. Please."

Concerned for her, I say, "What's wrong?"

"I just attended a delivery. The baby boy was stillborn." Tears stream from Violet's eyes. "His mother bled to death. We couldn't save them." She sobs as if the loss of her patients is a personal tragedy. Perhaps it is.

"Oh, dear. I'm sorry." Moved by her grief, I say to Barrett, "Maybe later . . .?"

"This is a murder investigation. It can't wait."

I'm dismayed to see a different side of him—the cold-hearted policeman who would take advantage of a suspect's vulnerable state.

Violet cringes from him. "I told you, I didn't kill anyone."

I have to admit, her manner and quavering voice make her seem much less credible than Severin Klosowski did when he made the same claim.

"Prove it," Barrett says. "Where were you and what were you doing between April ninth and eleventh?"

I gather that those dates cover the period when the police surgeon estimated that the latest Torso Murder victim died. Violet says, "I was working."

"Can anyone confirm that?"

"My patients. I attended them in their homes."

"I'll need their names and addresses, in a moment. What did you do during the hours when you weren't working?"

She shakes her head. "I went out to the market. I cooked my meals and washed my laundry. People in my building saw me. We share the facilities."

"What about at other times?"

"I was in my flat."

"Can anyone vouch for you?" Barrett asks.

Violet shakes her head. "I live alone."

I think of Charlie Holt, the horse knacker's driver, who was lucky that prison gave him an alibi for the new Torso Murder. Violet isn't so lucky.

Barrett mentions other dates that correspond to the other Torso Murders. "Do you remember what you were doing then?"

"That was a long time ago," I say. "*I* don't remember what I was doing."

Barrett frowns at me as if to say, *"Whose side are you on?"*

"I can check my diary." Violet picks up the brown leather bag she dropped.

"Let me see that." Barrett snatches the bag.

As he and Violet tussle over it, the clasp comes open. The bag overturns, spilling the contents. Forceps, scalpels, hooks, and scissors clink on the pavement. Other metal instruments skid under the wheels of a passing carriage. A glass bottle of medicine shatters, releasing sweet, nauseous ether fumes. Violet moans, scrambling to retrieve articles that fell in a puddle. I glare at Barrett and crouch to help her. I salvage a sewing kit that contains needles and spools of thread. Bandages and cotton wool are soaked, ruined.

"I'm sorry." Barrett seems genuinely appalled by his own destructive action.

Violet picks up a small brown book titled *Midwifery Practice*. She wipes the covers on her sleeve, but the pages are stained with mud. She drops the book and bursts into tears. "All right—I'll tell you." The other day, the successful delivery of a child empowered Violet to stand up to Barrett. Today it seems that the damage to the cherished tools of her trade, on top of losing the mother and infant, has broken down her resistance. "I didn't mean to kill her. But it's my fault she's dead." She buries her face in her muddy hands.

I gasp with shock because I didn't think Violet was guilty. Barrett looks shocked too, as if even though he thought she was guilty, he hadn't expected to get a confession this quickly. He says, "Do you mean the woman who was just found by the river?"

Violet sobs so hard that she can't speak. Barrett reaches down, pulls her hands away from her face, and raises her upright. "Tell me!"

He's breathless with urgency, on the brink of solving the case for which he ran afoul of Inspector Reid. I'm grieved to learn that Violet is a murderess, but eager to hear the identity of the victim whose remains lie in the morgue.

"Elizabeth Jackson," Violet blurts.

Fresh shock stuns me. Violet has laid claim to the third Torso Murder victim, not the latest. Then again, I shouldn't be surprised. Elizabeth Jackson had been pregnant, and Violet is a midwife—facts Barrett had pointed out during our first encounter with Violet. It stands to reason that if Violet knew any of the victims, it would be Elizabeth. I'm disappointed because we still can't put a name to the latest victim, can't inform her family and lay her to rest.

Barrett's expression alternates between contrary emotions. He's thrilled to solve at least one case, but bewildered and incredulous. I know what he's thinking: If the Torso Murderer is a single individual, did Violet Pearcy commit all the crimes? Did she slay and butcher not one woman, but *five*? We stare at each other, then at the broken, sobbing woman before us. *How is it possible?*

"What happened?" he asks Violet.

Her face streaked with tears and mud, she says, "We didn't mean for any of it to happen."

Barrett and I gape at each other, surprised to learn that another person seems to have been involved in the murder. Barrett says, "Who was with you?'"

"Tim Porter. The nurse at the lying-in ward. There weren't any patients that night. He and I were the only ones on duty." Violet gasps for breath, swallows a sob. "It was after ten o'clock when a cab brought Elizabeth to the gate. She was in labor. She said it had started that morning, and the baby wouldn't come. She was in terrible pain and begged us for help. She said she had no money, she'd been living on the streets, and she had nowhere else to turn. When we put her on the bed and undressed her, I saw the umbilical cord protruding from her."

I picture the cord like a bloody gray snake between the woman's legs. I feel dizzy and ill.

"It's a rare condition that can be fatal for the child. The pressure from the contractions squeezes the cord, he can't get enough air, and he suffocates." Violet's voice is steadier now; focusing on the technical matters of her profession calms her just as taking photographs does for me. "I'd never seen it before, but I heard about it during my training. I knew I needed to deliver the baby right away. But when I did an internal examination, I discovered that the baby was breech. Its feet were pointing downward instead of its head. While Tim tried to calm Elizabeth, I tried to turn the baby, first from the outside, then the inside."

My own stomach muscles clench as I try not to picture Violet palpating the woman's belly and inserting her hands into her womb.

"But it wouldn't move. Then suddenly Elizabeth lost consciousness. We couldn't revive her. She needed a Caesarean delivery, or both she and the baby were going to die."

"A what?" Barrett says.

I recall a conversation I overheard between two women in a train. One had experienced a Caesarean delivery, which she'd described in such awful detail that I'd moved to another seat.

Violet says, "A Cesarean delivery is a surgical procedure used to remove the baby through incisions in the abdomen and womb." Barrett winces at the image. "I'd never performed a Cesarean. Only physicians are allowed. I'd only assisted during my training. But the doctor wasn't on duty, and there was no time to fetch him. I had to do it myself."

This was how and why the baby had been removed from Elizabeth's body—not as a monstrous act of mutilation, but in a desperate attempt to save two lives. I'm ashamed to realize that the police, the public, my comrades and myself, and the newspapers had been cruelly wrong about the motives of the persons involved in the deaths.

"Tim tried to talk me out of it," Violet says. "He reminded me that I wasn't qualified, and something could go wrong, but I convinced him there was no other choice. I said he could leave if he wanted. But he insisted on staying in case I needed help." She draws a deep, tremulous breath, as she must have had to do to brace herself that night. "So I made the incisions. I lifted out the child—a little boy. But he didn't cry; he wasn't breathing. Then Elizabeth began to hemorrhage. We couldn't stop it." Violet moans. "She bled to death."

And the deaths weren't deliberate murders, but the result of a medical procedure performed too late, by inexperienced hands.

"I was devastated. I sat down and wept." Tears sluice the mud down Violet's cheeks.

I can't help picturing the scene—the woman sliced open, the dead infant on her breast, the blood on the bed, the floor, and Violet's hands.

"Tim said, 'Violet, you've got to pull yourself together. If someone comes in and finds this, you'll be in trouble.' I said, 'I don't care. I broke the law, they're dead, and I should accept the consequences.' He said, 'But *I* don't want to get in trouble.' And I realized I couldn't let him suffer. He's a good man, and he'd stood by me during the operation, even though he was reluctant. So, when he said we had to cover up the deaths, I went along with him. I said, 'We'll bury the bodies.' But he said, 'It will take too long to dig a grave, and someone will catch us.' I was ready to give up then, but Tim said, 'We'll dump them in the river. We'll use the ambulance to take them there.'"

Violet explains that the infirmary had an ambulance wagon and horses for transporting seriously ill patients to the hospital. "I asked how we could smuggle them past the guard at the gate. And that wasn't our only problem. Tim was afraid Elizabeth would be reported missing and her body would be found. The cab driver who brought her might come forward to identify her. Or she might have told someone else where she was going for help with the birth. The police would order an autopsy. The surgeon would see the incisions and know she'd had a Caesarean section. We couldn't let her be traced to us. So Tim came up with a plan. We moved the bodies to the operating room. It was empty; the surgeon doesn't come in until morning. Tim cut the bodies into pieces."

The person with anatomical knowledge and dissecting experience, who'd dismembered the corpses, wasn't Violet Pearcy. It wasn't a ruthless killer, but a nurse desperate to protect himself and his colleague from the consequences of a failed medical procedure. I feel so sorry for Tim and Violet. They were dedicated, hard-working people whose compassionate intentions had made them accomplices in a "murder" and a cover-up.

"I cleaned up the blood in the lying-in ward and burned the sheets in the stove. When Tim was finished, we cleaned the operating table and tools. We bundled the remains in Elizabeth's clothes and brown wrapping paper. Tom fetched the ambulance. We loaded up the bundles, covered them with a sheet, and I lay down on top of them." She retches as if the memory made her ill.

Barrett and I cover our own mouths, sickened as well. To lie atop the remains of a woman and her infant who'd been butchered and packaged like meat! I shudder as I imagine the lumpy sensation of skull and bones, dead flesh and organs, still warm, pressing against my body.

"Tim drove the ambulance. He told the guard I'd fallen ill with appendicitis, and he was taking me to the hospital. I groaned and writhed as if I were in terrible pain. The guard believed us. He didn't check inside the wagon. As soon as we were far enough from the gate, Tim let me out. He went to the river, and I ran home to my lodgings as fast as I could. I never went back to Garratt Lane Workhouse infirmary again."

Garratt Lane Workhouse.

In her vision, Anjali had seen a woman running away from buildings that Reid later identified as the workhouse. The woman was Violet Pearcy, not Irene Muller. My heart swells with my relief at learning that Anjali's vision is true. Her psychic talent is real, not a figment of wishful imagination.

And Inspector Reid wasn't as far off track as I'd thought. Had he not jumped to the conclusions and decided Irene was the latest victim, and her beau Charlie Holt was the Torso Murderer, perhaps he eventually would have solved the Elizabeth Jackson case.

"We thought that if the remains were found, they would be so decomposed that no one would be able to recognize Elizabeth," Violet says.

"You were wrong." Barrett sounds dazed, as if he can hardly believe what he's heard. "Her mother recognized the scar on Elizabeth's wrist."

"Tim said, all we had to do was keep quiet, and nobody would ever know," Violet says.

If Barrett hadn't singled her out as a suspect in first the Ripper case and then the Torso Murders, perhaps nobody would have known. I'm astonished that the circumstances of Elizabeth's death were so far from what I imagined. The person responsible wasn't an evil, perverted madman, but a kind woman who risked her own life and liberty to save a mother and child. Barrett takes off his hat and rubs his head, as if someone had clubbed him, or perhaps to show respect. He glances at the traffic on the bridge, the mist-shrouded city, and the river as if in search of guidance. Then he sighs.

"Violet Pearcy, I'm sorry, but I must arrest you."

Dismay floods me. "Must you?" That good intentions should result in punishment!

"What else can I do? She performed an illegal operation that killed Elizabeth Jackson."

"Elizabeth would have died with or without it!" I protest.

"According to her." Barrett gestures toward Violet, huddled and weeping amid her ruined possessions. "It's for a jury to decide."

Public opinion won't favor her. She broke the law; she overstepped the narrow confines of a midwife's duties and trespassed on territory reserved for doctors. If she goes to trial, she'll be convicted and hanged. I plead with Barrett.

"We're the only ones who know what she did. Can't you just let her go?" It wouldn't be the first time we looked the other way when someone was responsible for a death. Under these circumstances, the same decision seems justifiable now.

Barrett stares at me in astonished disbelief. "You know I can't."

I know that he, a police officer, is held to a higher standard than myself. But I say, "Just this once?"

Obviously torn between his duty to uphold the law and his wish to protect a good woman from the consequences of an impossible choice, Barrett shakes his head and speaks with regret. "Sarah, I have to take her in."

"No. Please!" I cry.

"It's all right," Violet says, hoarse from weeping. "I should have turned myself in that night instead of covering it up." She staggers to her feet.

Barrett exhales with relief that she's not going to resist arrest and make his job harder. "We'll tell the task force that one of the Torso Murders is solved." He raises his hand to hail a passing cab.

I grab his arm and pull it down. He says, "Sarah. Don't interfere." A new, obstinate tone of command harshens his voice, and he yanks his arm away from me. I've run up against a line beyond which things aren't negotiable.

"Now I must pay for my crime." Violet turns to face the river, grasps the parapet on the side of the bridge, and boosts herself up.

In the moment when Barrett and I realize what she means to do, she scrambles over the edge.

We shout in alarm and grab at her.

She falls the twenty feet down to the river and lands with a great splash.

I'm left gasping in horrified shock, holding a torn strip of her skirt in my hand. Violet sinks beneath the muddy water, out of sight. I hear cries from other people who saw her jump.

Barrett climbs onto the parapet. Without hesitation, before I can think to stop him, he launches himself into the river. His instinct to save a citizen who's in danger is as strong as his duty to put a criminal behind bars, no matter that the endangered citizen is the criminal. Terrified for him, I yell his name as I lean over the parapet and see him splash down. He sinks, bobs up, and dives under the water.

Around me, along the bridge, people watch in clamorous suspense. The water roils as Barrett searches for Violet. Panic grips me. Barrett comes up, spits, and gasps while he treads water. He dives again and stays under for seconds that seem like hours. I hold my own breath until he surfaces again, farther downstream, carried by the current. There's no sign of Violet. Has she sunk to the deep bottom or drifted beyond his reach? Barrett dives under, and long moments pass. Spectators murmur uneasily. I can't hold my breath any longer. I cover my mouth and moan as I pant.

Has he drowned?

I gaze at the water that's visible, a stretch of some twenty feet between the bridge and the point beyond which the fog gets too dense to see anything. If only the force of my will could lift Barrett to the surface! But of course it can't. I climb onto the parapet, ready to jump in after him. I think of the man rescued from the Tower Bridge the day I found the torso. Surely Barrett will be as fortunate. But he doesn't appear. The Thames is full of treacherous currents and submerged objects that can injure a man or trap him underwater. My quarrels with Barrett pale to insignificance. My body fills with a terror as cold as the water that swallowed my husband.

Chapter 24

I'm about to hurl myself into the river, in a desperate, foolhardy attempt to rescue Barrett. If he's dead, I don't want to live.

Then he shouts, "Help!"

My heart leaps. I sob for joy. I hear splashing and other men's voices. Excitement ripples the crowd of spectators, which has grown so large that it's blocking the bridge. I watch the hazy shape of a tugboat glide out of the fog toward me. Aboard the boat, men crouch by a figure that lies on the deck. One of the men is Barrett. He managed to rescue Violet! The crowd cheers. I moan with relief, then whisper a prayer of thanks.

The boat chugs toward the north bank of the river. I run along the bridge, onto the street. Spectators follow me down the steps to the London Bridge Wharf. We meet the boat as it draws up beside the quay. On the deck, Violet lies sodden and still, her face pale and eyes closed. Barrett, dripping wet, frantically pumps her chest, trying to push the water from her lungs. But she doesn't move. The other men shake their heads, and I hear one of them say, "It's no use, mate. She's gone."

Barrett looks up, and his gaze meets mine, his face so distorted by anguish that he looks like a painting of a tortured saint. He keeps working on Violet until two local police constables arrive. They pull him away from her, despite his protests. When I reach him, they're telling him that the death by drowning of a person who'd jumped off the bridge is their business, not his. They override his arguments and take charge. I persuade him to come home with me before he catches pneumonia.

We ride home in a cab. He's wrapped in blankets that someone at the wharf gave him, but he's shivering from the cold. Water from his drenched clothes seeps through the blankets; a puddle forms around our shoes. He smells of the river, fishy and rotten. I squeeze his hand through the blankets, but he flinches from my touch. He turns his face away from me and stares out the window.

"It's not your fault," I say.

He shakes his head. "If not for me, Violet wouldn't have jumped."

I can't argue with that, but I try to downplay his role in her death. "I think she couldn't live with her guilt, and she wanted to die."

"I don't want to talk about it."

For the rest of the way home, his silence is as impenetrable as a stone wall.

Luckily, no one is at the house to ask questions. In the kitchen, I fill the boiler with water to heat for his bath, but he says, "I have to get to the station and tell Inspector Reid about Violet before somebody else does." Upstairs, he strips and scrubs himself with cold water and soap, then dresses in clean clothes.

"I'll go with you," I say.

"No." His manner is as sharp as if he'd pulled a knife on me. Then he's gone.

It's two o'clock. I bundle up his rank, wet clothes and take them to the laundry. At home again, I make a late lunch of bread, cheese, and tea and force myself to eat it while I wonder what's happening at the police station. Inspector Reid will learn that Barrett not only drove one suspect to suicide, but he locked up another just because three of the man's regular streetwalkers seem to be missing. I dread imagining the retribution Reid will exact.

I still think the truth about the Torso Murderers lies at the Haven of Love. If only Barrett hadn't insisted on questioning Severin Klosowski and Violet Pearcy again! And if I hadn't been so scrupulous about honoring our bargain to give his theory a chance, I might have dissuaded him. I feel a certain resentment toward Dr. Lewes, even though I chose to follow his advice.

At five o'clock, Barrett still isn't back. I begin dinner preparations, and my family comes home—first Fitzmorris, then Mick with Sally, then Hugh with Dr. Lewes. I tell them the news. We're at the table when Barrett finally returns and drops into his chair. Warned by my briefing, they say nothing about the day's events. In silence, we pass him platters of fried ham and potatoes; I pour his tea.

"Thanks." He chews and swallows mechanically, as though he doesn't taste his food.

No one ventures small talk. Barrett doesn't look at the rest of us. We look down at our plates, bursting with questions we dare not ask. At last he says, "Inspector Reid said he's going to investigate the 'incident on the bridge.'" His sardonic tone puts quotation marks around the last four words; apparently, that's what Reid is calling Violet's suicide. "But it was obvious that he's already decided the outcome of the investigation: I as good as drowned Violet with my own hands, and he'll bring me up on a murder charge."

No one speaks. We're all too horrified, without words to soothe Barrett's pain or our own. I think he must have anticipated what would happen at the police station, and that's why he wouldn't let me go with him. Not only did he not want me to witness his humiliation; he must have been afraid of how I would react and of what Reid might do to me.

"But look on the bright side," Barrett says with bitter humor. "If Reid makes the murder charge stick, then losing my job will be the least of my worries."

I'm speechless with fear that Reid finally has Barrett—and me—where he wants us: so deep in trouble that we can't get out.

"That's so unfair!" Sally cries.

"Sod the bastard," Mick says.

"Second that," Hugh says.

Dr. Lewes watches with somber concern. I wish Hugh hadn't brought him tonight. I don't like an outsider seeing my husband's distress, and if Dr. Lewes weren't here, at least the rest of us could speak candidly.

Fitzmorris gets up and fetches a bottle of whiskey. He pours a glass for Barrett, who says, "A last drink for the condemned man? Thanks." He drains his glass in one gulp.

I struggle to collect my wits. "But Violet confessed to murdering Elizabeth Jackson. She knew that if she was arrested and put on trial, she would be convicted and sentenced to death. She decided to die on her own terms. Reid can't blame you for that."

"Reid weren't there," Mick says indignantly. "He didn't see what happened."

"That's the problem," Barrett says. "He doesn't believe Violet confessed. She didn't sign an official statement. He thinks I hounded her, and she was so scared, she jumped off the bridge to escape me. Then I made up the confession to cover my behind."

Furious at Reid, I protest, "I was there too. I heard Violet confess."

Barrett regards me with scornful pity. "Do you think Reid will believe you? He'll think you're lying to protect me."

"There must have been hundreds of people on London Bridge," Hugh says. "Someone must have overheard what Violet said. When Reid investigates, he'll find witnesses that will debunk his version of events."

"He'll choose the ones who didn't hear anything and think I pushed Violet off the bridge," Barrett says.

Mick snorts in disgust. "You solved one of the Torso Murders for him after he ran around chasin' false leads. And this is the thanks you get."

"Reid's decided Elizabeth Jackson's murder isn't part of the series, and the Torso Murderer is still at large." Barrett reluctantly admits, "I hate to say, I think he's right about that."

I too agree with Reid on that point, but I refuse to say anything in his favor. The man is determined to see the end of Barrett, and if my husband dies, my life won't be worth living.

"He still believes the Torso Murderer and Jack the Ripper are one man," Barrett says. "Nothing will convince him otherwise."

"Reid is so vexatiously blinded by his obsession," Hugh says.

"Yeah," Mick says, "he wouldn't see the truth if it punched him on the nose."

Sally frowns in puzzlement at Hugh and Mick. "So, you and Barrett and Sarah are all sure he's wrong. I don't understand why."

"I must say I don't either," Fitzmorris chimes in.

Dr. Lewes raises a quizzical eyebrow. It's obvious that he, too, wonders why Hugh, Mick, Barrett, and I take such strong objection to Reid's theory. The air sparks with danger as we remember that three people at this table don't know the secret and can't be allowed to know.

Hugh is first to dissemble. "Reid has a history of looking for the truth in all the wrong places. It's a safe bet that he's way off track in the Ripper case."

"Ten pence says that when we solve the other Torso Murders, the guy will turn out not to be the Ripper." Mick holds out his hand to Hugh.

"I'm sure to lose, but I can't resist a gamble. You're on." Hugh shakes Mick's hand.

Fitzmorris nods; his loyalty to Hugh trumps his doubts. But Sally and Dr. Lewes look both unconvinced and suspicious. I can tell they think we're hiding something. I had wondered whether Hugh told Dr. Lewes our secret. It seems he hasn't, but now Dr. Lewes is aware there is a secret, and woe betide us if he should induce Hugh to tell.

"I wish I'd left Violet alone," Barrett says. "If I had, none of this would have happened."

Nobody contradicts him; that's one point on which we all must agree. Barrett pushes back his chair and leaves the room. The rest of us sit in troubled silence, listening to his footsteps mount the stairs. His misery fills the house. I can't even be glad he ended a conversation that had wandered into dangerous territory.

Chapter 25

The next morning, I go downstairs to find Hugh, Mick, and Fitzmorris at breakfast. Outside, the weather is gray, and rain drips down the window. Hugh says, "How is he?"

"Still asleep," I say.

Except for the days I'm called to photograph a crime scene, Barrett usually gets up earlier than I do. The change is troubling, and not only as a stark reminder that he's suspended from duty. I'm afraid he's lost his sense of purpose and believes he has nothing worth getting up for. And I'm not sure he's really asleep. Last night, when I tried to console him, he said he was too tired to talk, but his restlessness kept me awake. I think now he's pretending to be asleep to avoid conversation. In our house, there's no privacy, no place for him to be alone with his thoughts.

My head aches and my eyes burn from my own wakeful night, and I'm sick with worry about Barrett. I pour a cup of coffee, hoping it will jolt me alert so I can think of what to do.

"I made pancakes," Fitzmorris says. "Barrett likes them. Maybe they'll cheer him up." He fills a plate and passes it to me.

"Mick and Sally and I will help you exonerate Barrett," Hugh says. "Sally is going to put a notice in the *Daily World*, asking anyone who saw and heard what happened between Barrett and Violet on the London Bridge to come forward."

"I'm headin' to the bridge to post notices and look for witnesses," Mick says.

"I'm going to track down Tim Porter, the nurse who cut up and disposed of Elizabeth Jackson," Hugh says. "He's the witness who can confirm Violet's story."

My eyes well with tears. "Thank you." I'm so glad to have my family's support. Things begin to look a little better. We've accomplished impossible things before; we can again. "I'll work on the Torso Murders case. If we can solve it, that should help Barrett."

Hugh smiles. "That's the spirit."

I eat Fitzmorris's delicious pancakes with more appetite than I thought I had. After Hugh and Mick leave, I wash the dishes, then go upstairs.

Barrett is still in bed, hidden under the quilts. The room is dim and cold, as if invaded by the weather outside. My spark of optimism fizzles, quenched by disturbing thoughts. Does Barrett feel so guilty about Violet that he *wants* to be punished? Instead of fighting for his job and his life, is he going to accept whatever Reid dishes out, because he thinks he deserves it? Despair is as dangerous as the river in which he could have drowned yesterday.

My fear provokes anger, toward both Reid and my husband.

I'd meant to offer Barrett breakfast in bed, but I say, "Get up."

He stirs at the sound of my no-nonsense command. "What for?"

The dull apathy in his muffled voice makes me angrier. "We've work to do."

"What work? I'm suspended, remember?"

"We can still investigate the Torso Murders."

"You go ahead."

"I'm not letting you lie here." I yank the covers off Barrett.

"Hey!" He sits up to grab the covers.

For the first time since last night, I see his face. His eyes are bloodshot in dark hollows. Bruises that he must have gotten while rescuing Violet have bloomed on his unshaven cheeks. He looks so heart-wrenchingly terrible that I almost relent and let him stay in bed. But I'm overpowered by a need to believe that if I can get him moving, he'll be all right.

"Sally, Hugh, and Mick are out there trying to exonerate you," I say. "Fitzmorris cooked pancakes for you. You don't get to loaf."

Barrett glowers with more pain than anger. I'm afraid I've only made things worse. Then, with surly reluctance, he swings his legs over the side of the bed, stands up, and reaches for his clothes. No matter how bad he feels, his pride and his respect for our family won't let him lie idle while everyone else is working on his behalf.

"I'll see you downstairs," I say, relieved but not daring to hope for too much.

In the kitchen, while I warm up the pancakes and wait for Barrett, I consult a railway map and timetable. Soon he joins me. He's neatly dressed and shaved, and he eats the pancakes without appetite. His complexion is so pale, I worry that he's physically sick, for he must have swallowed all manner of filth while swimming in the Thames.

"How do you feel?" I ask.

He shrugs. "There's something I didn't tell you yesterday. I missed Severin Klosowski's court hearing. The magistrate released him because I wasn't there to testify."

"Oh." This is more bad news. Klosowski is guilty of assaulting a police officer, if not the Torso Murders, and the dangerous man is back on the streets—another professional failure for Barrett. His hard expression tells me that any sympathy I offer would only rub salt in his wounds, so I keep quiet.

After he finishes breakfast, he accompanies me to Paddington Station. He doesn't ask where we're going until after I've bought our tickets. Then he says, "Why Swindon?"

"It's the closest station to Ashlade, Reverend Patrick Eden-Smith's former parish."

A glimmer of resistance shows through Barrett's apathy. Right now, I would welcome an argument about whether investigating Eden-Smith is a wild goose chase. It would be a sign that Barrett is regaining his old spirit. But all he says is, "Open mind." He taps his finger against his temple and falls silent.

On the train, we find seats in an empty car, and as we ride west out of London, I try again to console him. "I think Violet wanted to be held accountable for what she did. She couldn't live with it forever, and she wanted to die. If we hadn't come along on a bad day, something else eventually would have happened to drive her over the edge."

Barrett turns on me. "Do *you* want to be held accountable for what *we* did?"

He means the night in the slaughterhouse. Caught off guard, I say, "That's different."

Barrett shakes his head to disagree. "Can you live with it forever?" He seems honestly curious; we never talk much about that night.

I force a laugh to lighten the dark moment. "What choice do I have?"

"If that were the only time, it wouldn't be so bad," Barrett says. "But there's also Cremorne Gardens." That was the scene of our last investigation, which had ended badly. "We seem to keep making choices that lead us farther into a place I don't want to be."

Certainly, I'm not happy with all the consequences of Cremorne Gardens and other cases we've solved, but I consider each unique, a one-time event, which makes them more comfortable to accept. I'm dismayed to learn that Barrett sees them as parts of the same foul swamp that grows bigger with every investigation that goes wrong.

"You don't seem to mind," Barrett says bitterly. "You just shrug it off."

"I do not!" I'm indignant that he thinks I'm so callous about events that cost people their lives or suborned justice or both.

Barrett chuckles as if he doesn't believe me. Since we never talk about those events, how would he know that the results of our actions trouble me every day? Fresh dismay fills me as I wonder about Hugh and Mick. They seem to carry many of the events in our past as easily as if it's lint they could brush off their clothes, but perhaps they too struggle with guilty consciences.

"Of course, it's different for you," Barrett says. "You're not a police officer. You haven't violated a professional code of honor."

I'm stunned to comprehend why Violet Pearcy's death affected him so strongly. He sees it as a new breach of his police honor, on top of earlier ones, like gangrene in a wound that hasn't healed.

"You did your best to save Violet," I say. "I don't blame you for what happened to her. Nobody should. And you know there wasn't anything you could do about the Cremorne Gardens case. Your hands were tied."

"Excuses don't change the facts." Barrett's tone is hard, merciless.

It's not only his professional code of honor he thinks he's violated. That he's also compromised his personal honor bothers him more than the prospect of losing his job and facing criminal charges. He can't forgive himself. Horror sickens me as I acknowledge that I'm part of his troubles. If not for me, Barrett never would have been involved in the Ripper situation—and probably not in the other cases that went wrong.

"Someday, will something happen to make you spill the beans and drive you over the edge, like Violet?" he asks, his somber gaze intent on me.

My mouth opens, then closes. He's turned my remark about Violet Pearcy into a question that I don't know how to answer. I recall times I've been pushed to the brink of divulging our secret about the Ripper. It could happen again and again until finally I break down. Is Barrett telling me that he's near the edge? Does that figure into his current mental state? I didn't realize until now how much my ability to accept the past depends on his, and Hugh's and Mick's. Now I see Violet Pearcy's suicide in an even darker light—as a possible harbinger of our own fates. This does nothing to ease my fear for my husband and my family.

We pass the rest of our journey without further conversation. Two hours later, we exit the train at Swindon Station and hire a cab from the rank outside the building. We rattle along foggy, smoky streets jammed with wagons, carriages, and pedestrians, but within the hour, the city gives way to expansive fields of wheat. The sky is clear blue between puffy white clouds, the cool air fresh. Along the roadside and in the pastures, yellow daffodils and pink rhododendrons bloom. Tulips in flowerboxes decorate farmhouses. It's an English spring such as we Londoners rarely experience. A shepherd leading his flock completes my illusion that I've traveled back in time to a simpler, bucolic age.

Ashlade is a quiet hamlet some five miles from Swindon. At the center are the church, schoolhouse, and businesses that include a post office, blacksmith, bakery, and general store. A waterworks stands beside a stream. Lanes bordered by stone cottages wind outward from the village center.

"Where to?" Barrett inquires in a voice that suggests he couldn't care less.

I tell the driver to let us off by the church. We pause outside the ancient stone structure that looks to date from the Norman era, with a square, crenellated tower. On the left side of it, old tombstones dot the grass in the graveyard. On the right, the rectory is a newer, brick Georgian-style mansion.

"This used to be Reverend Eden-Smith's church," I say. "We'll start here."

Across the street is the Lamb Inn, a whitewashed, half-timbered building, the local public house. Through its window I glimpse men at the bar, their faces turned toward Barrett and me. The few people outside the shops pause to scrutinize us. Ashlade seems the kind of small, insular town in which strangers are noteworthy. There can't be more than a few hundred inhabitants, and I can understand why Patrick Eden-Smith moved to London. Trouble or no trouble, he needed a richer hunting ground to satisfy his grandiose ambitions. I turn to Barrett to share my thoughts.

He's watching a constable ride by on a bicycle. "Maybe I could get a job in a place like this."

I laugh because I think he's joking. He loves London and the rough-and-tumble of policing. He's never lived anywhere else, never expressed any desire to move. "You would be bored to death."

Barrett doesn't laugh. I'm surprised to see that he was at least half serious. Has Violet Pearcy's death changed him so that he craves peace rather than the excitement he once thrived on? Or maybe the change started long ago. Where will it end? I'm suddenly frightened. What does this mean for our marriage?

In the church, the air is colder than outdoors, as if the thick stone structure retained the chill of winter. The memorial tablets on the walls and floors look as ancient as the building. Dim light filters through narrow windows divided into many small panes. Stone arches rise from columns capped with worn carvings of saints. I see a man dressed in black standing in the chancel. He walks down the aisle, between the dark wooden pews, toward Barrett and me.

"Good morning." He's bespectacled and stout; his clerical collar digs into his thick neck. He must be the vicar. His smile thins as he notices that we're strangers. "Welcome to St. Mary's." His manner is less hospitable than wary.

We return the greeting, and Barrett falls silent. I introduce us and say, "We're here about the Reverend Patrick Eden-Smith."

"I'm afraid you're too late for that," the vicar says coldly.

Puzzled by his comment, I say, "Late for what?"

"Mr. Eden-Smith is no longer the officiant here."

"I know."

Before I can explain that Barrett and I are investigating Eden-Smith as a suspect in a murder case, the vicar says, "If you came to visit the scene, you wasted your time. By all means look around, but there's nothing left to see."

I realize that he thinks Barrett and I are tourists lured by tales of disreputable events that happened during Eden-Smith's tenure. Intrigued, I say, "Why did Reverend Eden-Smith leave?"

"Why do you want to know?"

I glance at Barrett. He's drifted away to study the baptismal font. "I'm a reporter at the *Daily World* in London. I'm doing a story about Reverend Eden-Smith."

"We've had quite enough of the press in Ashlade, and he's no longer honored with the title of 'Reverend' here," the vicar says, downright hostile now.

My curiosity increases. "Did you know him?"

"If you'd like to worship at St. Mary's, feel free to do so. Otherwise . . ."

"What about his wives? Merciful Saint, Anointed One, and Light of Heaven?"

"Go away. Leave us in peace."

Outside the church, after we bade farewell to the vicar, I say to Barrett, "Reverend Eden-Smith apparently departed Ashlade under a very big, dark cloud."

"Apparently."

Barrett's lack of interest frightens me. Where is his usual eagerness to solve a crime? Will it ever return? I take refuge in anger, a more comfortable emotion. "I could have used some help with the vicar."

"What was I supposed to do?" Barrett says. "Slap him around?"

His sarcasm stings. "You could have told him you're a Metropolitan Police detective investigating a murder, and Patrick Eden-Smith is a suspect."

"I'm not working for the Metropolitan Police. I'm suspended. Did you forget?"

"Of course not." Although sorry I touched his sore spot, I hope that if I can get him to participate in the investigation, he'll revert to his normal self. "But the vicar doesn't know you're not on duty."

"*I* know."

I feel a mixture of anger, concern, and helplessness. Glancing across the street at the Lamb Inn, I say, "It's lunchtime. Aren't you hungry?"

The Lamb's public room features dark timbers and worn brick walls, a stone hearth blackened with soot, and rough-hewn tables and chairs. It looks as if Shakespeare might stop by for a drink. As we pause at the threshold, conversation ceases. At the bar, the publican, a bald man with a goatee, is polishing glasses. All the tables are full except the one in the center of the room. The customers—men and women, mostly old—gaze upon us with expectant smiles or speculative curiosity as we hesitantly move toward the empty table. It appears that word of our presence has gotten around, and everyone with nothing better to do has turned out to meet us.

Barrett pulls out a chair for me. I feel as self-conscious if I'm an actress on stage and I've forgotten my lines.

The publican brings over two glasses of ale. "On the house." He sets the glasses on our table.

"Thanks." Barrett smiles for the first time since before Violet Pearcy's drowning.

I smile too, grateful for the kind gesture after our chilly reception from the vicar. But as we sip the tasty, strong ale, I suspect the drinks are meant to loosen our tongues. Sure enough, the publican says, "From London, are you?" His other patrons listen eagerly.

Barrett lets me speak for us. Nervous in front of our audience, I introduce myself and say, "Yes, I'm a reporter from the *Daily World*. This is my husband—Mr. Thomas Barrett." I barely remembered not to call him "Detective Sergeant."

The villagers murmur in anticipation. One man, with a pipe stuck in a mouth hidden by a gray beard, says, "Haven't had a reporter here nigh on eight years."

"What brings you to Ashlade?" the publican asks.

"We met Reverend Patrick Eden-Smith in London. I'm writing a story about him. We heard that this is his former parish."

Friendly laughter ensues. The gray-bearded pipe smoker nudges the fat man seated next to him. "I told you that's why they came. I win." He holds out his hand. His friend feigns disgust as he hands over a coin.

"Sorry, but you missed all the fun," the publican tells Barrett and me.

I think I've found witnesses amenable to gossip. "What sort of fun?"

"We saw you go into the church," Graybeard says. "The vicar didn't give you any satisfaction, did he?"

"No," I say. "He as good as told us to get lost."

"Well, of course he wants to sweep it under the rug."

Tamping down impatience, I say, "Sweep what under the rug?"

"I suppose you folks in London haven't heard about our little scandal," the publican says.

I smile with eagerness I don't need to pretend. "We would love to hear about it now."

Chapter 26

No further prompting is required. The villagers settle in for a leisurely story time, glasses filled, pipes and cigarettes lit. The publican, who introduces himself as Dick Norton, sets plates of bread, cheese, pickles, and cold meat before us. We're an honored audience as well as sources of fresh gossip who need buttering up.

"Before Reverend Eden-Smith came, Ashlade was always a quiet, peaceful place," Dick Norton says.

"Not always," says a woman at the table next to me. She's as petite as a girl, not much over four feet tall, but with an hourglass shape, gray streaks in her brunette hair, and laugh lines around wise brown eyes. "There was the time the circus came to town, and the Stevens girls ran off with it."

"Exception to the rule, Mother," Mr. Norton says. He's far too old to be her son; he's among those men who take to calling their wives "Mother" after they have children. "St. Mary's church was no tourist attraction. The old vicar was a good man, but a dull preacher."

"Don't forget the sermons when he passed gas," Mrs. Norton says.

"He wasn't trying to be entertaining," Mr. Norton says.

"Credit where credit is due, Dick."

Their audience chuckles, and so do I. They're as comical as a London music hall skit. I'm glad to see Barrett's face relax.

"Well, when the old vicar retired, we were all curious to see who we would get next," Mr. Norton says. "The squire at the manor house decided to give the living to his daughter's new husband. Miss Julia met Reverend Eden-Smith while she was studying at Oxford and married him there."

So far, this is the same story Eden-Smith told Barrett and me.

"We'd never seen the likes," Mrs. Norton says. "The Reverend and Julia rolled into town in a splendid carriage, with liverymen and white horses, and wagons full of expensive new furniture for the rectory. And he was so handsome, like a stage actor." Clasping her hand over her heart, she sighs.

"Don't get all fluttery now, Mother." Mr. Norton takes up the story. "We all turned out for his first Sunday. Now, St. Mary's church has been around for seven hundred years, and if the walls could talk, they would say his sermon was the best ever given there."

"What he said wasn't anything we haven't heard before," Mrs. Norton says. "All about heaven and hell, and sin and repentance, God and Jesus and the Holy Spirit, and love and mercy. It was the way he delivered it. So dramatic!"

"You ladies were certainly bowled over," Mr. Norton says. Women among the audience giggle.

That certainly sounds like the big splash that Eden-Smith bragged about.

"Word spread," Mrs. Norton says. "The church was packed to the gills every Sunday. The donation plate overflowed, and after the service, the charwoman swept money off the floor."

"It was good for local business," Mr. Norton says." People came from near and far to hear the Reverend. I've never had so many customers before, or since."

"Reverend and Julia had two children," Mrs. Norton says.

A pang of surprise ripples through me. I saw three children at Haven of Love, not two, and Merciful Saint said that Humility, Fortitude, and Atonement are Eden-Smith's daughters by his first wife. Where did the other girl come from? This is the first discrepancy between the stories told by Eden-Smith and the Nortons. Catching Barrett's gaze on me, I try to be objective and give Eden-Smith the benefit of the doubt. There could be a logical, innocuous explanation for the discrepancy. Perhaps he'd adopted an orphan girl after he left Ashlade.

"Then Julia died in the carriage accident," Mr. Norton says. "At her funeral service, the Reverend had a spell."

"A revelation, it was," Mrs. Norton says. "He said he was the Holy Ghost, made flesh."

"His preaching was so powerful that it drove the women mad," Mr. Norton says. "They were wailing and sobbing and tearing at their hair and fainting. The next week, he started healing the sick. That really brought in the crowds. He had to add an extra service every Sunday."

Perhaps he'd truly loved Julia, her death had sparked a religious epiphany, and the Reverend is guilty of nothing more than delusions of grandeur.

"Then the trouble started," Mrs. Norton says. "There was a big difference of opinion about the Reverend. Some thought he walked on water. Just as many thought he was a downright fraud." Mutters among the audience suggest that the controversy hadn't ended with Patrick Eden-Smith's departure.

"The believers clashed with nonbelievers. Husbands fought with their wives." Mr. Norton's narrow-eyed glance at his wife says they'd been on opposite sides of the controversy. "Boys and girls quarreled with their parents, servants with their masters. The drunks and no-goods seized the excuse to brawl in the streets. Friends became enemies. Families split up."

"It wasn't all love and sunshine between the believers either," Mrs. Norton says. "They fought over the Reverend's attention. He invited people to special prayer sessions at the rectory, but only men who were rich and women who were rich or beautiful." She sounds miffed, likely because he hadn't included her among his favored few.

Eden-Smith had left out that part of the story, but I'd seen the jealousy between his current brides and Emily Clifford, his fiancée. What else did he leave out?

"The Reverend remarried not six weeks after Miss Julia was in the ground," Mr. Norton says. "A railway heiress."

"God sent me a new partner to share my vocation," I remember Eden-Smith saying. A partner with a conveniently large dowry.

"That caused some bad feeling in the church," Mrs. Norton says. "Women who'd been around longer thought they deserved to be his wife."

And now that Patrick Eden-Smith plans to wed another new follower, he's engendered jealousy among his current wives.

"Meanwhile, reporters had been flocking to Ashlade," Mr. Norton says. "Newspapers printed stories about the Reverend. The bishop got wind of it. He and his men came to the church to investigate."

"They got an eyeful," Mrs. Norton says with relish. "The Reverend made a lame man walk. There was a fight between a dozen women. His enemies shouted curses and lobbed bricks through the window."

"A brick hit the bishop," Mr. Norton says. "He ordered the Reverend to stop the service. But the Reverend said he was the Holy Spirit and answered only to God."

Well, that's one answer to my question. Eden-Smith had neglected to tell Barrett and me about the fracas.

"The next Sunday, he proclaimed that God had told him to spread his love around," Mr. Norton continues. "He married two more women. He called them his spiritual brides. I thought I'd seen everything, but I have to admit, I was shocked."

"So was everyone else," Mrs. Norton says, "even his most faithful believers. Some quit the church, while new ones joined every Sunday. There were rumors about what went on in the rectory during those prayer sessions." Her hushed tone hints at sexual orgies.

"People went in and didn't come out," Mr. Norton says. "Mostly women. A few escaped late at night, looking pale and shaken. One was kidnapped and dragged home by her brothers. The Reverend bought bloodhounds to keep trespassers away."

"A man tried to rescue his wife," Mrs. Norton says. "Those dogs tore his trousers. They almost took off his leg."

I think of Louisa Nussey, kidnapped by her relatives and committed to the Ticehurst asylum. But no disturbances of the other kind have occurred at the Haven of Love, as far as I know. Perhaps his experience in Ashlade taught Reverend Eden-Smith to keep up a decorous front.

"We didn't know what happened behind closed doors until . . ." Mr. Norton pauses for suspense. Barrett and I wait eagerly. The publican looks across the room and says, "You tell it, Joe Hanks."

All eyes turn to a lean, gangly man seated by himself at a corner table. He's in his forties, dressed in a shabby business suit. His spectacles and rounded shoulders lend him a scholarly air. His mouth sags, as if he's appalled to find himself the center of attention. He flushes, shakes his head, and waves his hands, too embarrassed to speak.

"Joe's a clerk at the law office," Mrs. Norton says. "He's one of them that escaped from the rectory. But his wife stayed. He couldn't make her leave. When he got out, he told tales."

Joe flushes bright red, mortified. Mr. Norton says, "Come on, tell our guests from London what you told the sheriff you saw at the rectory—that's a good lad."

Put on the spot, Joe hangs his head and mutters. Someone in the audience says helpfully, "The deflowering."

We sit back in surprise. As far as we know, "deflowering" has but one meaning.

"Her name was Annie Morris. She was a baker's daughter from Swindon." Joe speaks in a low but clear monotone, perhaps as he did when he reported the incident to the town authorities. "She was sixteen. The Reverend gathered everyone around the altar, his wives and all us followers, and she lay on it while he preached. He said he was like a refiner's fire, and he was going to purify Annie. He was going to channel the Holy Spirit's love from heaven to earth, through his flesh to Annie, from his soul to hers. Then . . ."

Joe raises his hands and drops them. The spectators murmur in disapproval.

"Wait," Barrett says, jolted out of his silence, his expression filled with disbelief. "You mean he . . . right in front of everyone?"

Joe nods.

"Yes, indeed." Mrs. Norton says. She and other women titter with scandalized delight.

Patrick Eden-Smith had sexual relations with a young girl, in a perverted religious ceremony! It seems tantamount to public rape, a crime far worse than bilking rich women out of their fortunes. Never mind that I already thought him guilty of murder; I'm still flabbergasted by this proof of his vileness.

"What happened?" Barrett asks. "Was the Reverend arrested?"

"No," Mr. Norton says. "It was Joe's word against his. Nobody else would talk."

"Annie kept mum," Mrs. Norton says. "She went around looking as innocent as an angel. All the while her belly grew bigger and bigger. Nine months later, she had a baby girl. She named it Humility."

Fresh astonishment accompanies my revelation. Humility, the third child whom Patrick Eden-Smith is passing off as his daughter by his late first wife, is his illegitimate child conceived during the sacrilegious rite.

"After Humility was born, the Reverend gave a sermon about her," Mr. Norton says. "He said the devil had fathered the child with Annie."

That explains why Humility is called "devil child." I pity the girl, born of Eden-Smith's violation of her mother. Detested and abused by his women, she's paying the price of his sin. Her existence, which I've verified myself, is evidence that the story I'm hearing now is true.

"The news spread like wildfire," Mrs. Norton says. "People from as far away as Yorkshire came to see the virgin, the devil child, the Reverend, and his wives."

"The bishop revoked the Reverend's license to preach in this diocese," Mr. Norton says.

"He should've defrocked him," Mrs. Norton says.

"Only the Roman Catholics do that, Mother. Not the Church of England."

"What happened to Annie?" Barrett seems interested in spite of himself.

"Skipped town," Mrs. Norton says, "with all the rest of them—the Reverend, his brides, and his other women who lived at the rectory. One night, they bundled themselves into carriages, went to Swindon Station, and boarded a private train car to London. They've not been seen in these parts since."

So much for Reverend's story about leaving his previous parish because he wanted to spread his gospel farther and wider and grow a bigger congregation. He'd fled to escape scandal and censure and to preach in a jurisdiction from which he wasn't banned.

"What's the Reverend been up to in London?" Mr. Norton asks.

The people in the room angle their chairs toward us, the better to watch and hear. It's our turn to tell tales. Barrett surprises me by speaking. "He's started a new church called the Haven of Love. And he's a suspect in a murder."

Our audience reacts with exclamations of surprise and disbelief. Mrs. Norton says, "Well, I never. He didn't look like a killer."

"Who's he supposed to have killed?" Mr. Norton says.

"One of his followers," Barrett says, "a woman named Louisa Nussey." He doesn't mention the Torso Murders. I think he's finally ready to consider the possibility that Eden-Smith murdered Louisa, but he draws the line there.

"Well, go on," Mrs. Norton says eagerly. "How did she die?"

Barrett explains that Louisa's wrists were slit during what might have been a murder staged to look like suicide. The villagers murmur in dismay. Mr. Norton says, "Nothing like that has happened in Ashlade in my time, and I've lived here all my life."

"Were there any unsolved murders while Reverend Eden-Smith was here?" Barrett asks.

"Not hereabouts," Mr. Norton says, "but in Swindon, yeah. Off the top of my head, there was a man pushed onto the train tracks and a woman beaten to death in her lodgings."

Those crimes seem unrelated to the Torso Murders, but I'm overjoyed to see Barrett acting the detective, taking part in the investigation. He asks, "Did any women go missing?"

"Some were never seen again after the Reverend and his people left," Mrs. Norton says. "We all assumed they went with him."

Barrett takes the names of the three women the villagers recall went missing. I hope the women are contentedly ensconced in the Haven of Love. No matter that I'm hanging onto my theory that Patrick Eden-Smith is the Torso Murderer, I don't want to learn that more women have been killed and dismembered.

"I'll say this about the Reverend," Mr. Norton says. "I never saw him raise a hand to anyone. Even when his enemies disrupted his sermons or attacked him in the streets, he didn't fight back."

"He turned the other cheek," Mrs. Norton says, "just like a good Christian."

My theory takes a serious blow. I think Dr. Lewes would suggest that a man who refrains from defending himself against verbal and physical assaults lacks the personality to murder and dismember women, and Patrick Eden-Smith also lacks the skill.

"Besides, he didn't need to fight back," Mr. Norton says. "His followers did it for him. The police had to break up the riots more than once."

"He did leave a lot of bad feeling," Mrs. Norton says. "Some folks who disagreed about him still aren't speaking. Two of the women he didn't take with him were sent to the insane asylum."

"So Louisa Nussey wasn't his only follower to meet such a bad fate," Barrett remarks.

"By the way," Mrs. Norton says, "Is Ruth still with the Reverend?"

"Who is Ruth?" Barrett asks.

"Ruth Talbot," Mr. Norton says. "One of the two 'spiritual brides' he married after Miss Julia died."

"The Reverend has three brides," I say. "Merciful Saint, Anointed One, and Light of Heaven. I don't know their real names."

"Merciful Saint, that's the name he gave Ruth when he married her," Mrs. Norton says. "The railway heiress, but she didn't act like you would expect an heiress to act. She went to medical school in London. She worked at a hospital in Swindon, but she gave it up when she joined the Reverend's church."

CHAPTER 27

Riding in the cab to Swindon Station, I say to Barrett, "Merciful Saint must have performed dissections in medical school."

"It could be a coincidence," Barrett says. "It doesn't mean she and Reverend Eden-Smith are connected to the Torso Murders."

My theory has evolved in response to the story we heard at the Lamb Inn. "Maybe he kills the victims, and she dismembers them."

Barrett shakes his head. "She was a doctor who took care of sick people. It's a stretch from that to murder."

"She's jealous of his other women. And I'm sure he doesn't want any more 'devil children.' Murder, dismemberment, and dumping the bodies would be a good way to get rid of pregnant 'brides' and prevent another scandal." I remind Barrett, "He was run out of Ashlade. He wouldn't want to be run out of London."

"Which would be the bigger scandal—pregnant brides or getting caught murdering them?" Barrett says, "The man's an unsavory character, but I don't think he's stupid."

"I believe he's vain enough to think he can get away with murder. And if he is the Torso Murderer, he hasn't been caught yet. It's time for another visit to the Haven of Love."

Barrett rolls his eyes, then cracks a wry smile and says, "Open mind."

⋆ ⋆ ⋆

Our session with the villagers enlivened Barrett's spirits, but on the train ride back to London, they sink again and my attempts at conversation peter out. By the time we get to Whitechapel station, he's lapsed into silence. His steps slow as we near our house. Home used to mean sanctuary, comfort, and peace to us, but now it's as if homecoming is, for Barrett, a return to all that's wrong and dreaded. My own spirits plummet as I fear more than ever for his mental state.

I unlock the front door, and we go upstairs to find Mick and Hugh standing in the parlor, all smiles, eager to greet us. Mick is tossing a coin in the air and catching it. "We thought you'd never get back!"

Excitement cheers me up, and Barrett's face brightens; our friends obviously have good news. "Did you find the nurse who disposed of Elizabeth Jackson's body?" I ask.

"Unfortunately, no," Hugh says. "Tim Porter quit the Garratt Lane Workhouse infirmary. Nobody there knows where he went. I checked some other workhouses and hospitals, no luck. I'll try other places tomorrow."

Gloom descends on Barrett again. "If he's smart, he'll have skipped town. He could be anywhere in England—or out of the country."

"Don't give up hope," Hugh urges.

"I went to London Bridge and talked to hundreds o' people," Mick says. "I found some who seen Violet Pearcy. None of 'em heard what she said before she went off the bridge. Sally's notice is in the *Daily World*, but it's too soon for any witnesses to come forward." He speaks fast, as if eager to get the bad news over with. "But look at this." He hands me the object he was tossing.

It's not a coin but a gold ring, sized for a woman's finger, set with a large, pale green stone that looks to be a peridot, surrounded by tiny white pearls. Black dirt clogs the setting, but the gem is as sparkly as the genuine ones in expensive shops, and the ring is heavy, surely made of real gold.

"Where did you get it?" I ask, puzzled regarding both the ring's origin and significance.

"From my friend Roddy. He's a dredgerman." Mick pauses; his eyes twinkle with glee.

"So he found the ring in the river. So what?" Barrett says.

"Yeah, in the river. With some other interestin' stuff." Mick grins as he draws out the story.

Sensing that the find is important, I demand, "What stuff?"

Hugh laughs. "Keep her waiting any longer, and she'll throttle you."

"Awright, awright," Mick says. "Roddy told me he found the torso when he was scavengin' along the river by Horsleydown Stairs. Last Thursday, at about seven in the morning."

"That's about three hours before I did." I'm surprised because it never occurred to me that I wasn't the first to discover the torso.

"Why didn't he report it to the police?" Barrett says, his interest roused by this new development in the Torso Murder case.

"Because he didn't want them to know he stole somethin' off it," Mick explains. "The torso were wrapped in a fur coat. The ring were sewn into the hem."

Comprehension stuns me as I gaze at the ring in my hand. "The coat and the ring must have belonged to the victim."

"Where's the coat?" Barrett asks. He's concerned about the evidence, a good sign.

"Roddy sold it," Mick says. "But he kept the ring. He's been showin' it around the pawn shops, tryin' to get the best price. I had to pay him six pounds."

Six pounds seems to me a bargain price for a such a valuable clue. "The ring could help us identify the victim! I'll take a photograph and run it alongside a story in the *Daily World*."

"Be sure to include the owner's first name," Hugh says.

I frown, not understanding. "How do you know her name?"

Mick's grin broadens. "Look on the inside of the ring." He hands me a magnifying glass.

Peering at the tiny letters engraved on the ring's inner surface, I spell out, "M-A-R-I-A-N-N-E." I laugh with sheer elation. "This could be the clue that solves the case!" I feel certain we're getting close to the Torso Murderer, whether or not it's Reverend Eden-Smith. "Good work, Mick!"

"Thanks." He bows with theatrical panache.

"Oh God." Barrett stares at me, as dumbfounded as if I'd whacked him for no reason. He claps his hands to his temples.

"What's wrong?" I ask.

He drops his hands; shakes his head. "It can't be. But—"

"Go on, man, spit it out," Hugh says encouragingly.

In a breathless voice, Barrett asks me, "Do you remember you stopped by the morgue on the day of the inquest? A man and wife came to view the remains."

"Yes." Confused, I picture the pale, bespectacled man vomiting and his wife with a silver rose on her coat lapel.

"Mr. and Mrs. Basil Winters," Barrett says. "The man's sister is missing. Her name's Marianne."

Hugh, Mick, and I exclaim in astonishment: "Marianne Winters!"

"You identified the Torso Murder victim!" I'm thrilled, not only because this is a gigantic step toward solving the case. It's also an achievement for Barrett at a time when his pride desperately needs a boost.

"Bravo!" Hugh slaps Barrett on the back.

"It could be a coincidence," Barrett says. "There must be more than one woman named 'Marianne.'"

I think he's afraid to hope too much, especially after he couldn't make a case against Severin Klosowski, and his investigation into Violet Pearcy went terribly awry despite the fact that he'd solved one of the Torso Murders.

"No coincidence," Mick says, adamant. "You put a name to the victim, and you did it while Inspector Reid had you stuck on the sidelines. While his old task force hasn't done squat."

"Maybe." Barrett tries to suppress the smile that tugs at his mouth.

"We should go talk to Mr. Winters immediately," I say.

"I brought my notebook home when I was suspended," Barrett says. "His address is in there."

⋆ ⋆ ⋆

Some four miles southwest from Whitechapel and a world away, affluent Belgrave Square consists of four splendid terraces of white stucco neoclassical houses ranged around a private garden several acres in size. Barrett and I walk past the hedge that encloses the garden, which contains plane, chestnut, and lime trees, wooden pergolas, gravel walks, and a tennis court, all veiled in fog. There's a white detached mansion at each of three corners of the square. The mansion occupying the north corner corresponds to the address that Mr. Basil Winters gave Barrett. It's four stories high, an asymmetrical but elegant study in interlocked geometric shapes. A bow front forms a half cylinder attached to the rectangular main structure. The main entrance is behind a portico built into a three-story octagonal turret. The mansion is even grander than the Nussey house in Mayfair. The Winters family must number among the wealthiest in London.

Barrett wields the polished brass knocker on the door. My heart beats fast within a band of apprehension that tightens around my chest. Far more than the identification of the latest Torso Murder victim rides on the outcome of this call. If Barrett solves the case, it could impress the top police brass enough that they'll accept his version of the circumstances of Violet Pearcy's death, thwart Inspector Reid's attempt to charge him with murder, and restore him to active duty. And then, I hope, he'll revert to his normal, steady self.

A gray-haired man, presumably the butler, answers the door and greets us with haughty courtesy. Barrett says, "I'm here to see Mr. Winters."

"Whom shall I tell him is calling?"

"Detective Sergeant Barrett, from the Metropolitan Police, and Mrs. Barrett."

I'm glad to hear my husband use his professional title. It suggests that he believes he'll soon regain his full right to it. The butler hesitates. I suppose the usual visitors don't include the police. He lets Barrett and me into the octagonal hall, which has a white marble fireplace and pink-velvet-covered benches. A staircase with a curlicue black iron railing leads to the upper gallery. The butler leads us to a large parlor. Within paneled walls painted mint green, a huge crystal chandelier with three racks of glowing gas lamps hangs from the high ceiling. A Turkish rug in shades of rust, green, and ivory partially covers a parquet floor. The butler gestures us to one of a pair of pink velvet settees by another white marble fireplace. He lights the fire but doesn't offer to take our coats or serve us refreshments; he presumes we won't be staying long. I'm happy to keep my coat on, since the fire provides scant warmth in the cold, drafty room.

"One moment, please." The butler exits the room.

While we sit and wait, we hear the noises of children shouting, running, and stomping upstairs and a man's laughter. The chandelier quivers; its glass prisms chime. Maids in black uniforms and white aprons and caps peek through the door at us. Word of police in the house has spread quickly among the help. After some minutes, Mr. Winters enters the parlor. The thin, pale man wears a gray pinstriped business suit and polished black shoes, but his white shirt collar and dark blue tie are crooked, as though he'd dressed hurriedly after his playtime with his children was interrupted. His damp hair, slicked back from his balding pate, shows lines from combing. When he sees Barrett, his eyes blink behind his spectacles.

"Oh. You're the officer from the morgue." His complexion turns greenish, as if meeting Barrett reminded him of the grisly remains. "What is this about?"

"There's been a new development in the Torso Murder case," Barrett says. "Perhaps you'd better sit down."

Mr. Winters perches on the edge of the settee opposite us. He sits very straight, braced for bad news.

"I'm sorry to say I believe I've identified the Torso Murder victim as your sister Marianne," Barrett says.

Mr. Winters jerks backward as if Barrett's words struck him like a battering ram. *"What?"* Disbelief tinges the horror that fills his eyes. "How do you know it's Marianne?"

"We've learned that the torso found on the riverbank was wrapped in a fur coat." Barrett reaches in his pocket and takes out the peridot ring. "This was found sewn into the hem. Do you recognize it?"

When he passes the ring to Mr. Winters, the man moans while his trembling fingers caress the engraving inside the ring.

"It belongs to Marianne. It was a birthday present from her godmother. The peridot is her birthstone."

Barrett and I murmur our condolences. Mr. Winters says, "But those remains in the morgue can't be Marianne! I just saw her. She isn't dead."

Barrett's expression shows the same surprise and concern that I feel. Is the victim not Marianne Winters? Have we made a mistake and troubled Mr. Winters for nothing? Moments ago, the solution to the case seemed close enough to touch; now it recedes into the distance like a train I've missed. But if the victim is someone else, then how did Marianne's ring turn up with her remains?

"When did you see Marianne?" Barrett asks. I perceive his effort to hide his disappointment. If Marianne is alive, that's a good turn of events for her family, and we shouldn't mind that she's a false lead for our investigation.

"On April second," Mr. Winters says.

That was two weeks before the torso washed up on the riverbank and the notices asking the public to identify the victim appeared in the *Daily World*. She could be Marianne Winters, murdered after her brother last saw her. Caught between hope, confusion, and pity, I say, "If you thought Marianne was alive, then why did you go to the morgue to see the remains?"

"I didn't want to go. It was my wife's idea." Mr. Winters flops his hands in a gesture of helplessness.

I'm more confused than ever. Barrett says, "Do you mean, your wife thought Marianne was still missing and might have been murdered?"

"Yes." Mr. Winters casts a frightened glance toward the door. "She's out visiting. She'll be home soon."

"Why didn't you tell her you'd seen Marianne?" I ask.

Mr. Winters rubs his hands down his face, distorting his features into a mask of horror and shame. "Oh God."

"You'd better tell us what's going on," Barrett says in a gentle but authoritative voice.

"I don't want her to know! You mustn't tell her."

I avoid looking at Barrett, although I can feel his gaze on me. The issue of marital secrets hits too close to home. Barrett says, "We'll keep this as confidential as possible."

Mr. Winters crumples, relieved to shed the burden of his knowledge, willing to risk the chance that it will become public. "Marianne never married. She was pretty and charming, and after she made her debut, she was courted by several eligible gentlemen. But she was more interested in books and learning. She wanted to study philosophy at Oxford. Father and Mother didn't want her to, but they couldn't stop her. She had her own fortune, an inheritance from our aunt, and she could do as she pleased."

I sense that Barrett is as impatient as I, but we let Mr. Winters talk, the least we can do for him. It seems possible, even likely, that he'll have to face the death of his sister.

"After she completed her studies, she obtained a position as a tutor to female pupils at University College. Our parents didn't approve."

Marianne had been another woman whose interests diverged from those of her family and caused an estrangement.

"She came to live with me," Mr. Winters says. "She and my wife never got along, but she loved our children, and they loved her. Everything was more or less all right until last year. Then Marianne started staying out late. Sometimes she didn't come home until the next morning. When I asked her where she'd been, she said she'd joined a new church that had evening services and prayer meetings."

Barrett and I turn to each other, startled by this unexpected turn in Marianne's story. I speak through the hope that rises in my throat. "What church is that?"

"It's called the Haven of Love."

I feel as if I've been tinkering with random gears, cylinders, rods, cranks, and pistons, and suddenly they've clicked together to form a steam engine that roars into thunderous motion. I see the stunned expression on Barrett's face, surely a mirror image of mine. *We've connected Reverend Patrick Eden-Smith to the Torso*

Murders! My heart beats wildly; every muscle, bone, and fiber of me tingles with electric excitement, and I can hardly sit still. I press my lips together to keep my expression calm and my voice from bursting out in a triumphant cheer.

Mr. Winters continues his story, oblivious to its effect on us. "At first, I thought that if Marianne wanted to stay out late, church was better than taverns and music halls. But this past February, she went and didn't come back. My wife was upset because she thought Marianne was ruining our family's reputation. But I said Marianne was a grown woman, and we should mind our own business. A week passed with no word from her. Then I looked in her room and discovered she'd left all her books. Then I knew something was wrong. She loved her books; she would never go off and leave them behind.

"So I went to the Haven of Love—by myself. I didn't tell my wife because she would have wanted to go with me, and I was afraid of a scene between her and Marianne. When I got there, I found Marianne at the rectory. I barely recognized her. She was wearing a plain gray dress and a white headkerchief. She looked like a nun." His face crinkles with the puzzlement he must have felt. "I asked her what was going on. She said she'd married the pastor and become his spiritual bride—or rather, *one* of his spiritual brides." Mr. Winters grimaces in revulsion.

A spinster like Louisa Nussey, estranged from her parents and at odds with the society into which she'd been born, Marianne had sought a place in another sort of family.

"I told her I thought she'd lost her mind. The pastor was a bad character, and he'd tricked her into immoral behavior. I said I was taking her home immediately. But she refused to go with me; the Haven of Love was her home now. And then she said . . . she said . . ."

Mr. Winters hunches his shoulders, looks around to see if anyone besides Barrett and me is within earshot, and lowers his voice. "She was with child. The pastor's child."

After my trip to Ashlade, the news that Reverend Eden-Smith's marriages to his spiritual brides aren't strictly spiritual comes as no surprise. Neither does the news that at least one of those marriages resulted in conception. But it's a new development in the case. Dr. Phillips didn't note any sign of pregnancy in the latest Torso Murder victim, but it would have been difficult or impossible to see because the internal organs were missing.

"I couldn't take Marianne home." Obviously, her pregnancy was a rude shock to Mr. Winters. "Not in her condition. What would our family and friends and the neighbors say? So I left her there. What else could I do?" He plaintively appeals to Barrett and me for understanding and validation.

Her pregnancy had made Marianne not just an inconvenience to Patrick Eden-Smith, but a threat. I want to tell Mr. Winters that he'd abandoned his sister to an evil man who murders and dismembers women, but it's not necessary. Mr. Winters breaks down and sobs. "He killed her, and her child! Oh God. If only I'd made her come home with me, she would still be alive!"

She'd been thrown away twice—by Patrick Eden-Smith, who needed to get rid of her before another scandal threatened his standing in the Church, and by her brother because she was a disgrace to the Winters family.

Barrett inhales deeply, exhales, and shakes his head. I can tell that even if he solves the case and regains his job, he'll regret this moment when he brought grief to this man. So will I. This is a painful reminder of the times when my own actions cost other people their lives. The images of Polly Nichols, Annie Chapman, Liz Stride, Kate Eddowes, and Mary Jane Kelly materialize before me, ghosts invisible to everyone else.

"You couldn't have known what would happen," I tell Mr. Winters.

Lack of foresight is no comfortable excuse for me, and it isn't for him; he weeps, inconsolable. Barrett says, "The ring is Marianne's, but that doesn't necessarily mean the remains are hers."

But I'm as certain as I've ever been about anything. As soon as Barrett connected the ring with the couple who came to the morgue, I knew to the core of my soul that Marianne Winters is the latest Torso Murder victim. Mr. Winters's story is mere confirmation, my belief as fixed as the planets in their orbits.

"Marianne, I'm sorry, I'm sorry," Mr. Winters laments; he, too, is convinced. "Oh God, how am I going to tell my wife? And the children?"

In the street, carriage wheels clatter to a halt by the house. A moment later, I hear the front door open and a woman's voice greeting the butler. Mr. Winters gasps and jumps up from his chair, his tearful eyes suddenly wide with horror.

"That's my wife!" he says in a loud whisper. "You have to leave before she sees you." He makes shooing motions at Barrett and me.

"You'll have to come to the Whitechapel Police Station and make a formal statement," Barrett says as Mr. Winters hustles us toward the back door.

"Yes. Anything you want. Just go now!"

Chapter 28

When Barrett and I arrive at home, nobody else is there. Barrett says, "We shouldn't go to the Haven of Love without Mick and Hugh."

"You're right." I'm impatient for action, but our previous confrontations with other murderers had required all hands on deck. If any of us hadn't been there to help the others, someone surely would have died.

I putter around the kitchen, fixing cold beef sandwiches with cheese and mustard. Barrett makes tea. The doorbell jangles, and my heart leaps as I hear our friends' voices. Mick and Hugh bound up the stairs, burst into the kitchen, and regard Barrett and me with expectant smiles.

"Well?" Mick demands.

I'm about to tell him and Hugh that we've identified the latest Torso Murder victim and connected her to the Haven of Love, but then I notice Sally behind them. This is one among a very few occasions when I haven't been glad to see my sister.

"I came to see if you've learned anything new." Sally bubbles with excitement. "Mick and Hugh told me about the ring."

"Did you talk to Marianne's family?" Hugh asks.

Barrett starts to answer. I step hard on his foot. He says, "Ow!"

"Sorry." To Sally, Hugh, and Mick, I say, "The family wasn't home. The servants refused to speak with us."

Barrett glances from me to Sally and back again. Comprehension dawns on his face. "We'll have to try again tomorrow."

Sally's face falls. Mick says, "Aww, rats."

"Next time's the charm," Hugh says.

"I made supper. Sally, would you like to join us?" I say, hoping we can get rid of her fast.

"Thank you, but I'd better run along. I've a few things to do." Sally blushes and hastily departs.

"Could 'a few things' include an assignation with a rival reporter?" Hugh says with a mischievous smile.

Any other time, I would eagerly speculate, but as soon as I hear the front door close, I slap sandwiches onto plates while Barrett sloshes tea into cups. "Eat fast. We're going out."

"Where?" Mick wolfs down his sandwich.

"To the Haven of Love." Barrett says with a rueful smile, "I hate to admit it, but Sarah was right. Reverend Patrick Eden-Smith is our prime suspect for the Torso Murders."

Surprise lifts Hugh's eyebrows. "How so? I thought you didn't get anywhere with the Marianne clue."

"I wanted Sally to think so," I say.

"We spoke to Mr. Winters," Barrett admits. "The ring belonged to his sister Marianne. Turns out, she was one of the Reverend's 'spiritual brides.'"

"Blimey!" Mick says. "But why'd you keep Sally in the dark?"

"Because I didn't want her going to the Haven of Love with us," I say.

"She wouldn't want to be left out," Hugh says.

"I know." Guilt fills me. This could be the culmination of the case, the climax of the big story that could win Sally her longed-for promotion. "But it could be dangerous."

Mick's expression darkens with comprehension. "Yeah. Remember all the bad stuff that's happened to us before. Killers don't like getting nailed."

"Like it or not, the Reverend will pay for his crimes," Barrett says.

* * *

The brick church blends with the fog, its steeple and towers invisible amid the darkness. The white marble eagle, bull, lion, and winged man above the entrance stand out from the murk as if liberated from their pedestals and ready to defend the Haven of Love against trespassers. Their stone eyes glare down at Mick, Hugh, Barrett, and me. Although it's seven thirty and the street is deserted, the stained-glass windows glow with brilliant color. I didn't look closely at them last time, and now I notice they're depictions of saints. Male and female, they all have Patrick Eden-Smith's face. We hear faint organ music and joyful singing.

"This must be the Reverend's wedding to Emily Clifford," I say.

"Well, then," Barrett says, "let's have a look in the rectory while he and his people are occupied. It may take more than Marianne Winters's ring and her brother's story to convince a jury that he's the Torso Murderer. I'd be happier with additional evidence."

While Mick picks the lock on the iron gate behind the evergreen shrubs, Barrett wanders out to the street. I accompany him and ask, "What's the matter?"

Raising his hand to silence me, he peers left, right, and straight ahead through the fog. "I thought I heard someone following us."

Not again. I stifle my irritation and my fear that his suspicious fancies have taken control of his mind. I didn't hear anything, but I don't want to say so and upset him. "If anyone is following us, it's not the Torso Murderer. He's in the church, getting married."

"Sarah. Barrett," Mick calls softly, beckoning us to the open gate.

We slip into the garden. Lamps on posts illuminate a gravel path that leads away from the back of church, into the fog. It seems an invitation to our destiny. I shrug off the notion. The Haven of Love folks must have lit the lamps so they could find their way home easily. Barrett pauses, looks around for his imaginary pursuer, then hurries to catch up with us. Our footsteps crunch on the gravel. The music in the church should prevent the Reverend and his flock from hearing us, but I hope there's nobody in the house. My pocketbook is heavy with the weight of my gun. We'd debated whether to bring our weapons, and we agreed that it's better to be prepared than sorry. As we pass the playground, the swings move in the breeze, their chains clink, and I imagine the ghosts of Humility and her sisters swinging. I'm becoming as fanciful as Barrett. The rectory comes into view, its chimneys, gables, and crenellated ramparts hazy in the fog and the glow from lights in the ground-floor bay windows. I lead the way to the door through which I entered last time.

"I'll do the honors." Mick makes speedy work of the lock.

Inside the house, the passage is bright with lamps that reflect in the mirrors and shine on Patrick Eden-Smith's portrait. White roses and lilies fill an urn on the hall table. Their scent overlays his fetid body odor. A glance into the dining room shows me the table set with silverware, crystal goblets, white candles and linen, and porcelain dishes for the wedding banquet. The Chinese vases that Anointed One and Light of Heaven argued over contain more lilies and roses. The elaborate white wedding cake, covered with a glass dome, holds pride of place under the Reverend's portrait. I put my finger to my lips. We stand still and silent for a moment, listening.

All we hear is the hiss of the gas lamps. Everyone who lives here must be at the wedding. I motion my companions toward the basement stairs. Mick uses matches from his pocket to light the lamps on our way down. There's no singing or machinery noise this time, and the hot, humid air smells of roast meat and baked goods. The laundry is neat and clean, but the scullery is a shambles of dirty pans, dishes, and utensils, crumbs and splatters on the floors. In the kitchen, pots simmer on the stove. I open ovens and see roasted chickens and legs of lamb keeping warm. Barrett examines carving knives. Mick peruses the bread baskets and the covered serving platters that sit on the worktops; he steals and munches a biscuit.

"How can you eat something that was cooked in this house?" Hugh exclaims. "They cut up bodies of murder victims."

Mick swallows, licks his lips, and shrugs. "They must've cleaned up before they cooked."

"Right," Barrett says. "We aren't going to find any evidence. Let's go to the church."

Heading for the stairs, I spot something I didn't notice previously—a door by the entrance to the laundry room. "Wait."

The wooden door is in a corner of the passage where the light from the nearest lamp barely reaches, and painted gray to blend with the stone walls. We gather around it, and I twist the knob; it's locked.

"I can't open that." Mick points to the shiny brass lock. "It's the newfangled kind that can't be picked."

We all look at each other.

A current of reckless daring flows between us.

I stand back while my companions kick the door. The thuds are so loud that I cover my ears and hope the noise won't carry to the church. The door bursts inward as Barrett, Mick, and Hugh exclaim victoriously.

Strong fumes of disinfectant from the room make us cough. Mick strikes a match, then locates and lights lamps. It's a chamber with tiled walls and floor that resembles a cross between an infirmary and a morgue. There's a metal table with a low rim around its sides, long enough to accommodate a human body. A pipe connects a hole in the tabletop to a drain in the floor. Glass-fronted cabinets contain bottles of medicine and chemicals labeled with skulls and crossbones. I open drawers to reveal an extensive assortment of knives, saws, scissors, and scalpels.

"This is where they did it. I can smell the blood." Hugh's voice is muffled by the handkerchief he holds over his nose and mouth. "Excuse me." He backs out the door.

We've found the scene of the dismemberments, if not the murders. I feel more horror than triumph. I picture a naked dead woman lying on the table; Merciful Saint in a butcher's apron, sawing at the corpse's neck; and gore trickling down the drain. A wave of nausea swamps me. Barrett opens a closet, releasing a stench of spoiled meat. I swallow acrid bile.

"This is where the parts must have been kept before they were dumped in the river," he says. It's a cold-storage pantry with brown stains on the wooden shelves. A melting block of ice drips into a drain on the floor.

"Ugh," Mick says as he and Barrett and I envision torsos, limbs, and heads crammed into the pantry.

"Evidence doesn't get any better than this," Barrett says with somber satisfaction. "Time to arrest Reverend Patrick Eden-Smith."

We find Hugh waiting outside the rectory, and we all hasten back to the church. When Barrett twists the door handle, it readily yields. "Wasn't this locked?"

We all look at one another; we shake our heads; we don't know. In the excitement of our find at the rectory, we can't remember trying the church door. "Never mind," Barrett says.

We steal into the church. The scent of flowers is sweet, cloying, and funereal. In the chancel, the Reverend and Emily stand face to face before the altar, he handsome in black clerical garb and white surplice, she rosy and plump in her white wedding gown and veil. The altar is draped with a white cloth and backed by a vase of white lilies on a plinth and white candles in a silver candelabra. Near the organ, the dozen women in the choir wear pale blue robes. On the opposite side of the bridal pair, Patrick Eden-Smith's three wives and three daughters stand, adorned in pastel spring frocks and hats, the wives wearing white rose corsages, the daughters holding baskets of flowers. Some twenty other women occupy the front pews; all I can discern of them is their oversized hats, suitable for a garden party. Nobody seems to notice Barrett, Hugh, Mick, and me as we slip into a pew at the back of the church. The organist plays the opening bars and melody of "Love Divine, All Loves Excelling."

"Love is boundless," Patrick Eden-Smith intones. "Love does not flourish within the constraints of mortal law, but within the infinite abundance of God. Love in marriage shalt not be restricted to one man and one woman, but generously spread. In the presence of God and this congregation, Emily and I have sworn our wedding vows. Now I proclaim us husband and wife." He takes Emily's hand.

"Thus are we joined," Emily says breathlessly. "Nothing and no one can separate us."

"God is love, and God lives in us," the wives murmur with syrupy smiles. They betray no hint that they mind sharing their husband with the new bride they hate.

"Male and female has God created us," the Reverend says. "Now the two shall become one flesh." He puts his hands around Emily's waist and lifts her onto the altar.

Now I notice that the white altar cloth is a sheet draped over a mattress. My companions and I exchange startled glances.

"How beautiful you are, my darling!" Eden-Smith says to Emily.

How handsome you are!" she responds.

In unison, they recite, "'I am my beloved's, and my beloved is mine.'"

I recognize the verses from the Song of Solomon. Girls at school used to recite them to each other, pretend they were talking to boys, and giggle naughtily.

Emily lies back on the altar. "Kiss me!"

Her bridegroom bends over her and kisses her passionately. "'Your lips drop sweetness as the honeycomb. Milk and honey are under your tongue.'"

"'My beloved is radiant.'" Emily strokes his head and face. "'His hair is black as a raven, his cheeks like beds of spice yielding perfume.'" She moves her hands down his body and gasps. "'His arms are rods of gold, his body is like ivory, his legs like marble pillars.'"

The Reverend caresses her bosom. "'Your breasts are like twin fawns that browse among lilies. You are a garden locked up, my bride.'"

Emily raises her knees, spreads her legs. I glimpse white satin slippers as she scoots her buttocks to the edge of the altar. "Let my beloved come into my garden!"

My companions and I stare in shock. Mick whispers, "Are they really gonna . . .?"

The Reverend pushes Emily's skirts and petticoats up to her waist, exposing her plump legs in white stockings and lacy white garters. He opens his trousers, positions himself between her thighs. "Open to me, my love!"

His three wives move to the altar. Merciful Saint holds Emily's right hand. Anointed One and Light of Heaven hold her left. They smile with tight lips. This must be tame compared to the deflowering that got Reverend Eden-Smith dismissed from his previous parish, but it's a blasphemous parody of a traditional wedding. Humility smirks; her sisters are solemn. The audience and choir murmur with anticipation, naked longing on their faces. I think there's not one of them who wouldn't trade places with Emily.

Emily raises her hips and moans. The choir sings:

"Love divine, all loves excelling,
Joy of Heav'n to earth come down;
Fix in us thy humble dwelling;
All thy faithful mercies crown!
Jesus, Thou art all compassion,
Pure unbounded love Thou art;
Visit us with Thy salvation,
Enter every trembling heart."

Breathless with arousal, the Reverend says, "If anyone objects to this marriage, speak now, or forever hold your peace."

Barrett stands up and raises his voice above the organ music and humming of the choir. "What happened to Marianne Winters?"

Chapter 29

Barrett's timing is perfect. Hugh and I nod in admiration, and Mick stifles a laugh as we rise from our seats and accompany Barrett up the aisle to the chancel. Patrick Eden-Smith, Emily, the three wives, and the entire assembly turn toward us. In the front pews, heads crowned with flowery hats swivel. Each face shows surprise, confusion, and displeasure. The music trickles off into discordant notes.

"Detective Barrett. This is a private ceremony." The Reverend remains standing between Emily's raised knees, his crotch hidden by her skirts. "Go away."

"Patrick Eden-Smith, this is a murder investigation," Barrett says. "We're not leaving until you answer my question: What happened to Marianne Winters?"

This is the first time I've seen Eden-Smith enraged, and he doesn't display the reddened complexion, blazing eyes, or bared teeth that ordinary angry men do. His features remain smooth and handsome, but it's as if they've hardened into transparent glass, and I can see through them to a snarling demon within him. The transformation is so discomfiting that my companions and I flinch.

This must be how he looked when he killed Marianne Winters, Louisa Nussey, and his other victims.

"Make them leave, Beloved Lamb," Emily whines. "They're spoiling our wedding."

The Reverend says to the women in the pews, "Escort these intruders out of my church."

The women rise and advance down the aisle toward us, their pastel taffeta dresses rustling, the flowers on their hats bobbing. With their white-gloved fists clenched, their expressions grim, they bring to mind soldiers marching toward battle.

"Holy hell," Mick says, half amused, half daunted.

The women are a few paces from us when we realize they won't hesitate to use physical force to obey their master's order. We know from experience that women can be as dangerous as men, and these are in thrall to a killer. Remembering violent incidents from the past, I start to suggest that we come back tomorrow with reinforcements. But Hugh, Mick, and Barrett succumb to the masculine impulse to stand and fight, to carry out their mission rather than slink away in embarrassed defeat. They draw their guns.

"Stop right there," Barrett orders the women.

Vivid memories of gunshots and screams, blood and death, make me dizzy. The old wound in my shoulder aches. My heart rebels against more violence, but my gun is in my hand. My body reacted on blind, involuntary instinct, a creature of bad habit.

The women stumble to a halt. They stare in confusion, as if they've never seen guns before. Perhaps they haven't. Alarmed, they look to their master for guidance.

With rough, angry motions, he fastens his trousers and steps away from Emily. She scowls at us as she sits up and pulls down her skirts.

"You would shoot my innocent flock, in my house of worship?" Eden-Smith's voice is harsher, deeper, and more resonant than his usual suave one, as if the demon in him is speaking.

"I can arrest you," Barrett says, "and we can have this conversation in jail if you prefer."

Eden-Smith glowers, torn between wanting to stand pat and fear of being hauled away in handcuffs and thrown in with the riffraff at the jail. "I don't know a Marianne Winters."

"But she was your spiritual bride," Anointed One pipes up. The Reverend furiously waves his hand to shush her, but she says, "Don't you remember her, Beloved Lamb?"

I realize she's unaware of his crime. In her innocent stupidity, she's confirmed that Marianne indeed had been a member of Haven of Love.

"Marianne went home weeks ago," Anointed One tells Barrett. "Leave us alone." She huffs with righteous ire.

Light of Heaven nods in puzzled agreement; the Reverend must have kept her in the dark as well. But Merciful Saint looks wary.

"Marianne never made it home." Barrett says. "She's dead."

Amid murmurs of surprise from the other women, Barrett explains, "She was cut in pieces. Her torso and left leg and foot were found in the river. They're at the morgue now. The rest of her is still missing."

"Well that's certainly terrible." Although Patrick Eden-Smith musters a semblance of his normal suave composure, his face still has that glassy, artificial look, and his eyes are black with the rage of the creature inside. "But whatever happened to Marianne has nothing to do with us."

"By the way, Marianne was pregnant when she died. The child she was carrying is gone, too." Barrett pauses. "*Your* child."

Gasps of shock burst from the women. Humility giggles while the other girls stare blankly. Light of Heaven blurts, "She was with child? By you?" She beholds the Reverend with wounded indignation. "Why *her*? Why not me?"

Emily clutches her stomach and looks both frightened and mischievous. I'm not really surprised to deduce she's not only having sexual relations with Eden-Smith; she's pregnant.

"That's not supposed to happen," Anointed One says. "It didn't happen." She sounds as if her denial is meant to convince herself. "Spiritual marriages are purely spiritual."

She must not have an intimate relationship with the Reverend. I bet that no matter how much money she gave him, her birthmark put him off.

Barrett asks Eden-Smith, "Did you kill Marianne so she couldn't bear the child and there wouldn't be a scandal like the one in Ashlade?"

The news that his past has caught up with him provokes only a sneer from Patrick Eden-Smith. "Checked my background, did you, Detective? How clever of you."

Merciful Saint sidles behind her fellow wives, as if to evade Barrett's attention. I call out, "Dr. Ruth Talbot. Did you cut up Marianne's body?"

Merciful Saint blanches at the sound of her real name. She quickly molds her features into an expression of contempt and refuses to dignify my question with an answer.

A babble of protests erupts from the audience and choir. "How dare you slander Beloved Lamb? "God should strike you down!" "Beloved Lamb is the Holy Spirit incarnate. He could never do such a vile thing!"

It's just as I thought—most if not all the other women are oblivious to their master's true nature. Either his charm has blinded them, or they refuse to see. But I don't hear anyone defending Merciful Saint; she must be unpopular.

"All you did was dismember a dead body," Barrett tells her. "That's not a capital crime. If you cooperate with me and testify against Reverend Eden-Smith, you won't even go to jail."

Merciful Saint presses her lips together, but they tremble; she's not as impervious to the accusations as she would like to be.

"If you don't cooperate, you'll be tried and convicted as his accomplice," Barrett says.

"You'll both hang," Mick says.

I hear the other women whispering frantically among themselves, see their worried looks. The church is like a beehive clawed open by a bear; the bees agitate while their home falls apart and the honey leaks out. The sharp, alert expression on his face says Reverend Eden-Smith understands that not all of his flock are as enthralled by him as Anointed One and Merciful Saint. We interlopers have undermined the other women's faith in him, and he'll lose them unless he takes fast action.

"My brides, my sisters—we're under attack from the forces of evil," he says. "Because we are not of the world, therefore the world hates us. Yea, and all that will live in Jesus shall suffer persecution."

"You ain't Jesus," Mick says. "You're a crook who rapes virgins."

Amid another outcry from the women, Eden-Smith points at Mick, Hugh, Barrett, and me. "These people were sent by the devil to destroy us. Blessed are we who are persecuted, for ours is the kingdom of heaven. They are blind and ignorant."

"You're the ones he thinks are blind, ignorant, and gullible," I tell the women. "Open your eyes!"

Undaunted, the Reverend says, "They don't recognize the Holy Spirit when He's standing right in front of them."

"He's not the Holy Spirit," Barrett says. "He's a murderer."

"If you stick around long enough, you'll end up like Marianne Winters—cut to pieces and dumped in the river," Hugh says.

"Having no happiness of their own, they envy us ours." The Reverend's voice and body swell with righteousness. "They would lay waste to everything we've worked hard to build together."

"*He* hasn't worked a day in his life," I say scornfully. "All he's done is bilk you out of your fortunes and wrap you around his finger."

"Though I be maligned by them, I have no fear, because you are too intelligent to fall for their tricks."

"Don't fall for no more o' *his* tricks," Mick says.

"With your clear vision and pure hearts, you see the light of the Holy Spirit in me." Reverend Eden-Smith spreads his arm, evoking Jesus on the cross. "You see the darkness of lies and malice, and sin in them." He points an accusing finger at us, then extends his hands to the choir and audience. "O beloved sisters, you can trust me to lead you away from evil, along the path of righteousness."

"Dr. Talbot, he's led you into a conspiracy to cover up murders," I say.

Merciful Saint appears not to hear me; her besotted gaze is fixed on the Reverend, who says, "Rely on me to interpret the mysterious workings of God. Have confidence that everything I do is for love of you, for our mission, and for God and all His creation."

How he must love to hear himself talk! His rich voice rolls through the church like a wave intended to wash out all disbelief.

"But not everyone is sympathetic to our mission. Satan himself seeks to destroy us because we're thwarting his aim of spreading hatred, strife, and misery throughout the world. This is a holy war!" Eden-Smith thunders.

"Amen," the women chorus. He's blowing smoke at the bees, stupefying them into obedience.

"Satan has mustered the forces of darkness against us. And even I, your Beloved Lamb, the manifestation of the Holy Spirit, is not invulnerable." The Reverend lowers his voice to the intimate tone of a confession. "Every man hath physical desires. So hath every woman. Those desires are weapons in the hands of Satan. He possesses man and woman, works his evil magic on them, and renders them unable to resist their desires. He causes illicit unions to occur. Nature takes its course, and those unions sometimes bear fruit."

That he blames Satan for his own impregnation of Marianne Winters! Outraged, I start to protest, but Barrett shushes me.

"Those fruits are not the issue of man and woman, but the progeny of Satan himself—devil children," the Reverend says. Everyone looks at Humility, who stares back defiantly. "They're put on earth to shame the righteous. I say, again, this is a holy war!" He pounds his fist on the altar. Emily giggles with delight. "We must not surrender. If a seed planted by the devil should take root in forbidden soil, we must employ every skill and talent among our flock." Eden-Smith casts an approving glance at Merciful Saint. "We must cut the fruit from the vine."

Merciful Saint smiles beatifically at him. My companions and I look at each other in astonishment. Hugh asks, "Is he saying what I think he is?"

I can't believe my ears. The Reverend seems to be divulging that after he got Marianne Winters pregnant, Dr. Ruth Talbot performed a surgical operation to abort the child so it couldn't be born, wouldn't besmirch his reputation, and the church authorities wouldn't ban him from preaching in every parish in England.

"In every war, blood is shed," he says. "Noble is the blood that flows in the service of God. I bless those who made the ultimate sacrifice. They have not died in vain. They rest in peace, their bodies and souls purged of the devil's issue."

Now he's saying Marianne bled to death during the abortion. I think of Louisa Nussey, and snatches of the words I heard from her at Ticehurst Hospital come back to me with stunning force: *"Behold, for the Holy Spirit has come upon you . . . You have conceived the son of God . . . When Rachel saw that she bore no children, she envied her sister . . . Where jealousy and selfish ambition exist, there will be every vile practice. Bloodshed followed bloodshed . . ."*

Another stunning revelation follows: Louisa too had been impregnated by Reverend Eden-Smith and subjected to an abortion by his wife. That's why he killed her—to ensure her silence. She'd told me her story, couched in Biblical quotes that I had failed to understand. Perhaps the traumatic experience was the cause of her madness.

"Bless those who perform the act of mercy." Eden-Smith favors Merciful Saint with a radiant smile. She clasps her hands in prayer, trembles with adoration.

"The thief came only to steal and kill and destroy." If I'd had any doubt that it was Merciful Saint who also dismembered the victims, it's gone now.

"And bless the handmaidens who travel by night to strew the earthly vestiges upon the waters." He gives his daughters a fond look, and they smile in return.

I picture them riding in a carriage filled with wrapped-up body parts, through dark, foggy London, to dump the parts in the Thames. The police wouldn't think to stop and search a carriage occupied by children and nannies. I remember Mr. and Mrs. Norton at the Lamb Inn, saying the Reverend had his followers to do his dirty work. Those include his own daughters!

"May the waters wash the sin from those who fell in our battle against evil. They are fallen angels. May their souls rise to heaven and take their rightful place with God."

This, then, is Reverend Eden-Smith's rationale for murder and cutting up corpses. He doesn't mention that the dismemberment made the victims nearly impossible to identify and trace to the Haven of Love. To admit such a self-serving motive would tarnish the glowing image he wants his flock to have of him. And he's so arrogant that he thinks he can not only get away with murder but with preaching a sermon that's tantamount to a confession.

"All hail holy love!" the women cry.

Emily joins in, standing beside her bridegroom, smiling up at him through tears of joy. She seems to have no idea that what happened to Marianne Winters could happen to her, that she could be the next fallen angel in the river.

Light of Heaven is wild eyed, distraught, tearing her corsage to shreds. Patrick Eden-Smith's spell over her has worn thin. But she stays in her place, bound by her habit of worshipping him. Now I understand why Dr. Lewes's profiles didn't fit the crimes. Multiple participants, both male and female, were involved. The man is the reckless seducer, and the women meticulously clean up his messes.

"Patrick Eden-Smith and Ruth Talbot, you're under arrest," Barrett says.

The Reverend laughs. His loud, feckless mirth rings through the church, echoed by titters from his women. "You think to lock me in a cell, drag me to court, and have me convicted and hanged? It won't work. You've no evidence against me."

"I heard you confess," Barrett says.

Mick says, "Yeah." Hugh and I nod.

The Reverend draws back with exaggerated indignation. "I certainly did no such thing." He asks the women, "Did I?"

Light of Heaven frowns and chews her mouth, but the other women chorus, "No, Beloved Lamb."

"My witnesses outnumber yours," Eden-Smith says smugly to Barrett. "If you arrest me, my solicitor will have me out of jail tomorrow. You'll look a complete fool."

"We've been in your basement," I say. "We saw the room where Merciful Saint operated on Marianne Winters and cut up her body and stored it after she bled to death."

The Reverend shrugs even as Merciful Saint cringes. "You *think* you saw. You broke into my house and found the infirmary where my wife attends to our sisters when they're ill. There's naught to prove anything wrong ever happened there."

"We'll see about that. Come along." Barrett pulls handcuffs from his pocket and beckons the Reverend with his hand that holds his gun. I'm glad to see him back on the job, performing his duty as if he has both the right and the enthusiasm for it. Still, I wonder whether a jury will convict Patrick Eden-Smith and Merciful Saint based on what we've seen and heard tonight.

The Reverend descends the three steps from the chancel and strides down the aisle toward Barrett. Emily, Merciful Saint, and Anointed One follow him. Only Light of Heaven remains standing by the altar with its mattress and rumpled white sheet. The organist strikes up a militant tune, and the choir sings:

"Onward, Christian soldiers!
Marching as to war,
With the cross of Jesus
Going on before."

"Chain me, and I shall break free." Eden-Smith advances until his chest is within inches of the muzzle of Barrett's gun. "Shoot me, and yea, though I might die, I shall rise again, just as Jesus rose."

"Christ, the royal Master,
Leads against the foe;
Forward into battle,
See his banners go!"

Barrett, Hugh, Mick, and I gape, dumbfounded by the most bizarre situation we've ever encountered. This man seems to truly believe what he's saying.

"The Holy Spirit is strong in me, invincible to the slings and arrows of mortal men. By the grace of God, I shall live for all eternity!"

A loud bang resounds. Patrick Eden-Smith staggers backward as if someone had shoved him. His eyes enlarge with astonishment, and he clutches his chest. A red stain on his white surplice spreads beneath his fingers. He opens his mouth to speak, but only a grunt emerges. His gaze goes blank, and he crumples to the ground and lies motionless. The sulfur smell of gunpowder overlays the scents of lilies and burning candles. After a moment of shocked silence, the women begin to scream. My comrades and I look at one another in confusion.

"I didn't shoot him," Barrett says.

"Neither did I," I say.

Hugh gulps, struggling to control the nausea provoked by the sight of blood. He and Mick shake their heads. We all stare at our guns, as if they might have fired themselves. Merciful Saint, Anointed One, Light of Heaven, and Emily drop to their knees beside the Reverend. My companions and I turn around to see where the shot came from.

Mick voices our utter bewilderment. "What the hell?"

Chapter 30

Not ten feet behind us, in the pews to the left side of the aisle, stands Inspector Reid. Clad in a mackintosh and derby, his face radiant with exultation, he holds a gun pointed at the spot where Patrick Eden-Smith had stood.

Barrett asks one of the questions among the many that flood my mind. "How did you get here?"

"I followed you. While you snooped around outside, I jimmied the lock on the door." Reid sounds impatient, as if these are trivial details for which he doesn't have time.

So Barrett was right when he thought someone was following us. I'm ashamed that I thought it a figment of his imagination. Reid had been here in the church the whole time, secretly watching and listening.

"Thanks, by the way," Reid says. "You led me right to the Torso Murderer. I heard his confession." He gestures with the gun toward Patrick Eden-Smith.

The wives kneel over the fallen man. Anointed One chafes his wrists in an attempt to revive him. Merciful Saint presses her hands to the bullet wound on his chest, trying to stanch the flow of blood, then feels his neck for a pulse. Emily cradles his head in her lap, crying, "Husband, speak to me!"

Eden-Smith doesn't answer. His body is limp, his mouth slack, his eyes half closed. The horror on Merciful Saint's face tells the tale. The other women begin wailing, tearing at their hair and clothes. The daughters whimper. To my dismay, the confrontation I hoped would end peacefully has ended in violence and death. My comrades and I stare in shock; this is so unprecedented, such a bolt out of the blue.

Shaking his head in disbelief, Barrett says, "You can't just kill somebody like that."

Reid laughs, triumphant and sardonic. "I just did."

After the Irene Muller and Charlie Holt fiasco, he must have been humiliated and desperate enough to step outside the bounds of police procedure. He figured that Barrett, although suspended from duty, wouldn't stop investigating the murders and might solve the case before he himself could. Reid had covertly followed us in the hope that we would discover clues he could use.

I'm outraged by Reid's actions but disgusted with myself because I never anticipated them. "You spied on us."

"I took a gamble," Reid says. "It paid off better than I expected."

"We should have guessed," Hugh says. "He thinks we're hiding secrets about the Ripper. Why wouldn't he believe we might be hiding secrets about the Torso Murderer? Why not follow the rainbow to the pot of gold?"

Alas, Reid knows us too well, and we didn't know him as well as we thought.

Barrett's face darkens with anger at Reid. "I was going to arrest Eden-Smith. Why didn't you help me instead of killing him?"

"You heard that 'confession' of his. He beat around the bush six ways to Sunday. It would never hold up in court. It was either kill the bastard or let him get acquitted." Reid bursts into crazed, ecstatic laughter. "By God, I got him. The Torso Murderer and the Ripper!"

He still believes the two are one and the same. Patrick Eden-Smith is dead and can't deny that he's the Ripper. Nothing will convince Reid he's wrong. But although he's proven himself incorrigibly deluded, my feelings toward him undergo a stunning transformation. He's taken the law into his own hands to deliver a criminal to justice. He and I aren't such birds of a different feather as I once thought.

Emily points her finger at Reid and sobs. "You killed my husband!" Her wedding gown is stained red with Eden-Smith's blood.

Anointed One raises a tearstained, stricken face. "You crucified him as the Romans crucified Jesus."

Women in the choir weep. "O God, how could you forsake us?" The daughters begin to sob.

Merciful Saint rises, a picture of hatred and fury. "I shall call the police."

Reid stops laughing long enough to say, "I *am* the police."

"Then what are you going to do?" Barrett demands.

Reid's exhilaration deflates like a balloon when the air is let out. Suddenly sober, he says, "I'll make a full report about what happened here. Things will take their course."

I feel a new respect for him. When he shot the Reverend, he must have known his actions would have consequences. Now he's ready to accept them, come what may.

"You shot the guy in cold blood." Mick speaks as if he still can't believe his eyes.

"I did," Reid says with no trace of the scorn he usually displays toward us. "And it's your duty to say so when you're questioned about this."

He knows better than to ask Mick, Hugh, Barrett, or me—of all people—to lie for him to his superiors. He's so confident that he rid the world of the Ripper and the Torso Murderer, so certain he did the right thing, that he doesn't care whether he loses his job, his reputation, and his life.

"Give me your gun." Barrett extends his open palm to Reid.

Without argument or resistance, Reid hands over the weapon. Barrett pockets it. My respect for Reid turns to something like admiration. It's a peculiar feeling, as if the world has tipped on its axis, and in order to stand up straight, I have to tilt my body at an unnatural, precarious angle.

The women pay no attention to our talk as they weep for their master. Anointed One wipes her tears and says, "Do not be alarmed. Beloved Lamb will rise again. He promised."

Her words provoke babbles of joyful relief. Emily cries, "The Lord will descend from heaven, and with the sound of the archangel's trumpet, the dead shall rise."

Anointed One takes hold of the Reverend's shoulders and shakes him gently. "You are the resurrection and the life. You will never die."

Hands clasped, their bodies swaying with passion, the women loudly pray, moan, and beseech, as if their noise itself could pull Eden-Smith back over the threshold between this world and the next. Reid looks astonished by the scene he caused.

Emily kisses the Reverend and begs, "Awake! Live again!"

Merciful Saint bends over him, puts her mouth on his, and blows her breath into him, as if to aid the miracle of resurrection. Anointed One, Light Of Heaven, and the other women lift their eyes, as if they expect a divine light to shine through the roof. Eden-Smith remains silent, motionless; Merciful Saint's breath fails to restore his. Prayers and pleas dwindle into moans as his flock realize he's a corpse that nothing can reanimate. Merciful Saint sits back on her heels, her lips stained with blood that oozed from the Reverend, her face white with shock. Emily keens as she cradles him and rocks back and forth. The children begin crying again. Anointed One stares in disbelief. The other women grope for one another's hands, seeking comfort.

They've all lost their faith as well as the man they loved.

My companions and I avert our gazes from them, ashamed to witness such a personal, shattering tragedy caused in part by our own actions. I feel a terrible pity for the women's ignorance and blindness, their innocence and misplaced loyalty. For their Beloved Lamb, they threw away their families, their fortunes, and everything else they had, and now that he's gone, they have nothing. But I'm sorriest for the children. That I lost my father gives me only a hint of the devastation they must feel. Their father was killed before their very eyes, and he isn't going to come back like mine did. Reid watches the assembly with derision, as if they're fools who got what they deserved. I abhor his callousness, but he and I can agree on something: The world is better off without Patrick Eden-Smith.

Light of Heaven wails, "He wasn't the Holy Spirit." She staggers to and fro, as if buffeted by the cruel wind of reality. "He was just a man—a mortal man!"

Anointed One and Merciful Saint bow their heads, their last hope of Eden-Smith's resurrection gone. The other women hug one another as the church fills with the sound of brokenhearted weeping.

"I didn't want to believe it," Light of Heaven blubbers. "He was a fraud. And I gave up everything for him. Oh God."

I remember hearing her express her doubts about joining the Haven of Love; now her disillusionment is complete. She looks around, like the survivor of an earthquake viewing the ruins. "I should have left long ago. But I loved him. I loved him so much, even though he never loved me, he only wanted my money." She clutches her chest and sobs. "I loved him even though in my heart I knew what he was—a selfish, vile, greedy, grasping cad."

Anointed One covers her ears with her hands. Merciful Saint looks bitter; and Emily, oblivious of everything except her own grief.

"I severed my ties with my family and friends," Light of Heaven says. "I have nothing; I have nowhere to go. All I can do now is tell the world what happened inside the Haven of Love, so no one else will be taken in by someone like him ever again."

She steps down from the chancel and addresses Reid. "I was there during the operations."

Caught off guard, Reid says, "What operations?"

"On Louisa Nussey and Marianne Winters." Light of Heaven points at Merciful Saint. "He made me help her."

Merciful Saint's head jerks up. She glares at Light of Heaven, who says, "She needed a nurse. The other sisters couldn't stand the sight of blood. But my mother breeds horses, and when I was young, I watched them drop their foals." She smiles briefly at the memory before she reverts to anguish. "I held cloths soaked in ether over Louisa's and Marianne's faces. I handed her the instruments."

Merciful Saint hisses and flutters her hands at Light of Heaven, begging her to be quiet. Heedless, Light of Heaven says, "She scraped them out. Louisa was all right, but Marianne started bleeding. It wouldn't stop." She closes her eyes for a moment, as if to block out the terrible sight. Guilt thickens her voice as she says, "I watched Marianne die. And I cleaned up after she was cut in pieces and taken away. I will testify to it in court."

Horror silences the other women. Mick mutters, "Gorblimey." Barrett and Hugh look as flabbergasted as I am. Reid smiles as if a gift-wrapped present just fell into his lap.

"Well, thank you, Miss, Mrs. . . .?" Reid now has a witness to the crimes traced to the Haven of Love, evidence that the man he killed was party to a murder. I can almost hear him thinking maybe he's not in as much trouble as he thought.

"My name is Virginia Lythgoe." Proud yet forlorn, Light of Heaven reclaims her own identity.

Barrett moves toward Merciful Saint. "You're under arrest for murder. Come along."

She backs away, obviously terrified by the knowledge that with Patrick Eden-Smith gone, she'll bear the brunt of the punishment for the crimes in which she collaborated. Nobody moves or speaks to defend her. I can't feel as sorry for her as for the other women. She's a physician, trained to save lives, but she chose to use her skills to spare a selfish, arrogant man the bother of illegitimate children.

Marianne Winters died at her hands. She carved the corpse into pieces for his daughters to dump in the river. No matter that Patrick Eden-Smith had ordered the crime; Merciful Saint is the actual Torso Murderer.

"You're coming with us too," Reid tells the other women and the daughters.

I suppose there might be other accomplices or witnesses among them. Barrett and Reid will figure it out at the police station.

"We can't leave Beloved Lamb," Anointed One protests. "We have to perform the death rites for him." The other women raise a clamor of agreement.

"It'll have to wait," Barrett says. I can tell he's as impatient to leave the church as I am. Patrick Eden-Smith's blood is fouling the air with its sweet, metallic, meaty smell, and Barrett and Reid will have a long night of winding up this fiasco.

"Let them," Reid says. Perhaps he's feeling magnanimous because he thinks he's gotten what he wanted—the Ripper and the Torso Murderer sewn up in one albeit messy package.

Barrett frowns. "I don't think that's a good idea."

"That's an order." Perhaps Reid just wants to pull rank.

"Yes, sir," Barrett says reluctantly.

"Methinks the good inspector isn't quite ready to face the music," Hugh whispers to me.

Anointed One rises. All the other women look to her. She's only wife number three, but they seem to accept that she's in charge now. When she speaks, her voice is hoarse with grief, but she exudes a new authority. "Holy Lord, please deliver our Beloved Lamb from evil." She's stopped weeping; her religious zeal has burned away her tears. "Let him safely pass through the gates of death to dwell in eternal life in your blessed kingdom."

"God have mercy on our souls," chant the women.

Mick, Hugh, Barrett, Reid, and I bow our heads as we would at a funeral. I'm moved despite the fact that I don't mourn the deceased. The women's love for Patrick Eden-Smith was genuine, even though his claim to divinity wasn't.

"Lift us from the dark night of despair to the bright dawn of hope," Anointed One says, then walks out through a door at the side of the chancel.

During the few minutes while she's gone, the women repeat over and over, "'I am the resurrection and the life," sayeth the Lord. "Those who believe in me will never die."'

Anointed One returns bearing a silver chalice that's large enough to serve a church picnic. Standing over the Reverend's body, she intones, "He died and lived again, so that he might be Lord of both the dead and the living."

Is she speaking of Jesus Christ or Patrick Eden-Smith? Perhaps she thinks they're one and the same, just as Reid thinks the Ripper and the Torso Murderer are.

"Let us receive the blood He shed for you, that we may dwell in Him, and He in us, forevermore." Anointed One hands the chalice to Merciful Saint, who drinks deeply then gives it to Light of Heaven. I don't expect Light of Heaven to participate in this ritual after she renounced her allegiance to Patrick Eden-Smith and his church, but she drinks, perhaps due to force of habit. The chalice passes to Emily and from her, to each of the other women. The wine's faint, sweet, nutty scent mingles with the odor of the Reverend's actual blood.

Anointed One takes possession of the chalice. "'Whoever drinks His blood shall have eternal life.'"

"Amen," the others chorus.

A fit of coughing besets Merciful Saint. She clutches her throat. Mouth open, eyes wide with fright, she gasps. "I can't breathe!"

The same coughs, gasps, and breathlessness afflict Light of Heaven, then the other women. Amid panicky cries for help, they fall to their knees, their mouths spewing purple wine.

"Good God," Hugh says as realization alarms him and Reid, Barrett, Mick, and me. "The wine was poisoned!"

Chapter 31

Anointed One watches her sisters choke, her face alight with unholy exhilaration. "We shall not die, but we shall be changed." She offers the chalice to Humility, Fortitude, and Atonement.

"Don't drink it!" Barrett rushes toward her, puts himself between her and the girls. Before he can snatch the chalice, she raises it to her mouth, drains it, and lets it fall. Wine spatters.

The women are on the floor, gagging and convulsing. As Hugh, Mick, and I hurry to help them, Anointed One laughs triumphantly, her mouth as purple as her birthmark. "We shall be reunited with Him in Heaven!"

"I'll be damned," Reid says, his voice hushed with awe and disbelief. "*She* poisoned the wine."

I crouch beside Light of Heaven. Her face is swollen and blue, her fingers curled into claws at her neck, as if she'd tried to tear it open to let in air. Her eyes bulge. She's not moving or breathing, and when I yell her name, she doesn't answer. I feel her wrist for a pulse; there's none. I look up to see Hugh kneeling by Merciful Saint, her wrist in his hand. The expression on his face reflects my horror. She too is dead.

Anointed One forces her voice out between gasps and wheezes. "Neither death, nor the powers that be, nor things present, nor things to come, can separate us from Him!" She crumples to the floor, grunting as her body spasms.

My horror collides with astonishment. She killed herself and her sisters! I'd known she was a fanatical worshipper of her

Beloved Lamb, but never did I suspect she would go to such lengths as to follow him into death and take the others along. She threw away their lives and her own just as certainly as his daughters had dumped Marianne's remains in the river. The sins of Patrick Eden-Smith and Merciful Saint are nothing to those of Anointed One. *She* is the Haven of Love's mass murderer.

Within seemingly the blink of an eye, all the women lie inert, lifeless, in unnatural positions, like dolls broken by an insane child. Barrett, Mick, Hugh, and I stand mute and dazed, as if we're soldiers on the field of a battle that ended in utter carnage. We're the only survivors except the daughters. They begin to sob.

"Don't be dead!" Humility cries. "I'll be a good girl from now on. I promise!"

She of all the children seems most upset, even though she was the least loved by her family. Perhaps she blames their deaths on her misbehavior, just as my childhood self once blamed my father's disappearance on my own.

"Excuse me." Hugh rushes out the door, and I hear him retching. The candles gutter in the draft that smells strangely of almonds.

"Cyanide," Reid says. "She must have used rat poison." He sounds detached, businesslike, as though he's surveying a crime scene to which he's just been called.

Barrett bends an angry, accusing gaze on Reid. "What now, guv?"

Reid shrugs. All his habitual expression—the anger and belligerence, the cunning and suspicion—has drained from his face. He has the vacant look of a man who's been hit on the head and is about to lose consciousness.

"You really cocked things up, Inspector," Mick says with stern disapproval. "If you hadn't let them have their funeral, this wouldn't have happened."

"If you hadn't come here, we wouldn't have sixteen people dead," Barrett says.

I flounder amid emotions so various, contradictory, and confusing that they rob me of speech. I'm horrified because out of all the dead, only Patrick Eden-Smith was truly evil; the others, including Merciful Saint, were his victims, enslaved by his power over their minds. I'm furious at Reid but awash in guilt because, in a way, the deaths are my fault. My inquiries led to the Haven of Love; I persisted in investigating it after Barrett tried to discourage me. If I'd left it alone, Eden-Smith would have gotten away with murder, but Anointed One wouldn't have staged a mass suicide.

Tonight's body count far outnumbers the Torso Murder victims. And we don't know for sure that Patrick Eden-Smith was responsible for more than the deaths of Louisa Nussey and Marianne Winters.

But my personal culpability doesn't end there. When Barrett thought someone was following us, I hadn't believed him. If I had, we could have caught Reid spying before tonight. My distrust of my husband put us all in the wrong.

"So what are you gonna do about this?" Mick demands of Reid.

The inspector shakes himself, first his head, then his whole body down to his knees, like a wet dog. When he stops, he's drenched in perspiration, pale, lucid, and sober, as if he'd been dunked in cold water. He says, "Christ."

No matter our role in tonight's events, the ultimate, official responsibility is Reid's, and he must realize that he has much more to explain besides the shooting of Patrick Eden-Smith. His friends in high places might have excused him for that, but an additional thirty-odd deaths resulting from his actions will cause a scandal for which they'll be after his head.

Hugh returns, wiping his mouth with his handkerchief. "Not only did you execute a man who hadn't been given the benefit of a trial by jury, you triggered a mass murder."

"I won't be the only one who's struck off the police force." Barrett gloats with satisfaction.

"I bet you'll hang," Mick taunts Reid.

"Which would get him off our backs for good," Hugh says. "Sarah, wouldn't you call that the silver lining in a very dark cloud?"

I don't answer. Some other emotion is rising through the horror, guilt, and regret in my mind, like a whale trying to surface in water covered by garbage. Something about this conversation doesn't sit right with me.

Reid straightens his shoulders. "So be it." His voice is clear, somber, and firm. He faces Barrett, Mick, and Hugh as if they're a firing squad and he's ready to accept his fate. "I took down the Ripper and the Torso Murderer." His eyes shine with pride. "That's worth whatever happens to me."

He looks noble, which disconcerts me. Nobility isn't a trait I usually associate with Reid.

My companions don't seem to notice anything different about him. Barrett says to Reid, "I'm arresting you for murder. We'll sort out the other charges at the station." He looks glad we've got the upper hand over Reid but distressed by the circumstances.

"Now you're in for it," Mick says with unabashed glee.

"Just deserts," Hugh says.

"Mick and Hugh, stay here and guard the crime scene until I can send out a police surgeon," Barrett says. "And keep a watch over the girls. Sarah and I will escort Inspector Reid back to Whitechapel."

He heads for the door while Reid meekly accompanies him. But I stand paralyzed by an emotion I never felt toward Reid before. It's a sympathy that rises above all the anger, hatred, and grudges I've stored up for more than two years.

"Wait," I call. "Can we talk for a moment?" I beckon to Barrett, Mick, and Hugh.

"You of all people should be chomping at the bit to see me take the fall," Reid says to me with a touch of his old scorn. "Are you getting soft in your old age?"

Ignoring him, I motion my comrades down the aisle. Hugh and Mick hesitate and glance at Barrett, who looks puzzled and impatient, then shrugs. He seats Reid in a pew and handcuffs his wrist to the short, sturdy pillar that supports the armrest. Then he and Mick and Hugh follow me. I stop near the door, my three men facing me across the aisle. The girls sit on the floor, ignoring us, lost in their own sorrow. Reid twists around in his seat to watch us while I speak in a quiet voice that he won't hear.

"We can't let him go down for this."

Hugh and Barrett frown, astonished. "Are you kidding?" Mick says.

"Sarah, what the hell?" Barrett's low, furious tone expresses the emotion that his stony face doesn't.

I feel a sense of inevitability, as if certain choices I made in the past all led up to this moment. The first click of my camera's shutter when I photographed Kate Eddowes naked in my studio was the spark that set an arsenal on fire, and gunpowder kegs exploded into a storm of events whose consequences weren't immediately evident. Now the dust from the conflagration has cleared enough for me to see what I must do. I struggle to find words to explain why I want to go against all common sense.

"Reid got rid of a murderer." That's only the simplest, obvious argument.

"Reid shot a man in cold blood," Barrett says.

"An evil, dangerous man who would have killed again if Reid hadn't stopped him," I say.

"It wasn't up to Reid," Hugh says. "It was up to the court to put the Reverend out of business."

I glance at Reid, who cups his free hand around his ear, trying to hear what we're saying. On the day that he and I first met, he was caught up in the explosion I'd ignited. He didn't know it at the time, but that day his fate fell into our hands.

"Reid should have arrested Eden-Smith," Barrett says. "He's such a stickler for correct police procedure; he should have followed it tonight."

"Eden-Smith and his followers would have denied everything," I say. "You heard him say so. It would have been our word and Reid's against theirs. And we're not exactly in favor with the police department."

"After everything Reid's done to us, let's give him tit for tat," Mick says stubbornly.

"Amen to that," Hugh says. "Sarah, let's not waste a once-in-a-lifetime opportunity."

"Reid has always used police procedure as a weapon against us," Barrett says. "Let him be hoisted by his own petard."

But I see Reid's cruel treatment of us in a new light—as an attempt to get justice for the Ripper victims and prevent more crimes from the killer he believed was still at large. "Reid only did what we ourselves did," I say.

It's as if a giant glass bell jar has descended on us, trapping us in a silent, stifling vacuum with the memory of the night in the slaughterhouse. My mind fills the silence with screams, howls, and terror. Then Barrett says, "That was different." He glances up the aisle at the dead women lying strewn across the chancel, the weeping girls.

Although I can't deny that Reid's actions caused more casualties than ours, I say, "He didn't know that was going to happen. Neither did we know what was going to happen when we took the law into our own hands."

"She's got a point there," Hugh says reluctantly. "I suppose the pot shouldn't send the kettle to the gallows."

"Yeah, well, I ain't helpin' him out," Mick says. "Not after how he treated Anjali."

"People helped us when we were in the same kind of trouble," I say. "If they'd turned us in, where would we be now?"

"Rotting under Dead Man's Walk, no doubt," Hugh says.

In Newgate Prison, executed convicts are buried under the paving stones of Dead Man's Walk, the corridor that connects the jail with Old Bailey.

"Yeah . . ." Mick shifts his weight from one foot to the other as his conviction falters. No matter how strongly he believes that one bad turn deserves another, he knows that without the help he received at crucial times in his life, he could have been dead—a victim of the streets—years ago. And now he's in a position to pass on the favor.

Barrett stands firm, arms crossed. "I'm not changing my mind."

This is the culmination of his war with Reid. Now Reid has made the mistake that turned the tide in Barrett's favor. I can taste the sweet, intoxicating flavor of his victory as if it were my own.

"Just for the sake of argument, suppose we don't turn Reid in," Hugh says. His soft heart balks at denying compassion to anyone, even the man who brought about the scandal that estranged him from his family. "What would we do instead?"

An alternative choice suddenly blooms like a strange, exotic flower in my mind, as if from a seed launched there by the explosion that I set off long ago. "We can have our cake and eat it too."

As I explain my plan, I feel sensations of brightness, lightness, and fresh air. It's not only a way to walk off the battlefield as victors without any more blood on our hands, but a chance to breathe easier from now on.

Barrett's eyes pop. "Of all the dirty tricks!" Revulsion twists his mouth.

Mick whistles in admiration. "Yeah, that's as dirty as it gets."

Hugh chortles. "I like it."

Appalled to find himself outnumbered three to one, Barrett says, "I don't want to be involved in another cover-up. Especially not for Reid!"

Barrett is my husband, and I love him and want to please him. I feel guilty because his association with me has compromised him so often, in so many ways. And here I am, asking him to besmirch his honor once again. Why not tell the truth about tonight's events and let matters take their course? Hugh and Mick will be as amenable as they initially were, Barrett will be satisfied, and as Reid will get tit for tat. But the prospect causes me a sensation of heaviness, darkness, and suffocation. How can I bring Barrett around to my point of view?

"Suppose we turn Reid in," I say. "Will it change the past?"

"Of course not," Barrett says impatiently, "but we can start fresh."

"How fresh a start can it be? Turning Reid in wouldn't erase Cremorne Gardens." I pause, then say, "It also won't erase the night in the slaughterhouse."

Barrett shakes his head violently, as if my words are wasps buzzing around it while his hands are tied. "Reid committed a crime. He deserves to pay."

"He isn't the only one," I say.

As Barrett stares at me, stricken by a truth he can't deny, Hugh says, "'For we are whited sepulchers, which look beautiful on the outside, but within are full of dead men's bones.'"

"Yeah, I heard that in church a hundred times," Mick says.

"The only way to clean the slate is for us to turn ourselves in," I say.

Mick and Hugh cross the aisle to stand beside me. Barrett gives me a brief, searching, chilling look. It's as though he's a constable on patrol, I'm a stranger encountered in a dark alley, and he's trying to figure out who I am—a harmless citizen or a dangerous criminal, friend or enemy. He glances at Reid, then back at me. Rebellion storms in his eyes. Everyone is waiting. Suspense hushes the air in the church.

Barrett expels his breath and slowly nods.

I feel no triumph, only that sense of inevitability and an uncomfortable premonition that this is another event that will have repercussions in the future. As we all walk up the aisle, Mick and Hugh follow close behind me. Barrett tarries after them, his reluctance audible in his every footstep. But when we gather around Reid, I see that Barrett's face is as stoic and unreadable as Mick's, Hugh's, and mine.

"Well?" Reid's eyes flare with hope. He must have imagined what's going to happen to him when we get to the police station, and the picture isn't pretty. He tries to hide his hope for a reprieve under an attempt at bravado. "What's the verdict?"

I speak the words he's said to me so many times. "I'm going to offer you a deal." I find neither humor nor satisfaction in turning the tables on him; I feel as if I'm reciting a line that fate wrote for me long ago.

Reid's puzzlement turns to suspicion. "What kind of deal?"

I hold out my palm to Barrett. He takes Reid's gun out of his pocket and gives it to me. I walk to Patrick Eden-Smith and put the gun in his limp, cold hand. Then I turn to face Reid.

Shock and relief vie with doubt on his face. "Why would you do me a favor? I never did you any."

"You haven't heard your side of the deal," I say, "but I don't think you'll turn it down."

Even before I explain his side, I watch enlightenment strike Reid. Dumbfounded, he shakes his head. Anger and incredulousness swirl in his eyes. Finally he speaks with grudging admiration. "You sons of bitches."

Chapter 32

The Working Lads Institute is located in a tall, red brick building on the Whitechapel High Street. Funded by charitable donations, it provides education and recreation for employed youths and beds for those without homes. It also serves other purposes, such as on this Friday morning, April 24—three days after the disaster at the Haven of Love.

In the library, rows of chairs are occupied by a chattering, noisy crowd of reporters, officials, and curiosity seekers. Photographers set up their cameras to aim at the end of the long, spacious room. There, Inspector Reid stands at a podium, beneath a portrait of the Princess of Wales. Barrett, Hugh, Mick, Sally, and I sit in chairs lined up on Reid's left. Reid talks to members of the task force, seated to his right. He wears a dress uniform resplendent with military-style decorations. The task force detectives are in dark plain clothes. My heart pounds with anxiety; cold perspiration dampens my hands and my skin under my clothes. I sit up straight, my face frozen in a stoic expression while inwardly I shrink from the audience.

My companions don't share my terror of being on public display. Mick calls to acquaintances in the crowd, all young men. He sometimes attends classes here and uses the gymnasium and swimming pool. Clad in a new suit, starched white shirt, and silk tie, he's delighted to be the celebrity among his friends, a star of this press conference. Hugh waves and smiles at Dr. Lewes, entering the room with other latecomers. Sally, seated at my right, happily exchanges greetings with other reporters. Only Barrett, on my left, is as somber and still as I am. He gazes straight ahead, his jaw tight.

Reid pounds the podium with a gavel. "Attention, everyone!"

The room quiets. Every seat in the audience is filled; latecomers stand against the walls. Flash lamps explode; sulfur smoke hazes the air; black afterimages pock my vision. I remember the last time I was in this room, more than two years ago. It was at the inquest for Polly Nichols, the Ripper's second victim; I sat in the audience, unnoticed and anonymous. Now Reid occupies the coroner's podium; my companions and I, the seats once used by the jury.

After introducing himself, Reid says, "I called this press conference to inform you about the new developments in the Torso Murder case." Puffed up with self-importance, he pauses to heighten the suspense that grips the audience.

I search the room for a friendly face to put me at ease. All I see are strangers who look as avid and predatory as hungry owls. I shift my attention to the landscape paintings on the walls.

"The Torso Murderer has been identified," Reid announces. "His name is Patrick Eden-Smith. He was the vicar of a church called the Haven of Love, in Primrose Hill."

Exclamations erupt from the audience, questions from the reporters. Reid holds up his hand. "Simmer down, boys. Listen, and you'll get the whole story." When the hubbub ceases, Reid says, "Reverend Eden-Smith held unconventional religious beliefs, including the idea that he was the Holy Spirit incarnate. He had several wives, a harem of vestal virgins, and other female followers. He came to our attention thanks to Miss Sally Albert, a reporter with the *Daily World*. Stand up, Miss Albert."

Sally rises, blushing and smiling as photographers take her picture and their flash lamps light her up. This is one part of the deal I made with Reid—credit where credit is due. I only regret that Reid had upheld his side of the bargain by including Sally, Hugh, Barrett, Mick, and me in his circus.

"Miss Albert had the brilliant idea of searching the personal ads for items about missing women," Reid says. "Her search turned up a Miss Louisa Nussey. Miss Albert and her fellow reporter and sister, Mrs. Sarah Barrett, investigated further."

He motions for me to stand. As I reluctantly obey, my legs quake. I endure flash lamp explosions and keen stares.

"Mrs. Barrett and Miss Albert found Miss Nussey alive, but not well, in the Ticehurst insane asylum," Reid says. "Her family had committed her there after she joined the Haven of Love and Reverend Eden-Smith induced her to give him her fortune. It seemed possible that the Reverend not only took advantage of other women, but also murdered them. He became a suspect. The Torso Murder Task Force thanks Miss Albert and Mrs. Barrett for their valuable contribution."

Amid enthusiastic applause, I gratefully sit down. Hugh smiles and nods at me; Mick gives a thumbs-up sign. Barrett's expression is cold. I catch Sally's eye, and the happy glow on her face dims. She's angry with me because I didn't include her in the expedition to the Haven of Love. She didn't know about it until the next morning, when I told her the official version of what had happened, the story that Reid has begun to tell. She's still upset because she missed everything. But how glad I am that Sally wasn't involved in the events of that night or my deal with Reid! When I explained that I wanted to protect her, she said she felt like a little girl left out by her older sister and her friends. Her big story for the *Daily World* is secondhand reporting, and I'm afraid that not even the coveted promotion Sir Gerald gave her will induce her to forgive me.

Sally focuses her attention on Reid, who says, "Another clue came from Mr. Mick O'Reilly, another reporter with the *Daily World*."

Mick stands up and grins for the cameras. His friends cheer.

"Mr. O'Reilly discovered that a dredgerman had found the torso before it came to the police's attention. It was wrapped in a coat. Inside the hem was a ring, which Mr. O'Reilly recovered. The ring was engraved with the name 'Marianne.' But the major break in the case came when Detective Sergeant Thomas Barrett linked the ring to a man who'd come to the morgue to view the torso. The man was a Mr. Basil Winters. His sister Marianne was missing. Stand up, DS Barrett. Don't be shy."

Barrett rises, stone-faced. He gazes over the heads of the audience while the photographers assail him with clicking shutters and explosive white flashes. He's barely spoken to me since that night. He comes home late from work, after I'm in bed. I know he and Reid have been busy with the aftermath of the Haven of Love disaster—the crime scene examination; the removal of and the autopsies on the dead; placing the three children in an orphanage until the proper authorities can figure out what to do with them; identifying the women and locating and informing their families. I've stayed out of it except to give my statement at the police station that night. Hugh, Mick, and Sally have been covering the story for the *Daily World* while I stayed at headquarters to develop and print the photographs I thought would never be needed. I let Barrett keep his distance from me. At night, I don't say, "I love you." I'm afraid he won't say it back to me.

"Inquiries by DS Barrett revealed that Marianne Winters had joined the Haven of Love. He promptly reported it to me." This is where Reid departs from the actual events that led up to the scene at the church. "Now we had a connection between the latest Torso Murder victim and Reverend Patrick Eden-Smith, thanks to DS Barrett and Mr. O'Reilly."

Barrett sits down, ignoring the applause. Ire radiates from him like heat from banked coals. Mick bows until Hugh pulls him into his seat. I think of the second visit Barrett and I made to Mr. Winters, the day after the Haven of Love incident. All we told him was that Patrick Eden-Smith had murdered Marianne, and a scandal was about to break. He heeded our warning and took his family to their summer home in Cornwall.

"On Tuesday night, DS Barrett and I went to the Haven of Love to arrest Reverend Patrick Eden-Smith." Reid's narration strays further from the truth about that Tuesday night. "Mrs. Barrett, Mr. O'Reilly, and their fellow reporter, Lord Hugh Staunton, came along to cover the story." That's the version of events that we and Reid fabricated before we left the church. "We interrupted Reverend Eden-Smith in the middle of his wedding to his fourth bride. When I accused him of murdering Marianne Winters, he broke down and confessed. He not only admitted that he did kill her, but he explained why he did it. At his previous church, his relations with female parishioners resulted in the birth of an illegitimate child. He was relieved of his post and run out of town."

The audience buzzes, titillated by this tale of ecclesiastic wrongdoing. The task force detectives wear the proud, satisfied expressions of policemen who've solved a major crime. But Mick told me they're furious because they were left out of the conclusion of the case.

"Reverend Eden-Smith couldn't afford another scandal here in London," Reid says, "so after he got Marianne Winters with child, he killed her. His wife, Ruth Talbot, who was a physician, dismembered the body. His daughters dumped the parts in the river." At the church, Reid had convinced the rest of us that simplifying the circumstances of and motives behind the crime would make it easier to understand and less likely to provoke questions. Above the excited chatter from the audience, he says, "DS Barrett, Mrs. Barrett, Lord Hugh, Mr. O'Reilly, and I all witnessed the Reverend's confession. But before I could arrest him, he took a gun and shot himself. His women drank poisoned wine. They all died."

That's how we had decided to explain the shooting and poisoning, to cover up Reid's role. I perceive a chill between Reid and the task force detectives. According to gossip that Mick heard at the station, when Reid told the detectives our story, they smelled a rat. They grilled Reid and Barrett, going over and over the events of that night, challenging every detail. Barrett stood by the story. That was part of the deal. But Barrett isn't happy with the cover-up, which was my idea. Hence, his anger at me.

"The Reverend couldn't bear to face public humiliation and death by hanging," Reid says. "His followers couldn't bear to live without him. But justice has been served. Without the expense and trouble of a trial, I should add."

A smatter of applause gains volume in the audience. Reid stops it by lifting his hand. "There were other developments in the case. Reverend Eden-Smith was guilty of one Torso Murder, but not all. DS Barrett discovered that victim number three, Elizabeth Jackson, died as the result of an illegal medical operation performed by a midwife named Violet Pearcy. He obtained

Miss Pearcy's confession." Reid briefly summarizes the story Violet told Barrett and me on the bridge. "Lord Hugh Staunton obtained a confession from a nurse named Tim Porter, who dismembered and disposed of Elizabeth Jackson's remains."

Yesterday, Hugh tracked down Tim Porter at the Essex Hospital in Colchester and persuaded him to turn himself in. He's in jail, awaiting trial for tampering with human remains and obstructing a police investigation. In exchange for his confession, he won't be charged as an accomplice to murder.

Neither will Barrett face charges associated with Violet Pearcy's death. That's also part of the deal.

Hugh stands and takes a bow. Barrett remains seated, his expression stormy. Reid explains that Reverend Eden-Smith's confession included the fact that he killed Louisa Nussey to keep her silent about the shady business at the Haven of Love.

"What about the Whitehall and Pinchin Street murders?" a reporter asks. "Was this Patrick Eden-Smith responsible for them too?"

"Those cases are still open," Reid says.

Mick, the font of gossip, says the task force is looking for connections between those cases and the Haven of Love. I don't know whether they'll find any.

"Previously you said you believed the Torso Murderer and the Ripper were the same person. Is it true?" another reporter asks. "Was Patrick Eden-Smith the Ripper?"

"We're investigating the possibility," Reid says.

He still believes it, but after a heated discussion at the church, he reluctantly agreed not to pin the Ripper murders on Eden-Smith—for the moment. That's because I pointed out to him that if he closes the Ripper case and then the Ripper kills again, he'll look a fool. Reid declared that he'll find evidence to prove Eden-Smith is the Ripper. Of course I didn't tell him how I know he won't.

Other reporters call out questions. Reid says, "Hold your fire, boys. I'll take your questions after Police Commissioner Bradford says a few words."

Commissioner Bradford, a tall, dignified man with white hair and mustache, rises from the front row of the audience. His empty left sleeve is pinned to the coat of his dress uniform. As he strides up to the podium, Reid motions for Barrett to join him and the commissioner. Barrett obeys, his face rigid with an expression that some might mistake for self-consciousness; I know it's a mask that hides disgust.

"In recognition of their exemplary service, I present Inspector Reid and Detective Sergeant Barrett with certificates of commendation," the commissioner says in his brusque voice.

A constable hands Reid and Barrett each a framed document resplendent with calligraphy, signatures, and official seals. Reid and Barrett pose for the cameras, holding their certificates and shaking hands with Commissioner Bradford. Sheepishness tinges Reid's smile. Barrett doesn't smile at all. I can almost smell the bad blood between him and the commissioner, the man partially responsible for the disturbing outcome of the Cremorne Gardens investigation, who put Barrett on the Torso Murders task force. The detectives applaud politely with the spectators. I can tell they resent Reid and Barrett for getting the major credit for solving the case. I think they also still have their doubts about the official version of the story.

Barrett and Commissioner Bradford take their seats, and Reid fields questions from the reporters. Hugh, Mick, and Sally contribute some answers. Fortunately, no one asks Barrett or me anything. I don't want to speak in front of so many people, and he doesn't want to lie in public. I know he's desperate to get away. I'm desperate to talk to him in private, which I eventually must, even though I'm afraid of what I'll hear.

When the conference finally breaks up, Barrett hurries out the door, leaving his framed certificate on his chair. I follow him, but people block my path, lingering to congratulate Reid, Mick, Hugh, and Sally. Constables clear the room, and I find myself alone with Reid.

We glower with our old antagonism as we face each other. Reid says, "You got what you wanted."

"So did you," I say, gesturing toward the certificate tucked under his arm.

He glances at it and says with a wry smile, "You charged me quite a price for it."

"From now on you'll leave my husband and friends and me alone," I say. That's the heart of the deal we struck. All the other concessions he made were icing on the cake. "Or we'll tell the world what really happened at the Haven of Love."

"You needn't rub my face in it." Reid speaks with a mixture of resentment and grudging respect. He knows we've bested him, and he can't afford to look a gift horse in the mouth. Then a touch of his usual malice brightens his eyes. "But you know, I don't need to hound you for information about the Ripper any longer. Patrick Eden-Smith was the Ripper. I know it even if that case is never officially closed." He's as mistakenly certain as ever. "Funny thing is, I don't think you ever had any information." He laughs and points his finger at me. "I finally believe you're as ignorant as you always claimed to be."

"Thanks," I say, thinking, *What a relief!* But so not worth the deaths at the Haven of Love. "Now, if you'll excuse me." I turn away from Reid and hurry out the door. I can't bear his presence; I feel soiled by the deal we made. I never want to see him again. That he must feel the same about me is no consolation.

Outside the Working Lads Institute, I start down the high street in search of Barrett and run into Hugh with Dr. Lewes, and Fitzmorris, who must have been at the conference.

"Congratulations." Dr. Lewes smiles at me. "That's a very interesting case you solved."

I force myself to meet his eyes as I thank him. The expression in them tells me the task force detectives aren't the only people who are skeptical about Reid's story. Once again, I wonder how much Hugh has told Dr. Lewes, but I really don't want to know.

"What's interesting is how we were right and wrong about the crimes," Hugh says. "Sarah was right to think the Haven of Love was involved. Barrett was wrong about Severin Klosowski but right about the identity of the most recent victim, Marianne Winters. We were all wrong to think all the Torso Murders were connected."

"Mick was right to believe in Anjali's vision, wrong about which case it applied to," Fitzmorris points out.

Hugh and I don't mention that Reid is wrong to believe Patrick Eden-Smith is the Ripper. We're not touching that thorny issue. Hugh says, "In the end, wrong plus right equaled justice."

Drawn into the conversation despite my need to find my husband, I say, "Dr. Lewes, of all the examples you described, the one that fits the Torso Murderer most closely is Martin Dumollard, the Frenchman. He had a female accomplice, his wife. So did Reverend Patrick Eden-Smith."

"The Reverend was the selfish, remorseless criminal who lacks empathy for other people," Hugh says. "Merciful Saint, also known as Dr. Ruth Talbot, was the disciplined, meticulous partner who covered up his dirty business."

"I can understand why she did," I say. "She was under his spell. But what made him what he was? The illness during his childhood? Overindulgence by his mother, his nurse, and the women he charmed?"

"Perhaps," Dr. Lewes says. "Or he may have been born that way. The human brain is a mystery. We psychologists don't have all the answers. But we'll keep looking." He sounds happy with the challenge.

Fitzmorris says he has an errand to run and excuses himself. Left alone with Hugh and Dr. Lewes, I say, "Where are you two heading?" I don't mean just at the moment.

The looks they give each other and then me say they know I'm talking about their relationship. Dr. Lewes says, "It's not uncommon for personal feelings to arise between a doctor and patient."

He seems to know Hugh told me that the two of them share the same sexual inclination. He also seems to be admitting they're not only more than doctor and patient but more than friends.

"But we're not jumping into anything," Hugh hastens to say. "Caution's the game. Mum's the word." He puts his finger to his lips as he smiles and winks at me.

That reassures me. A scandal would damage Dr. Lewes's reputation, and it's the last thing Hugh needs. But I'm also hopeful that Hugh has found true, fulfilling, enduring love.

"Sarah!" Mick hurries up to us. With him are Anjali and Dr. Lodge.

I greet them and say, "Were you at the press conference? I didn't see you."

"I wouldn't have missed it for the world." Anjali bubbles with happiness. "I'm so proud of Mick!"

Dr. Lodge's manner is characteristically grave. "Thank you for saving Anjali from Inspector Reid," he says to me.

"You're welcome," is all I say.

He knows I told Reid that Anjali's vision applied to the Elizabeth Jackson case. But he also thinks Reid isn't going to press fraud charges against Anjali because he now believes she really is psychic. However, Reid still distrusts Anjali, and he only let her off as another part of his deal with me. But Anjali is safe, Dr. Lodge is placated, and I gladly let the matter rest.

"Father and Mick and I are going out to lunch." Anjali says to Hugh, Dr. Lewes, and me, "Will you come with us?"

This is part of a new arrangement in which she and Mick will keep company only in the presence of Dr. Lodge or another chaperone he's approved. Everything will be proper and chaste while they see if their love will stand the test of time until she grows up. Dr. Lodge still doesn't consider Mick an ideal son-in-law, but he wants Anjali to be happy.

I wish the best for them, but I say, "I'm sorry, I can't go to lunch."

Hugh and Dr. Lewes accept the invitation. As I go off in search of Barrett, I see Sally standing on the corner. She beckons me. I hurry over; perhaps she's ready to make up. Then I notice Jasper Waring beside Sally.

"Jasper and I have something to tell you," Sally's eyes are bright and her cheeks pink with excitement.

Jasper smiles admiringly at her. Noting that they're now on first-name terms, I feel a pang of alarm. Could they have progressed so quickly from adversaries to an engagement?

"Jasper has a new job," Sally announces. "He's a reporter at the *Daily World*."

"We're on the same team now," Jasper says.

I stifle a sigh of relief. "That's wonderful." Although Jasper seems a nice young man, and perhaps not a bad match for Sally, she seems to be less keen on him than he is on her, and at any rate they need more time to get to know each other before making a major life decision.

"But that's not all," Sally says. "We're going to investigate the Ripper case together!"

"Oh." The alarm I felt a moment ago was nothing to the alarm that clutches my heart now. The last thing I need is anyone investigating that case. The last person I want to do it is my own sister.

Puzzlement creases Sally's brow. "What's wrong?"

"Nothing. I'm just surprised." I scramble for a way to dissuade Sally. "The Ripper investigation petered out a long time ago. There can't be any new clues to discover."

"Two pairs of fresh eyes might find some," Jasper says.

Stalling for time to think, I ask, "Did Sir Gerald give you permission?"

"Yes, I did."

Speak of the devil. It's Sir Gerald, accompanied by two of the tough, silent men who work for him as bodyguards and only he knows what else. He too must have been at the press conference. He says, "At first I thought it was a waste of my new senior reporter's time and my money, but Miss Albert talked me into it."

Jasper beams proudly at Sally as I regret the influence that she has over Sir Gerald.

"By the way, good job." Sir Gerald holds up a copy of the new extra edition of the *Daily World*, headlined, "*Torso Murders Solved!*" Illustrated with my photographs, the front page bears the story that Reid told at the press conference.

As soon as I told Sally the story, she wrote the article. Sir Gerald had the extra edition printed and ready to distribute that evening, but in cooperation with Inspector Reid, he held it back until today. His deal with the police is back on. Now he looks around with satisfaction at the newsboys hawking the extra edition, and he smiles at Jasper.

"We scooped all the other newspapers, including the *Chronicle*."

"Good." Jasper shows no loyalty to his former employer.

After Sir Gerald leaves us, I say to Sally and Jasper, "Chasing the Ripper really isn't a good idea. If you come up empty, Sir

Gerald won't be pleased. And he fires people who let him down. You could both lose your jobs."

"We won't let him down," Sally says with the overconfidence of youth. "I've learned a lot from the Torso Murder case, and Jasper is experienced with crime investigation. I think we've a good chance at solving the case."

"I would bet on you to accomplish anything you set your mind to," Jasper says.

Unfortunately, I would too. My little sister is just as determined as I am. *Oh God, how can I keep her from finding out the truth about the Ripper?* "Well, I wish you luck."

"You can do more than that. Sir Gerald said you can help us." Sally sparkles with enthusiasm.

My heart sinks. "I don't see how I can. You know Hugh, Mick, and I dabbled in the Ripper investigation. We didn't get anywhere."

"But you knew the victims. You might have information that you've forgotten."

"I don't think so. And the Ripper's trail is more than two years cold."

"The three of us working together would be able to shine a new light on the cold trail," Jasper says hopefully.

I shudder to think what a new light could reveal. "You'd better not count on me."

Sally's eyes brim with hurt. She thinks I don't believe in her and I want no part in a venture that's doomed to failure. Then her brows draw together, and I recall her asking me if I'm hiding information about the Ripper. As she opens her mouth to ask again, I say, "We'll have to talk later. I need to find Barrett."

I hurry away from her. She's stirring up a hornet's nest that I thought my deal with Reid had buried, stepping right into the shoes he vacated! It was one thing to keep secrets from Reid. Now I'll have to lie to my beloved sister. I tried to keep her out of danger, and now Barrett, Hugh, Mick, and I are in danger from none other than Sally.

I'm almost home, and Barrett is nowhere in sight. Probably he's gone off somewhere to avoid me. The thought of the cold, empty house fills me with desolation and slows my pace. Then I happen to glance into the alley beside the Angel pub. Barrett stands against the wall, in the murky shadows. He turns and sees me. Dare I hope that he's waiting for me, ready to talk? He looks uncertain whether to stay or run. I hurry toward him despite a flood of trepidation. How can I get us past everything that happened during the investigation? What can I say that will restore our harmony, our happiness?

Stopping a few paces from him, I blurt, "I'm sorry I forced you into it." I can't spell out the deal we made with Reid; someone might overhear, but Barrett will know what I mean. But although I am sorry—for coercing him, for putting my own wishes ahead of his—I don't regret the deal, and I can't say I do.

He stares at me, his face unsmiling, and I tremble with sudden fear. Has my refusal to say I was wrong offended Barrett past the point of no return? Did he wait for me so he could tell me goodbye before he leaves me?

Then he shakes his head. "I'm not upset with you. At least, not anymore."

"Then what . . .?"

"I wanted Reid to get his comeuppance. I still want it."

Is Barrett saying he's going to renege on the deal, to tell the truth about the night at the Haven of Love? My fear constricts my heart.

"But what does that make me? The pot who would send the kettle to the gallows. No better than Patrick Eden-Smith, who did away with people just to serve his own interests." Barrett's expression is dark with self-contempt. "That's not the man I want to be."

I'm astonished because I read him so wrong, never suspected he was feeling any of this. I hasten to correct his mistaken opinion of himself. "You're a good man. You didn't send Reid to the gallows. Thanks to you, he's alive and a certified hero."

"I didn't only because you stopped me." A rueful smile twists Barrett's mouth. "You were right, as usual."

Enlightenment strikes. "You let me stop you because you wanted me to. Because you aren't the pot, and you aren't like

Patrick Eden-Smith. If you were, I wouldn't love you." I move closer to Barrett until our faces almost touch; I infuse my voice with all my passion for him. "And I do love you."

I feel him relax as the familiar tenderness fills his eyes. "I love you, Sarah." But he still looks troubled. "Reid's done awful things to you. I'm a man who let him get away with tormenting my wife."

"He's done awful things to you, and to Hugh and Mick. But he didn't get away with it. We've got a hold over him now. Isn't that the best revenge?" Seeing Barrett's eyes brighten, I drive home my point. "If he were dead, he wouldn't care. This way, he has a long time to think about how you bested him and how indebted he is to you."

"Yeah." For the first time since that night, Barrett smiles. He says gruffly, "I'm sorry for shutting you out."

I smile too, and breathe easier. "I'm sorry for not understanding."

I reach out my hand, and Barrett takes it. Our tight, fervent grasp warms our cold fingers as joy swells my heart. He's the man who isn't leaving me. I'm not like Louisa Nussey, Marianne Winters, or Patrick Eden-Smith's other women who felt they needed to escape their unsatisfactory existences in search of something better. I'm a woman anchored by love, by marriage, to the place that's exactly where I want to be.

"Hugh and Dr. Lewes went to lunch with Mick, Anjali, and her father," I say. "Fitzmorris is out on an errand. Nobody's home."

Barrett raises his eyebrows. "Nobody's home."

We exchange flirtatious, suggestive glances as we remember that an empty house provides the opportunity for uninhibited private pleasures.

Hand in hand, we run home.

Enjoyed the read?

We'd love to hear your thoughts!

crookedlanebooks.com/feedback